To my wonderful family and friends who have supported me during all the exigencies, downfalls and uplifts of living with Multiple Sclerosis. Also, to the old timers in Outback pubs from whom I heard many great yarns of Aussie folklore. I salute the inspiring people of the Outback, known for their resilience and determination.

Judith Emmerson James is an artist, arts lecturer, editor and journalist. A writer since childhood, she was educated at U.S.Q. and Q.I.T. in Queensland, Australia. A child of the bush, she grew up with indigenous people, and roamed around much of Outback Australia. Having contracted Multiple Sclerosis in the 1980s, Judith was aghast at the lack of help for people with all types of disabilities in country areas. She helped form aid groups across Australia, dealt with all levels of government, written, edited and published disability newsletters and bulletins for nearly thirty years, as well as film and stage scripts, having had a play produced, with short stories and poetry published in Range Writers Anthologies.

Receiving many awards and medals for her work for so many years in the disability sector across Australia, Judith writes for Government submissions and Disability Organisation websites. She was nominated for Australian of the Year in 2012.

On her desk is a pave of purple amethyst crystals which came directly from the lost cave in the Flinders Ranges…the inspiration for her first full-length novel.

Judith Emmerson James

LEGEND OF THE OPAL DRAGON

AUSTIN MACAULEY PUBLISHERS™

LONDON ∗ CAMBRIDGE ∗ NEW YORK ∗ SHARJAH

A CIP catalogue record for this title is available from the British Library.

ISBN 9781398471634 (Paperback)
ISBN 9781398471641 (ePub e-book)

www.austinmacauley.com

First Published 2022
Austin Macauley Publishers Ltd®
1 Canada Square
Canary Wharf
London
E14 5AA

Many thanks to Austin Macauley and Associate Publishers for their continued help, advice and much valued assistance. Furthermore, my thanks go to my Journalism Associates and Disability Organisations who, over the past 30 years, have long upheld my writing abilities.

Prologue

Around the vast blue of the Australian inland sea, lagoons and streams had shores of abundant warm green proliferation. Insects buzzed, small reptiles ran and fed though the wealth of palms, cycads and conifers, where reeds, sedums and mosses coated rocks, sands and banks of clay.

Along the hidden paths that ran through the densely covered shores, a great lizard paced his stately way along under the groves of pines and gingko trees, where flocks of large flightless birds gathered to feast on the cycad and gingko nuts. He ignored their strident cries, not interested in hunting for the moment as he had eaten his fill earlier from the upturned carcass of a massive horned tortoise. In life, the tortoise had roamed the forests and lagoons around the inland sea with lordly impunity, his armour-plated shell and heavily spiked tail defence from would-be predators.

Having alarmed a raft of small megapodes digging round the edges of the lagoon, where their running three-toed footprints would be imprinted in the surrounding clays to declare their existence for millennia; the great lizard turned to see another lizard of his ilk creeping forward to cast eyes at the remnants of the tortoise shell turned to the sky.

The great dragon raised his immense body of armoured shining scales to a threatening stance, balancing on his hind legs and hissing ferociously. His smaller would-be opponent seemed awed by this display to change course, disappearing quickly into the scrubby surrounds. He surprised a very tall flat-faced kangaroo-like animal, who shied away, not hopping but in a bi-pedal fashion that would also leave his footprints for posterity.

Lizard superiority having been established, the great reptile decided to move to a sheltered spot amid a stand of conifers to rest after his meal, but this effort became hotly debated by a large flock of the great flightless birds, flapping their tiny wings and stamping their horned three-toed feet, making fake rushes at his progress, rending the warm air into shreds with their shrieking calls.

It seemed to be a diversional tactic to perhaps cover up nesting areas of their huge eggs. Having no interest at the present in eggs or birds, the lizard lazily regarded this offensive behaviour with a jaundiced eye; so being an animal that preferred his own company, he turned to a different path.

Just then, the calls of the insects and birds ceased abruptly. The waters of the sea and the lagoons began to shiver, sending small waves of froth to coat the sands and rocks. Suddenly, the sands along the northern sides rippled and seismic shocks made the trees snap and sway. All life stood as though frozen in space, while underground rumblings shook and growled beneath them.

There was a hiatus for some moments until the land stood still and quiet once more and the shrill cries of the small megapodes again rent the air. The great lizard continued on his way towards the uplifting land that had folded into rocky outcrops and weird coloured strata. It had a jewel-like surface reflecting in the sun, all the micas and minerals that the seismic uplifts had shaken from beneath the ground.

None of this wonderland was of interest to the great lizard as he was intent upon some repose, until thrusting his way through the foliage with the impunity that his bulk gave his progress; his way was barred by a two-ton heavy weight that lumbered along tearing herbage with its big jaws.

It was a massive wombat-like creature, who certainly had the weight to cause the lizard some thought. The two giants stopped and surveyed each other, one immersed in the mouthful of fresh greens he wanted and the lizard wanting to pass by without trouble after his large lunch. The furred giant growled in its throat, champing its massive, stamping its inward turning feet in annoyance at being, the strong claws raking the earth into furrows.

The great lizard surveyed this colossus barring his path and though when not already fed, usually ate more medium to large size animals, birds and eggs; his serrated teeth built for quick execution. At present, he was not in the mode for a test of strength and stamina, so he hissed his displeasure, waving his armoured head from side to side, turning away to wander through new patches of scrub land that headed up a rising path towards a rock outcrop, which he used as his own domain.

In the late afternoon glare of the intense heat of the unforgiving sun, a great thunderstorm raged in fury over the blistered terrain. As lightning flashed and reverberating noise rolled over the upthrust hills around the sides of the waterways, the dragon-like creature crawled into his lair in a cleft in the cliff face and relished the dim interior of the cave in the rocky ramparts.

The beast had no eyes for his cool cave covered in walls of many thousands of minerals of every hue and formation, interspersed with florets of sparkling crystals and glittering mica amid the rocks. He clambered up on his favourite cool ledge of rock away from the heat of the entrance and settled to sleep.

A mighty earth tremor shook the dragon awake; as outside, rocks and debris hurtled down the mountain slopes.

The dragon's cave suddenly became black as death.

Chapter One

The wild, serrated landscape of the Flinders Ranges in South Australia had always revealed its timeless landscape of tectonic activity, which pushed heights out of the area that had once been an inland sea. A feast of uranium, gold and enormous mineral deposits encrusted the undersides of cliffs and rocky ramparts, where inroads had been made by miners since the early century.

The combined native tribes that had inhabited the ranges area had lived in any number of caves during bad weather and Archaeologists had found evidence of feasting in one of the biggest caves of the area, which contained bone digging sticks and stone grinding tools for making flour from different seeds.

The Zamia palms in the closed valleys provided giant seeds, which had to be washed in running water for quite some time to leach out the toxins before being dried and ground into a paste for cooking. The biggest cave had petroglyphs incised into the rocky walls and many drawings made with charcoal, as well as red and white clay and yellow ochre.

It was the area that provided the most dateable evidence of occupation and revered by the local tribal people. Their sacred sites held stories from their dreamtime, that echoed across the ranges and their songlines held the knitted fabric of their lives.

Bon Campbell had been a prospecting drilling surveyor for a number of mining companies for many years in the desert area of south Australia. He and his trusty big drilling rig had traversed the primitive tracks and inroads of the Flinders Ranges and had come across evidence of those ancient seas left over from the millions of years of evolution.

Bon had seen the Ediacaran fossils, the oldest in the world dug from the ancient rocks. He had also seen evidence of habitation in the caves and found he had a reverence for the past lives and left everything where it had lain for millennia.

In his latest explorations, Bon had been drilling mining core samples in a remote area in the declines near Mt Painter, when upon following one of the disused mining tracks he came upon two stringy, elderly prospectors with their shaggy tan camel in tow. They were dressed in dusty overalls, check shirts and big boots, with daggy hats that seen many an Aussie summer.

Each man had a kitbag slung over a shoulder and the short stocky man was wielding a short pick on a red boulder attempting to shave off a sample. Bon got down stiffly from his rig and walked over to meet the men. He was a tall, rangy man in his forties, clad in dust and rubble all over his form, with lines of fatigue etched into his face. His work trousers and dark shirt exuded dust and sweat in even proportions.

He extended his hand and exclaimed, "Great to see somebody on two legs in this lunar landscape, camel excluded! I'm Bon Campbell."

The red-haired man, with a shock of red curls and short curly red beard, came forward, put his pick and sample down, shook Bon's hand and introduced himself.

"I'm Michael Martin, commonly called Ginger for obvious reasons. This is Mungo Jack Johnson. You been in this area for long? Hadn't seen your truck around here before."

Mungo saluted with his hat, shouting commands at the camel. The camel groaned and folded herself onto the ground like a deck chair. She groaned again mightily, as though she were being tortured but seemed content once she subsided. She blew through her nostrils at the squadrons of flies and then proceeded to chew her cud with great aplomb.

Mungo came over to shake hands with Bon and squat under the shade from trees at the side of the track, waving away the flotilla of flies that had surrounded himself and the camel.

Bon wiped his sweaty face on his old blue shirt sleeves and pushed his hat back on his head, "Just about finished this tour of test drilling work, then I head back to Adelaide to deliver my core samples. Via Windani for fuel first. After about 6 weeks out here, I'm looking for a good feed at the Café and a good wash at the pub! Otherwise, my friends won't want to know me!"

Mungo laughed.

"Where you been camping? You're welcome to come back to our camp and we can show you a fine waterhole and some good outback feed. Reckon you can almost get there in the truck along this old track."

Bon looked quite surprised.

"What, are you magicians pulling water out of the air?"

Ginger scratched his head then said slowly, "We've been taken to a certain waterhole by some of our local tribal friends. They have a legend about the maker of the waters called Arkaroo, who it seems, had done a great job. We just about had enough heat and dust for today, so we'll put our gear on the camel and you can follow us along to our camp."

Mungo nodded and though the camel groaned her displeasure and showed her great yellow teeth, the men tied on their equipment and kitbags. They trudged off leading the camel, who once mobile, plodded meekly behind. Bon started his motor, following slowly behind so as not to worry the camel, but finding the going tough even for his big four-wheel outfit. After a half hour or so, the men signalled to Bon to stop where he was.

Ginger yelled, "That's as far as you can go, mate. You can make your camp here under those bull oak trees and walk the rest of the way. Not far now."

The men trudged down a narrow, hardly seen path between rocky outcrops with the towers of the hills looming over the terrain so that dark blue shadows filled the declivities. Bon had pulled over his rig, jumped down to follow the slow pace of the camel.

They all walked down a decline that had the first lush greenery for many a mile. Turning a bend, Bon was startled to see a beautiful watercourse filling the valley, which was lined with many varieties of palms, a myriad of ancient-looking cycads, plus verdant greenery, where songs of parrots filled the air.

Pretty speckled finches were drinking at the water edge and a number of furry, golden rock wallabies bounded up the steep rocky walls and when safe, stopped to eye off the strangers.

Mungo halted the camel, took off her halter and packs setting them down near a makeshift camp under some palms. He hobbled her on the sandy edge near the water, where she drank copious amounts, then munched at the plentiful green reeds. Ginger showed Bon the camp, made of two tarps slung under the palms over a couple of bedrolls and some cooking gear. He soon had a fire going with palm fronds with a billy of clear spring water over it.

Bon could not believe his eyes at the length of the deep dark blue water contained in this hidden valley.

He gestured to it and said in amazement, "I thought I had explored most of this area in my work, travelling all over the old mining roads but never knew this was here, nor had I ever heard of it."

Ginger smiled.

"The locals are pretty cagey just who they tell, but we have some good friends among them and have helped get some of the sick ones some help, so we hear plenty of talk-talk. Plus, we don't offer any outside news of these things. So, it would be a good service to them if you kept this bit of heaven to yourself when you go out of here."

Bon said quietly, "Right you are. I'm pretty good at staying mum as my work is private business and I would hate to see traditional places like this trashed by the great unwary. I've seen some hot springs in odd places round here but the water was caustic and with dead vegetation around the springs, I would hazard a guess there could be radio-active contamination in the water as well."

Mungo agreed.

"I've found a couple of those types of soaks in some odd places, hot as hell, smelling terrible. It's no wonder the tribal people refuse to go near those areas. In times gone past, they have said those bad waters made their people very sick."

Ginger said, "None of it is surprising really when you think how close this is to where the old uranium mining went on. I often wondered if the old miners got sick in later life."

The billy boiled, tea leaves were added, plus a couple of gum tree leaves. The men decanted the brew into pannikins and sat sipping their steaming tea, the camel collapsed her legs to sit down on the sand to chew her cud, looking over the water contentedly, watching small plops making rings on the surface.

Bon was transfixed looking at the marks on the gleaming silent water, enquiring of the men about the marks.

Mungo explained, "There are small turtles, small freshwater fish and plenty of spiney crays, which we can have as a meal now and then. We hang a cray bag in a sheltered place with a bit of bone in it and the crays can't get enough, scramble into the bag and they make great eating. There are also fresh-water mussel middens round the sands here where the tribal people used to feast on those, but they're not my best tucker—tough as boot leather!"

Bon looked pleased and said quietly, "Thanks for your hospitality—all I need now is a wash and I'd be fit to come for a meal."

Ginger laughed, dumped his pannikin and wrenching off his clothes and boots shouted, "Last man in does the washing up!"

The others followed suit and ran splashing into the water, yelping at the cold after the heat they had endured during the day. Bon swam gently through the clear water, watching the small fish darting about his feet, lying on his back, gazing at the walls of the rocky mountain surrounding the deep valley. The edges of the mountain were clad in late afternoon sunshine, glowing red, orange and yellow with dark blue shadows. The crest of Mt Painter loomed on the ridge and its interesting profile beckoned Bon to further investigation.

The other men were out and dressed, coming along the edge of the waterhole dragging a wet hessian bag behind them when Bon got back to camp. The bag was bulging with hidden movement. Mungo dropped the bag near the fire and turned the contents onto a piece of palm leaf. It was crawling with good sized, very spiney crays, which were dropped into a large pot of boiling water.

In a few moments, the crays were tipped out and a tin of salt produced. The men sat eating the fresh food with relish, along with damper from the camp oven, which had been toasted on the coals of the fire.

Bon was pleased with the change of food, plus the company; so the men sat for some time, discussing the area and the type of minerals found, as well as the old uranium deposits that had been mined around Mt Painter in the early part of the century.

Ginger waved his hands in the air expansively.

"A big area of the Mt Painter and Mt Gee was open to copper mining, starting around the late 1800's. Then Douglas Mawson found samples of torbernite, a uranium phosphate mineral from an area they called Radium Ridge."

Bon nodded.

"I've seen plenty of the remnants of old mines in strange places when on my surveys, but they seem to be so decrepit from so long ago."

Mungo added, "I think the Mawson samples were found around 1910 and that made exploration a must during the first world war. But they were not big deposits and were quickly worked out."

Bon thought for a while.

"Over my various forays into this whole area, I found so much of interest, outside my actual work and yet there is always something wonderful to turn up in the most amazing sites. Like the time I saw my first Ediacaran fossils when I stopped near a rock wall for some food. My eyes nearly fell out of my head when

I pushed away dirt and dust and there were these elegant fossils, dating from around 500 million or more years ago! Curious early life forms, leaf shapes, amoebas, skeleton of perhaps first fish and round curls of shapes unknown to us."

Mungo and Ginger both laughed. Mungo nodded.

"Know what you mean! The best thing for me is that being a blood brother of one of the local tribes, I understand how come they have such great stories to explain these happenings. I've been privileged to have been shown a cave where ancient fires had been lit and the remnants of Gerynormis, the huge Pleistocene bird and its eggs could be seen half burnt."

Ginger added his variety of geological explorations.

"I was delving into a likely-looking place to take samples, when I saw as indented arches across a rock face the stromatolite fossils believed to have formed from bacteria present during the Cryogenian era, around 50 to 70 million years earlier than the Ediacaran fossils. The Adelaide Museum geologists were up here quicker than fleas on a dog!"

Mungo added, "We can never reject any ideas what we might find as new areas get uncovered all the time."

Bon mused, "Because the Norwest and Paralana fault have caused many folds during seismic activity, so anything can happen round here and often does. No one could know what will be opened up next."

Ginger remarked quietly, "Only thing we never found were diamonds, which were supposedly found here. Mungo found a piece of blue corundum, which might polish into a rare sapphire but he refuses to sell it!"

Bon was amazed. He said, "Wow! That's a new one on me! I was test drilling further north in a flat area and brought up two tiny macro-diamonds—only two and the core samples don't belong to me, only to our scientists and they disregarded them."

As the night closed in with the first stars coming to light the purple and indigo sky, Bon started to yawn.

"Many thanks for everything. I'm clapped out after a big day's work. I'll bring breakfast over in the morning as I have some decent tins of stew you might like to go with the damper. This area has boggled my mind. I was looking at the ridge of Mt Painter and thought I would like a look up there tomorrow. Should be able to see forever."

Ginger looked at his mate, who nodded.

"We can show you a way to get up the ridge, which is not as tough as some other directions. We got plenty of time and a morning off is always welcome."

Bon considered for a moment.

"That'd be great. I have to change my surveys to a new site shortly, but a day off is good news."

He shook hands with both men and wandered off into the starlit night to his own very dry camp. He rolled out his swag in the sand and lay pondering the mystery of the long waterhole from a geological point of view. He listened to the flying foxes flapping round the fruit in the palms and the lonely call of a dingo echoing somewhere in the mountains.

Chapter Two

In the fresh morning air, before the sun had reached the deep valley, Bon rolled up his swag, tossing it into his rig, fossicked through his food boxes and found a couple of tins of stew. He laced up heavy boots, donned his wide hat, stuck two water canteens in his backpack and trudged off to meet Ginger and Mungo for breakfast. As he rounded the rocks into the valley, he let out a long 'coo-ee'.

There was an answering coo-ee, so Bon continued down the track until he could see the water of the hidden valley shimmering in the morning breeze. Ginger saw him coming in from the dusty track, sang out a greeting and Bon handed him the stew tins to put next to the fire. Ginger stabbed a couple of steam holes and left them to heat in the coals. Mungo came up from the water, where he had been having a wash in a basin and shook the drops off his head in a fine spray.

"Gooday, Bon. Ready for a decent trek up the mountains this morning? How're your leg muscles, good and strong I hope?"

Bon laughed.

"Think my legs are pretty good for going up those heights but dunno about coming down. Murder on the calves! Reckon it will get hot after a while, so I'll fill my canteens before we get going."

The other men nodded and they sat around the fire as Mungo opened the tins and decanted them into a billy, where they could help themselves eating while the water for tea boiled. Ginger had made a fresh damper in his camp oven on coals he had raked out to the side, plus he had a ring of coals smoking on its lid.

The smell of baking bread combined with campfire smoke was a great whet to appetites. The oven was removed and the aroma of baking bread filled the air. Ginger placed it on a metal plate and tore it apart so they could add it to their stew. The billy was boiled and decanted and they all sipped their tea with satisfaction.

Bon wiped his mouth, saying, "Many thanks for a good breakfast. Fresh damper is such a boon! I'd just about run out of flour in my stores and couldn't make any more. Been living on dry biscuits this last week. It'll be good to get into Windi to restock."

He shaded his eyes and gazed up at the ridges before them.

"I'm looking at the heights we'll be scaling. Bit of a task ahead of us. When do you want to get going?"

Mungo looked at the sun appearing over the mountains and thought for a moment.

"We'll pack a bit of damper and syrup, in case we're not back by lunch and Ginge has some dates there. Give us ten minutes or so."

Bon said, "I think I also have dried fruit left in my tuckerbox, so I'll bring them too. Back shortly."

He helped place sand over the fire, took his empty tins with him and walked back up the track with light heart, thinking of the day off with companionship and new exploration.

As the sun rose higher, the hills had changing colours turning to ochres, tans and browns, small scrubby areas looking like badly shaven beard, with indigo shadows reflecting in the water. The three men started round the northern side of the waterhole and made their way up a declivity that would take them higher and across some rounded peaks, without having to scale the rocky ridges running down towards the waterhole.

As they ascended the terrain became more rugged and made it hard climbing, so they stopped now and then for a drink and a few dried fruits. The scenery from the ridges looked westward across rows of hidden valleys, some with evidence of tiny water courses with trees and green reeds around sandy beaches.

There places were full of corellas, calling their weird wavering cries, flashing white in their aerial sorties in the early sun. There were also great flocks of swooping green and gold budgerigars, shrilling at the top of their songs before flowing down to drink. There were fluffy yellow-footed rock wallabies combing their fur, but shy, retiring up inaccessible slopes when the men came into view.

Bon was awestruck.

"Wow, fellas! I have never been in this part at all and though it's a good climb, what a sight!"

He shaded his eyes and gaze in all directions, turning right around, looking over the vast expanse of the old inland sea. The foothills and lower peaks of the ranges under his feet were speckled with scrubby patches of spinifex running down inclines of red rocky areas. Patches of white gum trees lined declines and gidgee and flowering shrubs showed up lining other areas.

He could see way beneath him an old road that led to two clapped-out uranium mines. The curvature of the earth could be seen against the almost flat undulating western skyline and Mungo and Ginger, sitting on the ground, watched him with interest.

Bon waved his arms to encompass the wide earth before him.

"Should've brought my binoculars. No brains! I could see forever!"

Mungo went over to his backpack and dragged out a small pair of his own, presenting them to Bon, who took them thankfully, scanning the horizons as far as he could see. The open blue sky was alive with great soaring eagles and whistling kites, zooming with outstretched wings on the thermal updrafts from the hills. Their piercing cries were the only sound in the almost foreign-seeming land mass below his feet.

Ginger said quietly, "We've combed all these ranges for years and this uplift here is good for many types of crystals and gemstones. We also make reports to our various institutions about the state of areas, be it degraded, pristine or under tribal lore. Jack is an Archaeologist and I am a Geologist. With our experience and learning we can find areas unknown to science to pass on south, plus what we find on our explorations we make enough to live on, so we can do it all again another day. Life is good!"

Mungo bought out the food packs with the remnants of the damper and syrup in a jar. They sat in quiet contemplation as they ate, while the great eagles soared above them on the rising thermals.

Suddenly the sound of the birds ceased and, in the peculiar quiet, the ground shook and the rumble dislodged rocks and scree sending it all down the mountain. The rumble seemed to roll along the heights of the mountains until it died away and the sound of falling rocks was all that broke the silence.

Mungo chuckled, "Old Arkaroo is wagging his tail again!"

Bon whistled through his teeth, "It was as if the old earth had breathed out for a moment."

They sat still, regarding the mountain for time, waiting to see if there were more tremors or rock falls. The birds took up their songs again and the dust settled, so the vista became placid once more.

Bon shook his hat free of dust and asked, "Who's old Arkaroo then? I'll have to speak to him about the tremors that play like hell with my surveying equipment—but luckily they come few and far between."

Ginger agreed.

"This whole area, because of the uplift that caused the ranges, is one of the most seismically active in Australia over millions of years, so that is why the whole area is rich in all types of uranium, minerals, plus gemstones and crystals. Arkaroo is the traditional owners' story about the making of the secret waters around this area. He wagged his tail and made the valleys and water holes they keep sacred. They don't want white people disturbing their ancient caves or traversing their sacred places and songlines."

The men got up, packing away the food, keen to fossick around, shifting loose rocks and shale. They stared at various rocks and crevices, scrutinising for mineral signs, digging here and there with bush knives, chipping off rock shards and examining them carefully.

Suddenly there was a shout from Bon, who was further away, scratching at the bottom of a rock face.

"Hey, you blokes, come and have a gander at this."

Ginger and Mungo scrambled over the scree and saw that Bon had been scrabbling at a dark fissure that had appeared after the tremor in a cleft. Bon pulled away rocks and scree and wrenched a handful of long crystals from the hole.

Ginger whistled and pushed the hat back on his head, while Mungo took the crystals and dropped a bit of water from his canteen over their dusty faces. In the sunlight, the men gasped at the rich purple of sparkling amethysts clinging to a piece of glittering crystal base.

"Hell's Bell's!" Mungo exploded. "That's top quality gemstone. Can we clear enough detritus to see into the hole there?"

Ginger took a collapsible spade from his pack and laughed at the surprise on Bon's face.

"Never go without a tool or two, so let's see what we can dig up."

The men dug and shifted rubble, until the edges subsided and left a reasonable hole, which looked enough space for one of them to wriggle his head inside. Mungo sized himself up against Ginger and Bon and offered to try.

"I'm skinnier, so I think I can shimmy in there. Be ready to drag me out by the heels if there be dragons!"

They laughed and Mungo lay flat, shuffling on his stomach, managing to get his head and shoulders into the gap. His long gangly legs stuck out like a grasshopper with boots on. There was a muffled exclamation and Bon started to pull him out by the legs. Mungo sat up covered in debris and dust with his eyes open wide.

"I been digging round here for half my life, but I've never seen anything like this! Ginge, you got a torch in your pack?"

Ginger went to his pack and sorted through to find a slim torch, which he tried off and on to make sure the battery was fine. He offered the torch to Bon, who took the spade and dug furiously until the opening widened. He wriggled himself in, having to manoeuvre his shoulders in a bit at a time. He took the torch with him, holding it in his teeth, until he disappeared inside.

There was another great shout, echoing eerily.

"Get yourselves in here, fellas, it opens out into a bigger cave."

He waved the torch around and the other men squeezed in and Bon slowly showed the floor and walls of the cave with the torch. The men crouched, struck silent, their amazed eyes looking at walls of the cave entirely covered in crystals of all colours and types, hanging from the walls and ceilings in great clusters.

Even the floor was covered in crystal formation like a luscious, sparkling, shimmering pavement fit for the Shah's throne room. There were pink quartzes, white quartzes, yellow quartzes in all formation as far as their eyes could see, interspersed with the green of beryls, aquamarine blues, red carnelians and flashes of flame, as well as blues plus the greens of chrysoprase.

The entire roof had a heavy encrustation of purple and lilac amethyst crystals of all shades ranging from small chunky pavement to huge crystals hanging down like stalactites.

The men sat back on their haunches and gazed in amazement. Shining the torch across the rear of the cave Bon spotted what looked like the brilliant colours of opal and beckoned the to see where he was looking. Ginger whistled and Mungo was dumbfounded at the sight which met their eyes. On a rocky ledge lay the skeleton of a possible megafauna animal, which, over the many eons it had rested there, had transformed its bones into almost all opal.

The men carefully shone the torch over the whole length of the skeleton, sizing up the flashing opal colours with silent reverence. No one spoke, awestruck by the magnificence of the monster.

Mungo finally found his voice but said in an almost whisper, "Look at the skull, Ginge. What great teeth! It's head shape looks similar to the perenties but the length is six times their size. It must be twenty feet nose to tail!"

Bon's voice was shaking as he muttered, "Let's get out of here and sort ourselves out. This could be Australia's version of the Komodo dragon and of national significance."

The men crawled out of the confined space and were pleased to get out in the fresh air. They sat in stunned silence, cogitating over the enormity of what they had seen.

Bon spoke quietly, "This find is beyond price, beyond money, beyond capitalists and tourists—beyond us! Do you agree?"

Mungo nodded furiously.

"This puts all our exploration into the shade. As you say, this is of extreme importance, but what the devil do we do next? It's not a discovery I would like any of my various departments to get hold of in the near future."

Ginger said very slowly, "Mungo and I don't need much to live on. We fossick around here because we enjoy what we do and love the area. We may give reports of worth to our various specific institutions, but this is right out of their league. The whole idea of the worth of that creature frightens the hell out of me and I would hate for it to be to be destroyed for capital gain, which is what would happen if exposed to the greater public."

Mungo looked thoughtful.

"There are the traditional owners to consider as well. They may know of these things and it may be considered sacred ground to them, never to be revealed."

Bon cogitated for some time. He scratched his head, ruffling his hair in his confusion.

"We all need to agree. I'm never going to tell you fellas what to do, but I have an idea that may be of use to all of us. We need first to find out just what it is we have seen there. I'm due back in Adelaide shortly and can quietly make enquiries from a Palaeontologist at the Adelaide Museum I know, who can be relied upon his oath to keep quiet."

The other men sat and listened attentively.

Bon continued, "My friend may have ideas as to what sort of thing this opalised creature might be and I can get back to you on the way here again. We could meet in Windani when I get back with news in a couple of weeks. I swear I will not give out any specific details in that time."

Ginger nodded.

"Mungo and I could get one of our tribal elders to meet with you when you get back and we need to talk with him before anything else could be done."

Mungo shook his head to clear his thoughts.

"So much to deal with all of a sudden, I feel quite boggled. Think we should roll some rocks across that crevice in case others see the hole and investigate. We'll go back to camp and mull over the whole thing."

Bon had a sudden thought.

"Would it be OK with you men if we took some samples at the front of the cave for proof I'm not talking twaddle? And can you blokes find this cave again, without me having scramble back up bringing my survey equipment to take co-ordinates?"

Mungo nodded, scanning the rock face.

"No trouble."

He scrabbled over to the hole and stuck his shovel against the inside wall, coming back with a handful of amethyst crystals.

"You want a few too, Ginge?"

Ginger shook his head, still too disorientated to think straight. Bon took the spade and made a thrust just inside the edge of the cave wall and came back with a piece of pavement with long purple crystals, which he hefted into his kit. The men then shoved, pulled, pushed and rolled rocks across the entrance, until they thought it looked entirely safe from prying eyes. Mungo swished his bag in front, until their footprints died in the dust.

They trudged back down the ridges, ravines and gullies, hardly saying a word, the enormity of their discovery weighing heavily.

When they arrived at the waterhole camp Bon said, "I'll go back to where I was working and give you fellas time to think. If you're happy for me to try and get more information, when I get back, you can tell me what you want to do."

Bon dug in the back pocket of his filthy jeans and hauled out a battered wallet. He extracted two business cards and handed them over.

"You can check my credentials any time—the official title being Bonnard Campbell, Resource Extraction Surveyor for IGF Mining, Adelaide. They will vouch for me and Ma at the pub will do so too, as she has known me for a number of years. I also know Morrie well, so you can check in town if you want to and I'll be staying with Ma as soon as I get back."

He shook hands with both men and hefting his pack with its load of crystals, waved and trudged back through the palm trees.

Chapter Three

Shouldering his heavy backpack, Bon made his way along North Terrace in Adelaide to the steps leading up to the South Australia Natural History Museum and looked up at the pillared entry, frowning. He was washed and brushed in his best jeans and a serviceable blue shirt but his rugged work boots and his tanned face bespoke his livelihood. He wasn't quite sure how to obtain information without letting on the knowledge of the opalised dragon form in the far away ranges but thought of an old mate who might be the person with greatest integrity.

Bon walked across the shining floor and stood at the reception desk, where a bespectacled, suited man, with very clean black shoes stood to attention. Bon felt a bit out of place and rubbed his desert boots against the bottom of his jeans in an endeavour to clean them.

He pulled himself up straight and looked the receptionist in the eye, enquiring, "Does Andrew Brand still work here, please?"

The informant nodded and pointed Bon to the row of offices on the left of the huge hallway. He hefted his backpack and strolled to the hallway indicated. He looked at the names on the doors until he found what he was looking for and knocked.

A disembodied voice beyond the door roared, "Come!"

Bon opened the door and laughed.

"I would know your stentorian voice anywhere, young Brand!"

The pleasant-faced man behind the desk leapt to his feet and thumped Bon on the back.

"By gum, it's the wild man Bonnard from the Outback! What're you doing in here?"

Bon smiled hugely.

"Well, old buddy, haven't seen you for ages, but heard you had progressed here from our time at Uni. Amazing where the great unwashed end up!"

Andrew chuckled and replied, "You're a great one to talk, always tearing round unheard of places in that rig of yours. What brings you to seeking my sage company?"

Bon was quiet for a moment.

"I need some info, but it's only for your ears, not to be heard by anyone else, especially in this august establishment."

Andrew looked puzzled for a moment, then suggested, "I've got a morning tea break. How about we go round the corner to a quiet place for a coffee and you can fill me in?

Bon nodded with relief and the two walked down the wide steps and headed to a coffee shop, which was cool and smelled delicious. They purchased their drinks and a couple pastries and sat at a table away from other people.

Andrew sipped his coffee and asked, "Now, young fella, don't tell me you got yourself into a spot of bother out in the sticks?"

Bon looked serious and said slowly, "You might say that, which is why I need to pick your brains and all your expertise—and your quiet. This a very serious matter, for your ears only."

Andrew looked surprised but stated, "I'm all ears and closed mouth."

Bon heaved his backpack on the table and slowly undid the lid, sliding the pack towards Andrew so he could inside the slab of the huge amethyst crystals.

Andrew drew back with an explosive breath and whispered, "Holy moly, where did that come from?"

Bon closed the pack and placed it under his feet. He sighed.

"I can only tell you part of the story as it also concerns others, including the traditional owners of the place these came from. This is why nothing of what I tell you must come out, until we work out just how this should be handled."

Andrew nodded.

"I think you have known me well enough and long enough to know I'm silent as the tomb when I want to be. Tell on."

Bon spoke slowly, "I was drilling core samples in the area of the northern Flinders when I met two old prospectors, who showed me to a wonderful waterhole known only to the tribal people around there. While we were at the waterhole I was looking at the ridges of the mountains and was interested to climb it for a gander. The two blokes were happy to show me the best way to get up and we clambered to the top, taking about half a day to get there."

Bon stopped to drink his coffee and ponder for a moment.

"It was a magnificent view and while we were having a bite to eat, there was an earth tremor that sent a lot of rock flying. We started finding crystals and minerals strewn about and I was digging into a cleft when I found a dark crevice that had been uncovered. We cleared the frontal rock and scree and one of the others, a skinny bloke, wriggled in through the hole and when he shouted, we pulled him out and he had a handful of these crystals."

Andrew whistled.

"A stash thus far undiscovered?"

Bon nodded.

"Not only that, we widened the entry and I wriggled in with a torch. The interior opened out into a small cave so we could stand and it was floor to ceiling in rock crystals, roses, yellows, green blues and huge amethyst. Even the floor was a pavement of glittering crystals. None of us had ever seen the like."

He paused.

"But even more astonishing was that at the back on a rocky ledge, we found the fully opalised skeleton of great reptile, almost entire. The thing may have been caught in the cave when a tremor brought down the entrance."

Andrew's eyes opened wide.

"Good gravy, Bon—it would have to be millions of years old. What sort of skeleton? Long, wide, clawed—what—what?"

Bon considered for a moment.

"One of my mates reckoned it had the look of a perentie, only huge. Massive teeth still intact. The skeleton was possibly twenty feet long and as far as we could see, the entire was intact and all opalised. But I know little of our megafauna, which is why I have come to you."

Andrew dragged out a pad and drew a quick sketch of what Bon had described.

Bon had a good look at the sketch and thought for a while.

"Reckon the head was different but bit like a wide goanna head, four goanna sort of legs, long neck and long tail. Give me the bit of paper."

He endeavoured to draw the outline in more detail.

"Here, I'm no artist, so this is the best I can do."

Andrew sucked in his breath when he was faced with the outline of the creature.

"Mate, I reckon you may have found a fossilised skeleton of a type of monitor lizard called *Megalania priscus*, which was the largest terrestrial lizard to have existed here. Maybe the biggest of its kind in the world. This type of megafauna inhabited the inland marshes of South Aus from the Pleistocene era and it would, without the added opalization be the most prized skeleton ever found in Australia."

Andrew paused for breath. He looked very serious.

"This beast would have been ranging round the water sources until the water evaporated and the sea turned arid and leaves behind clumps of hydrated 'silica gel', which, over millions of years dries up and hardens. The result is opal. There are plenty of opalised fossil bones around Coober Pedy and Lightning Ridge but not a whole skeleton."

Bon looked bewildered.

"Geez, Andrew, I don't know what to do for the best. I will note your info. I have to take back this to the two prospectors who helped find this and who are rather terrified of it being turned into greed for the big quid if it fell into the wrong hands! It could mean a capitalist war! Plus, the traditional owners will have the final say and if they wish it to be unmoved, that will be the end of it."

Andrew looked thoughtful.

"I can see where it might lead if the traditional owners refuse entry to the area, but I stress that this may be the most important find ever in Australia or indeed the world. If it is all opalised as well, the great and greedy would make World War 3 over it! You can imagine what would happen to the fossil and the whole area if the press got wind of this. Not to mention the forces of the underworld. Of course, you need to get back and see what eventuates, but would you let me know if we could bring myself and another bloke in my trade to verify this find? The other thing, can you get back there and measure the skeleton, length and side to side to give me a more complete idea of what we would be dealing with? I will be totally silent until I hear from you again."

Bon nodded.

"I'll be back there on my next sortie for my Boss, so I'll speak to the people concerned and let you know what eventuates. Give me your phone number, will you?"

Andrew produced his work card and handed it over. They shook hands and Bon closed his backpack, shouldering the heavy burden, going out into the noonday glare, trudging away as though the cares of the world were on his shoulders, while Andrew looked at the sketch and whistled.

He took it and tore it into small pieces, thinking of the disaster for the Museum if someone else got news of the find. He dunked it in the remnants of his coffee and swirled the lot into an ashtray. He prodded the sodden lump, until he was satisfied it had no evidence to offer anybody; rolled the bits into a paper serviette and took it away with him.

Chapter Four

On the way back from Adelaide, though the dry and desiccated desert lands, Bon drove his drill rig while in a state of mental puzzlement, thinking of the information he had to tell Ginger and Mungo and possibly the tribal elders he was to meet.

He drove into Windani and refuelled the truck and his jerry cans. He did his usual check of tyres and his spares, in case of being staked out in the rough terrain. He parked at the side of the pub, refilled his water containers and then went into the bar for a cold beer.

Bon quizzed the pretty blond barmaid for information. Clad in a black apron over her white blouse and red skirt, she was a treat for sore eyes.

"Hi, Gina, what's going on? There seems to be a lot of activity here at present? What's the big load of grog for?"

Gina laughed, waving her hands around to encompass the town.

"Don't you know the camel races are on in three weeks' time and Ma is getting supplies in early, so we've been really busy. She doesn't trust the transport to get here on time if it's not done early. There'd be a riot of we ran out of grog!"

Bon though for a moment.

"Right, I forgot, been bush too long! Is there a comfortable bunk out the back for me for a couple of nights?"

She checked a list on the bar wall and grinned, "You're in luck if you call them bunks comfortable!"

Gina wrote him on the list and took some money, ringing up the till.

Bon drank his beer an after a minute or so asked, "Have you seen Mungo or Ginger lately? I need to get in touch with them."

Gina shrugged. "I dunno where they're at, but they're pals of Morrie at the Café, so he'll know."

Bon thanked her, finished his beer and went out into the heat of the day to call into the Café. There he found Morrie, a short, stocky, heavily built man, clad in t-shirt and shorts, sweating profusely, taking in supplies and stacking them in his big freezer. Bon picked up some of the packages which felt like some sort of meat and helped pass them to Morrie in the door of the freezer. When it was all stacked, Morrie came out wiping his sweating head and gave Bon a handshake.

"Thanks, mate, that's made life a bit easier. Let's sit out the back for a minute while I recover. Just passing through again? Welcome to stay for tucker if you like Buddy's cooking. You running more tests round here then?"

They went out to the cool of the back veranda and sat on a long bench, while Morrie settled down.

Bon said, "New lot of tests for my bosses, but that's not why I'm in town at present. I need to get in touch with Ginger and Mungo fairly quickly, as I have some news for them. Any idea how I could get hold of them?"

Morrie shook his head, "Not at the moment, but I can pass the nod to Buddy, who can let his mates on the hill know and the blokes will call in when they're able. How long you in the area."

"Be here for a couple of days to take on supplies and have a rest at the pub. Be good if you can pass the word."

They shook hands and Bon left to go around the back of the pub to the Men's Quarters for a well-earned rest. Later in the cool of the evening, a group of men sat around on the old chairs and talked in a desultory fashion about the upcoming camel races.

Somewhere outside the yards there was the hoot of an owl. Bones, the yardman, listened and when a second hoot came, he vanished into the surrounding dark. He was gone for some time and when he came back, he beckoned Bon from the side of the building. They walked a little way off.

Bones muttered, "That was one of Ginge's tribal mates. Message is for you to meet them at Arkaroo water tomorrow if possible. That make sense to you?"

Bon nodded.

"They say what time?"

Bones shook his head.

Bon said, "I got a couple of days off, so I may as well go out there tomorrow early. Can I leave my gear here? Gina booked my bunk for two days."

Bones muttered, "Leave it under your bunk if you're OK with that."

Bon shook hands with Bones and went to his bunk to pack up his gear, placing water canteens and dried food in his backpack before heading to the showers before bed. The semi-enclosed men's shower was out to the side of the yard with a plentiful supply of water which came from the mound springs, though hot in the morning, it was cold in the evenings which made the men coo-ee.

Ma often told them they were a lot of sissies and refused to take any notice of grumpy blokes who went without showers while working in desert conditions, so they should be thankful for her showers, no matter the temperature.

Ma always shouted at the complaining bathers, "Are you men or mice to be afraid of a bit of cool water?"

Of course, there was no answer for that and they shut up meekly and used the cold showers. The pub, like many places in Windani, sported a filtering system to take out the minerals from the mound springs out of the water, making it palatable for the kitchen and the bar. Long-time residents of the town didn't mind the brackish taste, seeing as it was such good water and reckoned boiling it made it good for the kitchen. The local animals seemed to thrive on the mineralised water, so the camels and horses went to the troughs and drank heartily.

Next morning, when the air was still cool, Bon followed the old mining track for time in the foothills, taking extreme care driving his rig in the rough going until he recognised his former camp under the bull oak trees. He parked his truck and taking his backpack, jammed his hat on his head and marched down the track until he smelled woodsmoke. He let out a coo-ee, which came back to echo round the walls of the valley.

Rounding the end of the decline, the beautiful waterway came into sight and with it, a camel sitting under a palm like something out of the Arabian Nights. There also was a small campfire with Ginger and an elderly white-haired black man sitting drinking tea.

Bon shouted with relief, "Good day, you blokes. Thought I had the right track when I could smell a cuppa tea."

Ginger came over all smiles and shaking hands introduced his friend.

"This is our good pal, one of the elders of a local indigenous group who are the landowners of the area. His name in unpronounceable, so we shorten it to Warra, which he doesn't mind, eh, Warra?"

Warra nodded his head and Bon stooped to shake his hand.

"Great to meet you. I'm parched—any more tea on offer?"

Ginger put the billy back on the fire and Bon produced his pannikin and dried fruit of out his backpack and they ate and drank for a while in quiet satisfaction, until Bon asked, "Where's Mungo? Not here this time?"

Ginger shook his head.

"He's off helping some Archaeologists for a few days, but he'll be back after that."

Bon looked a bit surprised.

"When I got your message last night I thought I would be able to let you both know what I have learned down south."

Ginger smiled.

"That's OK. Mungo and me are of the same mind about what we have seen. But tell us your news for Warra, as everything now rests with the custodians of the place."

Bon said with interest, "Warra, give me the lowdown on your tribal lore of this area. I've been doing some testing in lower ranges but never seen the Mt Painter/Mt Gee area before."

Warra looked into the fire for a moment.

"Whities think we been 'ere some sixty t'ousand years, but we been come from dreamtime and lived as in the beginning. So many rocks and hidden caves 'ave sacred drawings and carvings and only for tribe."

Ginger agreed. "That's why I wanted Warra here when you got back to hear what you learned. Mungo is OK with this as he is a blood brother belonging to Warra's mob."

Bon recounted how he found his friend from Uni. days at the Adelaide Museum and though he had not told any details, his friend, a Palaeontologist, was very excited that the skeleton may be the rarest one of its kind in Australia and could be famous around the world.

Bon quoted Andrew, "*I reckon you may have found a fossilised skeleton of the type of monitor lizard called Megalania priscus, which means 'ancient lizard' and was the largest terrestrial lizard to have existed here. This type of megafauna inhabited the inland marshes of South Aus. and even without the added opalization, if it is intact, be the most prized skeleton found in Australia.*"

Bon continued, "Andrew reckoned this beast would have been ranging round the edges of the former inland sea. As the water source evaporated, the sea turned arid and eventually the desert appeared. There are plenty of opalised fossil bones around Coober Pedy and Lightning Ridge but not a whole skeleton."

There was absolute quiet for some time while the three men digested the information.

Bon remarked, "This friend has sworn he will not mention this discovery to anyone and he is man of his word. The only thing he would like to know at present is that if we can get back to the site, that we take some measurements for him to be certain of what it is. Without disturbing anything, of course. This is where we need tribal advice, Warra."

Ginger looked at the impassive Warra.

"Told you everything we know for now, mate. You wanna climb to the top of the ridge with us and have a looksee at the cave? Bit of a scramble getting up there, but you look pretty fit."

Warra looked scornful.

"Me been walking them hills all my time. You white fellas better look out if I beat you!"

The men laughed and started packing the kits with water, torches and the collapsible shovel. Before they began their ascent, Warra went to some bushes and selected twigs and pungent leaves that he placed on the ashes of their fire. He then took the smoking twigs and wave them around the men and intoned a ritualistic address to the surrounding mountain spirits, introducing the white men to the area.

Chapter Five

The heavy going up the declines towards the ridge of Mt Painter held no joy for Ginger or Bon, but Warra stepped out with the born ease of a local bushman. The landscape seemed to have dried out and become more desiccated since their original trek up the mountain, so the birds and the wallabies congregated in families round the edges of the valley where the palms offered coolness near the water.

Bon stopped for a drink from his canteen offering to the others who declined.

Warra laughed at him, "Knew you whities were pretty soft, matey. Need to be a black fella to survive out 'ere. See how happy me!"

As they were clambering hand over fist up the final ascent of the ridge, it was noticeable that the bird calls had suddenly ceased. Warra signed for the men to squat close to the ground. He then lay flat and the others followed suit.

The earth tremor that shook them was quite severe, rumbling along the lengths of the ridges sending a shower of rocks and scree belting down over them. The noise was fearsome with large boulders cascading down to end up crashing into the valleys. The very aspect of the folds and ridges seemed to have changed shape, with sharp edges and precipices emerging to file new horizons against the sky.

When the dust had cleared and the tremors ceased, Warra dislodged some of the rubble that had fallen on him and whispered hoarsely, "Old spirit Arkaroo no welcome we. Make trouble. Me go back down."

Ginger looked at Bon and asked, "Warra, is it Ok if we take a look up ahead and then meet you back at camp?"

Warra was quite upset, his concern written on his face.

"If you must, but touch nothing and come down quick. May be more falls."

Bon looked askance at Ginger and found his voice trembled a little, "What you reckon, Ginger? We're so close—all we need is some measurements?"

Ginger was shaken, but still willing, if very cautious.

"That was a close call, mate. Don't like to go agin Warra, but we can be quick and get down in short order."

They scrambled up the last ascent, finding the terrain so full of scree, with heaps of rock and boulders they had not had to traverse the first time they had been there. When they reached the top of the ridge, it was to find great shards of cliff they had searched before had fallen and the place, though quiet as a graveyard at that moment, looked ready for more falls to follow again with any following tremors.

Ginger shook his head at Bon.

"Don't like this, Bon. It's all loose now. I can't see the bit of cliff where we found the cave entry. Maybe I'm looking wrongly."

He shaded his eyes, turning in every direction, but found nothing that resembled their original site. Bon scrabbled at rubble and scree but making no progress, so he sat back on his heels and pushed his hat back on his head.

"I can't make head nor tail of the site either, Ginger. Reckon I'm crawling in the area where that fissure, but it's either covered in boulders or fallen in itself. So much has changed, I can't believe my eyes!"

Ginger also sat despondently.

"Perhaps we'll never find that entrance again, Bon. Maybe we were never meant to be here a second time. Maybe we should go down and sit with Warra and see what he thinks."

Bon nodded, dusted himself off, looking round in disbelief at what had happened and his vision of the magnificent opal skeleton being preserved slowly ebbing from his mind. The two men clambered over the rocks and rubble, slowly making their way down, sliding down new areas where shale and detritus had fallen, which took them much longer than expected.

They were getting very tired and went on without speaking until the tops of the palm trees at the waterhole came into sight. The bird song had recommenced and the tethered camel was sitting contentedly munching on greens. The waterhole seemed quite disturbed and the men were amazed to see great boulders had rolled right into the edges of the waters where, not so long ago, they had been swimming.

The men found Warra at the campfire, billy boiling, smoking and talking with two young bucks who were drinking tea. He refused to speak about what had happened, so they all sat quietly, until all of a sudden, he stood up and vanished into the darkening evening. The young bucks followed more slowly round the stand of palm trees.

Ginger sighed and looked at Bon.

"I hope the old man doesn't feel bad about what has gone on up on the mountain. Perhaps, he feels we intruded where we were never meant to be. Maybe the opal dragon still needed to be hidden from mankind for some time yet."

Bon stared into the fire, still shaken at what had happened.

"I can't believe we were right at the area we thought the cave entrance was but couldn't find the entrance—but there was a helluva lot of rock and shale displaced. I'll have to let my mate in Adelaide know there'll be no measurements of the dragon for the foreseeable future. Maybe another tremor will unearth the cave again. Do you think Mungo will be upset?"

Ginger spoke softly.

"Mungo is rarely fazed by anything and will take it in his stride. You going back to Windi tonight?"

Bon yawned. "Think I'll stay at the truck and get away early. You staying here for now?"

Ginger nodded.

"Tomorrow, I'll take the camel and go along to a small escarpment I've been meaning to look at for a while. Mungo'll be back the day after, then later we'll go into Windi for the camel races—always a bit of fun. Might see you there."

They shook hands and Bon traipsed off into the night. Two dark faces watched Bon go from behind the stand of palms and their eyes had opened wide at the news of the opal dragon on Mt Painter. They drifted away into the bush without a sound.

Chapter Six

The desert air had been perfumed with the scent of saltbush and wattle flower, spiced with red dust haze against the sky of sapphire blue and toasted to perfection with shimmering heat. Far past the curve of the horizon's rim, a distant rumble of thunder shook the dust into quavers, with a flash of lightning making its ancient track across the sky. The heat hung so heavily even the gum leaves dropped in despair and the thorny devils sought refuge under reluctant rocks.

A sudden fresh smell, a drift upon the small breeze became a reminder of lush days long past. The ants halted their scurrying, a pause to feel the air with waving fronds of antennae. The desert seemed to pause for a moment and the silence thickened so that the bird song and the creak of grasshoppers stilled.

Somewhere distant, there came a hushing and rustling like that of the waves of a seashore, a rattle of dried bones and things long gone. The heat wavered and the earth waited. The footprints of the night embedded their images in the sand: claws of goannas, splayed left and right, devil's tiny running toes, the rail tracks of a scorpion scoring deep. A flash of owl feet marked the sand in a tribute to the end of a tiny life. Flat dingo pawmarks broke over the tracks where the Lord of the Desert had smelled and marked his territory.

Into the tracks in the golden sand, an exploratory finger of water forged a new line. It frothed at the foremost edge like lacy frog spawn, then disappeared without trace. Another runnel appeared, stronger, collecting sticks, stones and detritus of leaf skeleton in its path.

The water widened, spread fat and sideways, the miracle of wetness eating up the gold dust of the creek bed. Gurgling, popping sounds, bubbling out of long-dry fissures, plops and sizzles and chuckling sounds of water ran over the rock bars.

Such an aura of change spread over the filling creek bed, splashing like quicksilver threading through the red of the desert. All the gullies filled with water and it spread in temporary relief across a wide area of landscape.

Welcoming birds shouted their praise to the sun and the water shouted back, flowing deeper and wider on its interminable journey into explorer's ghostly territory.

Next morning, the ice-cold crystal of early light showed the tiny creek flowing softly as a mirage, its first foray of flood calmed and serene. Finches in gorgeous coloured robes like those of vanished Indian princes flocked in rafts of thousands to chirp and flirt, bathe and drink at the shimmer of water's edge.

Galahs in pink and grey dresses hung thick from branches like mad cherry blossoms against the brilliant sky, their raucous call rending the air into shreds. They gargled and squabbled and flew sorties and wrote happy music of the creek. The red kangaroos came shyly to drink and comb and scratch sweet fur coats. They batted their long eyelashes at the flies, their whiskers coated with diamonds of dewy water.

A lone eagle soared over the creek, his kingdom the desert. He wrote sky writing in magnificent arches of Pegasus wings, the first wind of the day lifting his tawny flight feathers into elegant gliding fingers. Only the eagle knew from whence the water came and to where it flowed, to whom it would give or withhold life and where its songline would end.

Chapter Seven

Away from the tiny creek running its life into many washaways, the reds and golds and oranges of the painted desert and sandhills were a surreal backdrop to a galloping herd of camels, which were jerking in and out of the stunted underbrush and gidgee trees dotted across the flat, arid land. The bright blue arc of the sky and the burning sun made the clouds of rising dust shimmer in the heat. A tiny fleck of a helicopter, looking like an agitated gnat, flew in circles over the terrain and amidst the flying dust, there was the roar of vehicles and thud of the heavy feet of fleeing camels.

Camels had been introduced into Australia in the 1890's to help develop Outback land. After motorised transport was established, the camels were left to fend for themselves and as they were perfectly adapted to desert living, they proliferated to around 1.2 million over a wide range of inland Australia. In the Middle East, the much-valued camels always belonged to someone, be it an Arab nomad, a small-holding settler or a Sheikdom. Because of Australian isolation, the camels were disease free and much sought after by Islamic countries.

The camel groups also were highly mobile and could forage on trees and shrubs across an area of around 60 kilometres a day. They could go without water if needed but preferred to drink every day if possible and this brought them into conflict with cattle producers, who found that camels had broken down fences, damaging water points and bores. Large herds of males also stampeded cattle who were looking for water and chased them away.

As well, indigenous people found the camels trashed their sacred sites and damaged special waterholes, so were looking for a market that could produce a profit by selling the camels in prime condition to the Saudi, where there was a burgeoning industry in supply of camel meat for Islamic people in the Middle East, as well as in Indonesia.

Many of the big cattle stations had set up their own camel catching industry and prime camels could be sent to Melbourne to be trained and quarantined before being air-freighted to Saudi. Other catching outfits could send their camels to be transported by sea. Special yards had to be set up with wide wings of hessian leading to the central fenced area.

The trucks which transported camels had to have a wide platform to be able to load the camels from the holding yards. As the camels trained easily, a few days in the yards with water and mates made them tractable and they followed up the ramps with little disturbance.

Camel catching was an adventure for those men who were hardy and had plenty of skills in handling animals, no matter how big.

Out on a huge flat paddock, two dust-covered heavy-duty bikes with dust-covered riders were jumping and roaring in and out of scrubby bush and spinifex in a heady endeavour to keep bunched camels together. The camel catcher's four-wheel drive truck was right behind the bikes with the dust covered driver, Pete, clad in a Jacky Howe singlet, shorts and goggles, hunched over the steering wheel.

Rangi, a huge, bronzed Islander, was riding on the welded seat over the front mudguard, with a long noose on a pole at the ready. The rough terrain threatened to throw him under the truck wheels as the driver fought the truck over gibbers and sand. Two ringers in filthy trousers and singlets were hanging on the back of the truck with a pile of ropes in their hands, cheering wildly at the mad ride. As the truck and bikes took over the roundup, the tiny mustering helicopter circled once more and dropped away into the distance.

A funnel had been made of hessian and star pickets leading into the disguised yards. The camels became slower as they ran out of puff and the bikes raced around and herded them into the holding yard. Once of the catchers was there to pull the gate shut, waiting to see if the truck was coming in. There was one magnificent male camel who had dodged the funnel and was charging off again, so the truck went after him, slewing and bouncing alongside.

The catcher slung the long noose over the camel's neck and the truck dragged it to a halt. The ringers dropped down and ran around the camel binding its legs with ropes, until it fell on its side. The captive had its legs very carefully untied, one rope at a time, with enough ropes to hold it down if needed. It was urged to get up and as the man at the yards brought up a tame gelded camel, the animals were then strung together and walked off to the nearby yards, where there were troughs of water so the animals could refresh themselves.

The bikes slowed and the young riders saluted each other and rode up to the big yards to inspect the current catches and check the animals were drinking well at the troughs. The new camel had been taken in and the ropes thrown off him and he was left to settle down. One of the ringers threw a rope around the neck of the tame camel and led it to a fenced yard behind the windmill, where two other camels rested.

The chaser's truck barged up in a great cloud of dust and the men clambered down, heading for the big shed, which held rooms of equipment with banks of shelving holding repair supplies as high as the roof. There was also a kitchen of sorts with a gas cooker and refrigerator. There was a shower outside over a concrete floor and a big generator with a high fuel tank beside. An earth water tank had been dozed out the back with a tall windmill spouting water into it, which led to the shed and troughs.

Jason, a fit, tough-looking young man, threw his hat off, banged his shorts free of dust and went inside to emerge from the shed with a large cold chest holding cartons of beer—a lifesaver for parched throats.

He shouted, "Hurry up, you blokes! I'm looking for a beer or six."

"Long as you don't touch mine, you might live a bit longer, young fella," retorted his riding mate, Mark, who was just as filthy.

Mark was also a fit, tanned, well-muscled young man, though his hair and clothes were all the colour of dust after the chase on the bikes. He opened a beer and swigged it, gasping with pleasure.

Pete, the foreman of the outfit, the driver of the catching vehicle and one of the ringers fell into a couple of rusty chairs and Pete banged the dust off his head with his hat.

"That last camel gave us a run for our money. He's a big bugger and should fetch really good cash. Transport is booked for the mornin' so they'll be in Adelaide tomorrow night. Boss'll be pleased with this good healthy-looking lot. Next stop for them is Saudi. Don't know where our next sortie will be yet."

A ringer came out for the shower, shaking the water out of his hair, looking spruce in clean shorts. He grabbed a beer and flung himself into a chair.

"Phew! That feels good after today's hard yakka."

Pete said, "We got a few days off now. I'm going down to Adelaide tomorrow to follow the transport and see the Boss. Anyone who wants to come is welcome."

The ringer thought for a moment and said, "Yeah, I'd like to come, been a while since I saw my Ma."

The other ringer said quietly, "After all the hard work, some down time is good. I stay here and clean up the place a bit."

Pete looked pleased.

"Good man! I'll be seeing the Boss for your pay, make sure you get a bonus. Good time for you fellas to have days off and relax. Anything you want brought up besides supplies, sing out."

Jason asked, "What about Rangi? He going with you this time? I think he's got a girlfriend down there and might like a few days off."

Pete said, "He's always good company, so I'll see if he wants to come."

"Where's Rangi?" Jason asked, shading his eyes from the last rays of the setting sun.

Pete laughed.

"He's gone for a dip in the tank to get rid of his dust as he reckoned his skin changed colour from red dirt. Rangi would rather swim than shower—comes of being an islander. He's also too hungry to wait for us beer drinkers, so he's lighted the barbecue right away. You're always hungry, Jase, you can do the cooking."

Jason looked indignant.

"You mob know I'm the worst cook in this place! Nah! I'll wait for Rangi."

Adrift of song and heaps of splashing came from the large earth tank behind the shed, the windmill lazily circling beside it.

Jason sighed, quaffing more beer.

"I couldn't eat for all the dust without some beers to wash my gullet out first."

The sun dropped below the horizon so the sky turned watermelon red, leading into a deep velvety blue, leaving a whisper of cooler air into the camp and the sandhills were bathed in purple shadows. Everyone came to life when Rangi banged the barbecue and aromas of cooking filled the air. He looked fit and refreshed after his swim and his clothes were the only ones in the camp that looked even half clean. His Islander fuzzy hair stood up all over his head, making him looked even taller than usual but matching his great strength and size.

Pete gave Rangi a slap on the shoulder.

"This smells great, mate—whatcha got? Don't tell me—camel steaks!"

Rangi smiled a great white smile in his bronze face and chuckled.

"This better smell than camel. Dig in. There's cold spuds, tomatoes, tinned carrots and plenty mutton chops. Hey, you guys, a sheep tasting ceremony right here!"

Everyone pretended to groan but all got stuck into the food, which was plentiful and hot, all sitting round the outside firepit with their plates on their knees. Once they were replete, they sat around relaxing on the old chairs in the deepening gloom. Rangi collected the plates and dumped them in the sink.

Pete finished his beer and asked, "Anyone want more beer—I'll put it back in the fridge otherwise."

One of the ringers sighed.

"Don't mind a beer now and then, but I'd really like a glass of good red wine like my pop could make, but that's no goin' to 'appen out 'ere!"

Pete laughed, "Not the right place for plonk out here, mate. Besides, plonk makes me sweat worse. Reminded me of a bloke I knew once who brewed his own plonk and used to sell it out the back of his shed. He was a one-pot screamer though. One glass and he thought it solved his problems, two glasses and he couldn't remember what they were!"

The men all laughed.

As the night sky deepened, the evening silence was broken by the hoot of an owl and somewhere over the sandhills a dingo gave his melancholy howl to be echoed by others across the terrain. Full of food and beer, the men sat smoking and talking but gradually slowing down.

Mark yawned widely.

"I'm off for a few zeds shortly, Jase and me'll be off as early as possible, as soon as we load our racing camels and fit up our clobber in my truck for Windani. Reckon, I lost a few kilos tearing in this heat so that should put my pretty lady Lucinda up front for the races, me being lighter and all that."

Rangi chuckled.

"What for you call you camel such a name. That make her faster?"

The men all hooted while Mark shuffled a bit and pulled a face.

"If you must know, it used to be one of my girlfriends but she left when she couldn't stand the smell of camel any more. Jase's girl ran off too, so I'm not the only one."

Jason bridled but looked serious for a moment. He had thought a lot about how the young camel Lucinda would behave.

"Matey, Lucinda is becoming a good runner, but she's so toey at the start, she loses time, whereas my old Dagobar is a calm old race veteran and loves the competition. I guess we don't know who is up for the races this year. Haven't heard any scuttlebutt from the Windani mob yet."

Rangi was curious about the racing camels.

"OK. Understand Lucinda name but why name Dagobar?"

Pete chortled.

"Reckon it's because his former owner thought he was a daggy bastard!"

Jason retorted, "Yeah, laugh if you like, but I won some good money off Dags. It'll depend this time who's in his age race for geldings."

Pete looked thoughtful.

"I did hear from someone that a bloke from around Cameron corner is coming with his couple of racers so you both might have more competition than you bargained for. I think that camel racing will expand into all sorts of places over the new few years. Bringing in plenty of tourists to these little Outback towns. People seem to enjoy it and let's face it, plenty of camels to choose from. Which way you boys going over?"

Mark yawned again.

"Down the old Youga track, which will take us to the turn-off to Windi. Shortens the time for the camels instead of going into Marree and down again. We got our truck pretty well sorted for a few days away. Rangi, you reckon the tyres are good on the camel trailer?"

Rangi nodded.

"Everything all checked yesterday, ready to motor. Two spares in case."

Mark saluted. "Righto, see you blokes when we get back on Monday."

Chapter Eight

Early morning in fresh air and the first rays of sunshine, there were already signs of activity round the big sheds where Kate and her father were packing a white four-wheel drive Ute with all necessities for a trip into town.

Kate was an attractive, sturdy girl of twenty-two years, with a round intelligent tanned face and dark hair pushed under her worn felt hat. She was clad in frayed denim shorts, T-shirt and sturdy work boots. She had robust arm muscles that denoted her life of hard work on the cattle property and she gave off an air of determination, that had stood her in good stead in tough times.

Kevin Brenna was a tall, lean, weather-beaten cattle man with a shock of greying hair under his big felt hat, with heavy khaki trousers and tough gaiters, ending in thick-soled desert boots. Kate's blue cattle dog, Deefer, was full of excitement at seeing the Ute being serviced, running under the rig and giving voice, until Kate gave him a nudge in the ribs and sent him under the vehicle to lie down.

He obeyed but lying in the dust, his eyes followed Kate's every move, determined not to be left out of whatever adventure was going to happen next.

The trio of working dogs in their wired-in pen were bellowing to be let out. Kevin shouted at them but, as they took no notice, he stepped onto the veranda where a leather whip hung coiled, went out into the yard and cracked it with ferocity. The three dogs stopped at once and watched the boss carefully. He pointed a stern finger at them and they sat back on their haunches, tongues hanging out, trained to obey the boss without question.

Two roustabouts came out of the men's quarters, saluted Kevin, heading for the big shed where a trail bike lay in various stages of disrepair, its innards strewn across an old bag on the floor with other bits arranged in tins. The older man, Fred, was a lean, stringy individual who had many years of hard work and cattle expertise behind him.

Fred had worked for the Brennas for many years and was treated as the 'leading hand' and considered part of the place. The younger man had come to Tindabulla after Ma Batley at the Windani pub had her brother, the Flying Padre recommend the lad from the Mission Orphanage when Zack reached sixteen, as a good worker.

The lad had some training in mechanics, so Kevin and Fred had been pleased to find Zack seemed to have a natural affinity with any types of machinery. He was not afraid of heights and would scale up a windmill with alacrity and once he understood the work to be done under Fred's expert eye, Zack would have it in pieces and repairs done pronto.

Mechanics were often considered most important people on remote properties when so much depended on machinery kept in good working order. Zack was also keen to learn the ropes for handling horses and cattle and seemed to be relishing Outback country life.

There was a call of breakfast from the veranda of the homestead and Mrs Brenna rang a cowbell hanging by the steps. Fred and Zack came out of the shed, washed their hands at the tub under the big tank and dried off on a towel hanging on a wire. They were dressed in heavy work overalls, carrying wide-brimmed hats, which were thrown on the rail, joining the family along the big table.

Mrs Brenna brought out a tray with platters of steak and eggs with fresh baked bread on the side, followed by a large enamel teapot and mugs for the tea. There was a big batch of fresh scones and plenty of syrup in a big tin to go with them. Everyone sidled onto the benches and the food was forked off the platters with gusto. The fresh scones were always a treat when plastered with the standard 'cocky's joy' syrup always available in the Outback.

Kate spoke through a mouthful.

"Ta, Ma. Great grub. Hope you can give me a tin of these scones to take with me, in case of holdup somewhere, so I can have a bit of lunch. Hope the tucker's good at the pub though Mrs Batley usually makes sure everything is up to scratch for the hired hands."

Kevin stretched his long arms over his head and gestured to his workmen.

"Could you give Kate a hand to load her prize possession, please—she refuses to go without her little washing machine. It's like a lucky charm for her."

Everyone laughed.

Kate winced.

"All right for you lot to chuck off, but I get grumpy if I got to work hard in dirty smelly clothes and you can guess with the camel races coming up it will be flat strap all the time."

Mrs Brenna looked a might concerned.

"I know you are used to that track to Windani, but I hope you don't have any serious holdups."

Kevin spoke quietly, "As soon as Kate and Deefer are on the road, I'll ring the pub and let Mrs Batley know to expect them around mid-afternoon. I'm sure that good lady would send out someone on the track if Kate was late."

After the breakfast things were cleared, Kate went out to the yards behind the house and whistled softly. A bedraggled young Magpie gave a carolling call and floated down from a gum tree to land beside her. She smoothed the ruffled feathers of a damaged wing and offered a couple of titbits from her meal.

Named Scruffy because his feathers were all out of place, he had been rescued after being blown out of his nest and he decided Kate was a good surrogate mother. He preened and called gently as she offered her arm for him to sit. Kate gave him a good talking-to about his personal hygiene and lack of grooming.

"I'll be away for a few days, young Scruff, so no pecking at the hens, right? That rooster will tumble you over again and you'll be a bigger mess than usual."

She gently placed the beady-eyed bird back on the rail and went to the fowl yard, where there was a ruckus from the big rooster, Major Tom, who considered himself lord of all he surveyed. His main opponent was a black and white magpie goose, obviously called Goosey, who could fly but refused to leave a good home after Kate had rescued him from the big dam when he had become trapped in the mud at the side.

The main contention between the two birds were the kitchen scraps thrown over the fence. They shouted and hissed and clacked at each other, while the hens ignored them and ate all the best bits before the argument was over.

Kate chuckled at the silly birds and climbing over the homestead back fence, trudged uphill to where her own horses were lodged. She let out a shrill whistle so the two stock horses, a mare and a gelding, resting under the shade of a stand of trees, pricked up their ears, turned and trotted towards her. The other half-grown foal decided he wasn't going to respond and ran, kicking his heels, tearing round the top of the paddock.

Kate laughed at his antics, pulled down the head of her mare, Miss Molly and combed the fringe away from the horse's eyes. Both the stock horses nudged Kate and the gelding, Bushie, nibbled Kate's shirt pockets to see if there were any titbits on offer.

She good-naturedly pushed him away, patting his shoulder, pulling out a couple of scones and dividing them into bits offered both horses a piece on her palm. They chewed with appreciation and nudged her for more, but she batted them away going to the small hay shed to drag out some good lucerne hay, stacking it in the wire feed holder.

The foal stopped his wild run and eyed the hay. Kate turned her back on him and pretended to talk to the other horses, which were already nosing the good hay. The foal walked carefully, almost seemingly on tiptoe behind her, but she refused to look at him. So he eyed her again, then gave her a nudge in the rear and galloped off.

Kate chuckled to herself, still refusing to look at the colt; went over to the water trough to make sure the float was clear, so the water ran well. The other horses took no notice of the colt, so he tried to get her attention by galloping up to her full tilt, this time nudging her under the arm. He bent his head in submission and so Kate slung an arm round his neck, speaking softly to him, rubbing his rough coat while she blew in his nose.

She offered the remnants of the scones. The foal was ecstatic, chomping them at once. He followed her down to the fence, where Kate grabbed a brush and ran it over his still furry baby coat. This time he stood stock still, quivering with delight.

Kate pushed him away as she climbed over the fence, saying, "You with all your nonsense and worry about imaginary Bogeymen! Perhaps, we'll call you Bogey and then you'll be stuck with it for life! You're a good-looking boyo, but I wonder if you'll have the temperament of your ma when it comes to hard work? See you when I get back so we can start some proper training. Then you'll know you're alive!"

The colt whickered, stamping his feet and took off again to tear around the paddock.

Kate went to the shed to check over her transport with her dad. He used a tyre gauge on all the heavy-duty tyres plus the spare. He also made sure to put in an air pump, that could be run off the engine in case of tyres being staked. The white Ute was well packed up with a tarp lashed over the back, with Kevin and

Kate making sure everything was not going to shake apart on the rough tracks. It was very dry at the present time and the cattle yards were a sea of dust.

Kevin looked across the never-ending landscape and shook his head.

"Be nice if we could get some winter rain shortly to fill the big dam. The cattle do well enough on the bore water but nothing like fresh to tart up the place again."

He pushed his hat back on his head and looked at his daughter.

"You sure you've got everything now?"

Kate looked at him softly.

"Don't fuss, dear dad, you know I'm capable of handling just about anything and the drive into Windi ain't the end of the world. Besides I have Deefer to back me up and defend my honour if needed!"

Deefer barked at the sound of his name and jumped up ready to get in the cab with Kate. She kissed her father, started the engine, tooted the horn to her mother standing on the veranda, who waved and kissed her hand.

Kate was pleased to be off and remarked to Deefer,

"Right, old son, only around 10 miles to the front gate, so settle back and relax. You can get out for a pit stop there."

Chapter Nine

They drove out along the well-designated station road, graded to suit the B-double trucks that had just taken away their loads of cattle from the last muster. On the way, Kate spotted some disturbance on a rise, where a line of gum trees filled the horizon and she pulled over. She was cranky and growled to Deefer,

"Reckon that's another mob of camels come in for the water in the dam. Wonder where they got in—let's just trek up here a bit and check the fence line."

She stopped her rig and they got out to view the lengths of fencing around the dam paddock. They soon found evidence of the camel entry with a whole panel of barbed wire pushed right down. Kate stamped in annoyance and Deefer barked.

"Have to ring dad when I get to the pub and let him know about this damage—it's never-ending, between tearing down fences and damaging watering points, the cost escalates all the time. We need the camel catchers back again pronto!"

At that moment Deefer spotted some movement in the long brown grass near some old tree trunks and roared his disapproval, tearing round the area flat out. Kate stopped short and placing two fingers in her mouth gave a blasting whistle.

Deefer dropped in his tracks but whined and scrabbled at the ground. She trod carefully towards the long grass to see perhaps a King Brown snake emerge. She jumped, as with a great rush and hiss a large goanna shot out and up the tree trunks to perch on the top, his mouthful of armed teeth on full display.

Kate started to laugh and Deefer got up from his crouch to add his voice to the disturbance.

She patted his head and remarked, "Lucky for you, mate, that's too big a meanie to take on. He'd give you a right good chewing."

"Thought it was a snake and I didn't pack the rifle so we'd have had to make a run for the Ute. Come on, we'll leave that blighter to his perch and check the mail box."

They drove in silence until the grid at the front gate came into view. Beside the big sign that pronounced 'Tindabulla' there was a large assortment of boxes, sturdily built to contain mail, as well as an insulated metal cabinet shaded by an awning to contain cold supplies left by the couriers. Plus, there was an open-sided box for any maintenance supplies.

Kate halted her rig and she and Deefer got out to inspect the boxes but found nothing that was needing to be picked up, other than newspapers which were always a week old.

She swatted the hordes of flies that surrounded them and hustled Deefer back into the cab.

"Blasted flies never give anyone any rest, young Deef! Let's get to Windi and hope they get left behind!"

He gave a short bark and employed himself by snapping at the flies left in the cab. The white Ute headed down the beef road until Kate spotted an old finger board denoting 'Windani', which turned onto a barely used track. Some clown had wired a lump of tin underneath which stated,

"Welcome to Shit Track!"

This was emphasised by the many bullet holes in it. Kate changed down to four-wheel drive and negotiated the heavy sand and alternating rocky bars, she and Deefer were jolted around like peas in a bottle. Kate kept listening to the gear stowed in the back of the Ute, in case tightening of ropes was needed to keep it firm and in place.

As she struggled with the steering wheel, she remarked to Deefer,

"This is getting so bad, Deef, that I'll give the local Council a serve when I get back so they can get their grader out here to clear this up a bit."

Kate wiped the sweat from her forehead and saw that her rig was entering a damp-looking runoff, where water from some far away storm had seeped overnight. The sodden length of ground made her front left wheel start to groan. She negotiated the truck through most of the section, but her traction got slower and slower and finally ceased.

"Bother!" she told Deefer, "that's not a flat tyre, that's bog!"

They both got out to survey the damage and Kate could see that both front wheels where packed to the hilt with sticky bog. She sighed and went around to her toolboxes to look for something to dig mud.

Chapter Ten

Out on the desert country, flat as the eye could see, the terrain turned into bright yellows, with orange sand in many old shallow water channels of past rains. There was a stranded white Ute bogged down in a washaway that contained a water soak.

Seen from a distance there seemed to be the figure of a fit-looking young lady in T-shirt, shorts, rugged work boots with her dark hair tied up under a wide hat. She dug at the encrusted bog under the mudguards of the Ute with a file and the point of a small shovel. Having come from their family property and used to desert conditions. Kate had no illusions about the tough country, knowing of those who died with their boots on simply because they didn't take enough care for their safety.

She was satisfied with her well-stocked Ute and had a water barrel, jerry cans of fuel and bedroll and supplies for herself and her dog. It didn't matter to her she had to dig away at the encrusted mud, it being just another job to get done. She dug away, resting now and then under the shade of an awning she had rigged up, sipping billy tea with a scone now and then to share with Deefer.

Somewhere in the distance, she heard the sound of a big truck. She cocked an eye at the dog and grinned.

"Deef, we might just be saved a lot of digging if whoever it is has a winch— that is if they don't get bogged as well."

The dog was very interested in the sound of the truck and stood at attention, his ears alert, ruff bristling while he made small growling barks. The girl made a gesture of quiet and the dog leapt into the back of the Ute and growled in his throat.

She said, "Gently, mate, till we see who it is."

Mark changed gears and he and Jason looked at each other and at the queer entourage ahead, a bogged Ute, a girl in work boots and big hat and a blue cattle dog ready to eat someone.

Kate walked carefully back along the track and waved to Mark, who brought his truck and trailer to a standstill. The two camels sitting on their haunches in the big trailer groaned in unison as the trailer came to a halt. Jason stepped out to greet Kate. Deefer leapt down from his perch, running up to Jason and giving him a welcome bark.

Mark got down from his cab and gave the tail-wagging Deefer a welcoming pat.

"Good day, Kate Brenna. What's a good girl like you doing in a place like this? Do you remember, we're the camel catching mob who were taking camels from your place last year. As you can see, Deefer remembers us. How's your folks?"

"All good, a bit dry. Great to see you." She smiled shaking hands. "I didn't recognise you boys for a moment but Deefer was on the ball. Bet he remembers the camel steaks you threw him last time."

Jason pulled a face and remarked, "Deefer was the only one who could get his teeth through that tough old stuff. It nearly turned me into a vego!"

They all laughed and Deefer joined with more tail-wagging and a bark.

Kate turned more serious about her predicament.

"As you can see this washaway looked solid but ain't! So you blokes need to stop where you are until you have a walk around the terrain to make a detour, if you can find a hard ridge. There must have been a storm north of here. Don't suppose you've got a winch?"

Mark nodded. "How long you been stuck?"

Kate considered. "Coupla hours. Heading to Windani to a job at the pub as Ma Batley can't get enough workers while the races are on—and I see you're going the same way."

The men nodded. Jason took a walk around the washaway, looking at the mottled ground, testing the area with a steel rod from the truck. Mark had a look at where Kate had been digging mud out from under her mudguards.

He whistled through his teeth. "You've done a pretty good job, Kate. Nearly there."

He saluted her but looked twice when he saw the washing machine in the back of her Ute.

"First time I've seen a washing machine going to the races."

Kate bridled.

"Don't know what it is with you blokes—everyone wants to comment on my washing machine! Well may you chuck off but where I go it goes! Hate filthy clothes when I gotta work hard and it's done me many a good turn. At least I won't have to cart water to it at the pub. I'll pack up while you explore the track."

She undid her tarp, put away the billy and food, nudged sand over her small fire, cleaned her digging tools and was ready to roll in a short time.

Jason gave a shrill whistle from where he was walking. Mark went to tread the new track he had plotted. The men sounded it out thoroughly and deemed it sturdy enough to take the weight of their truck and trailer.

Mark looked ahead of them and said, "That's about as good as we can get, Jase, so we'll soldier on through in low gear and see if we can winch out the Ute from the other side. Then Kate can follow us into Windi and we can keep an eye on her rig. Not far now."

Mark started the truck and following Jason's directions, carefully manoeuvred across the new ground, making sure the camel trailer didn't stray from his tracks. As he arrived on stony ground, around the front of Kate's Ute, Jason came to undo the winch cable and led it out to attach it to the tow point under the front of the Ute. With a great sound of grinding the Ute slowly came out of the bog and onto hard ground.

Mark was pleased and he and Jason had a high-five and they fed the winch back on its reel. They went to see Kate.

"Reckon that's the last of the boggy washaways, Kate and if you follow us, keeping in the truck tracks, you'll be right to get into Windi."

Kate was very thankful for the help and she and Deefer seemed to be smiling all at once.

She said to the men, "Good job! See you at the pub later on and I'll shout you a beer or two."

Jason grinned.

"That'll be great. We gotta get our camels settled first and find a place to doss down, probably make a camp at the back of the showgrounds, but we'll be over later for certain."

The convoy started off in low gear, the truck and trailer going ahead while Kate drove her rig following their tracks. There were still some washaways but, luckily, these had rocky bottoms so the drive into town went without mishap.

Chapter Eleven

The former mining town of Windani sat on the edge of the gibber plain with a backdrop of brown, orange and gold mountains lacing the northern area of the Flinders Ranges. Besides some opal being found there in early days and the forays into uranium mining, with the smaller mines around Mt Painter being called 'Radium Ridge', the back country of that area became a maze of old mining tracks and disused sites.

After the old Ghan railway line went through the area, the town became a Mecca for fossickers and a few hardy tourists, its main claim to fame being the natural mound springs that watered the town. The eternal bubbling artesian waters dribbled over the edge of the mound into a permanent wetland.

The locals long ago had dammed the run-off so the precious water did not waste into the desert sand, so the waterway was quite substantial. As oases in the desert the mound springs were of vital importance to Indigenous people, as well at the settlers, plus like gold for the early camel drivers taking their teams across the desert.

There could be as many as around 5,000 of these springs surfacing the northern area of South Australia. Where the springs have been flowing for thousands of years, the accumulation of minerals have created the mounds and the overflow makes wonderful depressions for all manner of wildlife, where the surrounding trees would be filled with cockatoos, bevies of brilliant coloured finches and green and gold budgerigars which flirted and sipped the waters.

These were joined in the cool of the evening by the red roos and shy wallabies, until the night brought out the dingoes to drink. Plus, there were all manner of tiny wildlife, such as dunnart, bilbies and bandicoots to feast off insect and grubs in the healthy grasses and shrubs.

Beside the wetland from the springs, there were red mineral rocks that accumulated the mineral over eons and the locals found them a great help in their efforts to contain some of the dust. Near the spring there was Windani's large generator for the town set in a shed plus a pump that sent water up to a tall tank, which supplied water to the town at a reasonable pressure.

When the first Ghan railway was established from Quorn to Marree, it followed the same track as the Overland Telegraph to Alice springs. Because the Government Bureaucracy of the time did not understand the nature of Outback harsh conditions there was strife right from the beginning. When the first wooden telegraph poles went up, they fell down pretty quickly and it was found that the white ants thought it was Christmas and had eaten the lot!

Some of the early Ghan tracks were laid straight on the sand without ballast, so the tracks subsided quickly with the weight of engines and freight. The sleepers were also made of timber so the white ants had a field day.

The passengers on the first trains got used to having a flat car hitched behind the tender to carry tools and spare sleepers so that passengers and crew could repair the line and allow the train to continue its journey. There were rifles and ammo as well, in case there were serious washouts; also, the passengers were sent out to shoot roos or goats for their own sustenance. The early services were notorious for delays so there was a saying among passengers that if *your watch said the Ghan was on time, you need a new watch.*

The steam trains had to have frequent water stops along the way and it was found that the heavily mineralised water caused scaling in the boiler tubes, so desalination plants were set up to decant good water into steel towers. Coal was found at Leigh Creek so that as the rail line headed further north coal fuel dumps were placed with the water towers.

The remnants of the old train line were found outside Windani with rusted rails and abandoned rolling stock, which entertained all the kids and made good photos for the tourists passing through, who souvenired the rail spikes for some unfathomable reason.

On coming in or out of the postage-stamp sized township, there were large signs stating that due to unstable weather conditions in the desert areas, all vehicles proceeding from that point had to register with the Police.

The Windani main street boasted a clutch of bigger buildings, including the old red corrugated iron pub and a general do-everything store with bowsers outside, that also had a side building which housed the only mechanic. There was a Café with good signs outside denoting the fact that it was the best tucker for 300 miles.

Besides the generator shed near the mound springs, there was a smaller shed which held the town's only small fire truck, really a Ute, with gear on the back. This was run by the caretaker of the generator and water supply and the fixit man for all electrical problems.

There were also a few demountable buildings, one of which had a timber lockup at the back with the sign denoting the presence of the local Policeman, Sergeant Dave Dawson and his side-kick, Constable Nick Taylor. Nick was on his first secondment from Adelaide to the life stream of the desert. Nick, a tall, genial young man, with close cropped dark hair and the good physique of a Rugby player, had a permanent residence at the pub's men's quarters. He seemed to enjoy meeting the locals, who had taken a liking to him as they thought Nick had no *side*!

Nick had been a keen footy player in the city, so had formed the first Rugby team in Windani out of a few would-be footballers gathered from around the pub on a Saturday night. After much begging from a bevy of schoolkids, including some very swift girls, Nick had agreed to coach junior touch footy on a Saturday morning. He had told the barely possible Windani Rugby team that if they continued to improve in their after-work practice on the oval at the showgrounds, he would join them up to the Western area League competition.

Both Policemen had a good rapport with the locals, being always on call in case of trouble, with help given to rescue those stranded in the desert through breakdown or injury. There were only a few dust-ups with drunken outsiders now and then during festivities like the local show or the camel races.

At the back of the town were the designated school grounds with a paddock for horses out the back, where there was a water trough and shade provided by a thicket of pepperina trees. The school house was a donated old miner's shack, converted as much as funds would allow, governed by an elderly teacher, who had lived in the town for many years after her husband had died and considered all the children belonged to her!

The kids responded to her kindness and were always seen coming and going from her little house at odd times, usually because she was a good cook and had a supply of fairy cakes for visitors.

Behind the school on a small rise there was an old cemetery, which held the remains of some of the intrepid first Ghan fettlers who had the heat and dry and dust, as well as poor provisions with which they had to contend. There were also old headstones of the former uranium miners who had lost their lives, working in very unsafe conditions in the early days. It was quiet place surrounded by the trees that people had planted there over the years, with newer stones denoting a passing of the town's inhabitants.

The school children had a nature lesson in acquiring local tree seeds, sprouting them and then planting and caring for them in the cemetery grounds, plus a history lesson from their teacher about the people of the past.

There was a host of old mining shacks around the town, some converted into elaborate sheds, plus the old tin cabins that were once filled with fettlers who had worked on the original railway line. Many of these hardy old souls were still in residence and cared for by the townspeople. As well, there were some well-appointed timber homes, where owners had attempted to grow gardens in front and on the outskirts there were shanties constructed of anything available from the mining dumps.

One of the demountable buildings in the main street had a big sign signifying the presence of the District Nurse, Jean Rogers, the town heroine, who was always in evidence, in case needed medical help. Jean for some forty years had tirelessly given sustenance to all ills and injuries in her jurisdiction. She had radio access to the Emergency operator at the royal Adelaide Hospital and the Royal Flying Doctor Service.

The main street led to the flattest area where there was a graded dirt runway and drooping windsock that announced the possibility of the RFDS plane landing in medical emergency. A small tin roof at one side housed a bench and drums of Av-gas. This hot and uncomfortable place was where some unlucky injured ringer or unseated camel rider had to lie when they needed to be airlifted to Adelaide hospital, sometimes along with a pregnant lady or two.

Chapter Twelve

The district nurse, after a morning's hard work with some tribal injuries, came out of her donga, closing the door against the eternal dust, wiping the sweat off her face with her bandana. Jean was stocky, grey-haired and very efficient. Always clad in tan trousers and beige blouse with big, rugged boots, her hair jammed under a rag, hat, she smiled broadly at one and all regardless of race or creed. If they had any sort of medical trouble, Jean was the first port of call.

She ambled into the pub to find the bar girls, Madge and Gina, washing tables and, generally, cleaning up ready for opening. Jean was thirsty, having been seeing to a tourist who was not aware of the prevalence of the grey galvanised burrs surrounding the area. She had to dig out the burrs in the behind of a fat American, who had decided it was too barbaric here for him, so he was dumping his hire car and leaving on the next available flight for the city.

The girls laughed at Jean's story, Gina asking, "How do you keep busy out here when all this race stuff is over and everything quiet again? Besides digging out burrs for fat Americans, that is!"

Jean replied, with a twinkle in her eye, "I've been on the spot for nearly forty years and never been without something going on. I've trained other bush nurses, some who went back to the cities, but others loved the desert and the people and like me stayed on for the duration to work in remote areas."

Gina was very interested, not having met such a knowledgeable nurse before.

"How did you get on when you first arrived here? Must have been hard so long ago, when there was mainly miners and station people around here?"

Jean was thoughtful for a moment.

"When I first got here as a very young, untried country nurse, I decided to grow vegies in my back yard but the first dust storm filled my garden to hip height and my veg were never seen again. I only had a generator at the surgery, which broke down periodically, so I had to learn to manage the inside of it and ended up doing the same for anyone else who had gen troubles. Once we got the big town generator, my skills became redundant."

Ma Batley came in at that moment and laughed.

"Sounds a bit like me, Jean. The first thing I had to learn when my husband and I arrived was how to change tyres. Plenty of stakes out there that are a curse for tyres. Being a former town girl I had a lot to learn, including not to try and kill a snake but to get out of the road quick! Unless it's in my bed!"

Gina looked horrified, but Jean laughed.

"Some of the rough desert tracks I've had to traverse were real tyre killers, so I got I could change a tyre quick as a wink. I also learned what could happen to those who took the desert too lightly, when a young Japanese man on a large motor cycle went roaring through the town, taking no notice of the Police signs—he probably couldn't read English—and he headed out along the track north. They found him much later dead beside his bike, with no sign of water or fuel having been on board."

Ma had heard Jean's stories before so remarked, "Tell the girls about the time you got an offer of marriage."

Jean chuckled.

"I've had to ride in the back of all types of four-wheel vehicles with injured people, once in the Mailman's old Leyland Badger truck. Now that was an experience! Old Tom Kruise is a real trooper of the Outback. Another time we were carrying an injured stockman, who had his horse fall on him and it had broken his back.

I sat for hours in the summer heat, trying to keep the man still in a bucking Ute, holding an umbrella over his head and shooing away the flies. By the time we got to town and the Flying Doctor came in, the man declared he was in love with me and asked me to marry him. I declined gently and the flying Doc took him away. I heard later the stockman made an eventual recovery."

The girls cheered, but Ma spoke with pride.

"That was just one episode. Jean nursed a child with meningitis for days by herself in town here, as the RFDS plane had bogged on a station strip. The child survived and the parents nominated Jean for an Australia Medal."

Jean smiled, her memories coming back.

"It all goes with this harsh territory. But I had a much harder victim to deal with. I was out on a mercy mission to one of the Outback stations when I found on the track a man whose car was burning. He had fallen out on the sand.

Somehow I lifted him, not knowing how I found the strength, got him into my work vehicle, which always carries jerry cans of fuel and water. I doused the man's burns with water, dripped saline into his mouth all the way back, calling the RFDS on my radio for help. I had to sit with him for twenty hours until the plane arrived in the night and fell asleep in the car to be woken by the police sergeant next morning when he came looking for me."

The women applauded Jean and Ma patted her on the back.

"That's why Jean is our local heroine—Windani couldn't survive without her! Give the good lady a cold beer!"

Chapter Thirteen

The old showgrounds on the northern side of the town had fenced off areas for stock, plus a high water tank that fed numerous troughs, and plank seats around the arena outside a K-wire fence. The interior had been graded to suit the camel race, taking away the goal posts that had been perched up to encourage the hopeful rugby teams.

There were sheds out the back with a sheltering of pepperina and bull oak trees, where horses drowsed under the sparse shade in a number of post and rail sided yards. There was a high broadcast box, where the announcer and the judges could spot the winners and award prizes. There was a temporary office, where the town's ladies did all the accounting and took the dues from the camps and race people.

The makeshift camping area was out the back of the yards, on a bit of flat ground with a bevy of all types of camping gear and trucks, tents, plus the odd caravan and bus. There was the smell of woodsmoke in the air and sounds of merriment from old timers quaffing beer under their tattered tarps. There was a good supply of water fed in from the high tank to somewhat shaky outdoor showers that only had half a door each and were open to the sky.

The effluent drainage from the showers ran into the bush along an old ditch. This was exceedingly smelly and seemed to attract a pair of young emus, who rolled in the ditch, covering their feathers with evil-smelling slime.

The nick-named Mad Morrie, Café owner, in a fit of good heartedness had taken in the emu twins after they got lost, stolen or strayed from their paternal nest. He put them in with his chooks, fed and watered them and watched them growing alarmingly tall and spindly legged. Those legs unfortunately were attached to a pair of mischief-making imps, who were beady-eyed bundles of ragged foliage with brains the size of a pea, plus a great propensity for trouble.

Morrie often pondered, *could this really be Australia's National emblem?*

The emu twins were of one mind—their own—right from the start and Morrie lived to rue the day he took them in. Everything that lay in their path was grist to their mill. The fowl house was never a place of peace again, as the twins scrimshawed the wooden door with their huge feet until it fell down, eating all the corn and sending the fowls into hysterics.

The café cook, Buddy, got cranky and threatened to leave, as the emus soon found out how to knock over the rubbish bins out the back to extract their favourite tipple, leaving a trail of destruction behind them. To add insult to this crime, the twins got into the kitchen when someone left the door unlatched and pinched Buddy's favourite paring knife.

Last seen the favoured knife was disappearing fast into the scrub, clutched in a grinning beak, beady eyes laughing, four legs pumping and the twins were pursued by Buddy brandishing a meat cleaver. The twins' joy on a hot day was the un-lovely drain at the back of the camping area. They rolled and lay in it in the most outlandish positions, until they were coated in sticky goo and their feathers stuck out like an echidna and the miasma of pong emanated for a good fifty feet around them.

The twins strutted round like mannequins, excessively pleased with themselves. Visiting tourists leapt out of buses and cars, cooing over the half-grown emus, cameras at the ready, to be greeted by the terrible smell and there was almost a stampede in reverse to get back into the vehicles. The twins pinched any sunglasses or dropped knick-knacks and hied off with them into their scrubby hideout to examine at leisure their pilfered booty.

Their mischief grew in size, as well as their feet. Any camp tent or cabin door left open was an invitation to be invaded, pecked over, with any interesting titbit to be consumed or stolen away. They had been forbidden in all camping areas around the main street on account of their propensity for thievery and bad smell.

Morrie, in desperation to assert his authority was often seen threatening the twins with a long fence paling. They would leave the precincts at a run, their large feathered rumps bouncing with indignation. The twins were careful to keep just out of reach of the paling and Morrie, until he ran out of breath and swearwords and gave up the chase.

On a calm morning as the sun rose, the mist was clearing from the rocky ramparts around the mountains. The man in the old canvas tent was seen peering into a small mirror hung precariously on his tent pole. Clad only in blue-striped pyjama bottoms, he was industriously shaving the half-grown beard he had accumulated in days of bushwalking. Two curious emus appeared behind him seeming fascinated by this weird shaving behaviour.

The emu twins stepped closer and closer, peering intently over the man's shoulder. He jumped and shooed them away several times but, as soon as his back was turned, they stepped closer as though drawn by and invisible string.

Then suddenly there was an almighty shout and the emu twins were racing away, threading their way at full tilt though the camp ground. They were hotly pursued by an irate man with no shoes clad in pyjamas pants, brandishing a razor. The whole camp stopped in amazement and held its communal breath.

The emus won by a long leg and bobbing bottoms. They fled into the scrub through a patch of burrs. That sent the bare-footed one limping back through the camp, red with exertion and frustration.

"Them rotten blighters pinched me shaving mirror!" he roared. "And I only got half me beard shaved!"

Chapter Fourteen

As they reached the main drag into town, Kate saw the old red-roofed hotel and waved goodbye to Mark and Jason as she pulled around the back of the pub, where the quarters were for the hired hands. It was a large fenced-off square and in the next door yard were a couple of cud-chewing camels looking over the fence, plus a horse sheltering under an old shed.

Kate and Deefer were pleased to get out of the Ute, stretching and stamping with Deefer running round to find who had been there before him. Kate gave him a drink of water, chained him to the rear of the Ute and went in the back door of the pub to find out where she was to sleep. It was a welcome change after the midday heat. She was welcomed by the cook in the kitchen, a rangy aproned man with a short bristle haircut and a big smile. He was defeathering a brace of hens on the long table and looking very hot and fed up with the task.

The kitchen was long, with red corrugated iron outer walls, plus a high tin-roofed ceiling fitted with yellowing fly papers. The big black gas range took up nearly half of the back wall. The other wall was festooned with hanging cooking utensils and large ground ovens.

The floor was a cobble of dark red flat stones from near the mound springs, made over centuries of the drying minerals and which were polished to a high shine after many years of industrious feet. There were a number of timber doors out of the kitchen, with swing ones into the dining room and another into the private quarters.

Kate was quick off the mark seeing the work going on with the hens. She took off her hat and hung it on a nail and said,

"I'm Kate, the new hand—and I'll help with that job if you like?"

The cook looked very pleased and grinned. He wiped his brow leaving a trail of feathers on his forehead.

"I'm called Pup by ever'one, give you a high five, but I'm messy!"

He handed over a damp carcass, so Kate washed her hands and got stuck into the defeathering. They worked away, Pup telling Kate about the forth-coming camel races and the influx of visitors that had been arriving for days.

He said, "Got some queer fellas arriving round town, reckon they just looking, but me, I smell 'em! They be takin' bets on the races!"

Kate laughed. "I guess there'll be plenty of all sorts around. Many staying here?"

Pup nodded his head. "Yep! Full up 'ere, Ma ben taking bookings for yonks."

Kate felt a bit shy about calling the cook 'Pup', though she liked him very much.

After thinking it over she asked, "Do you mind if I ask, why you're called Pup?"

Pup laughed and said, "I born Polish with no good name for Aussies, so they call me P.U.P. after my initials and it stuck. Suit me quite OK."

They chatted in a desultory fashion until the birds were done, with Kate clearing away the debris, when Ma Batley came in. She waved a hand in greeting. Ma was a short, fit and feisty lady of indeterminate age, always clad in a green smock over her dress, with a shock of white hair and bright blue eyes that missed nothing.

"Good on you for arriving, Kate. I've been speaking with your dad on the phone. You had no trouble getting through? There's been some rain further north which might cause trouble for people coming down that road."

Kate chuckled.

"I did run into a bit of muddy patch, but two blokes I know in a big truck pulling a camel trailer saved the day and here we are."

She went to wash her hands while Ma went to the back door, putting two fingers to her lips, let out a great whistle. A sturdy, but somewhat bedraggled, tall thin elderly man, with a web of wrinkles radiating from his eyes and across his forehead, came around the corner and into the kitchen. He was wearing somewhat tattered trousers, faded check shirt and a bent old hat.

Ma waved at Kate.

"Bones, this is Kate, my help for the race weekend, so show her to the end room and give her a hand with her gear."

She turned to Kate, "The other girl, Gina, is in the room next to you for good company. You can help the girls in the bar, as well as clearing up after meals, plus helping now and then with the kitchen. My lass, Madge is home for a spell and will help in the bar. Have to warn you, though, her fiancé, Frank, is staying as well. He's nice enough, sleeps in the men's quarters, but sings all darn night when he gets on the grog!"

Everyone laughed and Pup clapped his hands.

"Like a good singalong, me!"

Ma smiled through her teeth.

"Yeah, right! I'll get the Sarge to sling you both in the pokey next time that happens!"

Bones beckoned Kate to follow him out to the row of tin-roofed rooms on the left side of the pub yard, which were the female quarters. He opened the creaky wooden door of the end room and gestured to the other end of the yard where a long range of iron clad rooms had derelict chairs and a couple of tables outside.

"Them's the men's quarters, miss. Hopefully quieter in these rooms."

As Bones opened the door, the hot air of the small room rushed out smelling of old boots and past inhabitants. Kate let Deefer off the chain and he ran into the room to check it out. He seemed to like Bones and leaned against him for a rub of his ears, but he growled when a couple of rowdy drunks started a ruckus in the outside yard.

Bones cackled.

"Good dog you got there, miss. I like good dogs. I'll keep an eye on him when you're busy in the pub. You keep him tied under your Ute, too and no one will touch anything belonging to you. Not that people are bad around here, just a bit easy with other people's stuff!"

Kate showed the gear in the back of the Ute and they sorted it out. She entered the sparse little unpainted room with a mossie net hanging over a bunk, old books on a dusty shelf in the corner, but with a clean set of towels, soap and sheets on the bunk. There was small cupboard in a corner with a tap, washbasin, kettle and tea bags. In another corner, there was a rod with wire hangers over it and a curtain in front that was the only place for clothes, besides a small set of drawers beside the bed. Bones showed Kate a wooden latch on the inside of the door.

"This is for the nights when the pub is full and rowdy, but if you keep your dog inside, he'll give any of the great unwashed some hell!"

They both laughed when Deefer, hearing his name barked and looked suspicious. Kate opened the push-out windows, then went over to the wash house at the side of the yard to get a mop and mop and cleaning cloths. She gave the room a good wipe over and washed the floor, so it already smelled much better. She and Bones wrangled her little washing machine into the room and set it beside the tap.

Bones went out and as Deefer was sniffing at his bag of dog pellets, Kate got his bowls out and gave him water and food. Just then Bones came back from the kitchen with a couple of meaty bones, which made Deefer his best friend.

Kate thought Bones seemed a nice man but wasn't sure she should call him by his nickname.

She asked diffidently, "I can't call you Bones like they do inside. My mother would go me crook!"

Bones smiled.

"I have to think about it, miss. Real name is Keith Burns, but I been called Bones most of my life 'cause of being long and skinny, so don't you pay any mind. Jus' don't call me late for dinner!"

They grinned and shook hands like old friends already. As they and Deefer went outside a huge furry ginger tom cat with a fat white tummy strolled out of the kitchen and jumped on one of the wobbly yard tables to preen his fur. Deefer always felt the need to chase any cats that were around with great doggy aplomb. This time as he galloped towards the table the cat raised itself to its full heights, glaring at the dog with huge orange eyes.

Deefer was sorely puzzled by this attitude unbeknown to him and skidded to a halt. He looked back at Kate and Bones with a frown between his eyes. The cat growled a hard, menacing growl and raised its fur to stand on end. Deefer slunk back to Kate and hid behind her legs, peering out at this ginger phenomenon of the cat world.

Bones cackled and said, "That's Zeus, who's ruled the roost here for all his nine lives and ain't afraid of nuthin' or nobody! Even the drunks don't mess with Zeus!"

Kate was vastly amused and nudged Deefer from behind her legs, "You big wuss, you're shaking like a poodle at a Rottweiler's party! Better stay away from that one, old buddy, or you'll end up cat's meat!"

Chapter Fifteen

In the arid Outback area of South Australia a futuristic, moonscaped land surrounded Coober Pedy, with the mining detritus of thousands of digs for the famous opal were scattered as far as the eye could see. It gave the huge area lining the breakaways of the old ranges a prehistoric aura of the possible unknown.

Great mounds of white underground spoil-heaps littered the landscape with all manner of derelict signs warning away likely thieves who came in the night to pilfer anything they might find. There were many warning signs at the edge of deep dark holes telling of danger and the locals were always on the lookout for anyone who may have fallen in while staggering home from the pub on a dark night. There had been some adventurous rescues and surprisingly few real damages, perhaps pertaining to the old adage that drunks always fell softly.

Some of the mining shafts had bigger signs, such as 'ATTACK KANGAROOS KEPT HERE FOR RATTERS!' who were the people trying to rat opal from existing mining shafts, sneaking round at night time. Some shafts in use also carried signs of crossed shotguns at their perimeter.

There was one brief, succinct sign which read 'BLASTING. KEEP OUT OR LOSE A LIMB!' While some wit had made a sign out of an old car door, painted it with green grass, of which there was none in the desert and which declared 'KEEP ORF THE GRASS!'

The sign that always caused great hoots of merriment from all newcomers and visitors was the one stating in no uncertain terms that 'EXPLOSIVES ARE NOT TO BE BROUGHT INTO THE PICTURE THEATRE!' The supposed theatre was a dusty compound with a booth at one end containing the projector and generator. Then there was an assortment of derelict chairs, stools, canvas bags and bare dirt with a bent white painted screen at the other end on shaky scaffolding.

The ban contained an epitome of truth, as there had been in the past some over-enthusiasm from the theatregoers, when an exciting Western reached a climax and someone threw a half stick of lighted gelignite at the baddies on the screen. The ensuing fracas nearly brought the house down, so the ban was put in place.

The early miners found they could burrow into their existing galleries to make reasonably comfortable homes, where the temperature even on the hottest days remained around a pleasant and moderate coolness. Now and then, a bit of paint was splashed around the interior walls in an effort to stop the eternal dust filtering down, but it was a lost cause so many didn't bother.

Ventilation holes were drilled through to take pipes which stuck into the air like sentinels. Water tanks were installed overhead outside to collect from the water tanker that arrived periodically from the nearest bore. The bore water was so hard and full of minerals it made the drying clothes stand up by themselves, but the miners grew beards to save from shaving and preferred to drink beer for refreshment rather than deal with the bore water.

Clean clothes seemed to be something of a fool's errand, so the miners wore their duds until they fell apart. Not much point in doing any washing of clothes when they were just as filthy the next day.

There was a permanent aura of white dust that covered the entire town and landscape, filtered through clothes, hair, eyes and mouths, if not closed. Whenever the wind blew which was most of the time, the white dust rose like a bomb cloud into the atmosphere and could be seen for many miles away. This mystified travellers, who often thought there had been new rocket blasts from the southern end of the Woomera Rocket Range.

There was an underground pub in the main street, which had been dug out an old horizontal mine shaft. It had a crudely lettered sagging awing over the steel bars of the door, which opened for business according to the wishes of the proprietor.

There was a corrugated iron tank perched on the roof ready for the next load of bore water, with a rudimentary piping system leading inside to the bar area. There was an old steel basin hung on the wall but the locals joked it had never seen water in it, let along wash mugs! There were rough recesses dug out of the wall behind the bar, which accommodated ranks of tin beer mugs, anything of glass being a dangerous thing of the past.

The main bar room had several ventilation holes to take pipes through the roof to assist the miasma of tobacco smoke that hung at eye-watering level when the bar was full. The room had been enlarged over the years and the roof drilled out to accommodate short and tall.

It was rumoured that when enlarging the pub was going on, Mine Host, Wossa, had uncovered a few good opals in his excavations, but he wasn't a man to open his mouth about it, in case the would-be opal gougers set upon his establishment to the detriment of the walls and fittings. He kept a loaded shotgun under the counter to deter any rabid drunken gougers from getting ideas above their station!

There was a permanent rumour also around the Pedy that Wossa had a secret moonshine still hidden somewhere in the labyrinth of his dugout passages, where he brewed his grog from a recipe that had come from his father's home country. Only Wossa's mates had ever tasted this magic elixir and they weren't giving anything away; Wossa being a powerful and hard man. No one wanted to get on his wrong side and, perhaps, have a trip down one of the disused mineshafts on a moonless night!

Chapter Sixteen

After a hot and heavy day's dusty work, the pub was full of drinkers and fag smoke, many seated at the scattered metal tables and some sitting on the uneven dirt floor. When there was a scarcity of seating, those on the floor had their beers delivered to hand by the bar boy, whose name was 'Pothole' because his boss reckoned he was always in the road!

There was a big fridge set into a dugout section of the wall containing kegs with all their systems in place and from outside there came the hum of a generator to supply both the fridge and the somewhat dodgy lighting system.

The actual bar was a relic of better times, a big slab of concrete that had a history of past drinkers on its top. Suspicious marks in the ceiling looked like they could be old bullet holes added to the decor.

Wossa was a hard-bitten older man, around six feet tall with a permanent scowl, a rim of grey whiskers and large moustache below a bald pate, who took no guff from anybody, drunk or sober. He presided over the hefty metal cash box welded under the concrete bar and gave orders to Pothole. Not many locals were game to play up in the pub, in case of being barred, a life-threatening ordeal, like being sentenced to Hell or worse.

Customers gave beer orders to Pothole, who ran around picking up used mugs, dunking them in the wash basin and ineffectually wiping off dust from the tables, plus supplying the drinkers with their sustenance.

A table full of drinkers, leaning over their beers were telling tall tales, each trying to outdo the others. The oldest of the men had a lean, wind-bitten face and arms and a mangy holey hat. The men with him called him Harpic, (reckoned he was clean around the bend) and he was shouting to be heard over the din.

"I tell you that Ginger and Mungo have been prospecting for years around Mt Painter! They know sumpin' they don't tell nobody! It ain't Lasseter's gold they found, or they would be weighing it at the Assayer's—but they go orf every now and then and only the blacks know where. I *know* they found the Opal Dragon because I know the black fellas who knows where as well!"

His mates all thumped the table and made derisory noises and rocked back in their chairs with laughing.

Harpic was adamant.

"I tell youse lot I heard the story from two young blacks I give a lift to outside Windani and they actually heard Ginger talking about it with a surveyor bloke."

The men around the table slapped their sides and made more rude noises and whistles.

Harpic gritted his teeth and exploded, "You hopeless lot should shut yer faces 'cause I know them old prospectors know Mt Painter to the Pedy like the backs of their hands—there ain't much they don't know about opals."

Robbie, one of his mates, who had sat quietly for a while, started to nod in agreement.

"I also heard the story 'cause I was in the truck with Harpic when he gave the black fellas a lift and I ain't no liar and any man who says different can have my knuckle sandwich!"

This affirmation suddenly silenced the other men. However, Robbie continued with some thought, "Just the same, them old fossickers is close bastards! Mates told me they know where the Opal Dragon is but don't never say to anyone. Tight as a duck's arse!"

When Harpic had the attention of them all, he milked the opportunity to tell his tale.

"I heard Mungo came into Windani with a load of crystals and the word around the ridges was that the cave of the Opal Dragon is loaded. A whole skeleton of opal, youse blokes—imagine what that would be worth, maybe millions."

The men all looked into their beers, thinking seriously about the fortune that could be there.

At the next table, Cosmo, a tall man with a shock of black hair and vestiges of stubble around his beard line, who was clad in white dusty dungarees, black t-shirt, with a dirty black bandana round his head, was listening. His brother, Chook, a plump, tattooed younger fellow who was short as Cosmo was tall. He also sat listening to the talk next door. He had brown hair falling over his rather vacant blue eyes and was also clad in dungarees. Both men had beers in hand and a big ugly dog under the table.

With them sat two Asian-looking men, who never offered any information as to where they came from or where they went to. These men turned up from Adelaide now and then buying opals. They were small men, sharp dressers, with slick backed hair, sharp black trousers and shirts, pointy shoes, gold neck chains and large watches. They were buyers of bad repute, always out for the quick deal and fast with a knife when crossed.

The Asians had been looking at a few pieces of opal potch that Cosmo had spread out for sale. They had been listening in to the drinkers at the next table shouting and their ears pricked up when they heard mention of the Opal Dragon.

Teo, the more outspoken of the two looked most interested and in a low voice said to Cosmo, "What this Opal Dragon?"

Cosmo yawned, as if bored with the effort.

"It's a mad yarn about an opalised fossil in a cave of crystals, but no one knows where the thing is, except maybe old Ginger Martin and his mate, Mungo Jack from Windani—and a few black trackers—and if they know, none of them is telling!"

Chook, who was half drunk on his one beer and slurping more, chipped in loudly, "Yair! Old mad yarn but a goodie!"

Cosmo said quietly, but with venom, "Shut yer gob, Chook!"

Chook subsided, looking hurt. The drinkers at the next table were getting more enthusiastic about the yarn of the fabled Opal Dragon and more blokes joined in the gabble.

The Asians and Cosmo moved a little closer with ears open for information. A big burly bloke wearing miners garb and a dirty hat that said 'Boof' avowed he heard about the best black tracker at Windani, who would know where the secret cave was as well.

Boof declared, "There's that old tracker, Fardy, one of the local tribes around Windani who knows the fossickers. I heard Fardy's so good he can track a ferret with a nosebleed on a dark night! He's a mate of Mad Morrie at the Windi Café. If you really wanted to know properly you might get it out of Morrie if you squeezed Fardy."

Harpic looked stunned.

"*That's* todays *bad* idea! Everyone hears of Mad Morrie and things he done to blokes who get on his bad side! Be a bloody fool to take on Morrie, 'cause his black mates would call out the witch doctor man on yer the next day and y'd die with yer boots on!"

The men looked serious at this proverbial threat famous in the Outback.

Harpic said succinctly, "I tell you, Morrie is as mad as a meat ant when crossed. One time, Morrie let it be known after a break in at his shop that anyone who tried it again would be hung out to dry. Of course, there's always some drunken lunatic who'd have a go to pinch stuff. Morrie happened to be out the back turning off the lights, grabbed the joker in a headlock, his black cook, Buddy, stripped off the guy's trousers and Morrie hung him by his shirt off a hook outside the front door, faster than lightning through a wet dog!"

The men around the table all hooted and laughed.

Rob said admiringly, "What happened to the idiot? Did he fall off the hook?"

Harpic chortled.

"Nah, the bloke was still hung by the time the town woke up and people came along to laugh and chuck orf at him. Reckoned he was crying by the time the Police Sergeant made Morrie take him down. Another time, some layabouts roughed up his cook, Buddy. Mad Morrie chased them down the main street, tickling their backsides with a bullwhip. He keeps the bullwhip rolled up hanging on a wall in the café, so blokes learned they doan mess with Morrie or his black fellas!"

The Asians were listening with all ears. Tong motioned to Cosmo and hissed, "Get over and ask them, find out where this opal cave. You find out dragon story—good money in it for you."

Cosmo, with Chook stumbling behind went over to the story tellers. He was all casualness and well-being.

"Good day mates—couldn't help hearing the bit about the so-called Opal Dragon—if I buy a beer round can youse fill me in on the yarn?"

Everyone nodded their agreement and Cosmo and Chook hauled their chairs over and yelled at Pothole for beer.

Cosmo went and paid Wossa for the drinks. The beers were brought over and the men started to swill them with relish. Teo and his mate Tong were straining to hear what was being said but then the men there had suddenly become quieter and were talking in undertones to Cosmo and Chook, huddling in to listen.

Tong muttered to his mate, "If they find out where fossil bones are, we maybe make big killing. The opal in it could be millions, more than we make with this lousy opal buying!"

Teo being more sceptical, whispered, "If! Maybe just these men damn fool ideas."

They looked searchingly at each other.

Tong hissed, "A whole opal skeleton!"

There was a shout from the next table and more beer was brought. Cosmo stood up, slapping a few backs.

"That's a good yarn, youse blokes tell, enjoy your beers and we'll see you round."

He beckoned to Chook, who was getting more tipsy by the minute.

Chook, starting to stagger leered at the men, "Yairs, we'll find the Opal Dragon and bring it back. Beers for everybody!"

He laughed hugely. The Asians looked horrified and made gestures to Cosmo to shut Chook up. Cosmo grabbed Chook by his singlet and shook him menacingly.

"Chook, you dopey bastard, if you don't' shut your gob, I'll smack you so hard all your pictures will all fall orf!"

The whole room cheered, whistled and stamped, while Chook looked shamefaced. They went back to sit with the Asians and the room resumed its normal hum.

Cosmo leaned in towards the Asian pair and quietly told them, "As far as the Bush Telegraph knows, the supposed opal skeleton is in a cave somewhere in the Mt Painter area in the northern Flinders Ranges. Two old miners Ginger Martin and Mungo Jack who hang out around Windani have been to the cave. One of the local blacks went with them to it some time ago."

Chook laying across the table added his bit, "Thash what I reckon too!"

Cosmo thumped the table right under Chook's nose and he reeled back and fell his chair. The three men ignored Chook, who went to sleep on the floor with his head on the big dog.

Teo asked, "Why not been found if others hear about it?"

Cosmo pondered for a moment.

"It's supposed to be in a tribal sacred place or sumthin' and the only whities who are their blood brothers have been taken there. The Mt Painter area is some rough bugger of a country!"

Tong shifted excited in his seat.

"You got map? How far from here? You take us there for big money?"

Cosmo went over to the bar and spoke to Wossa, who gave him a dirty creased map. They spread it over their table. Cosmo traced along the map with a filthy fingernail.

"Have to think about that. It wouldn't be easy. Here we are at the Pedy— quickest way is across an old desert track to Anna Creek. Shit track but passable in dry weather with four-wheel drives. Chook's truck can go through anything but my rig cannot. We could veer off onto the old Younga track south and come out to the cross roads near Windani. Mt Painter is in the ranges behind that area."

Chook started to snore loudly, so Cosmo gave him a kick in the ribs. The others turned back to study the map, which was all double Dutch to the Asians, who only knew the main road from Adelaide, so had never been off the beaten track.

Teo tried to make sense of the markings.

"This track, how far, how many days?"

Cosmo scratched his head and considered the mileage on the map.

"It's about fifty, sixty maybe seventy miles across country before the turnoff, but the tracks are hard going and some sand—given no storms and if the dry holds it could be done in three to four days."

Teo asked, "Where go from there?"

Cosmo was trying to work out the directions across country.

"The old tracks are slow but faster than going into Marree and then down the northern road. It's better down the southern end to Windani. We could be faster that way than a piss in the wind."

The Asians looked at each other with raised eyebrows, mystified.

Cosmo smirked. "Nah, never mind."

Tong found the area on the map and stabbed Windani with his finger.

"So, where this painted mountain from there?"

They turned the map around and Cosmo showed the roads and tracks marked with dotted lines around the northern ranges.

Cosmo told them, "All them old mining tracks lead all over the place—we'd have to get local knowledge to sort them out."

Teo had trouble trying to fit the enormity of the place in his head.

"Why so long to get to this Windi place?"

Cosmo shrugged, not wanting to put off his possible paying clients.

"It would be rough going to the turn off, depending on how fast we can manage. Can't really hurry through desert country. Don't want to be stranded broken down. After the cross roads it'd take another coupla of days to get to Windani. Have to camp there to refuel and get local info about the Mt Painter area. All the desert is the hardest country around and have to be careful about water—the blacks are the only ones who really know where it is. Though the word is Ginger Martin and Mungo Jack have explored plenty of times around Mt Painter."

The Asians were silent for a few moments. They conferred in their own lingo and looked at the map again.

Tong said, "We get these people who know about the dragon to take us to the painted mountain for money. We pay well."

Cosmo looked very unhappy.

"Nah, mate! I can take youse over there but don't think you got a bloody chance! Too thick with the black fellas, those blokes. Like I said, It's their sacred ground or sumpin."

Tong said with some force, "We offer *big* money to them, we see! You take us if we hire your outfit. We cut you in for bigger money when we get the dragon, more money than you ever see in your life!"

Teo reached into an inner pocket of his vest and flashed a big wad of money in front of Cosmo's eyes. He was startled, silent and thinking very hard. Usually, he and Chook took fossickers touring round the Coober Pedy minings and, sometimes, camped out with them. The idea of being hired for an across country stint was a new concept. He felt a bit dubious but he could use the money to keep his vehicles and equipment in good order.

Tong gazed at him with hard eyes.

"We need bush knowledge and you to help us find these persons so we get to the dragon cave. How we find this ginger person at Windani? How long till we get ready?"

Cosmo looked again at the map and spoke slowly, "Weeel—if we could get trucks and gear ready and get away termorra, the camel races are on in Windani in a week's time. As long as the weather holds, we could make it there—everybody and his dorg goes to the races so those old blokes should be in town."

The Asians breathed out slowly. They looked at each other and nodded. Tong got out his big bank roll and gave half to Cosmo. Tong took out a very deadly looking flick knife, shot out the blade and displayed it to Cosmo.

"We partners from now on. We trust you but never, never do the double cross or the knife will take your soul to Nirvana."

Cosmo looked horrified and wondered what the hell he had agreed to do. He gurgled, "Yairs, yairs, mate! No need for that. I'm in it for the trip to Windani, OK? All agree?"

They shook hands. Chook still snored loudly under the table. Cosmo nudged him again.

Tong pointed under the table.

"But you get rid of that one!"

Cosmo shook his head vehemently.

"Nah, mate! Chook's got the biggest and best rig around and once we're out of town, he's fine, a great driver. Besides, he does all the heavy stuff like loading and unloading, refuelling, plus the cooking—unless you wanna do that all yerselves every time we need to stop. If my rig gets bogged it'll be Chook's Blitz that pulls me out. He could save our lives. I'll take care of Chook, no worries. He does what I tell him."

The Asians looked at each other, then nodded. Chook was doused with what was left of his stale beer and Cosmo hoisted him up. He shook himself, staggered up and he and the dog lurched outside into the noon day blinding heat.

Chapter Seventeen

The sun baked the landscape around Coober Pedy, turning the white mullock heaps that surrounded the town into burning white discs that blinded the eyes. In the main street there was a big, ugly, dusty four-wheel drive truck with a large quantity of gear all over it, looking like something out of Mad Max.

It was for the most part a WW2 4x4 Chev Blitz but had so many other additions and variations over the years that other than its pug nose and downward facing windscreens and magnificent suspension, one would be surprised it was a traditional Blitz. The rear had been stripped down many years ago and a rim of welded metal surrounded the tray to hold drums and equipment, with racks on each side containing spare tyres.

There were also racks holding tools and a large metal locker welded to one side. The rig was much envied by many around the area, but was Chook's pride and joy, once he learned to drive it, so it was not for sale.

The truck was being loaded by a sweating Chook, who knew exactly what he was doing from long practice. He and Cosmo lifted two all-terrain motor bikes onto special racks and chained them in. There were tents, jerry cans of water, two fuel drums, a fuel pump and wallaby jack, plus boxes of food supplies, all being lashed down with tarpaulins and heavy ropes.

Chook loved his truck and so Cosmo had reorganised the cab to contain a donated long passenger seat and installed it to replace the two old canvas ones, so Chook and the big dog could ride in comfort. Though, according to Blitz aficionados, because of the crash gear box and a non-standard placement of the brake and accelerator pedals, it was a fair devil to drive. Though the Blitz was tough and more reliable than most modern trucks in the desert, it had a propensity to try and cook the driver, plus to try and throw its passengers out of the cabin while cornering.

None of this mattered to Chook, as he was up to the mark when it came to handling the truck over rough terrain. He crashed the gears cheerfully, roared the engine to change gears and now and then on straight road managed to achieve the amazing speed of fifty miles an hour!

The truck never bogged, even on the worst mucky road, took on bulldust and potholes and rocks with aplomb and roared up sandhills without delay. The whole shebang had never given a moment's trouble over the many years since Cosmo had found it discarded by a deserted mine.

Cosmo was an experienced mechanic, having worked for years around mining industry machines and he was adamant about keeping his vehicles in tiptop condition. He had arranged two dongas just out of town, roofed the space between them and so made a comfortable home for himself and his brother. He had also put up a tin shed made out of discarded bits and pieces, where he did all his mechanical work.

Cosmo had found other derelict Blitzes, whose owners had left the Pedy thoroughly disillusioned, leaving the old trucks to turn into dust-covered heaps, where he could cannibalise bits and pieces for his own Blitz. This had turned the outfit into such a reliable machine that men had offered good money to sell it to willing buyers, but it was Chook's baby and there could not be another to replace it.

Another smaller four-wheel drive vehicle with bull-bars, heavy duty tyres and radio antenna was being loaded on its roof racks with more equipment by Cosmo. He quietly slipped his much treasured ex-Army 303 Enfield rifle and box of ammo in the back, along with bedrolls and duffle bags belonging to himself, Chook and the two Asians. He had been teaching Chook how to use the rifle out the back of their bush donga, firing at tin cans.

Chook didn't like the noise much but obediently did as Cosmo showed him, proving in the end to be quite a good shot. He was made to help clean the rifle afterwards, making sure no sand got near its polished barrel. He was told it was all because of the need for safety in the bush, like falling foul of the King Brown snakes being found in camp or being broken down in the desert needing to shoot a kangaroo or goat for tucker.

The two Asians had been into the general store, where they had changed their city clothes and black shoes, dumping the old clothes into new kitbags. They came out clad in stiff new desert type khaki clothing and boots, plus Akubra hats which sat incongruously on their small heads, so they looked like mushrooms walking.

The new outfits made them look even more out of place among the general mining crowd and opal gougers, where no one knew what a new pair of trousers looked like, let alone a new flash hat not yet covered in the ubiquitous white dust.

For the locals it was only newbies and tourists coming into town in new clothing, which denoted them as fair game in the selling of opals, not always of good substance.

A four-wheel drive Police truck passed the vehicles being loaded and the two men inside took great interest in the goings on. They made a quick report as to what they had seen on their radio. They did a U-turn and came back to stop beside Chook's big truck. He leaned on the front of the truck with great casualness and took his hat off to wipe his sweating face.

The Police sergeant had his name on the front of his shirt in readable letters— *B. J. Jeffries*. He was a big, beefy man in the standard Police blue clothing and wide hat and he looked like he took no guff from anyone. Jeffries walked around the truck looking at all the supplies and preparations, taking his time, kicking the heavy-duty tyres to test them for correct pressure.

He beamed at Chook with a false smile on his face.

"You off again, Chook? Where to this time?"

Chook was miffed by the close inspection and answered truculently, "What's it to youse?"

Cosmo spotted them and hurried over from his own rig before Chook got flustered and said something that would dob them all in as what they were proposing to do. The Asians spotted the Police wagon and quickly turned away, looking into the front of an opal display shop.

Cosmo shifted his old hat back on his head and drawled, "Howse yer goin', Sarge?"

The sergeant was not a whit taken in by Cosmo's nonchalance, having a nose for possible trouble and noted the presence of the Asians coming and going to Cosmo's rigs. He was looking over the supplies with practised eyes.

"Going bush for a camp? Hope you were gunna let us know your track and destination?"

Cosmo pretended he was not very interested in what the Sergeant might think.

"Yairs, no worries."

The Sergeant was gazing into the cab, walking round the rear, checking in the back.

"Your radio working? You got a license for that rifle?"

Cosmo was starting to look cross and dragged out a paper and showed the Policemen.

"Of course! We need to get goin' today and not flamin' termorra!"

Jeffries perused the paper, handed it back and looked stern.

"Keep your hair on, mate. Just make sure you call into the station, before you leave and give your call sign and ETA."

He saluted, climbed back into his wagon and drove off slowly, still eyeing the trucks and all the preparations. His offsider spotted the Asians trying to look innocently at the shop and spoke to Jeffries, who eyed them as well.

Chook was cranky and spat in the dust. He exclaimed, "Them blokes think we're newchums and can't look after ourselves!"

Cosmo was suddenly all business.

"Get them Asians, Chook and let's skedaddle before the pigs decided to check the vehicles and find things wrong to keep us from leaving."

Chook opened the Blitz door and gave a shrill whistle. The big dog leapt into the front seat and Chook sounded the horn. The small men ran back looking all around them to see where the Police were going and quickly got into Cosmo's waiting rig. He waved to Chook to follow and they trundled out of what passed for a town.

Chapter Eighteen

Cosmo's rig led the way and as they left the last of the mineshafts and mullock heaps, the red of the desert took over. Cosmo heaved a sigh of relief, though still not quite sure about the trip he was doing for these unknown people. He negotiated bulldust and gibbers, which made his passengers shake and roll around and hang on for grim death.

The going on the Coober Pedy road was rough enough but reasonable except for the heat, which pressed down like a lead blanket. Any bulldust swirled around the convoy and penetrated every crack and corner, so the only part of faces left clean was under sunglasses.

The Asians coughed and sneezed and gasped for air, covering their mouths and noses with what passed for neckerchiefs. Cosmo pulled up his black bandana up over his nose, showing no sign of discomfort but, now and then, wiping his sunglasses free of the dust.

The Blitz was following, Chook singing at top voice, glad to be out of town and on the move again. He didn't care about the dust, even though the dog, Bitzer, born and bred in the dust, kept wiping his eyes with an equally dusty paw.

After some time of rough going, Cosmo signalled with his blinkers that he was turning off to the cross track that would take them down towards the town of Windani. Chook followed and after around a half hour they pulled up to have a drink and wipe the bulldust off their faces.

Chook siphoned water from a jerry can into his hat and gave Bitzer a drink, tipping the rest of the water over his face to let it drip onto his shirt. The men had some still cool cans of soft drink from an Esky in the back of Cosmo's rig. The Asians wanted some water to wash their face and eyes and wanting to have a rest from the rough road.

Teo whined, also pointing to Tong, "We all over dirt. Need water for cleaning eyes and faces."

Cosmo refused point blank.

He growled, "Look, we only just got started and youse blokes are complaining already. We don't use water to wash in out here, until we come to a bore drain. Until then you just gotta wait like the rest of us. You see the dorg complaining?"

The two Asians looked askance at the big dog, which was sitting under Chook's truck panting happily, seeming to be smiling all over his doggy face. They turned away in disgust and got back into Cosmo's vehicle, grumbling to each other in their own lingo.

Cosmo went around checking both rigs, looking at tyres, making sure everything was tightly secured on the back of the Blitz and the top of his own rig. He patted Chook on the shoulder and they got back into the driving seats and started off again with Cosmo leading.

The old track across country was in a really bad way, so the vehicles had to use four-wheel drive to negotiate their way over gravel, dust, rocky bars and old washaways. Cosmo got out often to carefully tramp through any dip that may have been too deep and boggy so cause his rig trouble, so he would signal the Blitz to drive through in case Cosmo needed Chook's winch to pull his rig through. He then followed in the wheel tracks of the Blitz and, thus far, had crossed without trouble.

They had been traversing the desert track for many hours in the heat of the day. The old track was hardly discernible in places and the trucks shuddered and jolted across the unforgiving terrain in the miles of fairly flat going and in areas of undulating country larded with boulders that could crack a diff or slash a tyre.

The trucks pulled over to refuel, decanting fuel from a drum on the back of the Blitz via a hose. The drivers also needed to have a good break. The big dog was given a drink of water and Cosmo pulled the Esky out and perched it on his bonnet. He and Chook pulled out some bread, slapped on a few slices of corned meat, handing some to the Asians.

They looked at the fare suspiciously and Cosmo growled, "Doan tell me this ain't good enough for youse? This proper bush tucker and there'll be more of this as we go along, unless youse want to die of starvation!"

Tong shrugged and tried to much some of the huge sandwich, while Chook and Cosmo ate with relish.

Teo looked at his food with loathing and after a few chews asked, "Too hard for me—any more drink?"

Cosmo looked in the Esky and dragged out the last of the cans and gave them to the Asians. He and Chook walked around stretching their muscles that had been pummelled for hours of the rough track. The Asians sat disconsolately on the side of the road in the sand with the flies for company.

Chapter Nineteen

Nearing the place where Cosmo wanted to stop for the night, they came across some small sandhills, which were a relief from the flat track. They wallowed up over the sandhills, roaring down the other side, bucketing over rocks and ditches and over rondels of spinifex.

The spinifex was a pest which pushed into the radiators with its sharp ends stuck, which could cause the radiators to boil. Cosmo called a halt to also check under the vehicles, in case there was a build up near the exhaust pipe which could catch fire.

Cosmo was stiff from the long drive to he asked the Asians to help get rid of the spinifex.

"Righto, youse guys could give a hand to get rid of the weeds stuck in the radiators. Chook and I need a break from driving for a few minutes. If you wind rags around your hands, you won't get stuck with prickles.'

He went to the big truck and hauled out some rags. These he gave to the Asians and showed them how to wind them round their knuckles and fingers. The Asians made a few desultory efforts at the weeds and cursed the spiky grasses, sucking their fingers as the spikes stuck in even though they had the rags on.

Tong shouted, "This devil grass. What we have to do this for, we not servants!"

Chook chuckled, "It makes good fires for my cooking though, so not to grizzle about a few prickles!"

Being used to the terrain, Cosmo and Chook took the low-lying spinifex as a given in the desert but treated it with respect when it came to their vehicles. Spinifex, the main cover of the lower desert areas had descended from a Gondwanan ancestral grass. The characteristic grass of the Australian deserts, it was well-adapted to the combination of poor soils and great aridity.

The plants were the only things stopping the deserts from becoming a pile of shifting sand, as when the spinifex hummock experiences its first dry spell, the leaves roll in on themselves reducing the area exposed to sun and wind. The ultimate desert survivor.

After the radiators were cleared, the two vehicles drove through a plain of wildflowers of all colours, a sea of white, yellow and pink, where some water from a shower had dropped. After this brief floral interlude, they had to drive through a rough sandy area and had to stop on the top of a sandhill as Cosmo could smell burning.

He told the Asians, "Need youse blokes to get out and give a hand again to clear the exhaust pipes, 'cause they have a build-up of spinifex and if youse don't want to die in the desert without the trucks, you need to give a hand and do your bit of clearing."

The men clambered out and shaken, gazing round at the never-ending desert. Cosmo and Chook took it all in their stride, but the Asians seemed terrified by the weird landscape where they could see nothing but the curvature of the horizon. They were huddled together in Cosmo vehicle clinging on for dear life most of the day, but got out to ease their bones and hobble round in the deep sand.

This time they refused to help in any way to clear the spinifex again, hating the sharp spines and the silicone-stiff, thin leaves.

Teo stood askance and screamed at Cosmo, his face enraged, shaking his bleeding fingers.

"Hurt my hands. We not your servants. We pay you, you do it!"

Cosmo signalled to Chook and they both charged to their vehicles, revved up and started rolling down the sandhill with the Asians having suddenly to run for their lives to catch up. They fell in a heap at the bottom gasping, when Cosmo casually got out of his cab and remarked to the sky,

"Blokes like you die quick out here without bush knowledge. We all in this together and got to work together. Now, you gunna give help to go on, or we leave you behind?"

The Asians were too winded to speak but nodded reluctantly and wove the rags around their hands and got sticks to scrape the spinifex from around the undercarriages and exhausts. Once Cosmo was satisfied, they stopped and sat grizzling to each other in their own lingo. Chook and the dog went off for a stroll round the base of the hill while Cosmo had a break. Chook came back with a very long brown snake skin hung over a stick.

He threw it on the ground and said to the other men, "This type of snake can kill out 'ere with one bite, so never, ever, mess with them. No doc's out 'ere to save you. Too far to get help."

The Asians looked at the snake skin carefully, dread in their eyes, but then Tong started to pretend some sort of bravado, pulling out his flick knife and waving it around.

"Not afraid of biting things—our country got bigger ones. I fix them with this!"

Cosmo sighed and came back from where he had been resting against his rig.

"Put that fool thing away. Next thing you be tellin' me you can bite the head off them snakes!"

Chook hooted and Tong looked at him with distaste. He said, "You no brave, bring us just a skin."

Cosmo snorted.

"Doan throw off about these desert snakes you never seen. Our death adders are small and fat and disguise themselves under things, so they can't be seen. The taipan or King Brown will come at you fast! One bite and you quick-fella dead!'

The Asians looked startled and were looking round at the clumps of grass where they had been walking without really noticing anything.

Cosmo got tired of this lack of knowledge and remarked, "Just look and learn. If you make a fair bit of noise or thump with sticks, the snakes would rather go somewhere else but will certainly strike if you corner them, so just keep your eyes open. Chook, let's roll, got to go a bit further to where I wanna camp for the night."

They found the track difficult enough, though it was covered sometimes by sandblows and Cosmo had to get out and mark the way again and he would signal Chook to drive his big truck through first, in case Cosmo got stuck. The two Asians refused to get out of their vehicle again, huddled together on the rear seat, looking at the barren terrain with loathing.

Chapter Twenty

As the sun fell below the horizon, the heat of the day dropped sharply, as in the desert it could become icy cold at night very quickly. Cosmo scanned the area they were driving across for a suitable flat camp site and eventually there came into view a few stunted gidgee trees, which had low undergrowth sheltering the place.

The trucks were pulled up parallel, Chook let the dog out and went to the back of his truck, where he untied and dragged out a tarp. He got some rope, tied it to the corners and strung it between the trees and the trucks. He untied another tarp and flung it on the ground under the trees, so when this was done he went to Cosmo's vehicle and found the bedrolls and tossed them onto it.

Chook was all business, in his element in the bush and happy to be out of town. The big dog was also in his element, running round and smelling the grasses, barking at nothing and generally making a nuisance of himself. Cosmo gave a whistle and the dog and he went off looking for old sticks and tinder, coming back with a good load.

He made a fireplace out a few rocks, started it going with spinifex tinder, threw the sticks on top, so soon a good campfire was going. He decanted water from the jerry cans and filled two black billies to place over the fire.

Chook dumped a camp oven down, pulling out some coals to the side. He placed the oven on the edge of the coals and soon had it filled with food out of the cold chest to make a good stew. He put the lid on placed a shovel of coals on the lid. The other men sat relaxed in the sand drinking rum out of a bottle they passed round. Cosmo had half-filled the bottle with water to reduce the rum but didn't offer Chook any, who was in disgrace over his last foray into beer in Coober Pedy.

Tong said to Cosmo, "He not get any rum?"

"Nah," said Cosmo, "only let him have a beer when we get into town. He's a two pot screamer!"

Both the Asians looked non-plussed, so Cosmo elaborated, "Two beers and he's drunk as a skunk, but never out of town when we're drivin'. He drives that big truck like a pro."

He shouted to Chook, "Hurry up, mate, or I'll be eatin' the camp oven. Smells great!"

Chook was proud of his camp cooking, ladling the meal into tin dixie cups and handing them around. Cosmo dug into the cold box and brought out the remains of the now hard bread which he and Chook broke into their tins of stew. The Asians looked sideways at the stew offered.

Teo said disparagingly, "This not our food. What else you got?"

Tong was also shocked at what he thought was not good fare and turned up his nose, looking down into his tin mug and the hard bread.

He said, "I don't want to eat this way either."

Teo placed his tin on the edge of the fire without tasting the stew. Chook felt mighty offended as he considered he could make a tasty meal of just about anything.

He grumped, "Wassa matter with it? The dorg'll eat it if you don't and I ain't cookin' anything else tonight, see!"

Cosmo, eating all his stew and bread with gusto, helped himself to more stew and said, "Youse blokes can please yerselves. Yer can eat what we got or go without—no skin orf my nose, but there ain't np fancy shops out 'ere so get used to it or starve!"

He gave a gasp as he saw Teo rinse out his mouth out of a canteen of water, upend it and tip the rest out.

"Shit, mate, you throw away water out 'ere and you're dead meat! We need every drop for us and the trucks. Could be no water for days until we hit one of the station bores."

He shook his fists at the man and looked menacing and even the big dog growled.

Chook was also upset and growled, "Me, I dong the next one who wastes water. I ain't gonna die because of youse fool fellas!"

Both the Asians backed off. They were so much out of their usual haunts that they were starting to wonder why they had thought of this trip anyway.

Teo looked abashed, "OK, OK—water careful—where we sleep then?"

Cosmo gestured to the bedrolls on the tarp under the trees.

"Bedrolls there if you want to make yerselves comfortable. Just doan go off into the desert too far at any time, might get lost or snake bite."

He strolled over to the fire, threw on some large branches and he and Chook dropped onto the ground sheet, took off their boots, rolled over into their bedrolls and were instantly asleep. The dog came and curled up on their feet.

The Asians dubiously tried to do the same but found the ground hard and the bedrolls not keeping out the icy air. The deep indigo sky was filled with twinkling white crystal stars that made the desert twinkle back, with an incrustation of frost forming on low grasses and bushes.

Both Teo and Tong could not get comfortable, shuffling round, though tired out, but when a dingo voiced its mournful howl close by, they both jumped up. They tried to stare out into the intense black undergrowth, not seeing anything. They went to the fire, pulling their bedrolls round their shoulders. They kept busy throwing more sticks onto the fire to light up the night, though their fronts were warm their backsides were still icy cold. Soon a white, cold half-moon showed its glittering face above the tops of the ranges to the east.

There was snuffling and rustling outside the perimeter of the firelight and the men looked askance at each other. They shot upright looking around wildly to find out what it was that might menace them. Just then a large, fat, spiny-coated echidna came bustling into camp, nose to the ground, following an unseen trail of ants.

The men stood together looking at this bristling intruder, but as it took no notice of them, they followed his progress to an interesting hole under the roots of one of the trees.

The echidna used his great claws to root out under the hollow and, suddenly, there was a stream of extremely angry red ants swarming over the whole camp area, biting, tearing at anything that they came against. This included the boots and trousers of the Asians, plus eventually landing on the dog and the tarp. The dog started to yelp, followed by the men and everyone rushed out of the camp swatting their arms, legs, trousers, followed by angry swear words from Cosmo, who was still half awake.

Chook's efforts were much more practical. He opened the truck door, brushing the dog down and it leapt in. Then Chook threw off his pants and making sure he was free of ants he also flew into the truck and slammed the door.

Teo and Tong took much longer getting rid of the ants, tearing off their boots and pants, dancing round shaking and detritus all over while they tried to dance above the hordes.

Cosmo grabbed a burning branch and waved it around the sand of the camp where the ants and their army were in full array. The men fell into the smaller vehicle, dispatching the odd ant and then tried to get some sleep. Now and then, a few left-over ants would bite someone and there was a swearing match until the intruders were killed and peace restored.

The remnants of the moon were declining, so the desert was a magical place, but the tired men refused to care. Outside the truck, there could be heard rustling of many tiny feet in the underbrush and the flash of a white owl's silent wings against the night sky. The echidna was not perturbed by the camp's sudden evacuation and continued on his forays, feeding on the myriads of ants until he was sated and he rumbled away to his next hideaway to digest his meal.

Chapter Twenty-One

Next morning at daylight the air was cool and fresh. The armies of red ants had retired to rebuild their nest. Cosmo and Chook were fit and ready to get going as soon as possible. The fire was built up again with Cosmo sweeping the whole area with a branch to dissuade any ants from looking at having breakfast with them.

Kookaburras overhead were shouting at the new morning, sounding as though they were laughing at the two bedraggled Asians, who looked very much the worse for wear, coming out of Cosmo's rig with bedrolls slung over their shoulders. They were looking all around the camp to see if there were any more biting things, while they shook out their pants and tugged on boots.

Cosmo noted the tracks in the sand from the night inhabitants and pointed them out to the other men. He showed them the tracks of splayed toes and wavy tail of a large goanna that had explored their cooking things from the night before.

Tong made a face and refused to see what was in front of him.

Cosmo and Chook laughed.

"Just doan have another fit—he's long gone by now. If you see one at any time, get well away as they have very big teeth!"

The fire had the billies boiling, while Chook was mixing water, dry milk and salt into a billy, making a thick dough. He got a shovel from his truck, cleaned the end off with a fire stick and laid it on the coals. He started cooking Johnny cakes, tipping them onto an enamel plate by the fire. There was a big tin with syrup in it to add to the fare.

Cosmo shouted at the sleepy Asians, "Wakey, wakey. Tea and cakey! Shift yerselves, we got a lotta bush-bashing to get through today."

The other men staggered over, hair standing on end, eyes still half shut after their disturbed night. Cosmo offered them their billy tea in large pannikins and though they sniffed at it suspiciously, they drank thirstily. They took their proffered johnny cakes, tried them out and then gave them to the dog. They went to sit with their backs against a tree in the sparse shade. After eating and swigging his tea, Chook was busy cleaning up his cooking utensils and shovel and stacking them in his truck ready to roll.

He looked over at the two men and started to cackle.

"I wouldn' sit there if I was youse."

Tong pretended to yawn with indifference.

"You tell *me* what to do? Hell, who died, made you King?"

He and his mate laughed uproariously as though it was a big joke and leaned back against the tree again. Over their heads a big carpet python was hanging from a limb looking for a way down to the ground, its large triangular head weaving to and fro for an easy path. It hissed in alarm as they jerked upright. Next moment, the pair were running for their lives across the thick sand, screaming like banshees, falling to their knees in panic.

The python kept its cool and flowed down the tree trunk like a coloured Persian carpet, sliding off into the undergrowth quite unperturbed.

Cosmo viewed this mad sortie with bafflement. He shook his head, smothered the fire with sand, grabbed the billies, throwing them onto the truck to be tied down.

"Bloody jumped-up fools. What the hell youse chuckin' a wobbly about now! That's just a python, won't hurt you—they're not interested in biting, just want to do their own thing. Stop and have a look at all the tracks around you from the night—look and learn!"

The Asians sat back on their haunches in the sand, while Cosmo pointed out to the tracks right in front of them.

"That's dunnart track, a small native, furry animal, see the four little toes out front and the big one behind. They eat insects and stuff like that. A dingo walked across in front of my truck, have a look at his footprints. The desert is full of life, so you need to get used to living with it—without ants just the same!"

The small men looked doubtfully at the tracks, wondering if there were snake tracks too. They just sat not looking as though they wanted to go on.

Cosmo suddenly shouted, "Chook, let's rock, fed up with this, we need to get going now!"

He went around both vehicles checking the tyres, feeling the tie-down ropes, throwing the bedrolls in his own rig. He started the motor, while Chook did the same. Suddenly, the small men came to life and ran to fling themselves into the open back door of Cosmo's rig.

As the day moved on, the trucks were making reasonably good time allowing for short stops to refuel. The flies were as thick as fleas on a dog. Cosmo and Chook took little notice, but the Asians were driven mad, flapping their hats at the flies, trying to protect their faces and so lagging behind when they were needed to help push Cosmo's vehicle out of a sand blow across the track. Chook was very careful driving the Blitz though the worst places but had no trouble, while Cosmo was getting very tired and fed up, not getting the help he needed.

When the small men declined to give a push when needed, Cosmo roared, "Youse blokes need to get your arses into gear and give a hand or we'll be stuck here for days. Or would you rather die here?"

The Asians were tired and dirty but, in the end not game, in spite of their bravado, to make any more fuss, learning fast that in harsh desert country everyone has to help or die. They got out to help and all were glad when the vehicles moved onto more solid ground.

It was a quick stop for drinks out of the waterbag on the front of Cosmo's rig and no one wasted a drop. Even the dog drank every bit of the water he had been given in Chook's hat.

There were plenty of big red roos and camels coming into view on the hot, dusty plains. Chook sounded his horn and indicated the presence of an artesian bore drain to their left. The men pulled up the trucks beside the bore drain and throwing off their boots, dropped into the water to refresh themselves all over, clothes and all. The big dog lapped the water with enjoyment and sprawled in a patch to roll in the mud at the side. Even though the water started quite hot as it came out of the pipe, it cooled as it ran down the drain.

The two Asians doffed their once spic and span shirts and splashed themselves. They carefully took off their new boots and felt the relief of cool water on their feet. The stunted trees around the bore were ringed with corellas, who echoed their weird quavering calls around the trees, flying and roosting like snowflakes covering the trees with white.

A few emus came up out of curiosity and strolled in to have a look, but the dog took exception to this and chased after them. The emus ran flat out, shaking their floppy wealth of feathers like huge dusters, leaving the dog well behind. He gave up in disgust and came back to drink again and flop under the truck in the shade.

Teo wandered round looking uncomfortable.

Cosmo asked, "What's the matter with you, mate?"

Teo looked at the ground.

"I need toilet quick!"

Chook chuckled but Cosmo said sternly, "Plenty of bushes round 'ere, mate. Just run behind one of them if you want to hide. But watch where you put your feet."

Teo started to jog on the spot in his anxiety.

"But got no toilet paper."

Cosmo said, "You're out in the bush now. No time to be fancy. You do your business in a hole, wipe with a handful of leaves and cover it. Easy."

Both Teo and Tong looked horrified.

Tong yelled, "What sort of backward place you bring us to?"

Cosmo remarked quietly, "I remind youse, you were the blokes who wanted to go look for this so-called opal dragon, so you need to learn things the way they are in the desert."

Chook also added seriously, "Never wipe your bum with spinifex, gives you what called sandpaper bum."

Teo went silently away into the shrubbery and was heard thrashing round the bushes until there was silence. He came back looking at the ground and went to the bore drain for a wash. The men decided to have a break beside the water and as things were being brought out for a meal, Tong spotted the big rifle Cosmo had in the back of his vehicle.

He was fascinated and asked, "What rifle this?"

Cosmo said shortly, "It's a .303, big and heavy, to deal with any feral pigs we see. It'll put down a big boar in full run with a punch to the heart or the brain. Not many wild pigs out this far, but we see them now and then and the boars have nasty tusks that can go clean through a man or dog. Besides, if we ran out of meat, we can shoot a goat for a feed."

He handed over the rifle and both the small men tried it out for size, finding it so heavy they had trouble keeping it steady. They aimed it at the tops of the trees making 'pow-pow' sounds.

Chook chuckled.

"Not much good making that racket—why don't yer have a go?"

Tong looked at Cosmo, who was undecided but, in the end he agreed, taking out the box of ammo from his rig. He showed the men how to load the bullet, how to use the sight, holding the rifle at the correct angle. Tong tried the rifle, holding it awkwardly.

Cosmo said, "Never, ever point the rifle at anyone, mate, even if you think it's unloaded. Now, aim at the crow's nest in that tall tree. Get the sight in place and when you're ready, pull the trigger back slowly. This rifle has a helluva kick, so hold the butt close in to your shoulder."

Tong did as he was told and though aiming high, in his excitement pulled the trigger too quickly, so the recoil knocked him over backwards on the ground. The limb of the tree where he had aimed fell to the ground and the bullet ricocheted back down to bounce off the metal siding of Chook's truck. It then flew along and tore the toe off Tong's boot. He shrieked and they realised he wasn't worrying about his boot but a huge wasp's nest that had fallen from the tree on the branch and the wasps were very angry aiming at Tong's head.

The other men didn't waste any time and they tore off and fell into the bore drain covering themselves as much as possible with mud. Tong flung the rifle away and joined them, brushing away the stinging insects and howling fit to kill. They all lay in the water and mud until most of the wasps had gone back to the nest, which lay too close to the trucks for comfort.

Cosmo looked ruefully at his prized rifle laying on the track covered in dust.

"Geez, you're a dopey bugger! What'd you do that for? I gotta get my rifle away from that mob and it'll be full of dirt."

He sighed and patting mud around any exposed skin, specially round his face and ears, he ventured out to pick up the rifle and then fled back to the safety of the other side of the big truck. He found a hefty stick near the drain and lit it with a match until it flamed. He roared around the truck flat out and set fire to the wasp nest and then fled back to the cover of the water. Tong was lying in the water feeling very sorry for himself, pasting mud over his head and face, which were covered in lumps.

Chook looked at him and said kindly, "That mud the best for stings. It'll make you good soon. Yer nearly put a hole in my back tyre, so just as well the bullet hit the metal."

Tong looked at his ruptured new boot.

"Don't like this mad country Austraya. Everythi' go bad here."

Chapter Twenty-Two

The country was much flatter in the new area they were traversing, with the outline of the ranges to their east becoming clearer. After a stop for lunch and billy tea, everyone was resting in the shade of the trucks. The Asians had admired the motor bikes on the ramps on the Blitz.

Teo asked if they could try out the bikes.

"We have best motorbikes at home and we good riders."

Tong nodded, recovered from his earlier trials.

"We might try these bikes to see how good they are?"

Cosmo looked serious.

"Maybe. We carry these bikes, in case of needing to get to a town for fuel or too many staked tyres. They're also in case of being stuck out 'ere because of breakdown that we can't fix, so they ain't for fun, but a lifeline."

Teo looked a bit startled, but said, "We used to bikes, so we take care."

Chook and Cosmo undid the straps, lifting the bikes down to give the Asians a go at bush-bashing. The small men sat down to put on their boots after taking them off to tip out dust and dirt, until suddenly one of the men gave an agonised cry and reefed his boot off and flung it away.

Teo shouted, "Somting bad in my boot bite me, how hurting!"

He was jumping around nursing his foot, howling with dismay. Cosmo looked bemused.

"Thought yer would be using yer loaf by now. Always tip out yer boots in the bush, mate, in case of snakes or scorpions. You won't die. Chook, get out a bit of fuel and put it on that bite."

Chook did as he was bid and gave Teo a bit of stick with a rag on the end to dip into a lid with a small amount of fuel in it. Teo swabbed the bitten area, which was already turning red. He sat with his foot in the air, showing the bitten place to Tong, who then was careful tip out his own boots and leapt up startled when a small white scorpion fell out.

He swore feelingly in his own language and shouted at Cosmo, "This very bad place, why you bring us here?"

Cosmo started to laugh.

"It's only a scorpion, buddy. Plenty of them around, so watch where you put yer hands and feet. Never mind that, it'll be right in a minute. Do you want a go on the bikes or not?"

The Asians nodded, putting boots on very carefully. Teo found the bite responded to the fuel and he limped a bit but was pleased to get out of the vehicle for a change.

Cosmo checked the fuel, then handed the bikes over. He and Chook stood to one side, arms folded, waiting to see the expert riders handle the rough conditions. The others started off well enough, but used as they were to good roads and flat country, the sand hollows and low spinifex gave them trouble and they both fell off frequently, having to get off and heave the bikes upright to get back on. Cosmo looked on impatiently, worrying about any damage to the bikes.

When Tong's bike hit a patch of deep sand, as he was skewing the bike this way and that, revving to get out of the sand, he fell off into a bed of galvanised burr.

He tried to stand up, then started to yell wildly, "I dead, bad tings sting me all over—help me—help me!"

He tried to wheel the bike back to the trucks but fell down again and the bike slumped over.

Cosmo shouted, "*You* wanted a go on the bike, so what're yer pushing the blistering thing for? I'll have yer guts for garters if you've staked a tyre."

The air was filled with howls from Tong and his mate rode back slowly to find out what the noise was all about. He parked the bike and went back to help Tong bring in the other one. Tong was riddled with the barbs of the burr, which were sharp and hooked and his backside and legs were full of them, adhering to his pants and making it hard to walk.

Teo asked, "Bikes OK—what is this stinging thing on his pants?"

Cosmo laughed, "He'll be right, mate, just a few burrs, but I ain't pickin' them out. I'm a bit choosey about backsides—you do it."

He gave Teo a pair of needle-nosed pliers out of a toolbox and showed him how to get the barbs out. Chook had stood by watching, quite amazed at the fuss, as he had often picked the things out of his legs by himself. Tong lay on the ground yelping as Teo pinched him now and the with the pliers and found he had a few burrs stuck in his own fingers.

The big dog seemed to think all the yelling was for him and he joined in with his mournful howling, so the scene was one of farce. Cosmo got fed up, so he and Chook loaded the bikes back on the Blitz, made sure of the straps ready to motor again.

Chook whistled the dog, opened the door of his truck and the dog bolted in. Cosmo motioned to the Asians to get in the back of his rig, started the engine, so they had to grab Tong's trousers which he taken off, plus the pliers and scramble onto the rear seat. They continued taking out the burrs out but, even so, Tong found it hard to sit with his mangled bottom in the bouncing vehicle.

The track to Windani started to improve marginally, though the red gibbers on the desert floor made everything on the trucks, including the men, rattle around hard enough to make their teeth chatter. The trucks were able to get up a better speed and charge through the various cattle properties closer to the town. The Asians were asked to get out and open and close the gates. Tong was the first to grizzle about this chore.

"I too sore to do this ting. Leave the gates."

His mate got equally cross, shouting, "What for you bring us, we give you money, just to do the gates? You do the gates."

While they argued about doing the gates, Cosmo refusing to enter into any discussion, pointed to a big sign beside a gate that stated—*UNCLOSED GATE TRIGGERS ELEPHANT GUNS.*

The Asians were shocked into silence and got out to open and close the gates without further ado as their convoy drove through. Teo and Tong were looking very much the worse for wear, their new clothes filthy, mud caking their pants legs, their flash new hats limp with sweat and one man limping with the toe out of his boots.

They hated the myriad of flies that settled all over them as soon as they got out to deal with the gates, coating their shirts, flies in their eyes and ears and noses refusing to be batted away. Chook was as happy as he had ever been, driving over the track singing at the top of his voice accompanied by the dog howling. Bitzer was also happy riding with Chook and very good at adding his own serenading.

Chapter Twenty-Three

In Windani many trucks, plus vehicles of all sizes, shapes and equipages were pulling in and setting up camp on the flat areas. Mark and Jason towed their own outfit round the back of the showgrounds to the camel camp. They got out stiffly, flapping their legs and hats covered in dust.

Jason went to the designated office to pay their dues and came back to help Mark unload the weary camels from their confinement on the trailer. They backed the trailer up to the camel holding yard, let down the wide ramp, asking the camels to stand, leading them down carefully. The animals were thankful, groaning their delight at being able to move and were taken to the water troughs for drinks.

Mark unhitched the trailer and he and Jason both shoved it, moving it away to a flat area, where they wanted to pitch their camp. The tent went up without trouble, a ground sheet thrown underneath it and swags thrown onto it. The cold box was moved in out of the heat of the day and a couple of kitbags also slung into the tent. They had a gas camp stove, which they set up on its legs off the ground to keep the ants at bay.

Mark went to their vehicle and switched it on to check the fuel content. He said to Jason, "I might go in and fill up before there's a rush. I could check out the Café for some good steak. You OK with that?"

Jason nodded. "I'll give the camels a good brush down shortly and give them some feed to browse on. They'll settle pretty quickly when a few others turn up."

Mark started his rig and moved into the main street to the store where two fuel pumps decorated a bit of cement that passed for a footpath. He refuelled the vehicle, checked the jerry cans, washed the dusty windscreen and filled the radiator with distilled water. Just then there came the yelp of an injured dog and he turned to see a half-grown pup of indeterminate parentage had been bowled over by a passing car.

The poor mite had fallen to the side of the road, whimpering. There seemed to be no one noticing or belonging to the pup. Mark could see the dog was in a poor state, as though he had been on the run for some time. He was once white with black spots and a black patch over one eye like a pirate, but now dirty and ragged. Mark could see his little paws were bleeding, as though he had been running looking for a lost master.

Mark scratched his head for a moment, but being used to handling all types of animals, decided he could look for the owner later on. He got a hessian bag out of his truck, picked up the shaking pup and rolled him in it. He could feel the little dog was all skin and bone and his ribs were sticking out. It seemed no one had fed him for quite some time, so Mark tucked the pup in the bag into a jacket, where close to warmth and coverage its shaking subsided. He went into the store and bought a bag of dog pellets, plus paying for his fuel.

Mark asked the attending lad, "Anyone looking for a lost pup?"

His lifted the edge of the bag and showed the lad the pup's head. The boy shook his head, so Mark recovered the pup and went out to shift his truck. He moved further down the side of the street and could feel the pup panting, not sure from fright or injury.

He said softly to the little animal, lifting the bag to check on the pup, "There, there, matey, we'll patch you up and then see if we can find your owner."

He drove quietly back to where they had set up camp, pulled up and got out cradling the pup to his chest. He called to Jason who was in the camel paddock.

"Come and have a look here, Jase. We might have to do some First Aid."

Jason vaulted the fence, as Mark undid his jacket and carefully unloaded the wrapped hessian bag. He was startled to see a pair of soft brown eyes peering out at him and the pup licked Mark under the chin.

They both laughed, while Mark recounted what he had seen, so they at first had to find out if the pup had sustained any injuries when he was hit. The pup whined softly as they undid his bag in the shade of their camp tree and the pup lay panting on the ground.

Jason was shocked at the state of the little fellow and growled in his throat, "Anyone who leaves their animals in this state needs a good whipping!"

He patted the small head kindly and the pup looked at him with gratitude in his big eyes. When the men examined the dog, they could see his paws were rubbed red raw from his exertions on the roads, but when they felt around for injury to his back leg, they could not find anything that was torn or broken and felt it would probably heal with a bit of help to keep him quiet for a few days.

Mark looked at the dirt covered pup and remarked, "Reckon we could give him a wash without hurting him too much? If we get some of this grime off we could maybe treat his feet better?"

Jason agreed, "I'll take him to the tubs near the shower and give him a quick clean, while you find our First Aid kit—think it's under the seat."

He folded the pup back in the hessian bag, taking him to be cleaned, while Mark came out with the First Aid kit and checked it to see if anything there would be of help to the raw feet. He found some Iodine, which would sting at first but stop any infection in the end. There were some swabs as well but nothing else seemed to be of use at the moment.

Jason came back with a shivering pup, who looked a different colour altogether. The men rubbed him down softly looking for further evidence of injuries but they found nothing, which pleased them. They laid the pup down, patting him all the while, swabbing his feet with the Iodine. The pup whimpered a little but seemed to understand at last someone was on his side to help.

The pup lay panting and Jason came with some water in an enamel dish and laid it beside the tired little head. The pup lapped greedily then sat up perkily, giving a small yip, which made the men laugh. Mark went to their rig and came back with the bag of dog food.

He said thoughtfully, "Maybe we should only give him a little at a time, do you reckon? If he's been starving, too much at once might make him throw up."

Jason nodded, "Bit at a time and often. We'll just watch to see that's OK."

They put out a small handful of the doggy pellets and the pup fell upon them with gusto. He looked at them with grateful eyes, lay back on his hessian bag and dropped off to sleep almost at once.

Mark considered how to find the owner.

"We could put up a notice at the race bar, but I don't like the chances of finding who owns this scrap. We can keep the pup till he is OK again. I saw down the street a bloke with a leather stall. Might amble down there and see if he's got anything in the way of harness or a leash to keep the pup quiet for a bit. You OK to stay here and mind the little guy? Don't want him trying to wander off with those bad feet."

Jason was fine with that and he was also ready for a bit of rest after their hectic morning. He stretched out on a swag next to the pup and dozed off at once.

Unbeknown to him, the pup crawled out of his bag and settled in the crook of Jason's arm, feeling safe and secure after his long ordeal.

Mark strolled along the stalls that were being set up on both sides of the main street. He stopped now and then to admire some of the polished stones and opal jewellery and other hand-made articles. There was a lady with a large box, which had advertising for two well-kept half-size blue cattle dog pups. Mark stopped to have a good look and spoke to the owner.

"These look in top condition. You breed them yourself?"

She smiled and looked proudly at her roistering pups.

"Yes. I'm from Mt Unite station north of here, been breeding this good stock for some years. Some of our pups have gone to the United States. We own the parents and train the dogs ourselves before they are sold. I also make sure I keep track of the possible new owners to make sure the dogs will be well handled and treated. Being such robust dogs, they are well-thought of in the USA."

Mark mused for a moment, then asked, "Just picked up a lost half-grown pup of unknown parentage, who had been injured, so if you hear of anyone looking for a small black and white one, could you tell them please, to come down to the camel camp and ask for Mark or Jason."

The lady was all smiles and nodded. Mark then went further down the stalls until he came to the bigger tent of the leather man, who had his stock of whips, harness, belts, hats and hat bands already hung up. There were also two beautifully fashioned saddles hung on stands in the back of the stall.

Mark introduced himself, shaking hands, "I'm Mark Garner, in town for the races and found an injured half-size pup that needs a bit of help. Thought you might be the man with some ideas how to keep this tyke still until he heals."

The grizzled older man, wearing a weathered leather hat and looking like his own leather articles laughed and said, "Good to meet you. I'm always full of ideas. Tell me the pup story, so I understand what the go is."

Mark described the pup's injuries, plus the bad feet, so there was a need to keep it quiet for a few days while they tried to find its owner. He described the treatment of the battered feet with Iodine.

"It's all we got in the fixit box that was useful and we'd been using it for years in the camel camps treating cuts and other small gashes."

The leather man nodded his head.

"Always good to try and stop infection first up. The District Nurse could give you something else if you're worried—she's a good stick and doesn't mind helping animals of all sorts of legs!"

The man walked to his equipment and found some offcuts of leather he had thrown in a box. He swiftly plaited some of them into a small harness that strapped over the chest and back, with a clip there to take a leash, which he took off his stall and clipped on.

Mark was pleased, pushing his hat back and marvelled, "Boy are you good! How quick was that! The harness should fit just fine."

The leather man also found two fine leather bootees fashioned for working dogs that had to run in burr country. They looked too big, but Mark was willing to take a gamble that these would help with a bit of interior padding.

"That'll be great. How much do I owe you?"

The man smiled, "Nah, nothing, mate, just hope the pup recovers. Just let be known I can make anything!"

Mark walked back to the camp, laughing when he saw Jason and the pup curled up together, asleep under the shade of the tent. He got out some bread, pickles, cheese and corned meat from the cool box and made hefty sandwiches. He lit the gas burner and put on a billy of water for tea. When that was boiling, he tipped in the tea leaves and gave Jason a kick on the boot.

"Wake up, sleepy head, food is on. You can bring your new mate."

Jason opened a sleepy eye, gathering his wits and looked down at the pup cradled in his arm.

"Nothing like making itself at home, is there?"

He yawned, stirred and the pup awoke, blinked his soft brown eyes and gave Jason a lick under the chin.

Mark, laughed through a mouthful of sandwich, "That might mean he owns you now!"

They both sat on the tent floor to eat and drink, giving the pup a few crumbs here and there, which were wolfed down with alacrity. They tried on the leather harness, which fitted remarkably well, but the bootees were too large, so they were put aside. The pup tottered outside to relieve himself and staggered back to lie on the bag again. Just that small effort seemed to drain him of energy.

Mark said thoughtfully, "Not sure what we're going to do with you, little matey, if we can't find your owner. But its early days yet. I'll put our plate number on our advert for the race bar so we can be found. Might tell Kate at the pub as well. They'll have plenty of people through there and the old bloke, Bones, might also have seen people with this pup."

Jason looked at him, "The pup seems to have settled down for now. Our own animals are going well, watered, brushed and fed. What about we take a stroll down to the pub and see if anyone there has heard anything about this tyke? Kate might have some ideas about his feet. We can take the burr bootees with us and show her."

Mark nodded, went into the tent, found his kitbag and threw everything out, finding an old soft jumper. He gave it to Jason.

"Put this in the bottom of the bag and roll him in gently, then we'll see if there is any news of him."

They put the pup in the bag gently, threw in the soft bootees and half closing the top, went to walk down the main street looking at all the preparations for the next day's races, with many competitions and stalls being set up. As they came to the leatherman's tent, seeing as he wasn't busy, Mark stopped to introduce his mate.

"This is Jason, my good buddy in the camel-catching business. Here's the pup we're concerned about."

He opened the bag wider and showed the pup's big brown eyes looking up quizzically, with the lopsided ear tipped over his face. The man started to laugh and the pup gave a yip of greeting, so he leaned into pat the little head and the pup gave him a good lick.

He said admiringly, "That little bloke may be in a bit of trouble at present, but he's got guts, that one! He'll survive with a bit of help from his friends."

Jason remarked, "Trouble is we need to find his owners if possible. We're not supposed to take dogs into our work camel camp, by order of the BIG Boss. We've got two camels entered in the races, so we'll be here until Monday at least, so if you hear anything about the pup we'll be at the showground camp. Cheers."

They waved and went further down the main street towards the pub, surprised at the amount of people already arriving, with kids running everywhere, getting into all sorts of mischief.

By the time they got to the backyard of the pub, time had passed quickly and they found Kate, Gina and Bones having a long awaited lunch break and cups of tea under the shade of a tree at the side. The girls looked curiously at the kitbag, which started to wriggle and at which Deefer was having a good sniff.

Bones started to laugh, "Bet I know what you got in there. You fellas want a cuppa tea?"

The men nodded, so he went off to the kitchen, coming back with the big teapot and mugs. While Bones looked on, Kate and Gina opened the bag and found themselves looking into a pair of bright brown eyes, one of which had a large black ear hanging over it.

Jason carefully lifted out the pup and laid him on his lap, explaining how it was found injured and the bad state of its paws. The girls gasped at the thought of such a small dog being almost run down, let alone running for so long he wore out the pads of his paws.

Mark explained, "We thought someone may have left a message in the bar from the owner? No message you know about?"

Bones and Kate shook their heads, while Gina went to look in the bar notice board but came back shaking her head. Kate patted the little dog's head gently and lifted him onto the table. She examined his paws, looked at the damage to his hind leg and hip and felt the bones there. The pup grinned amiably at them and sniffed at the left-over food on their plates so the girls broke off small pieces of meat and bread for him to eat.

Kate said slowly, "Can't feel anything wrong there, so perhaps it is all bruising and needs to be kept as quiet as possible to let it heal better."

She said to Bones, "You've probably had good experience with this sort of thing. Could you have a look at this mite?"

The old man ran his hands over the pup, who seemed quite happy at the attention.

He said, "Think that's right, Kate. Nothing broken but needs good rest and feeding which should help him to get going again. The feet will take long to get right, but he looks like a good little dog with a nice nature."

Mark patted the small head and said, "The only thing we could do in the beginning was to give him a wash to clean him up so we could put Iodine on those paws. I got burr bootees from the leather man thinking that would protect his bad feet, but they're too big for him."

Kate shook both hands over her head in a fighter's cheer, saying, "Hooray! I've got just the thing in my kit. There's an old pair of soft woollen socks I can cut the toes off, so we should be able to bind his feet and to stuff the rest down to the bottom of the bootees."

She went off to her cabin and came back with the socks and some small scissors. They measured the pup's front feet, the worst injured, cut the toes off the socks and pushed them down into the bootees. They placed the pup's feet into the bootees and strapped them on.

Bones then made strips of the soft wool and bound the back feet as though it was the pup wearing the socks. He then placed the pup on the ground and while he looked a bit surprised, he managed a few steps before he fell over. Deefer came to sniff and lick the pup, who wagged his stumpy tail but couldn't rise. Jason picked him up and placed him back in the kitbag.

"Reckon that's enough excitement for today, young fella. We've given him a few dog biscuits, Kate, but not game to give him too much at a time as he's been starving. He drinks water well, so that's a good sign."

Kate nodded. She was very cross, having grown up with animals, moving to the family cattle station when she was five years old. She seemed to have an affinity with every animal that came into her sphere. Her mother was an educated woman who conducted Kate's home schooling through the School of the Air.

Though the girl protested mightily, she was sent off to Adelaide to further her studies with two years of High School. Kate returned to the property every holiday, enjoying the break back to her home environment. She had learned in Adelaide what she did *not* want to do, so moved home for good at the end of her sojourn.

She growled, looking into the kitbag at the waif, who grinned up at her.

"Poor little mite, he doesn't deserve this trouble. Good idea not to give him too much food at a time until he gets stronger. You going to keep him or what? I hate to see animals abused like this! I'd like to take shotgun to the feet of anyone who hands out this sort of bad treatment!"

Gina was looking at the group of friends with their caring for the pup and suddenly said, "You guys should call the pup Lucky! Lucky, he found some people who care about animals!"

They all laughed and shouted, "Lucky, it is!"

Chapter Twenty-Four

Kate was out in the shade of the trees in the pub backyard as the evening drew in, having her late supper with Mark and Jason, with glasses of beer all round. Deefer was under the table watching for any handouts, cheerfully bumping a knee now in in case. Bones brought out some small pieces of meat from the kitchen for the pup, who ate them with relish and then went to sleep in his kitbag under the table.

Bones came in from the camel yard, where he had been checking water and feed. He was fond of his older camel, having had her for many years. She knew him well and, now and then, when Bones had his back to her, she nipped his shoulder. She almost smiled when he took off his hat and flogged her with it. She batted her eyelashes at him in a most feminine beguiling fashion, which made him laugh.

Jason was most amused at this bit of side play and gave Bones a bit of teasing.

"You want to watch that one, Bones, there'll be the day when you upset her and she'll take a piece out of you!"

Bones put his hat back on and grinned over the fence.

"Not my Dandy 'ere. We got an understanding, we 'ave! She does what I want her to do and we get on fine. Very quiet and placid old lady. Often been teaching the kids to ride her."

Mark snorted into his beer and sang out, "Yair, right! Bet she won't take any other person on her back except you!"

Bones bridled and said with some asperity, "I been a cameleer before you were born, mate. You can bring anyone here that wants a go and we'll see how good Dandy is!"

Kate looked at her friends and chuckled.

"I've ridden horses most of my life but never been on a camel, but I'd like to try. Reckon, I can stick on anything with four legs. My dad reckons it comes of having an affinity with animals and maybe that runs to camels as well. I'd like a go!"

Mark and Jason sauntered over to the fence and Jason said to Bones, "Kate reckons she would like to learn to ride a camel, if you're certain about your old girl being pretty quiet and won't bite her?"

Bones looked at Kate for a moment and nodded his agreement. He went into the old shed and came out with a halter and reins, a heavy cloth and a queer-looking saddle. He gave Dandy a command and she groaned and started to sit, folding up like a deckchair, kneeling her front legs first followed by the back legs, until the whole assembly collapsed to rest on her calloused chest pad. She chewed her cud with disdain, ignoring the people about her.

Kate took Deefer and chained him under her Ute, much to his disgust, so he lay with his head on his paws watching every movement. She climbed over the fence followed by Mark and Jason.

They were interested to see that Bones used no nose peg for his camel and Mark, thinking out loud, remarked, "We don't use nose pegs either, Bones. Often wonder if too much nose peg makes camels grumpy."

Bones replied, "It'd make youse blokes grumpy too with drongos pulling your nose about!"

He placed the cloth on the rear of the camel, with the small saddle over it, passing two long leather straps, one under the withers and one over Dandy's chest. She took no notice till Bones placed the halter and reins in place and she knew he meant business. She fanned her great eyelashes at him and made as though to chomp at him but he kissed her on the nose and she subsided like a coy matron.

Bones walked quietly about, saying to Kate, "Always walk on the side of the camel so they can see you, no matter how tame one kick can break your leg. You see how Dandy sits, so when she gets up, she raises back legs first, so in the saddle you lean back, then the front legs come up and you lean forward."

Kate nodded and picked up the carrots Bones had taken out of his pocket, standing to one side offered them to the animal, who took them with her big soft lips and chewed with relish. Kate was calm and showed no fear. Bones nodded approvingly and the other men saluted the air.

Bones said, "Sling your leg over and hold the front of the saddle, legs against the animal."

Kate did and settled herself well, Bones walking up to the front of Dandy, holding the reins and called to her, "Yalla, yalla!"

Dandy grumbled but raised herself to her full height. Kate firmed herself in the saddle and to her surprise liked the feel of the rough coat under her legs. Bones led the camel round the yard and Kate soon became accustomed to the seat. Pup and a couple of drinkers came out of the kitchen to watch. Kate felt at home with the sideways swaying motion of the camel and after a few gentle rounds, as Bones called to Dandy to sit, with "Hooshta, hooshta," all the men gave a shout and a clap.

Kate got off, gave Bones a hug and stated, "Wow! That's the best thing I've ever done!"

The old man looked shyly pleased but busied himself with taking the tack off to the shed.

When he returned, Mark shook his hand and remarked, half joking, "Kate has a good seat, alright. Used to riding anything out on the property except camels. Here is a thought. Can you teach her quickly just to run straight on Dandy? She could be entered in the Ladies' race with a bit of tuition."

Bones looked at him seriously.

"I could give Kate some lessons if she is willing. It's all fairly easy on a tame camel like this one. Kate, what you think about learning to ride Dandy? You need long pants and socks on, as the rough coat can take the skin off your legs."

Kate was bubbling with enthusiasm.

"I'd love to have a go. I like the feel and motion of the camel. I'm willing to learn if Bones thinks it would be OK."

Bones looked at her eager face and nodded.

"Camels tame easily but never take your eye off what they're up to. Dandy is in her prime years and well trained, but always be careful of the young ones, specially the males. They tend to play up if you don't know what you're doing. The big feral males are tough buggers, but the tame ones have been gelded for easy handling. I've had all type in my strings at times."

Jason looked at Bones with respect.

"You really know what you're talking about, mate. How long you been handling camels?"

Bones considered, counting on his fingers.

"Makes about forty years, I reckon."

Kate whistled, "Phew! Come and sit down and tell us about your experiences. I'm all ears and ready to learn."

The older man grinned as he pulled up a chair.

"I came up from Port Augusta when I was a raw lad, mid-teens and got a job at Marree with one of the leading Ghans who had a camel transport business up the Birdsville and Strzlecki tracks and everywhere in between. I learned the hard way. How to walk camels, tame camels, treat camels and the outdoor life suited me. We walked many miles in terrible heat, besides having to unload the camels each night and reload them in the morning. Tough stuff but good. Made me very strong. After some years I bought two of the teams from the Ghans for myself."

Mark was interested.

"I had heard that the Police at Marree used camels to go out on patrols from the turn of the century as well."

Bones nodded, "Yeah, because of the lack of roads in the desert, the camels were well suited to the land and they were used by Police until the early 50's, I think."

Kate asked, "How come there are such huge numbers of camels roaming around today?"

Bones said thoughtfully, "Part of their great ability to adapt to harsh environments comes from the camel's coat, which acts as an insulator in winter and reflects the heat in summer. You've felt the tough hair, Kate, which is why I advise newcomers to wear good leggings. The hide can withstand thorns and spinifex and forms hard pads on knees, elbows and brisket. Added to this, the hump, made up of fat and gristle, is used for as a fat store during hard times. Doesn't hold water like some dills say! Pity human animals aren't as tough as camels!"

Mark was impressed with the lengths of time the old man had experienced the camel trades in the Outback.

He remarked, "Jase and I are part of a camel-catching team for a firm in Adelaide. They are sending their best camels to Arabian countries, some by boat and some by air. Aus now has the best disease-free camels in the world."

Jason added, "Our catching team goes to cattle stations, like Kate's, where the camels are making a pest of themselves around water points and fences, so we lighten the load for the cattle men. Hard work, but we are part of a good team and we like what we do. Of course, we also managed to get a bit fond of these weird animals and now own one each we have been teaching to race."

Mark laughed.

"My young filly, Lucinda, has a good nature but gets a bit stressed out by too many people being around her all at once. Jase was lucky enough to buy his old gelding, Dagobar, from a bloke leaving the area and Dags had some racing experience, not bothered by anything and is a good ride."

Kate asked Bones, "How did your camel trains manage for water in remote areas of the desert?"

Bones frowned, trying to remember.

"The original camel teams usually consisted of maybe seventy camels with four Afghan drivers. Water was always the biggest concern, both for animals and men. The teams could travel, fully loaded with around fifteen tons loaded on their backs for twenty miles a day. They were used in the early days to transport goods for the construction of the Overland Telegraph line, as well as supplying right up to Alice springs."

Bones paused for consideration.

"I can think of various waterholes that we had info about from the local tribes, plus there were a number of mound springs, like here, on the northern side of the Artesian Basin. Up at Beltana, there was a really deep well where the Ghans had placed a couple of wheels over ropes. With a camel on each wheel, the buckets would go down and the camels pull them up full of water to fill the stone troughs there. Something, they used in their home country, I guess."

Kate clapped.

"Too clever! You got your learning first-hand and now you keep your favourite camels in good nick. Good on you!"

Jason said, "I guess you eventually gave up the big treks when the roads got better. How did you end up here at Ma's place?"

Bones cackled, "You might say it was Providence! I used to call in here to the pub when Mrs Batley's husband, Eric, was alive and do the odd maintenance jobs he wanted."

Kate also laughed, "Just like now!"

Bones said, "After Eric died, Mrs B asked me to stay for a few days to help out and get stuff done for her and here I still am after some years. She was happy for me to keep Dandy and the other lady, Sadi, as a companion, in the outside yard. Ginger and Mungo use Sadi now and then for short treks around the area, where their old four-wheel drive can't go. These days I do the odd job work, keep the Men's Quarters clean and free of drunks and, generally, help out where needed, like the races, which will make us all work hard."

Kate said admiringly, "I would love to dig into your camel wisdom and learn about these animals. Warn you, I'm a bit of an animal frantic! I tend to fall in love with them all!"

Bones chuckled.

"Just common sense, most of it. If you want to ride, we'll do a bit every time we can. Dandy is a quiet old girl and will do anything for carrots. Sadi is a bit more temperamental at times but nothing I can't get over."

Mark grinned, shaking his finger at Kate, "Just remember, when you get in the saddle to hold your knees tight when she gets going or you'll come of at first bounce. Tight knees makes the beast hear you better!"

Bones snorted.

"And bite a bit better!"

Chapter Twenty-Five

The cloudless sky was deepest blue, highlighting the red of the sandhills on the edge of the desert. The vast saltpans were sparkling white in the morning light and the grey-green spinifex bushes ringing the pans looked like they were smoking in the sunshine.

The usually sleepy little town of Windani had spread its wings out into the flat country, with droves of caravans, tents, four-wheel drive vehicles, small parked planes with flocks of children running with excitement, mobs of camels and horses coming into the yards in a cacophony of neighing, braying and moaning amid the back ground hum of people.

There were also a number of bedecked old buses opposite the pub, parked close to the tin-sided amenities and a tap from the mound springs. These buses were fully equipped for living and mostly sprouted elderly white-haired people, who liked the buses for comfort. They also kept an eye on the kids playing on and around the derelict old rusting hulk of a railmotor on the unused siding that once serviced the town in the early days before the rail was rerouted.

A big truck with pictures of Boxers in shorts and gloves on the sides had arrived towing a large caravan. It had also stopped at the flat space on the other side from the pub. It seemed to mesmerise all the youngsters who stood around watching developments.

Firstly, all manner of equipment was unloaded by some strong, well-built fellows, all directed by a small man in yellow overalls with his logo on the front. Soon a large tent was erected, with a few locals giving a helping hand with guy ropes and pegs. There was a flat walkway and a ladder being unloaded out of the truck, sited at the front of the tent.

The luridly painted front of the tent soon aroused a lot of interest from gathering roustabouts, as it stated, "FELLOWES BOXING TROUPE, *with all the best boxers ready for bouts.* FIVE POUNDS WINNERS PRIZE."

There were large paintings of boxers, clad in their short and gloves, in appropriate fighting stances. Little kids were entranced by the paintings and copied the stances and tried to bop each other. The word about the boxing troupe arriving in town spread like wildfire.

After a great deal of hammering and pegging, the tent was made secure. The ladder was placed up to the ramp at the front. This was where the professional boxers would strut their stuff to draw in the would-be opponents from the crowd. The big truck, once emptied, with a boxer in his boxing shorts banging a drum and another ringing a brass bell, drove through the main street to refuel at the garage.

It took ages to get this done, as men of all ages crowded round to ask questions of the man in yellow overalls. They were told the bouts would take place on Saturday, starting at 2 p.m.

Would-be contestants were told to offer themselves for bouts at that time. There were four professional boxers ready to take on all comers, including a well-built aboriginal boxer who looked like being the next Aussie champion.

The Boss was soon shouting his spiel to the eager listeners—

"Give it a go, what you got to lose! Survive three rounds and win five pounds!"

Of course, this whetted the appetite of the locals, so there was nothing but big talk about who was the fittest and strongest men around who would be ready to give it a go. The younger men coming in from properties for the weekend were very fit and considered themselves strong enough to last the three rounds and the possibility of winning the five pounds was a great incentive when a whole week's wages for many were around five pounds.

Chook's big truck was following Cosmo's four-wheel drive round the perimeter of the town and past the showground camping area. They passed the mound springs and the lovely waterhole of the artesian run-off. Teo and Tong gazed out of the window, longing for a wash and clean clothes as they were a messy pair.

After Tong lost the toe off his boot, he was forced to limp around trying not to get burrs of bits of stick in his foot but his boot had filled with sand, so he was all agog at the water. They looked in amazement at the racing camels now resting in the big yard and at all the campers already set up in so many varying tents and camps and vans.

Cosmo drove past the last of the camps and went to an unused flat area around a half mile out on the low foothills surrounding the ranges. There was some good gum tree cover, plus they would be out of sight of the general camping areas.

Chook pulled up the Blitz, letting the dog out, who went at once to investigate the area, while Cosmo cleared the ground under the trees with a branch. The Asians stood together gazing around, feeling dazed after their rough ride. Chook soon had a tarp strung between under the trees, a fireplace of rocks set up, the groundsheet laid under the tarp and bedrolls and cooking equipment set out.

Cosmo told the Asians, "We got to go into the town and fill with fuel. We'll have to take the Blitz. Youse blokes want a wash, go down to the showgrounds and pay someone at the office to have a shower. Take your duffle bags, but doan hang around when you're done. Don't want to bring notice to yourselves. We'll bring some fresh tucker back and get some more food supplies with some drinks and good water."

The Asians collected their bags without a word, staggering down the hill to find some decent washing facilities after their dirty trip. Chook and Cosmo whistled the dog into the Blitz and they motored carefully into the main street to attend to their chores, hoping they were not particularly noticeable among the gathering campers and race goers starting to throng around the town.

They drove out again to the new camp with fresh food and fuel to find Teo and Tong had showered and looked remarkably fresher. Tong had changed his torn boots for his city shoes, which looked a bit incongruous, being black and shiny and too clean. They had changed into other clothes, washed their filthy duds, which Cosmo threw over bushes to dry.

He gave out cans of cold drink, while Chook made big sandwiches out of fresh bread, ham and pickles, which once the Asians would have refused but were now happy to dig in. The dog was also happy to get fresh water and some left-over food. Chook and Cosmo also took their kitbags down to the showers, paying their dues. Chook washed the dog in the shower with him, so all came back to their camp feeling like a good nap, letting out the bedrolls on the groundsheet and soon snores filled the afternoon air.

Chapter Twenty-Six

One of the biggest touring equipages arriving in town was that of Hector and Evie Ferguson, who travelled round from event to event across the country. Hector was engaged as a rodeo and race announcer. His big rig was a converted truck, the body of which had been made into a full self-contained living unit, so they could stop anywhere.

When in Windani they had a permanent spot to camp just outside the pub side yard, having had special dispensation from Ma Batley to use the pub facilities, as she had known them for many years.

Hector's big white truck home had been set up with its outside flyproof annex and awning. Evie, though, had a constant battle to keep the flies out every time friends came in to visit. She could stand most things thrown at her by the Outback, but she couldn't abide flies. Now and then, when she got fed up with the uneven fight, she went into the pub to see what she could do to help Ma Batley and Madge, her daughter, so they could gossip while Evie polished glasses, wiped tables down and mopped the floor.

This time around they were engrossed in preparations for Madge's coming wedding to her fiancé, Frank, so it was the main subject for the ladies. Evie looked at the young and attractive Madge, slim, with a lovely head of deep auburn hair curling round her face.

Evie said, "Not long to the big day now, Madge. You'll look stunning in whatever you wear, but I'd love to know what that might be, if it's not a secret. Such beautiful hair, Elsie."

Elsie Batley grinned, fluffing up her white hair, "You'd never guess it, Evie, to look at this white mop but, as a youngster, I had hair the same colour as Madge. Got it from my Scottish grandmother. Also got my stern backbone from her too!"

Madge sighed, looking at Evie.

"I had thought of doing the white dress stuff, but Frank's parents had passed away, so there will not be many of his family to bring here. We agree to keep it all low key."

Ma Batley laughed, "Yeah, right! So far as being low key, I can imagine half the town turning up in the end, so we're having it in the backyard and I've ordered a big marquee from Adelaide to do duty."

Evie was curious.

"Is Frank bringing this up on one of his loadings for Marree. If it will fit on one of his trucks, that is."

Madge chuckled, "Yup. Being a bloke, he reckons he can put it up by himself, but we all know what that means. His cronies will be around to help and they will want plenty of beer to lubricate them, while they do it! If we get a willy-willy it'll all fall down!"

The women laughed and went to sit around the bar for a lemonade. Evie was all ears as to what Madge was going to wear and the supposed honeymoon.

"Now, can you spill the beans about your dress. I vow to keep silent about it if you wish?"

Madge looked a bit wary but said, "Well, it's a simple outfit I can use later on, but pretty and with a cute flowery hat. Himself refuses to wear a suit to that put the kybosh on anything that might be flash. Besides we are travelling down to Adelaide the next day in Frank's truck for a few days, so I have to use some common sense about it all."

Ma Batley explained, "I offered to shout a longer holiday, so they are thinking of having a week at the beach sometime later but as Frank's transport company is short of drivers at present, no one knows just when that might be. My brother, Father Pat, will be coming in for the races so I'll see him about coming back to do the honours."

Evie asked, "Hope you're not thinking of doing the catering, Elsie!"

Ma Batley shook her white head with emphasis, "Considering half our locals would love to be there, it was bothering me, as Pup is good with short order stuff, but wedding catering is not in his line. So, some of our good ladies have offered to do the wedding breakfast, which will be only for a certain number of invited guests. The marquee is for the evening after party."

At the scene of the camel races, Hector was involved at the showgrounds with the Stewards, seeing the paperwork was all set up correctly.

The two Stewards were local men, volunteer hands and having had many years of organising the show the men needed little help but were keen to show Hec the year's main prizes. They were tall, elegant rock crystals set into polished wooden bases, made and donated by a local artisan, plus some donated cash monies by businesses in the town. There were also camel printed t-shirts and rock crystal key rings for runners-up. They were pleased with the number of entries and fees paid for such a small camel race meeting.

One of the Stewards remarked, "Thought there'd be only three entries in the Ladies race, but that lass, Kev. Brenna's girl has been helping at the pub and is a late entry. Had old Bones coaching her on his camel."

The men laughed, but one was more serious.

"Maybe we should give Bones more merit, seeing as he was a cameleer in his early days, carting to Outback stations. Be interesting to see what he has taught the lass in a short time. Heard via the grapevine though, she can break in tough horses and just about ride anything with four legs, so she may be fine."

Hec looked at the list for the race day and they sorted out their schedules. The Steward held up a leaflet.

"You decided on a Judge for the Fashions on the Field yet? What about a bloke for a change?"

Hec snorted, "No bloke from around here in his right mind would do that job and have his life shortened by his wife! It'll be Jean again, as at least the women know she's always fair and a darn good judge of an eyeful."

The others agreed. Hec continued, "Besides, Jean takes no nonsense from anyone and I can't imagine any of the girls arguing with her. They know well they might need her to give them some nursing at any time, plus many of the ladies with babies have made it to the Adelaide Hospital in time because of Jean. She was hopeful that one of the people from RFDS would be here to accept whatever money we collect to donate. It would depend upon where they are flying at the time."

The men sorted out some tins from a cupboard and brandished them in the air.

"Here's the old RFDS donation tins—plenty of these left from last time. We'll stick them on the bars. People round here are pretty good at wanting to keep the RFDS flying."

The men went back to sorting out their paperwork, ignoring assorted noises coming in from around the camel yards. Some of the locals had rounded up likely camels and brought them into to be tamed down for the brave to have a go at racing, but a lot of groaning and moaning filled the air from these.

There were always some riders who preferred to bring their own trained camels, specially taught to race, in belief their own animals could take away the prizes. A man from Cameron Corner had travelled down with two of his rather elegant looking well-groomed racing camels. These brought enthusiasts to the camel holding paddock to discuss general camel business, which needed a foray to the bars now and then to oil the process.

The bookmakers had set up their stands along the track into the grounds, made up of a roof of fresh green gum tree boughs. The races also had outdoor bars set up the same way so that the clear air was scented with eucalyptus, with other smells of camels, red dust and wood smoke from the campfires dotting the landscape.

There were plenty of events going on in the main street while the crowds waited for the main race events the next day. As well as many street stalls, a few makeshift awnings had been set up over tables where there were displays of all manner of gemstones, some uncut and some polished and set.

Many of the old fossickers were sticky-beaking round the stalls, arguing the merit of the agates, crystals and various mineral samples. The young girls were trying out the necklaces and bracelets in front of a mirror, aware the stallholder was awake to the possible disappearance of a trinket or two.

There were donkey rides for children, plenty of fairy-floss, plus the smell of coffee and barbecued treats. The 'catch-a-greasy-pig' race had a teeming flock of children running like the wind, urged on by cheering friends on the side-lines. The pig squeals caused the camels to bellow out their own indignation and the roar of the crowds signalled that the pig had been caught, after a fashion. The eventual winner was seen rolling on the ground with armfuls of kicking, frantic pig, each of them almost indistinguishable from each other, covered in grease and red dust.

The heat at midday made the surrounding desert shimmer. A number of cameleers were begging the announcer and the stewards for the races to start early next day so they didn't have to ride in the heat of the day—but were waved away with the news that all would begin at the scheduled time of 10 a.m. with no mercy shown for softies.

There was sudden uproar from the penned camels at the showgrounds and the siren in the generator shed was sounded as an alarm. There was an almighty sound of impending chaos from the edge of the yards, where a party of feral male camels had come in to harass the penned animals and were trying to kick the fences to pieces.

All the local menfolk, their offsiders and anyone else that wanted a good fighting trip after the feral camels, were seen to jump into any truck, Ute, motor bike and even on foot, armed with whips and shotguns and even bits of paling fence.

With the noise of shotguns, vehicles and shouting and whip-cracking they drove off the feral camels right back towards the low hills and a posse of willing helpers were given the job of keeping an eye on the ferals, in case of would-be interference again. The men had come back in pleased with their efforts and were quick to have some cold beers to restore themselves while the town resumed its normal hum.

The children's races were going well, with kids hobbled together in the three-legged race, while mothers were in the thong throwing championship, where the rubber sandals landed just about anywhere but in the designated area. The teenagers were dancing and singing to a Country and Western band set up near the Boxing tent.

Chapter Twenty-Seven

Whenever there was a spare moment from the rush of pub work, Kate had practised with Bones in charge, giving her the best information, to help understand the methods of riding a camel as well as knowing its peculiarities.

She had quickly become used to the sway and could ride around the big yard herself. She had also given Dandy the proffered carrots to get used to her smell and the camel seemed to be complacent about Kate's presence. Kate learned how to saddle her as well, so Bones was pleased with Kate's handling of Dandy and gave his full encouragement.

Jason and Mark were there to watch at times and Jason remarked to Bones, "You've done such a good job with Kate in such a short time, but then she has a natural seat with animals, I guess, from all the cattle work on her property with horses. Bet you never though she would be good to enter the Ladies Race on Dandy? You reckon Dandy will be up for it?"

Bones bridled, "Of course, she's up for it. It's only a short straight run and as camels can only canter for a short time; they have to be encouraged to race. Dandy is in good nick and likes to stretch out with me in the bush sometimes."

Mark and Jason gave themselves a high-five and Mark said to Kate, "You sure enough now to give the Ladies Race a go, Kate? Don't' think there will be much opposition and Jase and I'll dob in the entry fee."

Bones nodded in approval, but Kate said decidedly, "I'm ready to give it a go, if that is OK with Bones. What you reckon, Bones? A bit of a canter is fine by me, as my stock horses have a lot more speed than that, but I can pay my own fees, thanks."

Each time Kate had a bit of time off from her duties, she and Bones had been seen making their way across the flat ground with Kate riding Dandy, towards the school and back again. Kate was found she could urge Dandy into a trot by flapping the reins and calling encouragement, feeling quite secure on the tall beast.

Bones gave his instructions and looked pleased with Kate's progress on the camel. She would unsaddle Dandy and give her a good brush down, so Dandy seemed to like the attention and regarded Kate with her big soft eyes, with their great long lashes, nuzzling Kate's pockets in case more carrot treats were in store.

Bones had more to say about the actual racing. He said, "The camels don't have stamina for a long flat out run and in fact their best flat out is usually a canter at the best, but the race track is short and to get her going give her a boot in the side. She'll do her best in a short run, but she'll pull up quick, so be prepared."

Kate was pleased, "I think Dandy and I have a good feeling between us and she'll be fine, long as I don't fall off too often and make a show of myself! Just the same, I've landed on the ground from plenty of horses while mustering, so it wouldn't be the first time for me."

Bones said, "We'd better clear it with Ma first, too, to see if she won't need you round 10 o'clock, start of the Ladies Race. We'll be back in half an hour."

In town the hotel bar was full and the Café next door was also running hot and Morrie and his helpers were flat out. There was queue forming into the street for the hot pies and chips in a paper bag, Chicko rolls and the toasted mutton sandwiches that were Buddy's speciality.

Further across the road the 'ride-the-sheep' contest had the children racing after a poor, beleaguered, heavy lamb. One boy hung on the back for dear life and almost made the finish line until he slipped under its belly and fell off.

He howled loudly in disappointment, "No fair, no fair, I the winner! I should get the prize!"

His father, picking him up off the grass and dusting him off, laughed and said laconically, "Pick up yer lip, kid. You got a face like a dropped pie! Here's some better prize money—let's get orf and enjoy it."

He proffered some coins and the lad's face cleared, so they were both happy and went off arm in arm, heading for the lady with the spun sugar treats.

The station hands and cowboys were right into the 'see-how-many-dogs-fit-in-the-back-of-a Ute competition, where the dogs had a fight a minute and the crowd bellowed with laughter. A tall, calibrated board was set at the back of a Ute where athletic dogs could have a good run up and be urged by their masters to try and scale the biggest height.

Chook had come in from his camp, unseen, while the other men were sleeping and stood watching, remarking to a bystander,

"Me brother's dorg would eat all them mutts. Bitzer's his name, big bugger."

The man beside him looked scathing.

"Is he in there, then? Don't see many Bitzers in there. These all good cattle dogs."

Chook looked truculent, he grumbled, "Just the same our Bitzer would murder 'em. He's a good dorg!"

The other man was not looking for a row and moving away, stated, "Don't get yer knickers in a knot, I was only making a comment."

Chook pulled his big hat down over his head and stalked off to see if he could find a beer, which as Cosmo wasn't around, though it was forbidden fruit, Chook decided to find some while no one was watching him.

Some big, burly ringers were engaged in the egg-throwing competition in the showgrounds, much to the enjoyment of the crowds, who whistled and cheered and made clucking noises.

The egg-throwing took a delicacy of hand and a good eye, as the men tossed the egg to their opposite number who had to catch it carefully. When the received egg was dropped on the deliverer, or he sent his egg awry into the crowd, it meant disqualification for being a public nuisance. Every now and then a fresh egg went astray and exploded in the hand, or sometimes on the head of the catcher at the other end, much to the merriment and catcalls of the audience.

In a bough-covered stall in the main street, two of the local school volunteers had been manning the Sausage Sizzle stall. They had a sign up over their stall stating that proceeds were to go to supplying the school with boots and shirts for the new school footy club. This brought in many people to spend their money wisely. The men had been frying up what seemed to be tons of sliced onions on a gas plate, plus frying sausages on a barbecue on the side. These were placed on a white bread sandwich, accompanied by tomato sauce if required. All this was accompanied by hordes of flies.

They had employed a couple of school kids to be the fanners to keep off the flies and the lads had done a sterling job. They had been paid off and were away like lightning to share the booty with their mates.

As the busy lunch time came to an end, the men were clearing up the detritus and cleaning the barbecue, when a tall, well-dressed man came to the stall and asked for sausage with the 'works'. The chef of the sausages stopped his work and forked the last of the sausages with the rest of the onions into slabs of white bread. The flash gent paid but looking into his sandwich, he was very put out.

He queried testily, "Is that all there is? I asked for the 'works' as I'm hungry."

The chef was worn out and too fed up by the end of his work to put up with useless palaver and he called to his partner for the tomato sauce, "Chuck us the Red Ned, mate, bastard 'ere think I'm Santy Claus!"

Chapter Twenty-Eight

After Cosmo had set up his own camp well away from the crowds, he went strolling round the campers, gathering any information he could glean about the local scene and also about the races. He was wondering if the men the Asians were seeking, Ginger and Mungo, would enter a camel if they were in town. He decided to look in at the pub as well. He whistled Bitzer, who jumped into his rig and they drove down the red dirt road full bore.

In the pub the thirsty throng was causing Ma and her girls to work very hard, but also the seasoned drinkers were happy to be inside in the cool. Ma had a rented cold room out the back as well as more kegs in the old beer cellar and Bones was busy keeping things set up from there.

Kate said to Ma, after one foray into the cold room for special grog, "What happens, Ma, if the cold room breaks down?"

Ma looked amused.

"It did once, when the town generator stopped for a time, so all the blokes reckoned they should drink all the beer before it got hot!"

Kate and Gina dissolved into giggles and went back to deal with the cold room.

There were various signs around the bar walls, giving notice of forthcoming events around the town. A larger sign above the bar state, NO DOGS IN THE BAR by order SA Licensing Commission.

A few dogs had sinuously stolen inside with their owners, not wishing to be seen, but Ma had her eyes everywhere. She rapped on the counter loudly with an ashtray and pointing to the sign, shouted, "Can't you blokes read!"

The smoky air was rent by raucous laughter and hoots of derision.

Bad language never caused Ma to bat an eyelid, so she rapped again, "Yes, yes, get back in your boxes! I know what you think about this old girl running the pub, but I been here before you lot came and I'll be here after you're all gone! Get them bloody dogs outside—NOW!"

The untidy draggle of assorted ringers and bums grumbled loudly but all the same the dogs were booted out the door. The fag smoke and flies resumed around the bar above the hum of contentment, with clinks of glasses and their cool pungent ales.

Outside, along the red road, Cosmo's truck barrelled up to the pub and halted in a flurry of dust. The big dog leapt out with his master and they stamped into the suddenly quiet bar. The patrons held their collective breath to see Ma's next move.

Ma shouted, pointing to the sign, "NO DOGS IN THE BAR!"

Cosmo, startled, growled, "Where I go, me dorg goes."

The big dog lifted his lip and stated his intent of staying put with glaring, piggy eyes.

Ma drew herself up to her full five feet in height and barked, "Then get yourself and the bloody dog outsider, pronto and toot sweet!"

Cosmo was nettled and swaggering, gazing round the suddenly silent room.

"And who among this bar full of pisspots is gunna make me?"

The dog growled softly in his throat, raising his hackles.

Ma said quite sweetly, "Just me!"

She whipped under the bar with the speed of a striking King Brown, pulling out a double-barrelled shotgun and levelled it right between his eyes.

"You can go out live or you can go out dead!"

Cosmo, falling backwards over the drinkers and white to the gills, yelled, "Sh-i-te!"

The dog cringed away and they both backed out the door, falling down the steps in their hurry and were last seen rocketing back out the red dirt road clad in dust and defeat. The pub rocked with cheers.

Ma fluffed up her white hair.

"Get's 'em every time!" she said.

Chapter Twenty-Nine

The sun went down quickly over the red desert, so the spectacular sky was lit with flames of red, orange and purple tufts of cloud. The youngsters and partygoers were revelling in the cooler breezes. Some had gathered a few guitars and were starting to sing. Others made their way to their camps to make their supper and swig beers with friends. The aromas of barbecued meats hung over the camps and made the dogs hang around looking hopeful in case of a good handout.

After Cosmo, Chook and the Asians had set up their camp on the outskirts, Chook had been surfing round the general camping area and listening to old gougers talk about the area and the locals. He came back, hid his beer cans on the Blitz, started a good fire going and was in full cooking mode with a camp oven on the side coals and plenty of sausages grilling and potatoes in their jackets on the edge of the coals. He turned these with his toe now and then and raked them out to cool.

While Chook was cooking, Cosmo had tried the pub for info, to his detriment. He had come back properly out of sorts and sat by himself, while the others sat around the fire eating. The Asians were hungry and last deigned to eat what they were given and Chook grinned when he saw them pull at his brown and delicious damper with enthusiasm.

Cosmo came to eat and mumbled with a mouthful of grub, "I heard those blokes you wanted to know about, Mungo and Ginger, are around here somewhere, word is they usually camp out of town."

Tong grated out, "You get them to see us quickly. We give you plenty of money for this and you tell them we got job for them and will pay big."

Cosmo looked doubtful, "Well, from what I hear about these blokes, I don't like our chances of finding them if they don't wanna be found!"

The Asians nattered together in their own lingo. Tong then stated, "If they won't take us to the cave for good money, then we take one of them along to *make* show the way!"

While all this was going on, Chook was singing quietly to himself by the fire, with a good chunk of damper and sausages on his plate. The dog liked to sing too and howled along with Chook. Cosmo threw a stick at them both.

Chook stopped singing and said, "Nuthin' youse can do to make them old geezers do anythin' they don't wanna do, from what I hear around the camps. I heard from some blokes in town that you gotta do sumpin' extra to make them fellas sit up quick. Yer'd do better to take that pretty sheila, who works at the pub called Kate—she's been seen on old Bones camel—he's a friend of them blokes. Then they come quick!"

There was dead silence while the other three took in this amazing bit of info from Chook, which made a peculiar rather dangerous sort of sense.

Cosmo clapped in derision, "Geez, Chook, what a thought! Nothin' like a bit of kidnapping to get us into big trouble. I need to go to see if I can find one of the black fellas that know that ginger fella and it'd all be sorted without getting into bad stuff."

Teo said, "We go and find!"

Cosmo shook his head, looked at the Asians and thought they were better kept right out of the way and should not be seen at all anywhere in the vicinity.

He said, "You blokes stay under cover if anyone comes around here. Don't want any trouble from the fuzz."

The Asians looked at him mystified and that made Cosmo cranky.

"Just stay right here, cause if you give any trouble I'm gonna give you back your money and go home. The Police often patrol the camps, in case of trouble. If the Police come past get in the truck and stay outta sight!"

The small men seemed a bit cowed by Cosmo's offering to pull right out of their deal, so they nodded and sat shuffling round a bit, waiting to see what Cosmo was going to do next.

He said, "I'm gonna stroll round and see what people might know about the men we wanna find. Chook, get this cleaned up, keep Bitzer with you and I'll be back shortly."

Cosmo went off, still feeling grumpy as he was right out of his depth. He went past many camps to see if he knew anyone that might talk to him and give him the info he wanted. He eventually got back to the camp feeling ripped off at not finding out anything of value and sat down to drink a beer, when Chook came over grinning, with the dog in tow.

Cosmo was cranky and threw a stick at the dog and growled and grumped at Chook, tired after such a big day and bothered by not knowing what to do next.

He said, "Piss orf, hairy legs! I'm fed to the teeth with these blokes. It was all their bodgy idea to look for some supposed opal dragon, which maybe just fairy stories. No one round here seems to know about it at all."

The Asians came back out of the truck and fronted Cosmo at once.

Teo said, "What you find out? We get hold that ginger man OK?"

Cosmo growled, "Nah! No one seen them in town. Yer can't make them appear out of the clouds."

Tong shouted, "If we don't get hold that man, we'll take the girl from the hotel to make them come quick!"

Cosmo shook his head disparagingly.

"I doan like that mate—I liked the idea of the opals, if they was real, but I would never get into kidnapping. Not my agenda at all. Big Police trouble if we get caught. We'll all be slung in jail and never heard of again!"

Tong hurriedly chipped in, "Not kidnapping, oh no! We just borrow the girl for a while, until those men show us the cave. No harm done to girl. We look after."

The Asians exchanged sly glances, but Cosmo was right against the idea.

"Youse mob got no idea how we could let this Ginger know we got the girl. Yer all bloody mad! Gonna get us into a big ruckus. More sense to get hold of Ginger and his mate first."

Teo said, "They would like our big money, so we wouldn't need to borrow girl."

His mate nodded, "Sure thing. Money always talks!"

Cosmo was fed up with all this mad talk and snapped out, "I ain't goin' in for any kidnapping, even if I can't find out anything. Not spending the rest of my life in the pokey because of your mad schemes!"

Tong leapt up, furious, brandishing his evil-looking switch-blade knife and grabbing Chook, held it against his throat. Chook's hair nearly stood on end and his eyes popped. He looked frantically to Cosmo for help.

Tong started to scream, "Our money pay for this, so I will hurt this one bad if you do not do as we want! I killed for less!"

Suddenly afraid for Chook, Cosmo, trying to stay calm, kept his voice even.

He said mildly, patting the air, "Calm down. Just try and think sensibly. Put that dang knife away. This also works my way too, 'cause if you hurt Chook I leave you in the desert to die!"

Teo was looking worried, but Tong, growling in his own language, was finally settling down, putting away the knife with a click, letting Chook go, so he went and sat with his brother, shaking all over.

Cosmo patted his arm and said, "Stay still, Chooky, no one gonna hurt you while I'm around. The only thing I heard talk about is that there is an old black tracker, who should know where Ginger hangs out. I'll go and see if I can find his camp and leave a message. Best I can do for now."

Tong agreed, "But then if they not help, we borrow the girl one night."

Chook looked up, "I got all the gen. Big party pub backyard after the races, plenty of beer and girls. Pretty girl be there."

Cosmo was exasperated, trying not to have anything to do with this eccentric scheme that had no good outcome.

"Gawd, Chook, you're a smart as a sock full of soup! Leave the planning to the men! I was talking to a bloke at the race bar, who found a good place to camp out of town where no one ever goes these days—even drew me a bit of a map. It's a waterhole with one big tree. We could go there and see if this Ginger plays ball and can meet us there. I was told he treks all over this area and would know it."

The Asians deliberated amongst themselves and nodded.

Tong said, "You go and find the black man and give message, then we see what next."

The mob of campers around the town were starting to quieten as the night drew on, so Cosmo went to Chook and said quietly, not wanting to leave him around the unreliable Tong, "Tie the dog under the truck and you come with me to see if we can find the old black fella. We got to go across the back of a few shops and I heard he camps out there somewhere."

Chook did as he was told, patted the dog and tied him up, so they could go softly out of the camp. The small men had finally gone to sleep in their bedrolls and were snoring gently.

The shops were very quiet, so when Cosmo and Chook went scouting round the edges of the town, they could hardly see, stumbling over uneven ground and through scrubby bushes, until they smelt smoke and eventually spotted a small fire behind a sandhill, where they found old Fardy, the blacktracker.

They squatted down by the smoky fire and gave Fardy some tobacco, who said nothing, kept his eyes on the fire while he took a bit of the tobacco and wadded into his mouth.

Cosmo tried to be as nonchalant as possible.

"Good day, Fardy, I got some news for Ginger and Mungo. You know where I could get hold of them?"

Fardy was no fool and eyed them suspiciously. He chewed his baccy slowly and deliberately. He spat on the ground.

"Nah, Boss. Dey around seeum Fardy not know. What you want dem for?"

Cosmo said placatingly, "I got some really good news for them, mate, that might earn them big money."

Fardy didn't shift from his fire and kept his eyes looking down, "I no seeum dis time round."

Cosmo tried to seem unconcerned and smiled ingratiatingly, "Reckon you might find them quick if I give you some coin?"

He jingled a few coins in his hand and dropped them by the fire.

Fardy said, "Naway, Boss."

Cosmo and Chook got up and drifted back the way they had come. The night was still dark with no moon up but now they were away from the firelight, the brilliance of the stars gave them enough light to find their way past sleeping camps. Fardy waited till they vanished out of sight and then took himself off casually round the camps as noise of footsteps declined. He followed the dark shapes of the pair without sound and came up behind a tree near their camp.

Cosmo woke the Asians and they sat groggily to hear if he had found the news they were waiting for. Fardy crept very close and heard them talking of possibly grabbing Ginger and making him show them the old track to Mt Painter.

Chapter Thirty

Fardy made off silently through the rough countryside, to the back of Morrie's Café, where Morrie was sitting out the back relaxing in the dark after a hectic day's work.

Fardy whistled like a night bird and Morrie walked out into the yard to meet him, saying quietly, "What's up, Fard?"

Fardy also spoke quietly, "That fella Cos, camping way out the back, reckon from Pedy, got bad men with 'im, look to get Mungo and Ginger into trouble. About the dragon stuff. Make Ginge take 'em to where he knows."

Morrie took in a deep breath and had a quick think.

"You know where Ginge's camp is?"

Fardy nodded.

"I'll get a bag of grub ready, you take 'em to Ginge and tell him to get lost quick time, eh? Bones' old Dandy has the camel they use in the yard with her, so they can get away at once. Tell Bones what you heard."

Fardy slipped away silently into the night, traversing a few low sandhills, until he smelt the smoke of a small fire. He whistled softly the trill of a nightbird until a whistle came back. He found the two white men in a good camp under a few trees away from the hubbub in town. Fardy spoke quietly to them handing them the bag of food.

They told Fardy to get hold of Bones and he could bring the second camel out with some of their gear on her. Then they would pack up their camp and get away shortly. They saluted Fardy and he sidled off.

Out beside the camel yard at the pub, Fardy made owl sounds and Bones, who had been clearing rubbish from the yard where the lights were still on, whistled back and went to the outside yard.

He listened intently to Fardy and told him, "I'll fit what gear they got here on the camel and bring it over to their camp and they can repack and get away to Arkaroo water, so no one but us will know where they are."

Fardy nodded and silently disappeared into the night.

Bones went over to the shed in the camel yard, found some packed gear along with girth straps and halter. He approached his second camel Sadi, who was not in the mood for night trips and made her loathing quite plain with groans and moans and showing of her teeth. As he was trying to be quiet, Bones kept talking to the recalcitrant animal, but she was in no mood for sweet talk.

Bones demanded Sadi sit, so he could load her, hissed her native language to her and when she half sat he started to load, but Sadi eyed him with abject loathing got up and shot her load everywhere. Bones dug in the pockets of his disreputable coat and found a couple derelict barley sugars. He whistled through his teeth and went slowly nearer, singing sweet nothings and offering the sweets, but Sadi was not having any of it. She lashed out, kicking sideways with feet the size of dinner plates.

Bones was cross with her antics.

"Bad tempered old biddy! Yalla, yalla, bust yer! Gorn and strewed the supplies all over the place and I gotta get it loaded, so Ginger can get away to his new camp."

The camel was having none of his sweet talk or offerings and was spitting and angry.

Bones sighed, "Well, old girl, can't fiddle round 'ere all night. I can see yer might cross, but by gum, I am gonna win this fight!"

He stripped off his old coat and plaid shirt, stepped out of his pants and piled them in a heap. He retreated to a safe distance, as with a roar of fury, the camel pounced on the clothes, stamping them in her rage, tearing with her teeth and grinding the clothes into the dust with her chest.

Finally appeased, she rose and quietened. Bones stood as still as a post, refusing to look at her, gazing out over the paddocks as though he was fully dressed for dinner with the Queen, instead of being clad only in a singlet and boots.

The camel made soft snorting sounds and went quietly to sniff and nibble at the man's hair with gentle lips. She sighed and knelt to sit before him. Bones grinned to himself. He retrieved his badly mangled clothes and donned the tattered remains.

Kate had come out near the saddling yard in the light from the pub to hang some bar towels on the line. She stared in admiration at the taming of the camel in such a short time.

"Geez, Bones, how'd you get like that? I thought the camels were your best friends?"

Bones stood up quite proudly.

"Yup! But it takes a fair bit of wit for a mad man to win a silly fight!"

Kate laughed, "Yairs, well—there's a lot of that about here at the moment!"

Bones nodded, "But look at her now, Kate. She's putty in my hands, so there are ways and means of handling camels that ain't in any book!"

He turned to gather the scattered camp gear and loaded the camel with great aplomb, putting on her halter and speaking to her gently. She rose and they walked sedately out of the yard. Shortly afterwards, Ginger and his mate were seen silhouetted against the icy starlit sky, leading the camel and disappearing behind the low hills.

Chapter Thirty-One

There was a bright shining morning over the desert landscape and the echo of bird songs came sweetly from the nearby wetlands of the mound springs. The town was already up and surging, cooking, plus grooming camels for the race day. Kate went to see if Ma was OK with her having a bit of time off around 10 a.m. for the Ladies Camel Race. Bones came along to offer his backup and let Ma hear his side of the story as well.

Ma said sternly to Bones, "You really reckon this girl is ready enough for the race when she's only had a few days of practice? I don't want to have to make excuses to her dad if she falls off and gets hurt."

Bones clapped and said, "This girl has a right royal seat and gets on well with Dandy, who is a cool old lady. Besides, there are only three others in the Ladies Race. Kate'll romp it in!"

Ma smiled, "I can see I have a lost cause with you two, just be careful."

She waved them away to get on with her prep for another thirsty day. Gina was backing out of the cold room, when Kate came over, with a borrowed bright Afghan throw over her usual jeans and shirt, pinned over one shoulder and holding a hard hat Bones had borrowed for her.

Gina was all admiration, "That looks great, Kate. Wish I could do what you're doing, but I'm not brave enough to get up on one of those great beasts. Reckon, I'd fall off as soon as it got up!"

"I've been riding tough stock horses most of my life, Gina, and this old lady is a doddle compared to them. We'll have fun and if I come off it wouldn't be the first time. I've been thrown, kicked, walked on and bitten by stock horses and that was just for a start! Give me a quiet camel any day!"

Bones and Kate put the harness, halter and saddle on Dandy and walked her sedately along the main street to the holding paddock at the show grounds. The crowds paused to give them a cheer.

Mark and Jason were in the paddock attending to their camels, brushing them down, checking feet and legs. They looked startled to see Bones, Kate and Dandy so early.

Mark shouted, "Good day, people, how's the Dandy lady this morning? We paid your fees, Kate, so I hope you are ready to have a go?"

Bones almost swelled with pride.

"We're all good and this 'ere girl will romp home!"

Jason lifted his arms and saluted the sky.

"Yay! You not feeling nervous Kate? Enough to fall off?"

Kate laughed but took the banter in her stride.

"Just a teeny bit, but more excitement than anything. Besides, I got to do well by Bones and I been getting on fine with Dandy. She's a real sweetheart compared to our tough stock horses at home."

The seats around the ringside were filling quickly with the crowd avid to see the first race. The race track had been graded to suit the camels, kids were running round like mad things, shouting and screaming, the bookies were taking the first bets of the day and the announcer and his offshoots were ready in the box to report on the various events of the day.

The District Nurse, Jean, had her emergency tent set up to the side of the yards. She had attended many an event there over the years and was always open to any sort of medical call be it lost children, squashed fingers in the yards or falls from the livestock. A kick from a camel could be serious or broken bones in a fall, so the Police Force were also on call all day.

They checked with Jean now and then to see if she needed any help. Jean was clad in her special outfit for the day, which consisted of navy trousers, a sparkling white shirt with a frill at the neck and a red bandanna round her trusty rag hat.

Hector, the announcer, clad in heavy jeans, big check shirt and wide hat, was getting his voice in to fine form. He rang the bell on his stand and bellowed into the mike, "Good morning, folks, the Ladies Race is the starter for today. The Ladies are all keen and the camels feeling fit. Get your bets in quick. A percentage goes from the race fees to the RFDS. Without the RFDS, this town would be the worse for wear! Support our Ladies!"

The crowd cheered and whistled. Jean was waving from the podium. The four women who were racing had their camels sitting on the far end of the track, with a handler to help. Upon Hec's call, they slipped into their saddles, calling the camels to stand. Some had bells and tassels and flowing robes, which brought applause from the crowds.

Kate looked quite sedate in her usual working clobber with the coloured wrap around her shoulders, plus gaiters to protect her legs. She and Dandy and Bones were keeping to the side of the general mayhem as the helpers tried to line up the camels.

When there was almost a line, the Steward raised his starter gun to the sky, letting a blast go and the camels were off.

There was trouble at once as one of the girls fell off right away and the announcer roared, "That's Tango who's misbehaving and lost his jockey."

The girl was unhurt, but the camel was running back down the track and tried to scramble over the fence, much to the consternation of the crowd sitting there, who parted like the Red Sea and left the fence for safer places.

The helpers ran with ropes to try and run the camel down and the announcer roared again, "Think that one should be called Tangles instead of Tango!"

The other three riders were trotting along at a good speed, but one of the leaders found her camel veering to the left all the time and was losing ground, while Kate and Dandy were steadily overhauling the other leader at a steady pace. Bones, Mark and Jason were cheering like mad and nearly fell over the fence in excitement, as giving Dandy the signal of slapped reins and a boot in the side made the good Dandy speed up into her canter. This got Dandy across the line a neck ahead of her opponents.

Kate spoke quietly to Dandy and as they slowed down, she pulled her to a stop, while Kate slipped off her back, passing the reins over Dandy's head and waited for Bones to appear. Dandy didn't seem the least bit fazed, either by the crowd or her exploit, standing quietly and fanning her huge eyelashes like a beauty queen.

The announcer roared into his mike that a newcomer, Kate Brenna and her mount, Dandy, had won the Ladies Race prize. The crowd was either cheering, whistling, collecting their bets or tearing the old wagers into pieces.

Bones and the boys came up to give a hand with Dandy and walked her away to the holding yard. One of the Stewards came out to escort Kate up to the podium, where she received a large, sparkling rock crystal set into a polished wood base and a cheque from the Race Committee.

Kate blushed, smiled a huge smile and waved to the cheering crowd, while a sash was placed over her shoulder.

Mark helped her down off the podium and lifted her off the ground with a big swing, shouting, "Great stuff, you clever girl, a really good ride. Nobody knew old Dandy could be such a good runner."

Kate dusted herself off, chuckling, "Makes a big difference that I've spent so much time on the backs of animals, so Dandy was just a walk in the park and I really enjoyed myself!"

They made their way after Bones and Jason who were guiding Dandy to the trough to see if she needed a drink, though Bones thought she would probably prefer to go back to her own yard to rest. He and Kate walked easily at the side of Dandy up the main street, where people waved and took photos and Bones saluted his mates as they ambled past. Many came to pat him on the back, though keeping a wary eye on Dandy, shouting offers of beers later on.

Mark was pleased as a dog with two tails, as he and Jason went back to readying their camels in the holding yard. There was the matter of putting on saddles and halters and girth straps, to settle all correctly.

"What a turn up that was, Jase. Hope we can get a bit of Kate's winning streak as well!"

Jason laughed at his exuberance.

"Yeh, good buddy, but we'll have a lot more competition. I been sussing out those in my Dag's age race and it may be OK for him as he's had a lot of experience. Dunno about your Lucinda—plenty of youngsters looming on her horizon waiting to have a go. At least Lucinda has had quite a bit of training at our camp, so she's not quite as novice as some I've been watching."

Mark nodded, saying, "I would have liked to try her out in more races, but they are so far and few between as yet. Reckon it'll become a much bigger thing around the ridges as time goes on as there as so many keen to have a go."

They went back to fitting out Dagobar with jingling bells, small flags on his reins and a flowered saddlecloth, which made the big camel look quite elegant. They chatted to other competitors while the races got into full swing, with the noise of the crowds filling the air.

The announcer roared out the numbers for the Age Race, so Jason marched Dagobar clad in his jingling harness and finery to the starting line. He murmured to the camel, who obligingly folded his legs, so Jason sprang into the saddle and got settled. Another command and Dagobar rose to his full height, looking stately and magnificent.

The helpers were flat out trying to range the camels into a starting line, but there was always a couple of goers who didn't like the fuss and ranged around hissing and groaning. Finally, when there was almost a line, the Steward raised his starting gun to the sky.

Soon as the gun fired, Dagobar was away at once, first ahead of the field of five camels. He never missed a beat and as soon as the cameleer who was clad in a turban and Arabic finery came close, Dagobar lengthened his stride and won by a head, looking as regal as ever and as though he did this sort of thing every day.

Jason turned his mount and walked back sedately down the track to great applause and congratulations from the other contestants. He slipped off and led his animal back to the holding yards, where Dags was patted by Mark and the men shook hands, laughing. Jason undid the saddle, girth and reins, pulling off the flowered saddle cloth, dropping them all beside the fence to bundle up later.

Mark was really pleased for his mate and said, "Don't know how much you've won, but I won some on the Tote, so I'm pleased. Old Dags never batted an eyelid, did he! Took it all in his great stride."

Jason was happy with his race, never mind the winnings.

He remarked, "Dags is clever with it, Mark and keeps an eye out for any competition, though I thought we were goners when Bryce came up so close near the end, but Dags was right in on him. I'll settle him down and come and give you a hand with Lucinda at her start, which we know she doesn't like. Not good with all the noise and confusion, which puts her off."

Jason led his mount to the trough where the camel refreshed himself, then ambled over to stand under the trees.

They listened for the announcer's call for the Beginner's race, so Mark and Jason walked Lucinda out to the start line, talking to her all the way to try and keep her calm. She was a splendid-looking young lady, brushed to perfection and in good health, but a little edgy about the other camels and helpers all around her.

Jason gave Mark a boot up, so he vaulted into the saddle at the last moment before the starting gun went off. In spite of her worry about the others in the field, Lucinda began well, with Mark whistling to her and urging her on and booting her in the side; she must have decided it was best to run at a good speed rather than be booted, so she cantered away to finish second.

Jason was hooting and shouting from the stands as the contestants brought their mounts back, Lucinda was frothing at the mouth and a bit disoriented, so Mark slid off the saddle and led her gently round the back, unsaddled her and led her to the trough. As she quietened he took her over to stand with Dagobar under the trees and left her to settle down.

One of the Stewards came over and asked the men to come and get their prizes. On the podium Hec announced their winnings and as they took their prizes and an envelope of cash each, the crowds gave them a good cheer.

Chapter Thirty-Two

After a few races had been run and lunchtime was approaching, Hec announced that the Ladies Fashions on the Field was about to be judged and asked the beauties to assemble beside the podium. There was much cheering and whistling from the admiring crowd, as a bevy of ladies in all their finery and prettiest hats came up the steps to stroll across the boards.

Jean, as Judge, was at one side of Hec and the Stewards, making notes in her little book while the ladies smiled and pretended they were not the least bit nervous. Just then, amid gales of laughter and cat-calling through the watching throngs, two extra beauties clambered up, hampered by their high heels. The two brawny ringers had begged and borrowed an assortment of female attire supplanted by elaborate head-dresses that looked suspiciously like emu feathers sprayed with paint.

Hec, who was in on the prank, seemingly unaffected by the laughter, solemnly introduced the first 'lady'.

"This is a late entrant in the Fashions on the Field. I would like to introduce Miss Bar-Sheila from Bullamakanka."

This sally just about brought the house down! Bar-Sheila was clad in a cut-off see-through purple nightie, large fake boobs protruding from look like a hay net, along with long frilled pink panties underneath, complete with garters and knee-high stockings. He did a curtsey to the crowd and nearly fell off his high heels.

From somewhere, Bar-Sheila had managed to find a long black wig with tresses he kept throwing over his shoulder to the whistles and stamping from the crowd. His face was gaudily painted with much rouge, blue eye shadow and lashings of bright pink lipstick. He sashayed over to the end of the line of laughing women, while his mate was introduced.

Hec was finding it hard to keep a straight face, but did not stumble over the next introduction.

"Here is another late entrant all the way from Kalgoorlie. As you can see it is a famous personality—I present Madam X!"

The crowd went wild!

The noise was incredible as Madam X paraded, clad in red fishnet stockings a red bustier stretched to its limits, with overhanging black bra filled with what looked like cushion stuffing, lycra bike pants and red high-heeled boots. Madam X's feathered hat kept tipping over one eye, which tangled the two-inch long false eyelashes, which made plenty of offers come from the crowd to come and fix it for her/him.

Madam X had thick pencilled eyebrows, which endeavoured to hide his own fluffy ones, plus a great deal of red lipstick and heavy powder, which didn't hide his chin stubble. He joined the other end of the line-up of women and they all looked to Judge Jean for her verdict.

Jean spoke hurriedly to one of the Stewards who came back with a small box for her. She then gave her notes to Hec who announced the winner of the most fashionable outfit. Jean placed a rosette and blue sash over the shoulder of a pretty, tanned girl in a lemon coloured outfit with a smart cloche hat with a white cockatoo feather at the side. An envelope of cash soon followed.

The crowd yelled its approval while Jean issued vouchers donated from the pub to the two Runners-up. She then unravelled the contents of the box and came up with two unused Australia Day red, white and blue sashes, which she draped over the shoulders of Bar-Sheila and Madam X.

Chapter Thirty-Three

At the other end of the main street, the crowd was surging towards the big tent, where four fit-looking boxers were posing on the high platform in front of the tent, clad in their boxing shorts, each with a long colourful dressing gown. The end boxer was beating on the big bass drum and the spruiker ringing a brass bell. Every now and then the drum stopped and the spruiker introduced one of his men to the crowd.

"This is Barry, powerful and fit, he's good and fast, but there could be some of you blokes who can beat him. Come on, come on, give him a go. Survive three rounds and you'll win five pounds. Anyone wanting to have a go at Jazzy there or one of his mates, put up your hands. We'll outfit you with gloves and shorts."

The drum boomed and the bell rang. The spruiker was in fine form, pointing out possible young men from the crowd, who he thought might be willing to have a go.

"Come on boys, you all look pretty fit. You there in the blue shirt, get up the ladder and show us what you're made of! Everyone welcome in the big tent, only five bob entry ticket—get your ticket at the door for the 2 p.m. bouts."

There was a fair bit of shoving and pushing amid the younger men, their mates ready to give approval if they had a go at one of the boxers. There were plenty of older men, not willing to try out, but wanting to see the sport inside. Some of the youngsters had girlfriends hanging on their arms, half excited and half dreading some damage done to their boys. One heavy, beefy young man put up his hand, so the spruiker waved for him to come up, followed by two others.

"Here's a likely lad to take on Barry in the first fight at 2 p.m. Climb up the ladder, mate and give everyone a good look at you."

Another young man came through the crowd, egged on and patted on the back by his mates and climbing the ladder to the platform. The spruiker made him shake hands with the boxer called Jazzy and they stood side by side, looking quite a good match in height and size. The crowd gave a rousing cheer for the contestants, who, while grinning and looking a trifle embarrassed, were not intimidated.

The spruiker started ringing the bell again, urging others from the crowd to climb onto the platform and 'have a go!', the crowd got bigger and bigger, with the kids rounding the side of the tent to look underneath at the big mat spread out, with stools, water buckets and towels ready at opposite corners.

For years, the boxing troupes had been a major spectacle at the Aussie shows and races and the atmosphere at Windani was no different, with touts offering bets on the contestants and a general cheerful crowd waiting to get their tickets. Usually, the locals were outclassed by the more professional and experienced boxers but all the same, there would always be a few incomers who could last the three rounds, get their winnings and be carted off by their mates, bloodied but unbowed and local heroes for all time.

Chapter Thirty-Four

Rising over the early morning sun-clad dunes, came the odd shape of a small helicopter, which flew a general recce of the town before landing on the end clearing of the airstrip, to park near small planes that had come in from neighbouring properties. The pilot waited for his rotation to stop, clambered out, easing his back from sitting so long.

Father Pat, the Flying Padre, wouldn't have missed the festive time for anything and had made a special detour from his Parish work to get there. Ma Batley heard the chopper noise and went out to the front of the pub to wave. Father Pat waved and grinned, going to pull out his guy ropes from a hatch in the side of the chopper. He tied down the machine securely, banging in the pegs with practised hands, making sure no sudden gusts of the desert wind could bowl his chopper over.

He took his kitbag out, making his way across to the hotel, where he was ushered into the kitchen for a late breakfast and many cups of tea. Madge and Ma gave Pat great hugs and he had a kiss on the cheek for Madge, who was his favourite niece.

Pup already had the kettle singing on the stove, went to shake hands with Pat saying, "What for you come to this bad place, Padre? You gonna convert the wicked this time?"

Pat laughed, "I came specially to see if you've been a good bloke, Pup and enjoy some decent cooking. Had enough of stew and beans in tins lately."

Pup chortled.

"No tinned rubbish 'ere, mate, good steak for tea tonight, my doing big barbecue before the yard party. Be there or be square!"

The men gave each other high fives and laughed.

Ma Batley shook her head at Pup.

"One of these days, you villain, your tongue will fall out, Pup! Once you've finished, Pat, come and see your bed for tonight."

They sat for a while over tea and Pup's large breakfast, full of steak and eggs and plenty of toast. Pat started to revive from his journey and looking much refreshed, was ready to help wherever he could. Going out through the door into the private rooms, Ma took Pat to a small room at the rear, overlooking the backyard. Here he could wash up and have a rest.

"Put you in here, Pat. This is Madge's room but she's bunking with other girls. Bit hot in here but the best I can do."

Pat smiled, not the least bit concerned.

"Lucky to get a bed here at all, my dear—thought I might have to roll out a swag on the bar room floor! And that wouldn't be the first time either, some of the places I've had to stay."

Ma Batley cackled, "Not that badly off, Pat. I could have chucked one of the fellas out of the men's quarters if really needed, but it's full up as well and even the floor space is taken. Reckon that lot will be carousing half the night after the barbecue party."

Pat replied, "After such an early flight, I will sleep like the proverbial log and not hear them at all. Now, anything you need a hand with, sing out, pronto!"

He dumped his kitbag on the bed, opened the window as far as it would go so after a wash and brush up, went into the bar to give a hand.

Pat, being Ma Batley's brother, often called in when on traverse across his huge diocese, for a bit of R & R and a catch-up with his family. He had been asked to officiate at Madge's wedding to Frank and wanted to know all the up-to-date news regarding this family event.

That night after the races had finished and the pub bar was closed, the town was still in party mode. The pub pard was fairly jumping, music from two guitars playing, some youngsters dancing, plus a big smoky barbecue at the back of the pub, where Pup was feeding heaps of party goers. Ma in her green apron, was taking money for the meals and grog; Pup was frying huge steaks and singing in Polish. Kate, Gina, Mark and Jason were seated together eating steak with all the trimmings, with lashings of beer in a big jug to wash it down.

Jason was in heaven.

"Gee, that Pup can cook—this is the best steak this side of the black stump!"

Mark was also doing a good job on his food.

"That Pup knows his stuff alright, Kate. Just a question, why's he called Pup? He's not what you'd call small!"

Kate laughed, "Nah. He was a polish reffo, came here after the war. No one could pronounce his name, so P.U.P being his initials, it stuck."

There was a keg of beer hung in the fork of a tree with several drunks reeling round its tap. One of them was Frank, Madge's fiancé. Frank was a tall, suntanned good-looking man with a big smile, clad in black jeans and a black T-shirt proclaiming 'Heavy-Metal' in gory lettering.

Madge, after working all day in the crowded bar, was feeling weary, with her deep red hair piled on her head, wiping her sweaty face with a hanky. She was still in her working clothes and apron. She and Ma were taking a breather on the back step of the pub, sipping a sherry prior going to bed.

Frank, full of beer and sloppy kisses, lurched up and fell on the step beside Madge.

Ma flapped at him with a tea towel.

"Enough of that, Frank. Hard enough trying to find beds and bunks for this lot without you playing up like a fool as well! There'll be no hanky-panky here the night. Wait until she marries you, you great loaf!"

Frank giggled, snuggling up to Madge.

"You're a hard woman, Ma. After all I am gunna make an honest girl out of this love of my life very soon. We'll share a bed if you're short!"

Ma said very crossly, "Like hell you will, Frank, especially with Father Pat staying the night— and remember I've dealt with bigger and harder blokes than you! You'll be in the bunk house and that's that!"

Frank and Madge laughed, then they got up and ambled arm-in-arm to view the partying mob who were singing to the guitars.

Ma thought out loud to herself, "I've put all the girls in the sleepout together and Pat in Madge's hot little room. He says he doesn't mind but we pushed the bed under the window to get more air for Pat, hot as blazes in there!"

As the night went on, most of the crowd were making off for further pastures, so Kate and Gina had begun cleaning up the mess, taking away glasses and trays, evading the more amorous drunks. Mark and Jason were giving Pup a hand to clear up as well, waiting for Kate to finish before they headed off to their camp. Some of the drunks had fallen asleep where they lay so Kate went in to turn off some of the yard lights.

The two Asian men were lurking in the shadows outside the yard in the dark, waiting to see where Kate would be sleeping. They had conferred between themselves that as Cosmo had not been able to find Ginger and Mungo anywhere in town, they sure they need a lever to get the miners to come to in with the information they needed.

Cosmo had his rig away in the dark, really worried about what the small men were cooking up.

Frank and his mate, Bob, were sitting on the ground under the finished keg with the last of the now hot beer in hand. They were both very drunk.

Frank clapped his hand on Bob's should and stated, "I'm gonna sneak in my lovey's window and get a goo' ni' kiss."

Bob, starting to giggle, slurred, "How ya gonna do that, mate. Yer need a leg up?"

Frank gestured elaborately, "Sssssssh. We'll get that 44 gallon drum an' use that."

They got the drum from the next door yard, rolled the drum across to under the window with lots of bang. Deefer, who had been shut in Kate's room, started to bark.

Frank tried to keep quiet, "Ssssh! Noisy bugger!"

With elaborate drunken caution the pair rolled the drum under the open back window and Frank clambered up. Someone in the bunkhouse roared at them to shut up and threatened a boot in the ribs. Frank and Bob stopped, holding their collective breathe until everything became quiet again. Frank heaved himself over the windowsill, falling onto 'darlin' Madge in bed and gave her a hefty, drunken, sloppy kiss.

All hell broke loose!

Father Pat, dead asleep, occupying Madge's bed, came awake, thinking he was being smothered by a beery, whiskery octopus that had slobbered on his face and dug him painfully in the shin with its boots on.

He shouted, "God in Heaven, I'm attacked!"

He flailed and yelled, banging Frank's head and the noise set Deefer barking again. The whole place woke up and Kate who had been dealing with the lights, switched them all on again.

The Asians, who were trying to keep an eye around the women's rooms quickly faded into the dark. They were aghast to see Chook turn up, falling over the pub fence when he was supposed to be back at the camp to have everything ready to roll. Chook was drunk, silly as a coot, stumbling round, singing at the top of his voice.

Frank, in his turn, fell onto the floor with a bang, horrified to see Father Pat, who wacked him with a boot. Frank, who had been totally drunk a few minutes before, regained some of his sense when the Batley family, sleepy and dishevelled, came streaming through the door.

Frank panicked.

He leapt over the bed and straight out the window, caught the big drum as he fell, breaking a rib on the rim. The drum came down on the concrete, the lid burst open and the entire contents of sticky molasses spread all over Frank. It filled his boots, his clothes, his hair, then oozed its way down the garden path.

By this time the entire bunkhouse was wide awake, the dogs were hysterical at the ruckus and Ma and girls, clad in night attire and hair curlers, plus Father Pat with a sheet around his shoulders, were all jammed in the windows and doorways to watch with open mouths.

Some of the men in the bunkhouse staggered out and seeing Frank covered in molasses, were hooting and cat-calling. They rolled the groaning, sticky Frank onto an old door, carted him out in the yard and turned the hose on him.

Mark and Jason were in the middle of it all, cutting off Frank's pants and T-shirt, helping with the hose with everyone laughing fit to kill. They hosed and scrubbed but still had to cut half of Frank's hair off as it remained stubbornly stuck upright with sticky goo. He was bundled into a sheet and carted into the bunkhouse very much the worse for wear.

Ma, the girls and Father Pat were starting to straggle back to bed. Kate lingered to gather away a few more lots of rubbish. Gina was busy stacking chairs.

Suddenly, to the Asians horror, a drunken Chook loomed large, thinking to himself he may as well take away one of the girls as the others from his camp didn't seem to be around. He staggered over the back fence and grabbed Kate as the closest one, tried to sling her over his shoulder, but she was one feisty lass. She yelled in outrage, clocked him with a stool and pushing him backward over the fence, dumped him half-witted in the water trough.

The Asians and Cosmo were horrified by the mess Chook had got himself into and faded out into the darkness, staying just on the edge of the paddock to see what was going on.

Kate was properly cranky. She snarled, "You, jolly mad bastard—keep your hands off the hired help. Nuff rubbish gone on around here already!"

Chook was singing loudly to himself, hat askew, sitting in the trough. Jason, who was fully sober, jumped up to give a hand, with Mark bringing up the rear.

He yelled to Kate, "What'll we do with this sozzled lump?"

She was quick to answer, "Can you and Mark pitch him in the cellar till the Sergeant nobbles him—just in case he wants to manhandle more girls. Some blokes go NO sense!"

Ma, in dressing gown and hair curlers, shouted from the back door of the pub, "I'll ring Dave and get this yob taken away."

Mark and Jason hauled Chook over the fence and into the beer cellar, slamming the door shut, while Ma put a call through to Dave Dawson, the Police Sergeant. He had his side-kick Nick Taylor, who stayed at the pub permanently, right at hand. Nick came out to see what all the shouting was about, so when Dave arrived in the Police vehicle, they went to see what the sozzled Chook was up to.

The cellar was like Utopia to Chook, who was happily sniffing beer fumes and singing at full voice, beating time on a beer keg. His clothes were sopping wet from being doused in the horse trough, but he was too drunk to notice. He yelled happily to see the coppers, who went into the cellar fanning their noses.

Dave Dawson, shouted over the noise, "Righto, my boy, you've had a skinful. Come on and we'll get you a dry bed for the night at Her Majesty's pleasure."

Dave had the police van at the gate and he, Nick, Mark and Jason shoved an unresisting Chook into the back, where he continued to sing and beat time on the sides of the van. They got a clap from bystanders who were still up and Mark and Jason went along for the ride to give a hand at the other end.

Dave parked in front of the timber lockup, with Mark assisting, almost rolling the cheering Chook into the pokey. They all decided to stay for a cuppa until he settled down, retiring to the office to boil the kettle as no one would get sleep with the racket Chook was delivering, hammering on the walls of the cell and singing out of tune.

Chook was searching in his pockets for a cigarette, still singing loudly. He liked to try and smoke now and then, but Cosmo always took tobacco off him and gave him a cuff round the head. It was a hidden delight to be able to hide a packet of smokes and have one when Cos was not around.

Chook stumbled round the cell, chuckling when he found his wallet, which was not wet inside. He found some half-mangled cigarettes and a box of wax matches. He tried many times to get the tobacco alight and threw away a half-lighted match in disgust, which happened to land on the fibre mattress of the cell.

The protruding bits of fibre lit up at once and soon the cell was filled with smoke. Chook started to sober up pretty quickly and began shouting for help. Dave and the other men had been ignoring Chook's noise but, all of a sudden, they smelled smoke and tore out to the cells to find Chook screaming in fright with smoke billowing from his cell.

David grabbed his keys unlocking the cell gate and Nick and Mark dragged the coughing Chook out and threw him on the grass out of harm's way. Dave flew back into the office and pressed a red alarm button on the wall, which set off the fire siren of the town.

Quickly, all manner of men, in ill-assorted clothing, pyjama pants and shorts turned out from the camps, as well as Todd with the fire Ute. They were manning buckets and a couple of hoses to try and stop the flames from catching on the wooden walls. Mark clambered up on the roof of the office and directed a hose at the tin roof of the cell to try and cool it down. Nick and Jason had another hose played on the walls.

Morrie and his off-sider Buddy, came tearing over from the Café with a couple of fire extinguishers and played them on the fire until the flames subsided and the drenched men could recoup and see what damage had been done. Nick and Mark looked for Chook where they had rolled him on the ground in case his clothes were on fire, but he had vanished. Dave came back dripping, pushing wet hair from his head.

"Thanks, fellas. Looks like it was mostly the fibre mattress, but it's now well and truly doused and can wait till morning to clear out. Rotten bugger, drunk as a skunk, set it all off!"

Mark said ruefully, "But not too drunk to P.O.Q. while all the fracas was on!"

Nick laughed, "Guess we'll find him somewhere around in the morning properly singed."

Morrie came over and shook hands with Dave.

"Good job, Dave, looks like mostly a few charred bits of timber but nothing that can't be sorted. Come over to the Café, you fellas, then we'll all have something cold to drink."

Those who were volunteers in the watery mess, slowly made their way back to various camps, while the Police helpers followed Morric to the back veranda of the Café where they rested on the benches and had drinks all round.

In the mayhem, Chook had half recovered his scattered wits, staggered up and vanished out the back into the night, heading back to his camp where, under Cosmo's instructions, he had been supposed to be stowing away the gear for a night trip. He had also stowed away a couple of cans of beer he had brought during the day, which he had drunk before his foray to the pub yard.

Chapter Thirty-Five

After Dave and the other men had departed, Kate had been finishing clearing up, turned out the last backyard light and made for her room. At that moment, she was grabbed from behind by Tong, who clapped a steely hand over her mouth. Kate tried to bite him, kicking furiously and Deefer, shut in her cabin, started to bark frantically.

Teo threw a stone through the window of Kate's room, which had a note tied on it. The Asians quickly bound her feet and hands and gagged her mouth and she was dragged over the fence, slung over Tong's shoulder and they soon found Cosmo's vehicle and slung Kate into the back. She was fighting and kicking as best she could, but Tong pressed a stiff thumb behind her left ear, pressing hard, so she lapsed into unconsciousness.

Bones heard Deefer continuing to bark madly, so he came out of the bunkhouse pulling on his trousers. He knocked on Kate's door but the only answer he got was more barking from Deefer. Bones shoved open the door, calling for Kate, getting no answer.

The dog flew out the door and pawed at Bones, who called sharply, "What's all the ruckus about, matey?"

Deefer ran across to the back fence and roared up and down pawing at the ground and the fence. Bones scratched his head and went into Kate's room calling,

"Kate, where are you? What's the matter with Deefer?"

When there was no answer, nor evidence of Kate being there, Bones went out to where the dog was trying to tear the fence down. He looked over the fence and saw one of Kate's ragged worn joggers she had worn that evening. There was also a shred of navy from her work trousers caught on the wires.

There was a hiss from the shadows and Deefer quietened for a moment. Bones replied and the old tracker Fardy emerged out of the gloom. He placed a hand on Deefer's head and the dog sat, suddenly quiet.

Fardy had heard all the ruckus, between Frank's sticky end and the fire at the Police Station. When passing back to his own camp, happened to see the Asians grab Kate and haul her over the fence. He looked at Kate's old jogger with the sole uppermost.

He said to Bones, "Them bad men I tole Morrie about, they took 'er. Can't see 'em now but day come soon and I find 'em."

Bones was horrified.

"What the hell they want with Kate? She's just a girl off a property!"

Fardy shook his head.

"Not 'er they want, but to make Ginge to come. Want him to take 'em to the opal dragon cave. Need to get news to Ginge quick."

Bones growled in disbelief.

"But we sent Ginger and Mungo off with the camel to get them out of town."

Fardy nodded.

"Naway, but Ginge needs to come 'ere to help. When I find which way the Pedy mob go I sen' our people to watch—they give 'elp."

Bones was still holding the fretting Deefer and he said, "I'll have to tell Ma, so she can ring Kate's dad and the Sarge first thing. You wanna wait, I make us a cuppa."

They sat for some time having their tea and conversing on low voices about what could be done to track the Pedy mob.

By then the first vestiges of dawn were lighting the eastern sky and Bones took Deefer out of the gate and round to the fence where they found Kate's jogger. The dog put his nose on them, then on the ground and sat down howling. Fardy came along and pointed out the scuff marks to Bones, so they tracked a little further out where Fardy pointed to tyre tracks in the dust.

"Him bad man's rig. Him the one asked about Ginge. 'ere his boot and two others. Little men carrying girl, tracks deeper 'ere, see?"

Bones looked alarmed.

"You get news to your mobs quick, fella?"

Fardy nodded.

Bones said, "I'll have to take the dog back to Kate's Ute and tie him up with some tucker. Can't have him running off trying to find her."

Deefer grabbed Kate's jogger and growled in his throat when Bones offered to take it off him, so Bones let it be. When he tied the dog up, Deefer sat with the jogger between his paws and was ready to eat anyone who wanted to take it away.

As the sun came up, Fardy could follow the tyre tracks into the bush. Not long after, Bones heard the sound of the bull-roarer stirring the early morning air into question marks.

Chapter Thirty-Six

When the pub showed signs of life, Bones went into the kitchen and told Pup, who was lighting the stoves, just what had happened.

Pup swore loudly in his own elegant language and waving a huge carving knife, shouted at Bones,

"What we do next? Me, I good at cutting throats! I help!"

Just then Ma Batley came into the kitchen, tying up her dressing gown, with her white hair standing up around her head like a halo. She saw at once the concern on both men's faces and her cook ready to take some serious action with a huge knife.

"What's going on Bones? Why is Pup ready to carve somebody?"

Bones told her about the dog setting up his alarm and how Fardy, going back to his camp saw the men from Coober Pedy snatch Kate and drag her over the fence, plus how they found her jogger and some threads from her work trousers on the fence.

"Looks like they snatched her sometime early this morning. Fard says they are really trying to make Ginger Martin come in to take them to the supposed opal dragon cave—using Kate as a lever. We need to get Nick and the Sarge out and ring Kate's dad."

Ma sat down on a chair with a thump and her face registered her disbelief. She ran her hands through her hair, "What a stupid thing to do! I can't believe someone has the gall to think the old cave story is true! Let alone, take one of my girls as a hostage! Mad buggers!"

Bones went on, while Pup and Ma were all ears, "We'll need the coppers quick as Fardy is tracking the Pedy mob tyres to see where their camp is. He won't let them see him—too risky."

Ma stood up, hanging onto the edge of the table, "Whoa, wait till I get dressed and I'll get on the phone. Reckon the Police fellas will have sore heads from last night but too bad! Pup, put that deadly weapon down before you take out

162

someone's eye! Nothing we can do till Dave has had a good look around. Bones, charge out to the bunkhouse and wake young Nick and tell him we need him pronto. Pup, get the breakfast on the go quick smart!"

Bones went and hammered on the door and there was a sleepy response from the young constable, who came awake smartly when Bones gave him a rundown of the night's events.

Ma, who was dressed by then, was on the phone in the office, speaking with Dave Dawson, who also came wide awake on hearing her news. He promised to be around shortly and asked Ma to make sure no one entered Kate's room or surrounds until he and Nick could take a good survey.

Father Pat was helping Pup with the breakfasts when Ma came back.

She said, "The police have to take a good look around before anything is touched and Fardy has gone already tracing tyre tracks. Bones, when you have eaten, could you go and stay with Kate's dog, I see he has her jogger under the Ute. Don't want him to eat the Sarge just yet!"

Father Pat, busy with the toaster, said, "I can also offer my help, if they need it, with the helicopter, which is a good bird's eye view of possible roads out of here. What else can I do?"

Ma thought for a moment, then said, "You could help Pup cut a big load of sandwiches and make the large thermos of tea. Put all the cool stuff in the big blue Esky, add some fruit cake and apples. Those blokes will need food if they are having to go out bush-bashing looking for those drongos. Goodness knows where they'll end up!"

The sound of the big four-wheel drive truck, which had plenty of carrying capacity on the back tray, echoed round the backyard of the pub. This coincided with Nick arriving in the kitchen in his navy work fatigues, lacing up big boots, combing his hair with his fingers and stuffing it under his bush hat with the police logo on it.

Sergeant Dave Dawson got out of the truck and was clad in much the same sort of gear as Nick. He came into the kitchen and saluted Ma.

He said, "Do I understand that Bones and Fardy were the first to know that the girl Kate had been snatched?"

Ma and Pup started shouting together until Dave, grinning, said, "Whoa, don't run me down all at once! I want to speak with Bones first—where is he?"

Ma stuck her fingers in her mouth and gave a gigantic whistle, so Bones came up from the yard pronto.

Dave shook hands with him.

"Good day, mate. Now I want to hear your story first. Nick here will take some notes."

Bones recounted what he knew, as he took the men across to Kate's room, telling them about Deefer sounding the alarm. They carefully pushed open the door, looking around. Nothing seemed out of place, so they went in. Nick spotted a lump of rock on the floor, obviously thrown in the window, which had a piece of paper tied to it. He pulled out some light rubber gloves from his pocket and prized off the paper. Dave also put on gloves and read the badly spelled message:

Ginger meet us Monday one tree—jus' wan' opal dragon info, then send girl back.

Dave folded the paper and gave it to Nick to place in a small plastic bag. He looked around further and said to Bones, "Does this all look the same to you, mate? Anything else wrong in here?"

Bones shook his head.

"Fardy already had the big bloke from Pedy questioning him about Ginger, reckons that lot up to no good. Fardy went out earlier to trace the tyre tracks if you want him now? Morrie's cook, Buddy, knows Fardy's camp."

The men went outside closing the door. Bones beckoned them over to the fence, where the dog had been howling and scrabbling at the site.

He said, "This is where Fard reckons some Asian-looking blokes grabbed Kate. There's the jogger she had been wearing, the dog's guarding it. There's a bit torn off her work trousers. Soon as he could see, Fardy pointed out the tracks of the Pedy blokes' rig."

Nick took the shred of navy cloth from the wire and put it in a sample bag.

He asked, "You remember what Kate was wearing last night, Bones?"

Bones thought for a moment,

"All her work gear, dark green pub shirt Ma gives all her workers, over her dark blue trousers."

The men clambered carefully over the fence and walking further along spotting the imprint of the tyres in the dust. At that moment Fardy sidled up and stood waiting quietly.

Dave saluted him, "Good day, Fardy. I was going to send you a message shortly, but here you are. You know about these tracks OK?"

Fardy hardly looked at the ground, he just pointed, "This where lady bin took. I trace tracks back to their camp."

Dave and Nick whistled in admiration. Dave said, "We going to need you, Fardy, so you good for some Police tracking work?"

Fardy nodded, looking pleased.

Dave said thoughtfully, "We need to get some news of the whereabouts of this mob and what direction they are going if they have scarpered."

Fardy gestured with his chin towards the rising sun over the mountains behind the town and silhouetted against the light sky there was a rising column of brown smoke making swirls and blobs in the still morning air.

Bones chuckled, "There's the Bush Telegraph already on the go. We whities not in the same league!"

Nick stared at the sky in amazement and even as they watched, further along the ranges came an answering column of black smoke, curling and weaving its ancient magic.

Dave said with admiration, "Looks like your mobs are already on the go, Fardy. Do we need to send someone to the big man, Warra? Can he get in touch with Ginger and Mungo?"

Fardy grinned, "Nah, Boss, him already know. Warra make smoke, Mungo read smoke."

Dave turned to Nick.

"Take the truck, remove the grill behind the front seats and tie it in the back. Get it all fuelled and loaded with camp gear out of the back lockup. Get tinned food from the Café and anything else we might need if we have to stop anywhere. See the radio is working well and tell Jean and Morrie where we will be going."

He looked worried for a moment, thinking ahead, "Don't want this to get out of hand, but it might be wise to put the gun box in and check the ammo. I'll take my sidearm but will keep it in the front of the truck till we suss out these perps."

Nick saluted, picked up the cool box from Pup and gave Ma Batley a kiss on the cheek. She laughed and waved him off. He drove the big Police vehicle away to load. He called around the back of Morrie's shop, where Morrie was already working.

The men shook hands and Nick produced a Police Requisition Form and gave it to Morrie.

"Dave said you know how to fill these out."

Morrie queried, "Buddy already heard about what has happened. You got any idea where those drongos have taken Kate? You'd wonder at the stupidity of believing that dragon stuff, let alone force Ginger to tell them anything!"

He shook his head, continuing to pack tinned food into boxes. Nick looked gloomy.

"We found a note to say Ginger must meet them at one-tree and Ginger is supposed to know where that is, as he knows all the waterholes around here. Hope that may be true."

Nick continued, "Dave is getting Fardy to track to where the Pedy mob were camped and from there find their direction. Fard says his tribal mates are already on the go, judging by the smoke signals. Dave is going to have a look at all the big maps shortly and Fardy says Mungo can read smoke, so he and Ginger will know what has happened. I'm supposed to let you and Jean know to monitor any of our radio calls, but there's no sign of her up yet. Can you let her know the gen?"

Morrie nodded, "Consider it done."

The men loaded the tucker into the back of the Police truck, tying it down with straps and Morrie waved Nick away.

He went to the Police depot and did his usual tyre, fuel, water and all checks deemed necessary, loaded the gun box and went to the office to find the biggest maps they had of the whole northern area of South Australia. He spread them out across the desks, tracing the roads out of Windani with his finger, making some notes to put past Dave and Fardy.

Chapter Thirty-Seven

Across the barren land at the back of the town, Dave and Bones followed Fardy, watching with amazement as the tracker followed what sometimes looked like bare rock terrain, but who noted broken grass stems, a stone or rock misplaced, until they came onto a more sandy area and could see tyre tracks again.

Dave pushed back his hat on his head and said to Bones, "I've seen Fardy tracking many times he has worked for us, but it never ceases to amaze me that he can see things that seem invisible to my eyes."

Bones agreed, "When I was a camel driver years ago, I would find the tribes in what looked like the worst dried out desert, yet they could take me to a waterhole without seeming to note where they were going."

Fardy stopped under a stand of bull oaks way at the back of the town camps. He showed Dave the same tyre tracks and that of a heavier vehicle, plus the remains of a campfire. He looked at the footprints and nudged the fire remains with his toe. He held up four fingers.

"This much white fellas, big truck, smaller rig. One fella with no boots, only city shoes. They left at small moon."

Bones calculated, "That would be around 3 a.m. after the party had finished. If they wanted to get away without lights that's when they could see enough."

Dave nodded, "So that's about four hours start on us. When did the dog start barking, Bones?"

"I reckon it was not long after Kate was turning out the yard lights after the last of the party. I tried to keep him quiet, but he was in full voice. I knocked at Kate's room but got no answer, so finally took the dog out with me when there was no one there. That's when Deefer started tearing up and down the fence. He must have smelt where they dragged Kate over the fence. Then we saw the jogger."

Dave looked carefully round the former camp site and said, "Fardy, where from here? We need a direction, mate."

Fardy began walking beside the tyre tracks, with the heavy tracks easily seen in the dust. He traced it down to the northern road, wandered up and down for a time and came back looking disgusted.

"No more good, Boss. Many tracks now, all mess, but gorn that way." He pointed north.

Dave said, "OK men, we'll go back to the office and look at the maps and try to make sense of them. Those blokes would want to hide somewhere not too far away if they want to have Ginger contact them."

The men trudged back into town and as they arrived at the Police office, spotted Ginger coming along from the pub.

Dave patted Fardy on the shoulder, "Your mob are magicians, Fardy, how did they let Ginger know so quick?"

Fardy looked at the floor shyly.

"Him Mungo read smoke quick."

Dave grabbed Ginger as he entered the room and shook his hand gratefully.

"Boy, are we pleased to see you so early. We really need your knowledge of this northern area, which I don't know a lot about. Did Mungo really read the smoke?"

Ginger chuckled, "No flies on that bloke! He gave me the gen, so I came back at once. He is in touch with our tribal mates, so they are on the go as well. Jack has starting trekking across the foothills with the camel, hoping if some of his tribal mates can rescue the lass, he can bring her home."

In an aside, Dave asked Nick, "Can you make a good big tea we're all parched from the hike. And get Fardy some overalls. He gets them every time he is on the payroll."

Nick saluted and went out the back to the small kitchen to make a big brew. He investigated a couple of cupboards and found some navy-blue overalls for Fardy. He found some biscuits taking the lot into the office, so the men could sit around and recover with a break.

Dave went in to contact the Coober Pedy Police on the radio. The others listened in.

"Mornin' Barry. Need a bit of help here as we have some of your bad boys from the Pedy. What you know about one bloke, short and sloppy, called Chook? Set fire to our pokey last night, drunk as a skunk. He has some other fellas with him in a smaller rig."

He listened carefully, making notes on a pad.

"You reckon the other driver is Chook's brother, Charlie Sims. When did they leave there? That, right, eh. Musta come across country then. They got any history? Well, they might have shortly when we catch up with them. You been keeping an eye on two Asians, they got with them doing some dodgy opal stuff. That seems to be all bad news—might have to add kidnapping to that lot as well! Keep you posted, thanks for your info."

He replaced the radio and looked at the others.

"You heard most of that. Not good news. Nick, get on the radio and give Headquarters in Adelaide the gen, but say we got the local indigenous and our best tracker on the go. We'll let them know if reinforcements are needed."

As Nick went to the radio, Dave remarked to the others, "Barry knows the Sims brothers but said they usually are OK, taking fossickers and tourists camping out round the mullock heaps. Makes me wonder why they have a couple of dodgy Asians with them this time, looking for the supposed opal dragon, as well as kidnapping!"

They spread out all the biggest maps and Ginger discarded all but one. Dave remarked to Ginger, "The note thrown in Kate's window said for you to meet them at one-tree—what does that mean?"

Ginger shrugged.

"I have a sort of an idea it is a waterhole off one of the old uranium mine tracks, if Fardy says they are heading north from here. Pretty rough those old tracks by now, so they'll have trouble getting through."

Nick said, "They have two four-wheel drive vehicles, one a big truck, according to Fardy, so that may limit how far they can go. Where is this possible one-tree?"

Ginger ran his fingers over the map, tracing the old small tracks leading off the road north.

"See here and here, these very old tracks. I have fossicked in all these areas but how to tell exactly which one goes to the one-tree, is a moot point."

He turned the map slightly and traced more marks until he found some likely looking spots.

"I reckon this could be the area they would try to go to as it's not too far out. They couldn't take the big truck too far into big bush."

Dave and Nick followed the lines on the map and made notes.

Dave said, "Thanks, that somewhere to start. Now, we'll need you and Fardy to come with us. We need all the help we can get. How do you feel about that?"

Fardy nodded with a big smile and Ginger was also good to go.

He growled, "I'm really angry about this nonsense—if these dopes want to find the opal dragon, they're all mad! I know for certain the dragon yarns are not relevant now, so I'm cranky that they saw fit to take the girl just to get leverage at me."

Dave said slowly, "That's what has made this so serious now, so we need to get to Kate before anything happens to her; though according to Mrs Batley, Kate is a proper bush girl and will get away if she can. Bones, can you go and tell Mrs Batley what we are doing and keep an ear out for anymore that'll help. Jean and Morrie will have our radio signals. Righto, you blokes, we'll get on the road and see if we can pick up the right tracks."

The men climbed into the Police truck, with Nick driving, reversed out of the yard and waving to Bones, set off to the northern road. The road was a reasonably graded red dirt road, but with all the recent traffic from the race weekend, there would be little hope of identifying the vehicle tracks until they got further out.

Chapter Thirty-Eight

Over at the pub, Ma Batley was filling Jean in on the morning's events and on the phone at the same time, ringing Tindabulla's satellite phone. After a couple of beeps, May Brenna took the call.

"Hello, Tindabulla here. May Brenna speaking."

Mrs Batley spoke clearly over the ensuing crackles. "Hello May, Just a query, have you heard from Kate this morning?"

May said quickly, "No, not at all, why do you ask?"

Mrs Batley replied, "Something's gone a bit awry here and Kate is missing this morning. Is Kev around? I need to talk to him."

May let out a gasp saying, "Hold on, Elsie, Kev's in the shed," and she ran with the heavy phone down to the large open-ended shed where Kevin and the two roustabouts were working on one of the trail bikes used for mustering.

May shouted over the hammering, "Kev, Elsie Batley's on the line, something about Kate."

She proffered the phone so she and Kevin went out into the yard for more quiet and better reception. May also pressed her ear close to the phone.

Kevin looked at his wife with raised eyebrows asking, "What seems to be the trouble, Elsie?"

Her voice came through the crackle quite clearly, "There's some mystery here as to where Kate has gone. She was here last night till late clearing up after the big party and no one has seen her since."

Kevin thought for a moment, "Is her dog still there? She always takes the dog with her."

Mrs Batley said slowly, "No. It was the dog that brought old Bones' attention to Kate not being there, as it started barking around 3 a.m. The dog was shut in Kate's room while all the noise was going on at the party. Bones went and knocked and when he got no answer, opened the door and took the dog with him to quieten it down. He found Kate was missing and so far there has been no sign of Kate anywhere as yet. In the meantime, Dave Dawson has been notified and he has Nick and Fardy, the tracker looking into the matter."

Kevin said promptly, "I'll be on the road as soon as I can, Elsie. See you then."

He closed the phone down and handed it to his wife. May looked very worried.

"I don't like this, Kev. Not like Kate to leave Deefer behind."

Kevin put his arm around her shoulders and they walked into the house.

"Things may work out, my dear. She may have gone off partying with friends, so there could be an innocent explanation for this. But we need to know our girl is safe. So, I'll see Elsie first and with Dave and the tracker on the job I'm sure they'll get to the bottom of it all. Pack me some tucker while I get the truck ready. I'll ring you as soon as I find out what's been going on."

He came into the kitchen shortly afterwards, gave his wife a peck on the cheek and took the food and thermos of tea. He went out to the shed and spoke to his hands, working on the bike.

"Got to go to Windani right away, boys, so see if you can sort out this bike trouble. I probably won't be back tomorrow, so take the working dogs for a run, plus a couple of bales of hay, up to the top horse paddock. Check the water there, clean the trough out. Take a wire brush and some tools and see the minerals haven't clogged the float end."

Fred spoke up, "That horse, Stalker, is in that paddock. He's a right mean bastard at the best of times, with his biting and kicking, but I think he needs his right back foot looked at. He seemed to be favouring it yesterday."

Kevin nodded. "Don't take any risks with him. I don't want the brute to take a piece out of Zack and put him off horses for life!"

Zack snorted, but Kevin said, "Don't take horses like Stalker casually, Zack. He's a great cattle worker, but if he keeps on with his biting and kicking, I might have to sell him off. Fred, see if you can get him into the stall for a look at the hoof, but take no chances.

Stalker likes the company of that red gelding, so you may be able to use that one as a ploy to get the big horse into the stall. Tie the red horse up beside the stall with a bit of grain. If the foot doesn't seem to be bothering Stalker too much, you might like to leave it till I get back and we'll all help to deal with him. Kate's the only one that has had much success with him so far."

The men nodded and Kevin turned to walk away, calling, "See you when I get back."

He went to check around his four-wheel drive Ute, which was always packed with jerry cans of fuel, water, tools and spare tyres, ready for whatever action was needed. He slung his kit into the back seat, jammed his hat on his head and beeped the horn to May, before heading down the road to the front gate.

Chapter Thirty-Nine

The desert night was lit with intense white starlight, which gave Cosmo and the Asians, with Kate trussed up like a turkey, enough light to see their way across the back of encampments, travelling as quietly as possible in low gear.

As they had driven across to the side of the pub, over low scrubby ground and over a pavement of low flat rocky areas, Cosmo was more or less following his earlier tracks back to their camp. The Asians were hanging on for grim death, while Teo was in the back seat trying to hold the unconscious Kate onto the seat. She lolled heavily, so he had to brace her with his legs until they reached firmer ground at their camp.

Cosmo turned off the engine, his face dripping with sweat.

He hissed, "Where's that fool, Chook, I swear I'll kill him this time!"

Tong whispered, "Think that him lying under his truck with dog."

Chook was snoring loudly, Cosmo kicked him in the ribs and dragged him out by the collar. Chook shook himself and emerged looking like an unmade bed, wet and smelling of grog. Cosmo was furious but had no time to do more than give Chook a slap around the head. He was slightly appeased to see the whole camp had been taken down and stowed away.

He snarled, "I hope to gawd you got that truck ready to roll, or I'm gonna take you apart. Get that truck started and follow me exactly, you hear? Use your side lights and try and keep it quiet!"

Chook was contrite, "Yeah, yeah, all ready to go."

Teo whispered, "We need to get away before girl make noise—she coming round."

Chook and the dog got into the truck and started the engine, which sounded a tremendous noise in the still of the night. Cosmo shoved the Asians into his rig and found Kate trying to sit up.

He said right in her ear, "Not a peep outa you, girl. Any noise and you get into big trouble."

They started out using their sidelights, jerking over the uneven ground. Kate groaned and fell about, as her hands were tied. Teo tried to hold her still, but he was a small man and had little success.

The two rigs finally came out onto the northern road, so Cosmo switched on his driving lights, signalling Chook to do the same. They travelled quite a way until Kate, coming to her full senses, spat out the gag and started to hammer and kick the back of the front seats.

She shouted and screamed, "What the hell you mob of lunatics think you're doing! You let me go NOW!"

Tong leaned over from the front seat and hissed, "You want go bye-bye again, shut mouth!"

Cosmo was trying to drive and see by dash light the rough map he had obtained at the races. He gave it to Tong.

"Here, see if you can see how far that turnoff is. The old guy marked it."

Tong turned the paper upside down and sideways.

"Not see where. There a sign post?"

Cosmo sighed, "Fair dinkum, I wonder how come I got stuck with youse blokes. I musta been a roo short in the top paddock. Here! Give me the cussed map!"

He pulled over to the side of the road, got out and perused the map in front of his headlights. He looked at the road ahead and shook his head.

He walked back to Chook's truck and said, "By the look of the map we got to turn off soon. Just watch me tail-lights. Reckon, it'll be to the right somewhere close. It's an old mining road."

They were able to drive at a fair rate on the graded road, plus being able to use the headlights. Though Cosmo kept checking that they were not missing the turnoff, being hard to see anything like it in the overgrown bush. He stuck his head out of the window now and then when there was likely parting in the scrubby trees appeared but with no luck.

Kate was trying to undo the thongs that bound her wrists without Teo seeing what she was doing. She worked at them, until she felt them loosen. The men were all concentrating on the road ahead when all of a sudden the thongs came loose and Kate gathered them in her strong hands. She let out a wild yell, lurched over the front seat and looped the thongs over Cosmo's head and pulled them back tightly around his throat cutting off his air.

The vehicle swerved wildly with both Teo and Tong fighting Kate for the thongs, while Cosmo coughed and snorted. He jammed on the brakes, while Kate caught a backhanded slap to the face from Tong and fell back stunned. That gave Teo time to rebind her hands more tightly and she was shoved down on the back seat.

Cosmo felt his throat and coughed and gargled some more.

He snarled, "Can't youse blokes even keep a sheila quiet! Talk about a pair of dills! Give me a drink quick!"

Tong offered a nearly empty canteen of water and Cosmo swigged it down. His voice started to come back and he dribbled some water over his face. In some small way, he seemed a mite impressed with Kate's verve.

He exclaimed, "Boy, that dame's got strong hands—she's tougher than she looks! You fellas better watch her, in case she gets free again and takes youse both on! No wonder she could dump old Chook in the horse trough!"

Just then, there was a toot from Chook's truck, which had pulled in behind them. He signalled with his right turning light, waving his arm out his window pointing ahead.

Everyone saw at once there was a break in the scrub where a track was barely discernible. Cosmo wiped the water from his face and turned thankfully onto the old road, which was little more than a track from not being used for years. It was hard going with dead stumps and bits of old trees fallen across the road.

There were also sandy areas, which needed four-wheel drive and slow careful driving. Kate was slumped in the back seat and though quiet for the moment, was weighing her plans for escape. It was very slow going, but Cosmo was being very careful not to injure either of the vehicles or stake a tyre. Kate was jolted and tumbled around with the rough terrain, so she knew it was away from her known territory. She had a fair idea they were heading north-east as she could see vestiges of the dawn over the silhouettes of the ranges.

The two vehicles picked their way slowly over the rubbish on the track, until Cosmo passed a track leading off to the left, but not marked on his map, so he flicked his right turning light at Chook and they kept to the right-hand track which became a little less tortuous, enabling them to move along at a better rate.

Having now put a fair distance between themselves and the town, Cosmo was pleased they were well into the bush away from any prying eyes. When he saw a stand of white gum trees away to the right on a small ridge, he felt he was going in the right direction. He pulled over under the trees, getting out, stretched and beckoned Chook to pull in. After all the engine noise cut out, the increasing daylight seemed to enclose them with intense quiet.

The small men also fell out of the rig, easing their legs and arms. Kate let out a piercing shriek that startled them all.

She was a mad as a cut snake, shouting, "Get me out of this car and get me something to drink, NOW! What the hell you think you're doing, you mad bastards! Who gave you the right to cart me off. I warn you there are severe retributions in place for kidnapping in this country—it means a Life Sentence for you all!"

She was struggling and spitting and kicking at the door of the rig.

Teo went back to the cab and found a canteen with a little water left, helping Kate to her feet and offered the canteen. She held it between her bound hands, drinking but watching all around to suss out exactly what her options were.

Cosmo shouted to Chook, who was letting the big dog out.

"We better get some fuel into the trucks, mate and something to eat. I'm famished."

There was a flurry of unloading and finding a funnel and hose line. Cosmo backed his rig beside the big truck and the men decanted fuel into it from the jerry cans on the back of the truck. They filled the truck with fuel and checked the radiator levels.

Chook and the dog fossicked round and came back with a load of underbrush and a few rocks, so in quick order had a good fire started. He sorted through the big store boxes and came up with a couple of cans of ham and assorted cans of beans. The hams were sliced, the beans dropped over them and Chook took a tin plate to Kate, who was sitting on the edge of the back seat stretching her legs out.

She looked at the food and at first felt like chucking it at somebody, but she was hungry and decided food was a better sustenance for her getaway. She shovelled the messy fare into her mouth the best she could and then yelled, "Hey, you blokes, I need drinks, NOW!"

Chook got a can from the stores and took it to Kate, tore the ring off, helping her to drink. She gulped the lemonade thirstily.

She then shouted, "I need to get some circulation into my legs, you morons. Take these leg straps off and let me walk around for a bit."

She rolled so she could stand up, grimacing in agony at her aching limbs and bruises from her rough ride. Teo bent to undo the thongs round her ankles and Kate jogged on the spot to get proper feeling back into her feet.

Cosmo said to Chook, "Chuck that black tarp down and a bedroll to sit on and we'll put missie under the tree where she might keep quiet for a while."

Kate snarled, "Don't bank on it! I got plenty of big voice from calling cattle for years, which have more loaf than you lot!"

Chook felt a bit abashed by this slanging and looked very down in the mouth. He remembered how strong Kate had been to dump him in the trough last night.

Cosmo patted his shoulder, "Ignore the bird. She can sit under the tree and if she gets funny we can tie her to it. That'll keep her shut up."

Teo squatted down in front of Kate and tried to quieten her down.

"We not harm, we just want man to come and see us and then you can go."

Tong growled his bit, "We send message to ginger man and we give girl back for cave news."

Cosmo smirked, feeling like Chook that they were involved in a lost cause.

"You gotta hope the Bush Telegraph works pretty quickly or we're up a creek without a paddle."

Teo looked pleased, "Ha! Bush Telegraph good idea—where here?"

Chook, now quite in charge, in his professional camping mode, shouted, "You mob sure are mad. Ain't nothin' out here, no telegraph—nothin'!"

Tong, losing patience, whipped his knife out of his pocket and brandishing the knife, grabbed Chook and held the knife under his chin. Chook looked astonished letting out a huge yell.

Tong screamed at Cosmo, "Better find that man quick or I make you all dead!"

Cosmo said quietly, "Put that piddling knife away and lay orf Chook. He's got all the water on his truck, so without his help you won't survive. You'll be the dead ones. We're used to this country and youse ain't."

Tong growled, stomping round the ground, swearing in his own language, but he let Chook go, slipping the knife away into his pocket.

Chook was white to the gills, shaking all over, going to sit with his dog beside the fireplace. Cosmo was feeling more and more irritated at the offered violence by Tong and was trying to think how to get rid of him or leave him behind somewhere. He sat with his head in his hands.

The Asians sat back on their heels and cursed to each other in their own lingo. Kate, regarding the knife-wielding Tong with new suspicion, was sitting on the bedroll, had her foot circulation back and standing up, shouted, "Hey, you guys, I need a pit stop and I need it NOW!"

The Asians stopped their argy-bargy and looked somewhat nonplussed as to how this would be achieved. Cosmo was not short of ideas. He went to the truck and took off a loading strap with a shackle at one end. He looped it over Kate's shoulder and around her waist and pulled the shackle reasonably tight. He hung onto the long end of the strap and motioned Kate to get around the tree.

Kate bridled. She growled, "Gee, don't give a lady any help will you!"

She vanished round the back of the tree battling with her still bound hands, managed to get her elastic-waisted trousers down, plus her knickers and was pleased with her effort. She pulled her gear back up and came back to the others looking as meek and mild as she could. Cosmo unlooped the strap and put it back onto the truck, thinking Kate was becoming nice and quiet.

Chapter Forty

After the food and refuel, the men pushed Kate into the back seat of Cosmo's rig, but though Teo followed, they all forgot about tying up her feet again, so she tucked them under her unseen.

Cosmo checked his scrappy map and leading the way again, felt they were at last on the right track to the place called One-tree.

The track was almost unreadable in some places, such as having a fallen tree across it, so Cosmo had to get out to find a bypass so they could get their vehicles round without damage. Chook was following carefully in his tyre tracks with the big dog sitting to attention on the front seat.

The old tracks were so slow and difficult, it took the two vehicles the rest of the day to negotiate them as until the sun was going down, they turned suddenly into a clearing that held a small amount of water in a reed-sided pool. There was a lone tall white gum tree on the edge of the clearing. The men pulled up to the side of the space where there was a stand of gidgee trees.

Chook and the dog did a quick run around the site, the dog running into the water and lapping thirstily, flopping down for a good bath.

Cosmo roared, "Geez, Chook, use some sense, get that dorg outta there! We'll have to fill our barrels with that water and I doan fancy the taste of dorg!"

Chook laughed but hauled the dog out and raced away with it. They went into the bush and came back with an armful of firewood to set up the fireplace.

Cosmo and the small men hefted the water barrels off the truck and rolled them to the water, scooping water in with a pannikin. It took effort to roll the filled barrels back and get them set on the truck. The night was closing in fast in the secluded valley, making the shadows very dark, so the men were waiting for the fire to take hold and give them light.

Chook was quick to get a roaring fire going, so it lit up the landscape around with its flickering flames making the shadows chase around the site. The tall flames sent up great eddies of smoke through the trees, floating up the mountain with its tell-tale aroma of eucalyptus leaves.

There was a sudden snarling, loud coughing and fighting in the trees above the camp. A fury of scrapping, fighting, warring possums fell down a tree and continued their fight, amongst flurries of torn fur, right up over the side of Chook's truck and into the back, where the stores were kept.

The Asians were horrified and tried to run away from the melee, but Cosmo yelled at them through the noise, "You blokes grab some sticks and throw them at the blighters, while Chook starts his rig. Be quick about it or we'll only have scraps left to eat!"

He grabbed rocks and stones and threw them at the fighting possums with good effect. Teo was fast off the mark, throwing sticks and bits of timber with good aim. Chook started his truck revving the engine loudly and let go blasts on the horn. The dog was yowling, trying to get up the side of the truck to the fighting.

While this noise was in full swing, Kate took the opportunity to get out from the vehicles, taking to her heels and running down the roadway as fast as she could go, hoping to get far enough away to hide in the scrubby bush. Unfortunately, she headed the wrong way and when Chook saw her figure in the gloom he switched on his headlights, so the men were transfixed at seeing the fleeing figure of Kate, running like the hounds of hell were at her heels, tearing back along the track for all she was worth.

Cosmo started to swear and shouted at the Asians, "Forget them possums, get the girl—see of you can do something right and run her down!"

He shook his head in disgust, fed to the teeth with the Asians and their dopey ideas of making Ginger come and meet with them, wondering at his own stupidity in allowing himself to get involved.

The possums departed for quieter pastures, chased by the dog. The Asians were running fast, being small and lithe and soon caught up with Kate, as she was hampered by only having one shod foot. They propelled her roughly back to the camp site and Tong found some stronger bonds, shoving Kate onto the tarp and bedroll thrown at the base of a tree. He bound her hands and feet and with a longer strap then bound her to the tree.

Everyone fell silent after all the ruckus and sprawled around the fire to get their combined breaths back. Cosmo was exhausted after his big day and lay stunned for some minutes while the fire spat and crackled beside him. Chook eventually got to his feet rustled up some grub from the stores, putting the billy on to boil. He passed some cold sausages and bread to the men, who toasted them on the fire and he took a small plate with some food on for Kate.

Kate was cross with herself, so shook her head and closed her eyes, sitting propped against the tree. She was quietly having another go at undoing her bonds, trying to keep her hands out of sight from the firelight.

She found her shoe-less foot bleeding from a cut made somewhere on her flight. She was about to make a fuss and get something for it, when in the sudden silence after all the possum fight had died away, there came the weird drone of a bull-roarer. The sound seemed to float here and there through the scrub, dying away, then sounding close then again far away.

The Asians started up, terrified and gazed around in panic, looking for the source of the uncanny sound. They were ready to run into the night.

Teo squealed, "Those bad spirits, I go 'ome!"

He moaned and held his hands over his ears, then both the small men started to back away from the fire and the clearing and were running down the track.

Cosmo started after them, groaning, "Come back, you idiots, bad spirits be dammed!"

He refused to run after them, but bellowed, "That's only black fella songs, come back before you get lost!"

Kate watched this small farce with a smirk. While the men were thus occupied, she saw a white feather fall into her lap. She looked hard in the flickering firelight and saw it was a cockatoo feather. She sighed with relief when she felt the bonds holding her to the tree loosen and she grinned to herself. A black hand came into her view holding some crushed leaves, pushing them into the billy of tea water. The hand signalled her to be quiet and gave her the thumbs up.

Cosmo was cranky after all the upsets, as the men trooped back to the fire.

The bull-roarer had ceased its melancholy call, so he said acidly to the Asians, "Kock off your damn-fool stuff, you silly buggers! That noise is just black fella songs. You lot are so much trouble, I'm sick of it. For two bob I'd take the kid back and leave you lot 'ere!"

He went to the Blitz, found a big tarp in the back and slung it on the ground and dumped more bedrolls on it, fell on one, exhausted.

Chook had poked the fire up under the billy and said, "I'm thirsty, billy's boiled, gonna have my cuppa tea—want some?"

All the men nodded in agreement, so he took the billy off, filled pannikins all round and gave them out.

Cosmo remarked from where he lay on the tarp, "Better give the girl a drink of water while you're at it."

Chook took some water in a canteen to Kate kindly washing her hands and face with a wet rag. He then tried to help her have a drink of clean water and patted her back when she choked a bit. The others ignored what Chook was doing, too concerned with their own worries. Kate was grateful for this small service, but was determined not to show it.

Chook said, "I get you some tea, maybe like that better."

Kate was tired but made out she was still cranky and shouted, "I'm not having your rotten tea. You can stick it in your ear!"

Chook was very offended and walked away.

He said indignantly, "Oh, nice! For that yer can go without!"

He went and sat with Cosmo, taking his pannikin and sipping his tea without looking at Kate anymore. She dropped her head and pretended to nod off to sleep. The men were thirsty and swigged their tea quickly.

Cosmo made a face.

"Geez, Chook, this water's gorn off! The tea tastes like swill. Have to clean out that last barrel with fresh water in the morning."

He drank his tea just the same and the others followed, too tired to care anymore. Kate was watching under her lowered eyelids, as the firelight died down. Chook and Cosmo dropped flat onto the bedrolls and fell asleep at once.

The small men were still looking around fearfully, worrying at the sound of a dingo howling somewhere close. They ended up taking their tea mugs and going to sleep in Cosmo's vehicle. Soon, the air was rent by snores and even the big dog was snoring, lying beside Chook on the tarp.

Kate watched as dark shadows flitted in the dying firelight. Some tribal men were untying her bonds, while a very old, white-haired man appeared, who had white tribal markings on his face and hands. He silently brought some white stones into camp, making a ring around the trucks and the sleeping men.

The big dog awoke, but the old man pointed into its eyes, so the dog dropped off again without a sound. Kate's eyes opened wide as she watched the old man, who had a small bark coolamon filled with white slurry, daub the unconscious Asians with white markings on the skin. He then brushed away footprints with a branch until the sand was pristine where he had been.

Two tribal men helped Kate to her feet, leaving the cockatoo feather in the middle of the bonds where she had been sitting. They took her hands and vanished into the night, leaving no print of their being.

Chapter Forty-One

At the remnants of the camping sites behind the showground, Mark and Jason were finally on deck, though a bit seedy after the excitement of the night, between the party, plus dealing with Frank's mishap and the fire at the cells.

They were washing up after lunch and seeing to the camels, when one of their mates, Roy, who had been at the party, came over and told them, "Just been given the nod that girl who was working at the pub, the one that won the Ladies Race—well, she's gone missing. Cops think she was snatched sometime last night. I 'member she was at the party and was OK then. She a friend of yours?"

Mark looked at Jason astounded. He said sharply to Roy, "What're you talking about? We heard nothing. You giving me a bad stick or what?"

Roy replied, "No way! Just heard the Police have gone out with a tracker and that old miner with the red hair. Gorn north. Mad Morrie can fill youse in if you want. Cheers."

Jason and Mark hurriedly put away their gear and trotted quickly down to Morrie's Café, where Buddy was clearing up after the lunch run.

Mark said to Buddy, "Need a word with Morrie—he here?"

Buddy nodded towards the back of the kitchen, so the men went outside to find Morrie sitting on a bench, feet up on the rail, with his hens pecking round about and one of his speckled hens in his lap. He was having his first beer of the day. Morrie had been impressed with the way both Mark and Jason had pitched in to help with the cell fire, so offered a beer for their efforts.

"Hi, you guys, have a quick one on me. You did good last night after that fool set fire to the cell. Mind you, we all seem to have a fit of the tireds this morning and are as slow as wet weeks."

Jason said, "No thanks all the same, had enough fluid last night for float me away!"

Mark was quick to ask, "Bloke we met last night has just told us Kate from the pub had been snatched sometime last night. She was there when we helped put that drunken yob into the cell before he lit it up. What the hell's been going on?"

More looked worried, "You mind the drunk who set fire to the pokey, name Chook or something? He scarpered while we were busy sorting out the mess. Old Fardy the tracker, who knows Ginger Martin, had already been approached by him and his brother—they're from the Pedy it seems. They wanted Ginger, but he had gone bush, so they took Kate to make Ginger and Mungo come back to meet them."

Jason whistled, "How did Dave find out where they came from?"

Morrie cocked an eye at him.

"You think we live in the bush or something? Dave radioed the Pedy cops and got the gen. Seems those two bad boys have another couple of suss blokes with them that are Asians, who've been noticed doing dodgy opal buying."

Mark frowned.

"So how did our cops find out these geezers wanted to get hold of Ginger?"

Morrie slugged his beer.

"Seems they threw a note through Kate's window—high class stuff that! The note was for Ginger Martin. Fardy traced their tracks to their camp, but they had scarpered. Fard got the word out to the tribes, so smoke was made along the ranges. Next thing, Ginger came trudgin' into town."

Jason and Mark looked at him in amazement. Mark said, "You telling me he got the message from the black fellas?"

Morrie nodded. "Yeah. Mungo Jack is a blood brother of Warra, the headman of his tribe, so can read the smoke, so Ginge came in soon as he could. Jack is trekking across the range to the north with the tribe from that area, to try and get Kate away."

Jason asked, "But how will the coppers know the area they are trying to find?"

Morrie smiled through his teeth. "Ah, secret ways around here. Ginger knows all the old uranium mining tracks off the road north, so he and Fardy are tracing the tyre prints of the old Blitz that drunken Chook was driving."

Mark was upset.

"What can we do to help? Can't just sit around here doing nothing when a friend is in trouble!"

Morrie waved a calm hand, caressing his pet hen, "Nothin' we can do for the moment. We have to wait for any radio calls. It's only a few hours since Dave left, plus Jack will be in touch with the area tribes. If anyone can find that mad mob, it'll be them."

They sat in stunned silence for a while, watching Morrie with his old hen.

He said casually, "You ever put a hen to sleep, boys?"

Mark laughed, "Not often, go on then."

Morrie gently took the speckled hen's head and tucked it under her wing. She quite happily sat still as a mouse.

Mark and Jason roared and Jason said with some asperity, "Pity you couldn't do that with your mad emus!"

Morrie sighed, "Yep, often thought of it, but can't catch them now they're bigger. But you shouldn't denigrate our National emblem. After all they won the Emu Wars against the Army."

Mark chortled, "Get out! Never heard that one—against the Army, you must be joking!"

Morrie took his little hen, undid her head and placed her on the rail near him.

"Nah, true as I sit here. In the 1930's the Western Aussie wheat farmers were sick of the throngs of emus eating their livelihood and begged the Government to help get rid of them. Government, in their wisdom, sent out a couple of soldiers, two Lewis guns and 10,000 bullets, just to let the emus know who was Boss."

He paused for recollection.

"If I remember right, they tried to herd the emus to where they could mow them down, but it was like herding cats! You know what emus are like, they run in zigzags everywhere, let alone stay to face noise and bullets, which seemed to bounce off their feathers."

Mark and Jason were starting to chuckle, looking sideways at Morrie to see if he was pulling their legs.

Morrie went on, "The soldiers mutinied, sick of feathers and went home. The emus continued being emus. I believe there were questions asked in Parliament why emus were not trained for the Army. So, you see, why our native emus perhaps deserve their place on the Coat-of Arms, as they won the emu wars against the might of the Army!"

Jason and Mark dissolved into shouts of laughter, while Morrie's emu twins, who happened to be listening over the back fence, seemed to be laughing too.

Or was it just the sun shining on their beaks?

Chapter Forty-Two

As the police truck traversed the old north road, now and then Fardy beckoned Nick to stop, got out and looked closely at the middle and sides of the road. It was slow, hot work, so they stopped at a stand of gidgee trees for a break and something to eat.

Nick produced fresh cut sandwiches, the big thermos and cake from Ma's big blue cold box, which made the men cheer. They sat around eating and drinking with great relish, all except for Fardy, who walked a way into the bush, coming back with a length of thick vine. He slashed the end of it and drank the fluid it contained. The other men looked on with interest.

Dave said admiringly, "What fella that, Fard? You make your own beer?"

Fardy giggled.

"Nah, Boss. This good for dry throats, black fella medicine best. Go all day on that one."

Nick took the vine and smelt it curiously.

"Be blowed. That smells like mint or something. The things I learn here never cease to amaze me. That knowledge could save a life!"

Dave laughed, "Yeh, right, but I'd rather have my own brand of beer with a lot of XX's on it. Come on you blokes, we'd better see what we can discover ahead."

The men cleaned up their site, placed the cool box back in the truck and started off again, with Fardy walking ahead and gesturing now and then. He got back in and pointed ahead, where they trundled over rough terrain, with many boulders in the way, which took a lot of negotiating. Nick had to be careful straddling fallen limbs, which could stake the tyres.

Ginger also got out now and then, conferring with Fardy, plus using his compass to decide just where they were situated. They were sure they were following the Blitz tracks but needed to find where they would turn off the main track. It was tortuous work and their own truck was in four-wheel drive a lot of the time. Nick was keeping an eye on the fuel supplies, knowing they would have to be topped up shortly.

While they stopped again, Nick said to Dave, "Somewhere soon, we got to stop for refuelling and I need to check the radiator as well."

Dave nodded. They were all feeling the strain, as the day had been long and tedious and the shadows were becoming deeper and longer as the sun sank into the west. All of a sudden there was a coo-ee from Ginger, who was pointing to the right.

He and Fardy came over, looking pleased.

"There! There's the old mining track I was hoping to find. Fardy says the Blitz tyre marks turn off there."

Fardy nodded, grinning, "This big truck mark going that way." He gestured into the bush at the right-hand side of the track.

Dave got out and clapped both Fardy and Ginger on the back.

"Great job, you blokes. Show me where you are looking."

They walked with Dave, while Fardy pointed out the tracks and Nick drove slowly along behind the men. Fardy followed the markings well but found it, more difficult to see as the light was fading.

Dave decided to call it a day.

"We'll give Fardy a break now and set up camp for the night. Ginger, anywhere flat enough to camp around here?"

Ginger walked along ahead and after a look around beckoned Nick to a small clearing where it was reasonably flat, with a couple of tall trees at the side.

The truck was positioned, so they had a view of the road both ways, if needed. Dave and Nick unpacked a tarp and they strung it between the trees, Dave rolling out another tarp under the trees, throwing on some swags.

Nick scouted around for sticks to make a fire in his ring of stones. He had trouble getting the flames to take, so Fardy came back with some flimsy paperbark, rolled it into pieces, which he laid on the smouldering fire, blew on it and had it flaming at once. Nick pretended to hang his head in shame which made Fardy giggle.

After taking some stew out of tins, plus raiding the rest of Ma's cold box, the men ate gratefully, glad to relax as they were tired and sore from their efforts all day. They lay around the fire and discussed what the morning might bring.

Dave yawned widely and said to Ginger, "This your old territory, eh, Ginger? You reckon there are a couple of side-tracks to the old uranium sites near here?"

Ginger nodded. "That's the pest, Dave. I can't be sure which one they might have taken, but hopefully Fardy can find their spoor in daylight."

Nick said quietly, "I'll clean up in the morning—I can't keep my eyes open now, I'm off for a zed, you blokes."

He went to the tarp, flung open a swag and fell on it like a sack of potatoes and was instantly asleep. Ginger and Dave soon followed suit, while Fardy sat watching the light of the dying fire. When the others were snoring, he took off his overalls and faded off into the night, flitting through the trees like a wraith.

Somewhere came the hoot of an owl.

Chapter Forty-Three

The silent figures helped Kate to navigate the rough terrain, walking beside her and pushing away scrubby branches, all faintly illuminated by the dying moon. As they moved away, the silence seemed to close about them. Only the rustle of the tree leaves and call of night birds echoed along the valley.

Kate felt as conspicuous as a blunderbuss when every step she took sounded loud and crackling, with the snap of broken sticks and crunched leaves, while the two men glided silently alongside her. She only had one shoe on, which made the going very difficult, harsh on her unshod foot.

Since her break for freedom along the road where she had torn her foot and it was now bleeding copiously. There were sharp blades of reeds and tough grasses plus the dry sticks under-foot but she was limping and trying to make as little sound as possible.

As they got further away from the trucks and into more open territory, Kate fell to her knees gasping, showing the men her bleeding foot and also indicated she was very thirsty.

The tallest man pointed to himself and whispered, "Perce. Fix foot. You stay."

Kate nodded and leaning against a fallen log was thankful to be still.

The smaller man grinned at her and whispered, "Me, Wane. Fix drink."

Of the old man there was no sign. He had spoken no word and vanished into the night, which made Kate wonder if what she thought she had seen was just imagination. She was too fatigued to ask any questions of her helpers and was content to sit quietly for a time.

Wane took himself off into the scrub and Perce took out his knife from his battered shorts cutting away a swatch of broad leaves, crushed them to almost a pulp and applied them to Kate's foot. They were cool and soothing so she signed her pleasure to Perce. He then went across to some tall reedy plants, cut some long leaves and came to sit by Kate, shredding the length of the leaves into long thongs.

She watched, fascinated, as Perce deftly wove the strips into what almost a shoe shape, with hardly any moon to see his work. He lined the bottom of his work with more of the broad leaves and then bound the assembly onto Kate's injured foot. She was astonished at how much better it made things feel and she tried the makeshift boot tentatively on the ground. It held quite strongly, so she felt it would help her to go on.

At that moment a silent Wane came back with a stout vine, which, as soon as he cut it, began to drip and he gave it to Kate indicating she was to drink. Kate looked surprised but was too thirsty to care what it was and had faith in her benefactors to know what they were doing. She let the drips run into her mouth and made appreciative sounds, which made the two men place fingers against their mouths. She smiled and nodded and drank quietly, pleased to find her thirst abating.

When Kate could stand again, they sidled through the rough scrub, where she could see the blackened edge of the ranges and the foothills. That gave her a fair idea of the south-easterly way they were heading. She touched Perce on the shoulder and mouthed the word 'home'?

He whispered, "Soon, get to hidden place known only to our people and make smoke for tribes. All look for you."

Kate made clapping hands without noise and Perce smiled. Kate did the best she could to keep up the pace, her makeshift boot managing to stay on her foot, but she got slower and slower, all her tiredness and bruises catching up on her system.

Wane and Perce could see she was on the point of collapse, so they took an arm on each side of her, supporting her weight so they could help her over the last of their trek. Just when Kate thought she could go no further, Perce, whispered, "Look Missie, see water."

Kate lifted her drooping head and could see the glint of water in a small hole at a rock face. She made a final effort and the two men helped her to sit on a soft sand bank under a couple of sheltering palms. Kate murmured her thanks, almost immediately falling on her side and into a deep sleep.

As the night sky lightened the two men also relaxed for a time, keeping an eye on Kate, who was very still, seemingly dead to the world. They went to the waterhole and drank, sitting quietly for a time waiting for the sun to rise.

Perce indicated to Wane, "Soon make white smoke for Warra and Mungo."

Wane got up, sauntered along the sand banks to where some tea-trees stood near the water. He sheared off long pieces of the white bark and left them in a heap. He then hunted through the reedy sedges until he found some whitish grasses and he piled these on the sand, helping to form them into a conical pile with the help of small sticks.

Kate stirred as the sun came up over the ranges, opening her eyes to see Wade tending a small fire, which was sending up a plume of white smoke in the still morning air. He watched carefully, waving his bark over it now and then, so the spirals waved and swirled above them, reaching for the sky.

As Kate sat up to watch, almost immediately she saw a plume of black smoke on a mountain seeming to answer, then closer to hand another drift of smoke along the foothills.

After the fire died down, the men came to sit with Kate. She asked in bewilderment, "You men are very clever. Did you rub some sticks? How long did it take you to make the fire?"

Wane giggled and shyly searched into the pocket on the side of his shorts, coming up with a box of matches. The three fell about laughing, which dispersed the tension they had endured during the night's rescue.

Kate asked tiredly, "Is it OK if I have a wash and a drink? I'm filthy."

The men nodded.

Perce said, "Wait till I fix washing stuff. Not put it in the water though."

Kate was used to the idea of being careful with any water supplies needed for drinking. She watched while Perce went into the scrub and returned with a fistful of leaves. He showed her how to rub the leaves fast so they produced a white froth to wash her face, hands and arms.

Perce said, "This time we got water to help. Dig hole at the side in the sand for water to wash. Only drink at waterhole."

Kate followed him to where she could see bubbles of fresh water coming from under the rock face into the pool. She fell down and drank the ancient water with great thanks, then moving over into the sand she scooped a small hole, which filled with water. She washed her face, arms and hands, feeling immense relief. She came back to the others smiling, though limping from her foot injury. The plaited reed boot was still in place so at least she could walk.

Wane and Perce were busy digging bulbs from under some lilies near the water. They cleaned the bulbs and threw them into the hot sand of the fire. Kate watched in surprise, going over to see what would happen next. They all sat quietly and watched the pretty firetail finches flitting round the water to drink, their jewelled plumage like little princes of old.

Many varieties of birds came and went and sipped at the edge of the pool, their piping and whistling filling the air with joy. Kate felt relaxed for the first time after such a tense night and lay back to watch.

She soon smelt the cooking bulbs and realised how long it was since she had eaten. Her stomach growled loudly and the men laughed at her. They scraped out the bulbs, shaking away the sand, placing them on pieces of paper bark and gave her a batch.

Kate watched as they carefully tore off the outer layers to reveal a fluffy white centre. She followed suit, pleased to find the bulbs tasted much like potato, so she chewed blissfully, giving the men the thumbs up in appreciation.

Kate was most interested in this hidden spring and asked, "Have your people always known about this little valley and the water? There seems to be so little water around these foothills."

Perce replied, "Our spirit ancestor Arkaroo made all the hidden waters by wagging his tail, so our stories handed down tell of this, all water in our country being sacred."

Kate said slowly, "This lovely little spring is so pure, though I had heard that there are many hot springs around as well."

Wane nodded.

"Tribal people always know where good water lies. Them hot water's really bad, make our people real sick. I seen 'em one place, with all dead stuff around the pool, water having bad smell too."

He said quietly, "We have plenty old ways through country. Make smoke so Mungo come soon with camel to take you home. Him know all tracks, him blood brother."

Kate said thankfully, "I can never tell you how grateful I am for all your help. You are so wise and I feel pleased to learn from you."

The men grinned bashfully and they all laughed.

Chapter Forty-Four

A long yodelling coo-ee came from the southern scrub and the men leapt up and answered. Soon Mungo Jack appeared plodding along with his camel in tow, waving his hat to them.

Kate waved back enthusiastically, almost leaping up and down in her relief, thinking she would like to run and give the good man a big hug, but suddenly felt shy. She remembered how Bones taught her about approaching camels, so she waited while Mungo brought the camel to its knees with a quiet 'hooshta, hooshta'.

He undid her packs and putting them aside, taking off the halter, he hobbled her front legs. The camel got to her feet and went at once to the water to drink then settled beside some reeds that were good chewing.

Mungo came to greet them all and Kate shook hands with him. He looked at her scratched arms and noticed her reed boot, otherwise she seemed unharmed.

He said mildly, "How you doing, little miss? Everybody has been on the lookout for you. The whole of Windani would be on the prowl given half a chance! Reckon, you'll be pretty famous round here by now. I heard around the ridges you were a race winner on old Dandy, so I feel you'll be able to ride Sadi going back to town."

Kate pretended to bristle.

"I'll have you know, Mr Mungo, I have been coached by the professional Bones—but stopping to think, it *was* on a saddle!"

The men laughed at her and Mungo asked if anyone was hungry. There was a shout all round, so he went to his packs and produced a bag of flour and some salt. He got clean strips of paper bark and mixed on it the flour, salt and some water into a firm dough. He then rolled the lot up in many sheets of bark and placed the roll into the ashes and covered it with ash.

While they waited, he asked how the rescue went last night and everyone filled him in on the happenings.

Kate said, "I knew something was going take place when these guys dropped a white cocky feather on my lap and I felt my straps around the tree being untied. Felt like shouting with relief, but kept my mouth shut! Those Pedy fellas wanted to have a billy of tea before nodding off and that is when these boys crept up and dealt with them. Don't know was in those leaves they put in the billy, but it did the job!"

Perce and Wane looked at each other and giggled.

Perce said, "We gave them a drink of tea they won't forget, dropped some tribal stuff in the billy and they soon all snored. They have *big* headache this morning—then it was easy to take missie away, except for her hurt foot."

He indicated the strapped bootee, which Kate held up for inspection. She was most enthusiastic about the help it had given her saying, "Perce made this in the dark, would you believe and I would never have made it this far without it! I'm going to keep this bootee forever, Perce!"

He laughed and shook his head.

Mungo said, "Now you are safely away, I'll take over from Perce and Wane, who've done a great job. I salute you boys! Dave Dawson, Nick, Ginger and Fardy are in the big Police truck tracking the brutes down, somewhere along the old uranium mining roads. They are in touch by radio with Jean and Morrie in town, so everyone knows what is going on. The Pedy mob have little chance of scarpering as Ginger knows all those old roads."

Just them the aroma of cooked damper filled the air and Kate's tummy growled again. The men laughed at her so Mungo went to scrape away the hot ashes, pulling out the roll of paper bark to lay it on clean bark. He went to his packs and brought out a small tin of syrup. The others waiting groaned with delight as they tore apart the warm damper and dabbed it with syrup.

Mungo remarked, "I always try to have a bit of Cockys' Joy with me so I can eat damper this way. Make life in the bush very agreeable."

When the damper was finished down to the last crumb, Kate licking her fingers to enjoy the last of the syrup, Mungo went to the spring, had a drink and filled his canteen with water.

He said to Kate, "You want to have a last drink before we start of again?"

She shook her head, "Had a super big drink when we got here and after the good damper, I'm full up for the time being."

They sat for a time, relaxed, watching the birds came and go, until Mungo sighed, picked up the detritus from their feast and put it on the remnants of the fire. He went to the camel, put on her halter and removed her hobbles. She made as though to nip his shoulder but he took off his hat and flapped it at her and she subsided.

He called "Hooshta, hooshta, girl," pulling on the halter. The camel groaned but sat down as she had been bid. Kate watched as Mungo flung a cloth over the rear of the camel, placed his few packs in a way that made the weight even and stretched a girth strap around her.

He said to Kate, "As I have no saddle, do you think you can stay on Sadi with one hand holding on under the girth strap? You can come and get on while I hold her head. Any time you think you might slide off, sing out and we'll stop for a bit."

Kate rose, holding out her two hands to her tribal friends saying, "I'll never forget what you have done to help rescue me and what you have taught me. Such clever people!"

Chapter Forty-Five

Remembering what bones had taught her, Kate walked quietly alongside Sadi, sliding onto the rear of the hump and fastened one hand under the strap.

Mungo clucked, "Yalla, yalla."

The camel groaned her displeasure but obediently rose and followed Mungo as though it was the normal thing to have another person perched behind her packs. Mungo and Kate turned to wave goodbye to the tribal men, but to Kate's surprise, they had vanished from sight, which made her wonder if the whole night had been a figment of her imagination.

Mungo was real enough though and he walked sedately along the old track, the camel following him meekly.

Kate liked the sway of the walking camel and remarked to Mungo, "After all my new experiences with camels I find myself becoming really fond of them. I thought I might like to get a camel and practice for next year's races myself. But of course, my dad might have a fair bit to say about that. We have a lot of trouble on the property with the feral camels doing such a lot of damage to the environment, as well as making a muck of fences and watering points. We are always having to repair heaps of gear."

Mungo nodded.

"If you've been getting good instruction from Bones, you couldn't do better with the years of cameleering he has under his belt. You could come into town and practice with him now and then."

Kate laughed. She said, "I saw how Bones dealt with this lady I'm sitting on when she wouldn't let him load. He was calm but it was funny as well. He took off all his clothes. She stomped them to death and when she'd got over her hissy fit, she almost came and whispered in his ear. He refused to even look at her. Then she knelt down to be loaded without a command. I could hardly believe my eyes!"

Mungo chuckled. As they progressed quietly down the old track they heard all the songs of the bush, with honey-eaters whistling in the scrub, pink and grey galahs shrieking overhead and a myriad of budgerigars swooping in unison.

He waved his hands at the beautiful birds and said, "They will all be heading to the mound springs outside the town for the water in the lagoon behind. Sometimes, I sit out there in the evening and count the birds in their hundreds coming in to drink. If I sit still as a mouse they even come and sit on my hat or my knees. Makes me wish I could take decent photographs."

Kate was most interested in the way this quiet bushman could blend into his chosen environment.

She asked, "How did you get the name Mungo I hear everyone call you?"

Mungo thought for a while.

"When I was a young fellow, I trained as an Archaeologist and at one time was involved in the work at Lake Mungo in western New south Wales, so I guess the name stuck. I was doing a lot of work with the tribes of the Flinders, cataloguing the finds in caves which dated back around 40,000 years."

He paused for a moment, adjusted the harness on the camel, then continued, "I met Ginger Martin who was a Geologist, working for some of the mining companies and we teamed up on some of the jobs and decided eventually to become our own masters. We've explored vast areas of this district and desert, sometimes sending in reports to various institutions, getting paid for same.

We've an old four-wheel drive Ute parked behind George's garage, which we use for longer trips, only using the camel for short treks that suit her feet. The whole area is such a special place that it never ceases to amaze us."

Kate was silent for a long time, digesting everything she had heard. She said, somewhat wistfully, "Makes my life on the station seem a bit less interesting, though I think I'll always be a cattle woman, as I love the animals and my dad has taught me well. It is splendid country, too, in its own way, but I can see I will be taking more notice of the birds and the topography after hearing your story."

She was becoming more and more weary, both from the strain of the night before and her rough journeys.

She asked, "Could I have some water, please?"

Mungo took his canteen from his belt and handed it up to her. He could see the strain on her face and the effort of hanging onto the strap.

"Not long, now, Kate. This ancient track cuts out a lot of road works, so is more of a straight line back into town as the crow flies."

Kate drank, awkward with only one hand free, then handed back the canteen.

She asked, "Just one more question and then I'll shut up. How did you know to come to the waterhole with no name?"

Mungo chuckled.

"I have been taught by the tribes to read the smoke and knew where I had to meet the men after they had rescued you. No trouble at all. There, can you smell campfire smoke from the town? Very close now."

Chapter Forty-Six

Kevin Brenna arrived at the pub after around four hours' drive and pulled in to the back yard to a vociferous welcome from Deefer. The dog had been tied under Kate's Ute, so Kevin went and let him loose and the dog ran around him with a joyous tail wagging but kept on running back to guard a tatty white jogger.

Bones, who had been helping two of the local girls with hanging out the washing, with so many sheets and towels to be sorted after the influx of visitors, came over to shake hands.

"How, do, Kev. That dog has been looking after Kate's shoe since she was abducted. He refused to let the Police have it either, so they had to give in. Come and have a cuppa and something to eat."

The men went into the kitchen, where Ma Batley came to give Kevin a peck on the cheek.

"Good news for you, Kev. The tribal men are on the job and will soon know Kate's whereabouts. Dave, Nick, plus Fardy the tracker and Ginger Martin are on board the Police truck. Fardy traced the tyre tracks across to where he knew the blokes from Coober Pedy had camped. So, our men are right behind them, traversing one of the old mining roads. Things are moving quickly."

Bones nodded, handing out fresh cups of tea.

"It seems the Pedy mob are not interested in Kate, other than to use her as a lever to make Ginger meet with them at some place called One Tree. Some Asians with them heard the old damn fool story about the supposed opal dragon, paid the blokes from the Pedy to bring them here, according to the Pedy Police."

Kevin still looked very worried and said to Ma, "Elsie, could I phone my wife, please, to let her know what has been going on. She will be fretting, until I tell her the tribal people and Dave are on the track of these fools, so we just have to wait for now."

Ma explained, "Come in to the office and let your wife know. Jean is monitoring the radio, expecting calls to come in from Dave and she will be the first to let us know where they are. Until then, we just have to sit tight."

Kevin followed her out to the front of the pub and into the office. As he expected, his wife answered the phone as if she had been sitting on it. He explained everything, as far as he knew, so May had to be satisfied until further news came in from Dave or the tribal people. He hung up and went back to the kitchen where Bones was waiting.

"Come along, Kev. You can stay in Kate's room tonight and doubtless Deefer will keep you company. He was the one who alerted us that Kate had been snatched after the party, as she had put him in her room while the party was on."

The men went out to the small rooms at the end of the yard and Deefer came out from under the Ute to bark his welcome.

Bones opened the door and said, "Deefer found Kate's jogger, where she had been hauled over the fence. Fardy, the tracker, showed Dave where the Pedy mob had been camped but they had already scarpered. Ginger got a message from the tribes, so came in at once, to help try and find the way to the One Tree site on the maps."

Kevin thrust a hand into his hair and ruffled it till it stood on end. He seemed a lot calmer than when he had first arrived.

"Wish I could help more, but everything that can be done at present seems to be already in place."

They went in to the little cabin, which seemed hotter and more lifeless, though Kate's belongings were around and her little washing machine sat in the corner. Kevin looked rueful, but thought that Kate would sure to be back to get her beloved washing machine. His daughter was known for her strength of mind and determination. There was the good thought as well, that the tribal people known to be such amazing trackers round their country, so Kevin had great faith in their abilities.

Bones heard his name called from outside, so left Kevin to look around, shutting the door as he left. Deefer had come in to keep Kevin company, so he lay down on the bed, suddenly weary from so much worry and the long drive over. He looked at the little washing machine, standing sturdy in the corner and fell fast asleep.

Chapter Forty-Seven

The morning light was infusing the east with pinks and golds, when there was a bashing on the cabin door and Deefer was barking at full voice. Kevin staggered to his feet, thrusting the door open to find Bones there with a great smile on his face.

"Come on, mate, you're the last to hear the good news! Look at the hills!"

Kevin rubbed his blurry eyes, not sure what he was supposed to see, but it became plain there was a stream of white smoke emerging from the northern foothills, to be answered by a stream of black smoke from higher on the mountain.

Bones clapped Kevin on the back.

"The tribal people have taken Kate safely away from the Pedy mob and Mungo has gone to fetch her on his camel. The tracker, Fardy read the smoke, so Dave has just radioed Jean and she has the news. Come on, quick!"

The men charged across the yard into the kitchen, which had become a war office. Jean was coming in the yard with a great map under her arm, Mark had arrived plus Father Pat was helping Pup get some breakfast ready.

Kevin looked at all the smiling faces and wiped his own face, sighing in relief.

"Phew! I've been running so many scenarios in my mind, wondering what the devil I could do feeling useless I could not be with the Police."

Ma laughed. "Some of us here also felt the same way. Pup has been brandishing his cleaver and wanting to chase the miscreants and do them some permanent harm. Meet my brother, Pat, the Flying Padre and this is Mark, one of Kate's friends, who is as jittery as a cicada on a hot wire!"

Jean came in wearing a big smile and brandishing her extensive map. She was pleased to see Kevin had arrived and came forward to meet him with outstretched hands.

"Good to see you, Kev. I bring the best news. Let's spread this map out. It's the one I have to use for my forays into local bush areas and is right up to date thanks to the RFDS. Just had a call from Dave—they had to camp for the night and Fardy, their tracker, picked up the smoke from his mates early this morning to say they rescued Kate and got her away safely."

The kitchen erupted into loud clapping and shouting all round. Pup even put down his cleaver to join in and Deefer roared from outside.

Jean went on, "Now Kate is safe, the Pedy mob will be in a panic trying to get away from the One Tree waterhole along the old Echunga mine road, which would lead them to the road north to either the Birdsville track or the Innamincka Track."

Jean stopped to draw breath and sip from a cup of tea thrust into her hand.

"Good news, too, is that there is an Army chopper at present at Marree and they have been seconded by the Adelaide Police headquarters. They are going to try and cut the Pedy mob off before they get onto the northern road. The old track they will be using is a real mess, as it's not been used for years and is probably in a terrible state, so will hold them up no end. Now, Pat, Dave asked if you could take your chopper over the roads I show you. You are to keep in touch with Dave, who is switching to VHF radio. Here is a card with his sign. If you can spot the whereabouts of the Pedy trucks that will confirm the way Dave and his truck are to follow."

Jean drank the rest of her tea, accepted a sandwich from Pup, munching for a moment before continuing.

"Dave says to list all your expenses and they will be covered by the SA Police. Far as I know there is still plenty of Av-gas at the airfield as it was resupplied before the race weekend. George at the garage has the keys."

Pat had been making notes and taking co-ordinates off the map, while Jean pointed out the roads north.

He looked at his list, turned to Mark and said, "How would you like to come and give me a hand, young fella? I have to do all the chopper checks, plus the Av-gas has to be pumped by hand. You can act as spotter as well."

Marl nodded enthusiastically.

"Boy, I've been wanting to help in any way. Anything I can do will be great. Always thought about getting a chopper Licence for drafting the camels we muster, so it will be good to get some first-hand experience."

They shook hands, preparing for the morning flight with a bag of sandwiches and a thermos of tea from breakfast, going off munching the biggest of the sandwiches of meat and pickles that Pup could make.

They went over to the airfield, which, in the morning light was serene, with the windsock as lifeless as yesterday's washing after all the hullabaloo of the weekend traffic.

Chapter Forty-Eight

The men reached the airstrip and Pat said to Mark, "Trot across and get the drum keys from George, please, I'll start here."

Mark ran across the main road, went into the garage and sang out a coo-ee for George, who appeared out from under a dusty vehicle, wiping his hands on a rag.

He said, "Guess Father Pat wants to refuel. What's the go so early?"

Mark was all excitement. He grinned.

"The tribal men have rescued Kate and now Dave radioed to say the Pedy mob will try to get away out to the north road. Dave is tracking behind them and they are expecting an Army chopper from Marree to head them off. We need to find where the offenders are and then find a safe place for the big chopper to set down."

George whistled.

"Sounds like a good morning's work! I wouldn't mind to come too but got too much on here. Great way to see over the country. Go well, you fellas," and he handed over a bunch of heavy keys.

Mark sprinted back to where Pat was making notes in a big blue book. Pat undid the padlock on the first Av-gas drum.

He explained to Mark, "The drums are set on a slant on wood blocks and all drums have vents are stored with bungs at three and none o'clock positions. This prevents water or dirty fuel from reaching the openings."

Mark looked mystified. He remarked, "Never thought of water being in the drums."

Pat was quite serious, "It could mean life or death for any fliers."

He took a small fuel hand pump with hose and filter out of his kit and showed to Mark, "See here, the pump standpipe should never reach the lowest point of the drum, so water or dirt will remain in the drum and not get into the chopper fuel system."

Pat then unravelled a lead from the chopper and showed it to Mark.

"Never forget to earth your vehicle while refuelling either. It's called grounding, as it only takes one spark and you and your craft become fireworks!"

Mark gasped and then helped with undoing all the tie-down ropes, rolling them into balls and stowing them in a hatch in the fuselage. Pat walked Mark around the machine testing all areas for possible malfunction, explaining what he was looking for. They pushed and pulled each part, checking all connections and mountings looking for cracks, so Mark learned never to take an inspection lightly.

Pat then remarked to Mark, "Never ever approach a rotating chopper from the side or rear. You can't see the tail roto-blades as they run so fast and they can slice you into bits in a minute. Also approach the main rotors from the front so you know where they are."

The men got hold of the chopper and rolled it close to the drums. The pump was inserted in the drum and Mark began the arduous task of hand pumping. When the fuel tanks were filled, Pat took a stick hanging on the side of the shed and dipped the drum.

He noted the amount, locked the drum and told Mark, "You take back the keys and tell George I'll settle with him later. I'll be charging this to the Police instead of the Bishop!"

Mark was impressed with all he had learned, so he said, "I never knew so much had to happen before you even get off the ground. A good lesson for blokes like me who have no nous about aircraft!"

Pat smiled, "You soon get used to the drill. The life you lose could be your own, simple as that. Choppers fly like a brick that wants to fall down all the time, as opposed to fixed wing aircraft which really want to fly."

Mark sprinted across to give George the keys and then he and Pat clambered into the aircraft, harnessed themselves in, donning headsets; Mark watching carefully while Pat went through his drill, indicating what he was doing.

"Power on, check the throttle, check oil and fuel gauges are registering properly, check the cyclic, spin up to 50% and all set, we notify Air Traffic Control."

Pat looked at where the fat orange windsock hung lifeless on its mast. He remarked, "Great to be able to take off without the desert wind causing battering. Can get really hairy sometimes, as it can blow the air out from under my rotors and dump me on my face!"

Mark was impressed. He said, "How long you been flying, Pat?"

Pat chuckled.

"Longer than your birthdays, young fella. Started off in the Inland Mission in light aircraft, then changed jobs and learned to fly these little beasts, as they can land on a handkerchief. Listen in while I call ATC."

Pat put in details on his radio and spoke with authority and a clear voice, "Helicopter VH-AFK departing Windani 900 hours, on recce north Echunga road for Police. SARTime 100 hours Windani."

The call was acknowledged and Mark asked, "What's SARTime? Never heard that term before."

Pat, busy with his take-off, was bringing the rotors up to full throttle, took his time in replying.

"That's Search And Rescue Time. Have to call in when we get back to cancel otherwise they come looking for a flat chopper splat on the ground!"

Mark chuckled, "I have every faith in your ability, Pat."

As they lifted skywards from Windani, Pat remarked, "With the radio calls the catch phrase is ABC. A-Accuracy, B-Brevity, C-Clarity. ATC has no time for rubbish calls, too busy."

Mark was watching all the handling of the aircraft with impressed eyes.

He asked, "What's ATC stand for, never heard that term either."

Pat laughed.

"It's not magic. That's Air Traffic Control, the big centre in Melbourne, who run all flights in the air for these areas."

They were silent, gazing out of the unfolding sunlit gold of the ranges, now turning the deep valleys into indigo shadows, with swathes of gidgee trees here and there among the short grey spinifex roundels. Patches of yellow button flowers were in bloom, which, after some storm runoff, carpeted large areas and white swathes of everlasting daisies added their own glory.

Pat said, "As there is no wind at present and no dust, we should be able to pick up these blighters quickly. I am following the co-ordinates that I got off Jean's map and maybe can pick up Dave and his contingent somewhere as well. If we see where the Pedy mob are going, then we can check out a landing site for the bigger chopper, which is a medium size twin engine job."

Mark was tracing the old tracks on the ground and could pick out the range behind where they were headed.

He remarked, "I'm surprised, Pat, it doesn't look all that far as the crow flies, but I hear the old roads are pretty bad."

Pat replied, "That's how come the tribal people were able to trace the Pedy mob and rescue Kate quickly, as they are so conversant with their own terrain. Reckon, the Pedy mob don't know the area at all and will be running round like cut snakes getting into all sorts of difficulties."

The men laughed and concentrated on the search, the chopper rising quickly into the early morning sun over the red, orange and yellow mountains, with only the swoosh of the rotors for company.

There was a sudden gust of wind that threatened to send the chopper off balance and Pat adjusted his machine accordingly.

Mark said, "I can see you correcting your cyclic all the time to the air outside. Looks like you can't take your mind off the controls for a moment!"

Pat replied seriously, "If there is any disturbance in the delicate balance between the main rotors, which give downward thrust and the tail rotor that counteracts the force to spin wildly, the copter stops flying, so pilots are continual anticipators of trouble. They know if something bad has not happened, it is about to, so be ready!"

Mark was shocked into silence.

The sides of Mt Painter loomed large as the little helicopter buzzed along its foothills. Mark and Pat kept their eyes focused on a myriad of seeming trails and old roadways, often skimming around to hover over a likely stretch of road that petered out.

Mark was still full of questions regarding the chopper, thinking of its possible service to the camel industry.

He said, "About using a chopper for mustering camels in the desert, how often would you have to have maintenance done?"

Pat nodded towards his logbook under the seat.

"Everything has to be notated in there. Reckon, the helicopters need four hours of maintenance for every flight hour. After this stint, I am off to Leigh Creek tomorrow and from there to Adelaide, where this machine will be overhauled while I am overhauled by the Bishop."

Mark suddenly made a quick pointing motion down to Pat and they circled a fairly good stretch of roadway below. They were pleased to see Dave Dawson's big truck, with his men out on the roadway waving. Pat got on the radio and put in the call signs for Dave.

Dave sprinted for his rig and came in loud and clear.

"VFH-Delta Navy Golf 302—come in VH-AFK. Fardy has been following tracks and we reckon the perps have already left One Tree waterhole. Need you to recce the old Echunga road north-west and find a safe landing place for the Army chopper to land at the junction with the northern road. Keep to 500 feet above the perps in case of firearms."

Pat replied, "Understood Delta Navy Golf, over and out."

The little chopper swung to the left, heading at once north-west, Mark following the barely discernible old road below and giving the thumbs up to Pat.

Chapter Forty-Nine

Out on the mining track, the police contingent was happily scanning the hills for more smoke signals. They were all relieved when Fardy picked up the white smoke from the tribal men to say they had rescued Kate without trouble and had taken her to the no-name water. There was also a red smoke feathering the skies from the foothills.

Fardy said, "There Mungo. He take Kate home on camel. All done."

The men cheered and shook hands all round.

Nick asked quizzically, "How come Mungo can read and make smoke? Thought that was your tribal business, Fardy?"

Fardy grinned.

"Mungo long friend of tribes and blood brother. He learn all things."

Ginger nodded.

"Comes from Mungo's long training as an Archaeologist and his working life in the Flinders for so many years with the locals—and he honours all the tribal laws and sacred sites."

Nick was busy sorting out food supplies from the stores, while Fardy got a good fire going and the men got on with the makings of breakfast.

Dave was in the truck on the radio to the Marree Police station. Reception was not good in the area, so the other men could hear him shouting.

"Can only just hear you, Jeff. We are in a deep section at present. The perps have certainly been this way and our tracker is right on their marks. Have had smoke signals from the tribal people to let us know that they have Kate safe and sound. Makes no difference, this case is still a kidnapping. Reckon, the Pedy mob will be slower than us because of the harsh road conditions. Bit worried how we can apprehend those four as only Nick and I have firearms and my other two men are civilians."

There was a pause while Dave listened carefully. He started to smile and gave his mates a thumbs up.

"Good news, Jeff. That'll solve immediate problems. The Flying Padre has been briefed and is doing a recce to see if he can see the perps on the Echunga road. Yeh he'll find a suitable place for the bigger chopper to land. Great stuff, over and out."

Dave came out of the truck with a big grin on his face, "Good news, fellas, guess you heard most of that. I'm starving and I need several cups of tea, pronto! What's for breakfast?"

Nick had hauled out a big frying pan, some butter and a tray of sausages supplied by Morrie, which, along with a dozen eggs, made a good filling repast, followed by slabs of toasted bread. Ginger put the billy on for tea and Fardy cleaned the pan with pieces of paper bark and stowed it back into its place in the truck. Ginger took the spluttering billy off the fire, added the tea leaves and a couple gum leaves and left it to steep.

Dave fetched the map out and laid it on the bonnet of the truck, while sipping his tea. The others came around to watch as he traced with his finger the old road north-west, marked only by dashes.

"Looks like we are starting to get on the winning side now, we know Kate is OK. There is an Army chopper at Marree on a training mission to Cameron Corner. The Police have requisitioned it for backup for us and will bring in Jeff and two Army blokes."

He made a victory sign and asked Ginger, "They might need more info about conditions that we are heading into, Ginger, but I have already asked Father Pat to recce it in his chopper. The Army helicopter is a twin engine job and needs more space to land safely, so Pat is going to see if there is a good landing site so they can block the access to the road north."

Ginger showed them his compass readings and he traced the markings on the detailed map, pointing to a place not far away.

"Reckon, this is the place they called One-Tree, where there's a small waterhole and people have camped there at times. It will be a hard slog from there to try and get to the road north. Those dashes on the map means the old road is hardly traversable, which will hold up the Pedy mob but maybe us as well. Have to be careful not to stake a tyre or hit a rock and damage a diff. Their Blitz will be OK but the smaller rig will not. Good if Pat can see them and let us know just exactly where they are."

Dave said, "Told Pat to stay out of rifle range, in case that lot have guns with them. This is where the Army men will be a good help—they will have plenty of fire power on board."

He went to put the map away, while the others drank their tea, tipped the billy out on the fire and packed up the camp so it looked pristine. There was a feeling of optimism among the men for the first time after the major worry about Kate had been lifted.

They were soon on the way and after a few miles Fardy got out again to scan the tyre tracks, he raised his hands over his head in a winning salute. He pointed to a small side-track, got back in and they turned onto this rough and difficult old roadway. The tyre marks from the heavy Blitz were easily seen so they followed them into a deserted clearing.

Fardy was quick to find the site of the camp, felt the fireplace with his toe, followed some invisible trail around the tree where Kate had been held and picking up a white cockatoo's feather said, "Dey camp 'ere. Tribal men been 'ere, take missie away that way. But she got one sore foot." He pointed to the dense scrub behind the clearing.

Fardy continued his search and pointed to the Blitz tracks. Dave and Ginger went to look. They walked a way along the old roadway branching off, where the heavy Blitz tracks loomed large in some heavy sand. Nick followed slowly while the men made sure they were right. They were just about to get back in their vehicle when the swoosh of chopper rotors broke the silence. They all waved at the tiny white chopper hovering above them. Dave got back on the radio and let Pat know the Pedy mob had departed and the police truck was on their trail on the old mining road.

Pat acknowledged the call and the chopper flew off towards the north.

Chapter Fifty

Mungo, leading the camel, with Kate perched precariously on its back, came around the mound springs wetland into the main street. Campers were moving out, the locals were cleaning up debris from the weekend and the street was busy with stalls and bough shelters being removed.

As Kate came slowly past the showgrounds, Jason, who had been attending to his own camels, saw her perched up high and ran out to jump up and down and whistle and coo-ee. This alerted the locals, so everyone came out to shout and whistle and clap as Kate and Mungo made their stately way down the main street. Everyone had spread the news of Kate's abduction right around the small town so there was great relief at seeing her brought back safely.

Mungo bowed his head regally at the applause and Kate triumphantly waved his battered hat that she had been wearing. As they passed Morrie's Café, he came out whistling and grinning.

He shouted at full voice, "Good onya, Mungo. Plenty of beers here for you later!"

Mungo grinned and bowed his head. Kate was not so blithe.

She yelled at Morrie, pointing to her dry throat, "And I want ice-cream!"

Everyone near the Café door laughed and Morrie's off-sider, Buddy, ran out the door with a little bucket of ice-cream with a tiny spoon, which he ceremoniously presented to Kate.

She waved the old hat and sat enjoying the cold of her gift. Sadi looked as though it were she, instead of Kate, that everyone was saluting and cheering and she walked in her stately fashion with her head held high, never batting an eyelid at all the noise.

The pub mob were out in the street cheering as Mungo walked past, taking the camel round the back to the big yard where Sadi's mate, Dandy, stood watching proceedings with interest.

Mungo gave the order for the camel to sit, then helped Kate off her precarious seat. She groaned in pleasure, stretching the arm and hand that had been holding the strap for so long. Kevin Brenna vaulted over the fence and grabbing Kate in a bear hug, was trying to shake Mungo's hand at the same time. In the pub yard, Deefer was yelping and barking and surging up and down the fence, beside himself with delight.

Kevin said shakily, "My darling girl, how wonderful to see you brought back safe and sound. I'll have to phone mum shortly, as she has been in a fret waiting to hear from me. Are you all right, my dear?"

Kate said shakily, perhaps more bravely than she felt, "I'm OK, dad, thanks to this wonderful man here."

She reached across and gave Mungo a hug and felt her eyes brim with tears. He hugged her back and said mildly, "Kate, you are a real trouper, so anything we could do to help you was all in a day's work!"

Kevin was all smiles, "Best come in and get some food and drink into you both. I'll take care of Kate, Mungo, while you sort out your camel. Doubtless she'll want a drink as well."

Mungo turned to take the harness and packs off Sadi, so she could go to the water trough. He pulled out a sheaf of hay for the hay bin, so that shortly both camels were eating contentedly, with Sadi looking no worse for her trek.

Kevin helped Kate around the gate into the pub yard where Deefer was yelping and standing on hind legs, ready to give Kate plenty of attention.

She laughed at his antics.

"You've put one some weight, old boy. Bones and Pup been feeding you too well, I'd say. We'll run that off you as soon as we get home."

The dog, pleased at being patted, ran around Kate's Ute and came out from under it with her old jogger in his mouth. He dropped it at her feet, his tail wagging nineteen to the dozen.

Kevin told Kate, "The Police wanted that jogger as evidence but Deefer refused to give it up and offered them violence if they tried to take it, so in the end they just took photos of it. Deefer has been taking care of it waiting for you to come back."

As they entered the pub kitchen filled with people, it was to find Bones trying to dance a jig, Madge and Gina cheering wildly, with Pup charging round, swearing in Polish, brandishing his big cleaver.

He bowed to Kate and declared, "By yimminy, missie, I ready to cut them bad boys' hearts out!"

Just then Ma appeared and shouted to Pup, "Put that damn knife back on the wall, Pup, or I'll have your guts for garters! Now, some common sense here. Pup and Bones, people are starving while you act like madmen. You're supposed to be in charge of eats, so get on with it! Madge and Gina, bar, please."

The men laughed and saluted, so she went out to give orders in the bar, where Madge and Gina were opening for the first drinkers of the day. The barflies had seen Mungo and Kate arrive and were keen as mustard to hear all the news and were badgering the girls for information.

One old man lifted his first pint of the day and said to Gina, "Where did that camel bloke get the girl back from?"

Gina shrugged, "You know as much as me, mate, at the moment."

One of his mates added his tuppence worth, "Reckon, there's sometin' been goin' on here that's behind it all. Who'd want to kidnap a girl out 'ere, I harsk you?"

Madge said to Gina, "I'll have a quick gander in the kitchen to see if I can hear anything—we're all dying of curiosity!"

She went out for a few moments, but there was such a hullabaloo there she came back none the wiser. She announced to the bar in general, "You'll just have to wait to get all the good news. Too much going on out there at present, talking all over each other."

There were some grumbles, but the men settled down to their usual morning tipple, trying to eavesdrop on the sounds from the kitchen but not having any luck.

Ma came into the bar and looked at the list on the wall of the current bookings in the Men's Quarters, finding there were already two bunks spare after many had left.

She said to the girls, "See that the cleaners put fresh bedding in there on two bunks, so we can give Mungo and Kevin a bed for the night. Mark them off the list and there'll be no charge."

Just then, Hector and Evie Ferguson came into the bar to say goodbye. They had been packing up their big rig and were ready to roll. They were all smiles.

"Great to hear the news that the girl is back safe, Elsie. Hope she doesn't suffer from her big ordeal. We're off to Adelaide now, to meet our new baby grand daughter. Then have a booking at Mt Gambier Show. That'll be a bit of a holiday for us, as we've been bush for months this trip. See you next time around. Hope all goes well for the wedding, Madge."

Evie came to give Elsie and Madge a kiss on the cheek.

"Thanks for having us. We'll be thinking of you on the wedding day and do keep us some photographs, please."

Hector nodded so they waved and sauntered out to drive off in a cloud of dust heading south.

Chapter Fifty-One

Jean arrived in her work Ute, parking it by the gate into the pub backyard. She came into the kitchen and gave Kate a hug. She was carrying her First Aid bag, dumping it on a side bench.

"Great to see you there almost in one piece, Kate. After you are fed and watered, my dear, next is a nice shower to get you clean, so I can look at that foot. Love the bootee, by the way. How clever is that?"

Kate waved her foot clad in the woven bootee and the kitchen fell to silence as she said, "The two clever tribal men who got me out, had crept in, put some bush stuff in the tea billy, which doped the Pedy men good and proper. My bonds were untied and we sneaked away quieter than mice, though I felt I trod on every stick that made a racket!"

She paused, thinking of the old man with the white clay, still wondering if it was real or her imagination. She thought perhaps it was better not to say anything about that weird happening.

"My rescuers realised I couldn't walk far with my injured foot, which got slashed when I was running away flat out from the first camp."

The people in the kitchen cheered and Bones smiled, "Knew you were pretty fit, Kate, how'd you manage that?"

She raised her fists, "I gave that mob hell whenever I could, nearly strangled the driver at one stage!"

The kitchen erupted with hoots and laughter.

Kate continued, "My foot was bleeding, so when we got far enough away, Perce found some broad leaves, mashed them up and laid them on so the bleeding stopped soon after. Then he made this bootee out of some reedy leaves and here it still is! They also gave me some moisture to drink out of a fat vine which quenched my thirst until we got to the water with no name. So clever, I was amazed at their knowledge."

Jean announced that she had news on the radio from Dave Dawson, that his contingent was going well with Fardy and Ginger doing the tracking.

She looked at Kate and said, "We'll help you across to your cabin, Kate, so you can get your clean gear. I'll peel that bootee off carefully, if you'd like to keep it. It's really like a talisman, it's so finely made, considering it was done in the dark."

Kate nodded, "I'll always treasure it for as long as it lasts. Look at the fat leaves the men tore up and put in the bottom. How clever they are to know just what to use. I wonder what they are."

Jean was also full of praise, "I had not seen that type of leaf before. Amazing what the tribal people understand and have used for years. I would like to know so much more about these botanicals, as I am sure there are a great many chemicals in them that could be put to use in modern medicine. Kate, have you got any rubber sandals?"

Kate nodded.

Jean said, "Wear them into the shower, so your foot doesn't touch the floor. Wear them even after I fix your foot up, to give it a chance to heal well."

Kate shuffled round her bags, found her rubber sandals, took her clean clothes, towel and bath items and limped off to the shower, followed closely by Deefer. He got in the shower with her, wanting to be by her side now she was back.

Kate laughed at him, "Righto, mate, you want a shower then it's bath time for both of us. I smell like camel and you smell like dog!"

She lathered them both all over, shampooed her hair and then sluiced them both down. When they came out, she was wearing shorts, clean T-shirt, with her hair bound in a towel. Deefer tore around the yard, rolling round the grass until he was covered in grassy fluff and looked like an echidna.

Kate sat on her bed, while Jean took out her kit and inspected the slashed foot. She was amazed at the healing that had already taken place.

She wiped the area with her alcohol wipes and said seriously, "Kate, I am bewildered how the tribal men have done this, but your foot is in fine form. I will cover it for a few days and bind it so it will keep healing well. Keep off it as much as possible and wear your rubber sandals to give a softer landing."

She found some soft padding, binding the foot with a light elastic bandage to make it firm and comfortable.

Jean spoke softly, "I have to ask this, Kate, so do not take this amiss, besides the Police will want to know—in all your travails, did any of those men interfere with you?"

Kate growled in her throat, "No, they jolly-well did not! They were too busy saying I was the bargaining point to get that man Ginger to come and give them information they were wanting. I was looked after OK other than a few bruises. The young fella, Chook, was trying to be kind all the time, but I hated the Asian pair, nasty lot, that! One of them threatened poor Chook with a switch bladed knife, so the driver bloke, Cosmo, had to smooth things down. The tracks were really rough so we got thrown about a lot, hence my bruises."

Kate was looking very tired by now and Jean could see she needed to catch up on some sleep, so she tucked Kate under a cover and the girl fell asleep almost at once, guarded by the faithful Deefer, who refused to be put outside. Jean shut the door softly and went back to the kitchen.

Next morning, Kevin went to check on Kate, who was sitting up in bed having a cup of tea, thanks to Pup's ministrations. She looked much brighter, so Kevin was pleased to see the change made by a good rest. He gave Kate a big hug.

"You look so much better, my dear and I hope your foot is on the mend."

Kate smiled, "Its fine, dad, thanks to the tribal men and Jean, plus Mungo giving me the ride home on the camel. I'll be up shortly and Jean said I was to wear the rubber sandals for now over her dressing, so I should be good to drive home in a day or so. I guess it will depend, though, on when Dave Dawson gets back. He will want to know all the ins and outs of what happened."

Kevin nodded.

"You'll have to make an official statement for them and maybe sign it in front of witnesses, I guess. Dave will let you know what he wants done."

Kate looked thoughtful, "I wonder who else will have to make statements. Are you going home today?"

Kevin said, "Long as you are OK. Your mother will be on tenterhooks waiting for news, though I phoned her last night. Besides, I need to get the boys out in the back paddock to round up the breeders and take them to Number Two, where the water is better."

Kate smiled, "There's never a dull moment on the station, dad and I know you're needed there, so off you go and you know I'll be fine with all the help here."

Kevin remarked thoughtfully, "If you don't feel your foot is healed enough to drive after the interview with the Police, I can send the boys over to drive your Ute back."

Kate laughed at him.

"Stop your worry, dear dad, everything is going fine now and I can phone you if needed. I don't think I will be needing the boys, the way Jean has said my foot is healing so well. So amazed at how those crushed leaves stopped the bleeding and cleaned up the wound. Jean would like to know more about their tribal medicine, I think."

Kevin nodded then continued, "OK then, I'll have something to eat with Pup and get away soon.

He hugged her again and went back to the kitchen, where Pup was frying quantities of eggs and bacon while Bones was in charge of buttered toast and the tea.

Pup said to Kevin, "I make tucker for you to take, but bread a bit stale, so put plenty of pickles on the corned meat. Morrie getting new bread supplies in from Marree if you want wait?"

Kevin tucked into the breakfast meal with gusto, but shook his head.

"No thanks, mate, I got cattle work to do today at home, plus a worried wife. I'll have a cuppa, then pay Kate's board and lodging for a few days extra."

He went to the bar to find Madge and gave her some money, then asked for Ma. Madge pointed to the office, where Kevin found Ma at her desk covered in the weekend's paperwork.

He laughed.

"Thought I was the only one, Elsie, that was always trying to get the better of paperwork!"

She sighed, "Nah, this seems to be my bugbear. I'd rather be doing anything else, but Madge hates the paperwork too, so it falls to me. You off, are you?"

Kevin nodded and shook hands.

"I can't thank you enough for all you have done for my girl. I've paid for two more days board and lodging for Kate, seeing as she can't help you at present."

Ma smiled, "Don't suppose she likes paperwork?"

Kevin laughed.

"Not at all, she's another one that would rather be outside, chasing cattle and riding horses, but that's her life. I'll be in touch and I am sure May sends her thanks to you too."

He saluted, went out to the kitchen to pick up his tucker and shook hands with Bones and Pup.

"You're good men so I'm really thankful you have been here for Kate."

Bones ducked his head, saying quietly, "Kate's a fine lass. Anything I can do to help you know, I will."

Pup pretended to bristle, drawing himself up to his full height, growled some imprecations in his native tongue, but smiled though his teeth.

"Me, I cut the heart out of them bad fellas, you wait and see!"

He put his finger to his lips and gazed around to make sure Ma was not in ear-shot. They all laughed, following Kevin outside, to wave him off. He started his Ute, Kate and Deefer went out to wave as well, Kate standing with her hand on the big dog's head, Deefer giving his 'I'm on duty' bark.

Chapter Fifty-Two

When Mark spotted Cosmo's outfit, Pat flew a circle overhead at the recommended five hundred feet. They could see the Blitz stopped behind the smaller four-wheel drive vehicle and the men running round it like ants.

Pat radioed Dave on the truck frequency.

"Pat here, Dave, we have a bird's eye view of the Pedy mob. They had some sort of trouble with their leading vehicle. But they are proceeding OK now. You're heading after them really well, the way you're going. Stick to it, though it looks pretty rough in places."

Dave replied quickly, "How far from the end of the old road are they?"

Mark was indicating with his hands the bigger, better, road north ahead of them. They could suddenly see where the old road came out to join it.

Pat replied, "Not far now but, I reckon, they are trapped. We'll have a quick look for a landing place for the Army chopper, but the good road evens out very well past where the old road joins it. If the Army can get there quickly, they'll be in front of the Pedy mob. There's a black bog on the right of the track so the Pedy lot can't exit that way. Thick trees on the left so that leaves no other way out."

Dave was pleased, "Good on you, Pat, thanks for the help. I'll radio the Army at once. You go back to Windani and they'll take over from now on. Over and Out."

With that, the little chopper melted away into the morning sky and silence prevailed. Fardy and Ginger got out now and then to check the Blitz tracks were still going the same way.

There were no other side tracks, other than where the Blitz had ploughed a pass through broken scrub and then come back onto the old road to allow the smaller vehicle to go past.

Nick had been driving the Police vehicle carefully, making good time as they came into more open spaces without having to get over rocks and fallen limbs.

The axle height of the Police truck was a boon in such difficult terrain and its undersides were made of stern stuff. The Blitz ahead would have little trouble with the rocks and tree limbs, other than perhaps a staked tyre but the smaller vehicle would find the going very slow.

Chapter Fifty-Three

At the one tree camp, in the early morning, the men had all eventually woken, staggering round with splitting headaches. They had no idea the tribal men had doped their last night's billy tea, which left them with intense discomfort.

Cosmo was suspicious that the water had been bad somehow so had made them all crook. He tipped out the remnants in the billy, got down the water barrel they had used, tipped it all out leaving it upended to drain. He went to the pool to fill the billy with fresh water while Chook made a fire ready for breakfast.

The sleepy Asians were still in the vehicle, where they had slept badly. When they finally tumbled out, they looked in horror at the white paint daubing their arms and faces. They both started to yell, which brought Cosmo back in a hurry.

"Youse blokes got shit for brains—what the hell's the matter now?"

The Asians were pointing to the ring of white stones around the truck and the place where Kate had been sleeping. It then dawned on the men that she had vanished. They stared at the tarp where she had been sitting, which had the white hand-prints in the middle of her of her former bonds.

In the centre of the prints there lay a white cockatoo feather.

Cosmo stood stock still, his headache throbbing like a hammer while he surveyed the site. There was dusty sand around the tarp and he could see no footprints.

He whistled through his teeth.

"The black fellas did this. How'd they get the girl away without leaving tracks!"

The other men stood stock still gazing at the ground in dismay. Teo started to blubber, tearing at the white marks on his arms, "Bad spirit come night-time, this time make me die!"

Tong, looking at the marks on his arms and across his mate's face, began rubbing them frantically.

He yelled, "I sick, I sick, they want make me into ghost!"

Poor Chook looked stunned. He looked where Kate had been sitting and then the ring of white stones.

He said, his voice quavering,

"Doan like this, Cos. Not right. Black fellas might have put our trucks out of action. What we do then?"

Cosmo felt baffled and angry. He stood scratching his head and even the big dog seemed cowed at not barking when he should have done so. He went and sat under the truck, head on his paws.

Tong was shaking all over, "This one bad, bad place, now we cursed by black fella."

Teo was in a proper panic and snivelled, "We go back now, no worth big trouble!"

Cosmo, though puzzled, tried to put on a brave front and was scathing.

"Yer a pack of big girls' blouses! This is only black fella nonsense to try and scare us. Doan let 'em put you off yer stroke! Shut up for a minute and let me think how to get us out of this."

He staggered across to his rig and found the torn map given to him by the old man, spread it out on the bonnet of the car. He also brought out the other bigger map of the area that they had used when coming across country. He traced a line to where they were placed and showed the others,

"Here we are now and there is the old Echunga mine road, which would take us out to the road north, where we could get away to Cameron Corner. We just got to get away fast. Chook, check the fuel and you blokes fill the water barrel from the pool. Don't let any leaves or muck get into it. We'll need it if we're gonna get through. I'll pack up the gear, so let's rock!"

Even though the men were still dopey, everyone felt they had something to do that would get them away from this weird place, where everything had gone wrong. The Asians filled the water barrel, while Chook refuelled the trucks and checked the water and oil. He raked over the fire and he and the dog got into the big truck, which to add to the confusion, wouldn't start.

Cosmo and Chook took the bonnet off, checked the carburettor and fuel lines, hoping there had not been sand placed in the fuel.

The Asians watched in horror, thinking their whole existence was coming to an end if they were stuck there forever.

Chook sprayed some fuel into the carbie, wiped the area, got back in. This time the truck started and roared into life, but not without coughing and spluttering, until it finally ran smoothly.

The other men leaped into Cosmo's rig and he drove off, beckoning Chook to follow his tracks. The men all breathed a sigh of relief as they trundled away from that place they felt was accursed.

They could follow the better old road out of the area, but it was very overgrown in parts, bits of low scrub had formed, with tree branches and debris strewn everywhere. They struggled through in four-wheel drive until they came across a fallen tree, though, while not a large one, it would have to be removed.

Cosmo halted his rig and got an axe out of the Blitz, yelling at the Asians to get themselves out and give a hand. They were looking terrible, still daubed in white, cowed out of their minds, with no idea how to handle an axe.

Cosmo grabbed the axe and slashing at the trunk, shouted for the Asians to hold the thing still, so he could chop properly. They complied and between chopping and pushing and pulling, managed to get half of the trunk from across the track. Chook put the axe back on the Blitz, so they could start off again.

Having to try and veer around the tree truck was awkward even in low gear and Cosmo was aghast to find one of his rear tyres slashed and he could hear the sound of air rushing out. Cosmo turned off the engine, put his head in his hands for a moment then got out.

Teo was trembling all over, he moaned, "We cursed by bad spirits, we cursed!"

He fell to his feet and banged his head on the ground. Cosmo swore and grabbed him by the collar and hauled him upright.

"Stop that nonsense or I'll give you something to moan about. Nothin' to do with spirits, it's this rough road, so we just have to fix things that go wrong. Go and give Chook a hand to get a fresh tyre out and find the jack. You've all gotta help, or we'll be stuck here the rest of the day."

At that moment a very large perentie strolled out of the scrub nearly at their feet and the Asians froze in fright. It opened its yellow mouth in threat, displaying a throng of formidable teeth while it reared back on its tail.

Cosmo stood very still and he said quietly, "Stand really still, youse mob and don't go near the blighter. They have a bad bite when get they cranky, but he might go about his business if we stand still."

227

Things were at an impasse, with the perentie surveying the strangers in his territory. He settled back down and went to move off, until the dog stuck his head out of the truck and let forth a volley of barks. The perentie stood up on hind legs again, hissing fiercely, so the men scattered. Chook leapt up on his truck, Cosmo jumped on the bonnet of his rig and the small men went tearing back down the track for all they were worth.

Cosmo shook his head in disbelief and said to Chook, "I'm not grubbing round under the Ute until that bloke has gone off, so we'll just have to sit tight for a bit. Shut that damn dog up. Where the devil did those mad fellas get to?"

Chook waved back towards the track they had come along and shouted, "Dunno, but they can stay away for all I care, proper mad mongrels them! We get on better without them. They want to hurt me! I done nothing!"

Cosmo nodded in agreement and they sat silent until the perentie settled down, at last marching into the scrub, where they could hear it scaling a tree. They looked carefully about, got down and finding the big wallaby jack, set about putting it in place so they could lever the rig off from the tree trunk and get at the tyre.

Cosmo took the axe down again and slashed at the sharp wood until it broke into smaller pieces and fell away. Chook and he heaved the staked tyre off, finally got the replacement on and they were standing on the wheel brace to tighten up the nuts when they heard a small cry from the bush behind them.

"Is the monster gone? We come out?"

Cosmo shrugged and disregarded this query, going on with the business of getting the tools and axe and dead tyre tied down on the Blitz. The two Asians came up almost tiptoeing, looking fearfully round for the supposed monster, who had gone about his own business. They decanted water from the barrel into canteens, while Chook watched them carefully.

"Doan waste not one drop of water, treat it like gold! That's all we got to drink for the rest of the day."

The men drank small amounts, this time listening to what they had been told, got back into the vehicles and the convoy started cautiously along the track again. They seemed to be travelling better along a more open section of the road when Cosmo thought he heard the sound of a helicopter. He switched off his engine, waving to Chook to do the same—and then they all heard it. The whoosh, whoosh of the rotor blades was unmistakable.

Chapter Fifty-Four

Cosmo shook his head at his passengers in disbelief. The sound of the chopper, though quite high, filled the scrubby landscape with an alien song that stilled all the birds.

Cosmo said, "That's torn it, youse guys. They've sent spotters up to find us and we doan have nowhere to hide from here on. We're all goin' down for kidnapping!"

Teo quavered, "Get the gun out and shoot them down!"

Cosmo shouted in exasperation, "For gawd sake, use yer loaf for once! They'll come for us anyway, so we may as well just keep going the way we are. Not gonna add armed conflict to all our troubles!"

Just then a mob of big red kangaroos, spooked by the chopper noise, barged across the road in huge running leaps, taking the men completely by surprise. They watched in horror as a huge alpha male, weighing more than a man, ploughed straight onto the bonnet of Cosmo's vehicle, leaping off the other side into the scrub.

All hell broke loose!

The bonnet flew back, breaking its tie-down straps, hitting the windscreen with a huge wallop that broke it into smithereens. The flying glass covered everything in shards and glass dust.

Cosmo killed his engine and yelled, "Sit quite still or you'll get glass in your eyes."

Chook had stopped the Blitz, got out and surveyed the damage.

"What the best way to get the glass out, Cos?"

They were sitting stunned, until Cosmo gathered his scattered wits.

"Chook, get a tarp down from the truck and some rags as well. Doan get too close here."

Chook did as he was told, wrenching straps off, found a rolled-up tarp and some rags and brought them over. Cosmo endeavoured to move out of his seat without getting cut.

"Now," he said to the Asians, "slide out of the car trying not to disturb the glass. Get some leaves and dust yourselves off much as possible. We'll spread that tarp right across the seat and try and clean it off. Have to break all the stuff left in the screen, so I can see out. We're just never meant to get outta here, I can tell youse!"

Tong scowled and raising his fist, growled, "Spirit men do this."

Cosmo groaned and shook his head with some violence, "Doan start that again. Get going and give some help like I tell you. Chook and I got to get the bonnet tied down somehow while youse lot get the glass out."

The Asians spread the tarp out inside the vehicle and were using rags tied around their hands and sticks for the hard parts. Cosmo and Chook were standing on the wrecked bonnet, jumping up and down to get it to the stage, where it could be tied down with wire and straps.

They had to struggle hard, as it had been badly dented by the weight of the big roo. They finally made some sort of impression that was enough to be able to get wire around it and some snatch straps as well. The Asians had found a brush, which had served to get most of the shattered windscreen onto the tarp. They bundled it all up and dragged it off to throw in the scrub.

Cosmo tiredly tried to start up his rig, so the Asians got back into the rear seat. There seemed to be some damage to the engine, so it spluttered and died a couple of times until it fired after a fashion. He was so fed up he refused to speak any more and they trundled along the bumpy old road with no hope in their hearts. The old track was levelling out and they were making a little better time and could see where it joined the good road north.

Tong was getting more and more agitated, beating his hands on the seats, cursing in his own lingo. Suddenly he yelled out, "Stop now! I not staying with you. Want that bike off and I go myself!"

He was screaming with his rage and pulled the knife out of his leg sheathe and waved it at Cosmo, who tried to be calm.

"Put that thing away. That ain't gonna get you nothin' We'll give you the bike."

Teo watched him with dull eyes, too stupefied to do anything more. Cosmo groaned, "I don't give a damn what you do from here on, we're all goners and it's all your fault!"

Tong screamed, waving the knife around, "They not catch me, give bike now!"

Cosmo turned off his faltering motor. He beckoned Chook who had pulled up behind him and said, "This maniac reckons he can run from the Police on one of the bikes. Crazy fool! Give us a hand to get the right side bike orf. We'll be well rid of that bloke!"

They started undoing the heavy straps on the back of the Blitz, lifted off one of the trail bikes and watched in silence as Tong strove to start the bike, which had been jolted around severely on the truck. The big dog had got out of the Blitz and made growling noises at Tong, who kicked at him. Eventually as the bike engine started, they heard the sound of a big helicopter somewhere close at hand.

Cosmo drew in his breath sharply.

"That's it then, fellas. I'm just gonna plead insanity! Nothin' else left to do now."

Tong tore off on the bike at full throttle but as he emerged from the shelter of the trees, the Army helicopter landed on the road in front of him, covering him with blasts of eye-watering sand. He veered wildly to the right, over the raised edge of the small rise in front of him, straight into the black morass of the boggy soak. The black bog stopped the bike in its tracks and the bog covered Tong from head to toe. He was immovable.

The big dog suddenly tore off after him, barking in full voice. Cosmo shouted and whistled, but the dog ignored him.

Cosmo groaned, "Gawd, more trouble I need like a third armpit!"

The dog became distracted from the bike when it spotted a big red roo at the edge of the morass. The roo stood on its tail and offered to hold the dog under, making grabs at him. Chook, coming to life, ran and grabbed the rifle out of Cosmo's car, jamming a round in the breech, aimed it and shouted,

"Good roo for lunch! I like roo!"

Cosmo grabbed the rifle, pushing it skywards, struggling with Chook, spluttering, "You're as mad as the darn dog. Gimme that before you hurt somebody!"

The rifle exploded, they both fell over with the recoil and the noise sent a tree full of parrots screaming into the air.

The Army helicopter had landed right in front of them, the side door opened and a large man in army fatigues and a Policeman in official blue uniform got out before the rotors stopped spinning. The great cloud of sand and dust covered everything until the final rotation, so the men on the ground hid their heads until it settled. The trooper saw the rifle, came over and pushed it away with his foot, making sure Cosmo and Chook could see he carried a much bigger weapon.

He shouted, "Hands on head, NOW!"

The men lay sprawled on the ground, too winded to get up, but sat slowly, with Teo coming to sit beside them. They all placed their hands on their heads. In the bog, Tong was screeching and screaming imprecations in his own language, until his voice gave out and he sat, trapped, finally silent. The trail bike had settled into the bog, so it was nearly up to Tong's midriff, anchoring him firmly.

The big dog came back and Chook sat crying, shaking all over, holding the dog, with tears running down his face. Just then, there was the sound of a truck engine from the road behind them and Dave Dawson's rig hove into sight.

Dave looked at the melee in front of them and said to Nick, "Get that gun out and load it, just in case, but looks like we'll have all the backup we need. Ginger and Fardy, stay in the vehicle until we get this sorted out."

Nick and Dave got out slowly, saluting Sergeant Poulsen, looking at the three filthy men sprawled on the ground, one of them with a big dog in his arms crying. One of these was a quivering Asian with hands on head and another one up to his middle in the black morass of the bog. Dave and Nick came around carefully, assessing where more firearms might be, patting down the men, but found nothing. The discarded rifle was under the boot of the trooper, filled with dust and dirt.

They went to confer with the Sergeant, who was carrying a sidearm in full view on his left shoulder harness. He was stern and looked like business, while the trooper covered the miscreants.

Dave was pleased the Army contingent had arrived before him and halted the two runaway vehicles at once.

He said, "Great we got here pretty well together. How do you want to handle these perps?"

Poulsen said quietly, "We've had info from Coober Pedy and Adelaide that the Federal Police have been watching this Asian pair. Seems they are illegals, arriving on false Passports and Visas and allegedly smuggling good opals out of the country. A Fed team is flying up from Adelaide, so there will be some interesting stuff going on in Marree when we get them sorted out."

He nudged Cosmo with his foot.

"What's your name? You in charge of this lot, mate?"

Cosmo, sitting with his hands on his head, nodded.

"I'm Charlie Sims, commonly called Cosmo and this is my brother, Eddie, but he doan answer to Eddie, you gotta call him Chook. He was dropped on his head as a baby and I look after him. We got into this mess when those two mad Asians hired me in the Pedy to bring them across country on some wild goose chase they heard about. Pox on both of them!"

He paused for breath, "We usually take fossickers for trips round the Pedy diggings and Chook does all the cooking and camp stuff, but I gotta tell him what to do. This is the first time we were offered such big money, to bring those lunatics over here, but I didn't know what mess they would get us into."

Poulsen and Nick were making notes as Cosmo spoke, conferring with Dave.

Cosmo spoke again wearily, "None of this mess is anything to do with Chook. He doan know anything, except what I tell him. Nuthin' is his fault. I'll be glad to give you all the info I can about these dickheads. Wish I'd never set eyes on them. That fool in the bog had been threatening me and Chook with a knife a few times, if we didn't do what he wanted—nasty bastard that one, so be careful!"

Dave Dawson said sternly, "We want to know what happened to the lady you lot kidnapped. It will go really badly for all of you if she has been injured in anyway."

Cosmo was aghast, "No way! I would never hurt a lady! I was dead against the whole thing, but that bloke in the bog reckoned he would knife Chook unless I did what he said. Chook and me were careful with the girlie, until last night the black fellas came and took her away, dunno to where."

They all looked down at poor Chook, still sitting with his big dog in his arms, with the tears coursing down his plump cheeks.

Sergeant Poulsen went and conferred with both the trooper and the Army Pilot who were standing on guard underneath the chopper. He gave them two sets of handcuffs so Cosmo and Teo were cuffed and left sitting on the sand. They all looked at where Tong was stuck over his middle in the bog.

Dave said, "Well, that one ain't going anywhere for the present, darned if I know how we'll get him out of there."

Sergeant Poulsen said, "He can wait. Those men must have kit with them.

He turned to Cosmo, "You got those fella's kit with you?"

Cosmo nodded, "More's the pity. In the back of my rig."

He stood up shakily and led the men around to his vehicle, opening the back, where they pulled out bag after bag, until Cosmo pointed to two identical new looking bags.

"Them's the ones."

The Policemen pulled the kitbags open and strewed the contents on the ground. They found in each bag a vest made to fit close to the chest of the small Asians. When they laid the vests out, Dave whistled. He and Poulsen felt in various hidden pockets in the linings and came out with many types of opals, both rough and refined, laying them on the cloth. There were wads of Australian cash stashed away, plus Passports and Visas in each vest.

Poulsen said, "This is what the Feds are on about. These two are the ones Barry at the Pedy and the Feds have been keeping an eye on. Nothing proven up till now. We can add kidnapping to all their felonies as well. That's a life sentence."

In the clearing there was dead silence.

Chapter Fifty-Five

Tong was a pitiful sight, stuck as he was in the bog, covered in black slime, but that didn't stop his bad language. He was red with rage and beating at the mire, shouting and growling non-stop.

Nick and Dave went to look at the state of Tong. Nick had an idea, going over to the bush and bringing back a stout branch. He went and got a coil of rope out of the truck.

He said, "Think I might be able to throw this rope as far as the bike. Reckon if I tie the rope to the end of this branch to stop it going too far, we might be able to haul the blighter out."

Dave hefted the branch, looking thoughtful.

"Well, that might work if we can get him to run the rope around under his armpits and tie it hard. He's got to come out one way or another, like it or not. He's mad enough to kill someone if we try and get in there, so that's not on."

Nick secured the end of the rope to a broken bit at the end of the branch, tested it for strength, then looped the rope over his arm. With a mighty throw like a discus thrower, he sent the rope coiling out to fall over Tong's head.

Dave shouted, "Tie this under your armpits and we'll haul you out, otherwise you can stay there and rot! We can't hang around here all day."

Tong shouted more imprecations, but in the end, they watched as he drew on the rope, fastened it under his armpits.

Nick took up the strain, then shouted, "Try to raise yourself up on the bike so you are on top of the bog and that might help."

Tong growled to himself but managed to get one leg out raising himself a little.

Nick, Dave and Poulsen started to pull, then heaving hard on the rope, which, through hard work, in the end Tong came out of the bog like a cork out of a bottle. They dragged him up onto the sand to lie like a stranded beetle. He was a mess of boggy detritus, clad only in torn shirt and underpants, having lost his trousers on the way in, with no sign of his knife.

Nick went over to the Army chopper and conferred with one of the men, coming back with a canvas bucket of water decanted from a valve in the side of the chopper.

He said to Tong, "Stand up and we'll wash you down, but don't try any funny business or the trooper will blow you away!"

Tong stood up, bristling with rage, but Nick dropped the water over his head and let it wash down as much muck as possible. Dave patted the remainder of Tong's clothes but no knife was in evidence. With the heat of the day the man would dry off quickly. Dave produced a pair of handcuffs and marched him over to Teo where he was made to sit with his mate on the ground.

While Dave and Poulsen were rolling up the secretive vests and the kitbags, Tong's eyes were following their every move. Suddenly, he started to scream and shout, yelling at full pitch trying to leap up and throw himself at the men.

The Army trooper pushed him back down with his foot, raised his big gun and aiming at the sky, let off two quick rounds.

The noise was so shockingly loud in the small area, that the cockatoos went off shrieking, flapping into the bush and the red roos fleeing in their masses to safety behind the nearest sandhills.

Dave, Nick and Poulsen turned in astonishment in the sudden silence that followed, to see the trooper standing with his feet apart, quite silent, with his gun pointing directly at Tong's open mouth. Tong's eyes nearly crossed looking into the barrel and his mouth dropped closed.

In the absolute silence, there came the distinct click of the safety being let off the big gun, which never wavered.

Cosmo said dryly, "That's the best thing I seen since this mob hired me! Shoulda thought of it meself!"

Dave said to him, "We got to take these kitbags into Marree for the Feds. As your rig will be here until we get it towed, is there anywhere we can stash this safely on the Blitz, which we need to take in now."

Cosmo took them to the side of the Blitz where there was a good secure metal locker welded to the back of the truck. He undid the padlock, which Dave took off him and then men rolled up the Asians' bags carefully, stowing them and the rifle in the locker, rehanging the padlock.

With the army trooper standing guard over the Asians, the men went over to Cosmo's vehicle to look at the damage. The wires had broken off and the straps fallen down, so the bonnet flapped. Dave and Nick tried to get the dented bonnet back in place with no luck. Nick had a look at the engine and said to Cosmo,

"Looks like the air filter is busted and some of the carbie and wiring, but maybe no major damage."

He went around, got into the vehicle and tried the starter but while there was whirring, nothing else happened.

"Nah, it's a no-goer."

Poulsen pushed his hat back on his head.

"Best I can do, when we get back to Marree, is to get someone to come out pretty soon and tow it in. Have to use it for evidence, Charlie."

Cosmo locked his rig and gave the keys to the Sergeant.

He said, what happens now?"

Poulsen told him, "We just got to decide how we are going to proceed. I have to charge you as an accessory, along with Chook and this will be for the time being. Both of you'll have the night in the lockup. I think, you'll be taken into town in the chopper with the Asians and you have to have cuffs on till be get into town. You know any legal fellow who will stand for you?"

Cosmo nodded, "Our uncle, Bert Thompson, has a mixed holding outside Maree and my cousin, Phil Thompson, is a big-name lawyer in Adelaide. If I can ring Phil as soon as we get in, I guess he'll start to sort things out, especially for Chook, who used to live with Thompsons after our mother died. They can take in Chook again."

Poulsen said, "I know Bert and his missus, nice people. You and Chook will have to give detailed statements before anything else can be done."

Cosmo nodded, "No trouble for me, but Chook can't do that, he can't read or write. He's good with cooking and camping and looking after the truck. When he settles down, he might be able to tell you how we were threatened by the Asians, specially that Tong, who wanted to kill poor Chook if I didn't do as they said. The girl saw that happen as well. Doan know why I didn't turn around the first time they gave trouble and give them their dosh back!"

Dave came over to confer with Poulsen and the Army trooper. They went to look inside the chopper and saw where there were two small dickey seats bolted to the floor.

Sergeant Poulsen said, "We can stick the two Asians in there so Charlie and I will take the back seats. The Blitz and the small vehicle will be taken to the Police yard and kept as evidence, with photographs taken tomorrow."

He turned to Cosmo, "If Sergeant Dawson rides with Chook in the Blitz, can Chook be made to understand he is to drive into Marree and meet you there? You and I and the perps will fly. Then I will arrange for the tow to come out get your rig, but dunno about getting that bike out!"

Cosmo sighed, jiggling his handcuffs, "That's about the least of my worries. But I tell you, Chook won't go without his big dog."

Poulsen said, "Can you talk to Chook, so he can understand what is going on?"

Cosmo nodded, "That'll work. I just gotta make sure Chookie understands I'll be there to meet him."

He went across to Chook and raised him off the ground. Poor Chook was still shaking but had hold of the dog's collar like grim death.

Cosmo put an arm across his brother's shoulder, "Now, listen hard Chookie. You gotta drive the Blitz into town, with the Sergeant and the dog and I'll be waiting for you there. I'm getting a ride in the big chopper so you can watch us taking off."

Chook looked scared but nodded and went to open his truck door.

Cosmo had a thought and sang out to Nick, "We better check the fuel before he starts. Old Blitz chews up the gas on the rough tracks."

He went to the Blitz, turned it on and checked. He nodded at the other men, sprang up on the back and handed down a jerry can of fuel to Nick. They decanted it into the tank and Cosmo tied it back in place.

He said, "That'll do to get into Marree."

The Army troopers came over to add their advice to the conference going on. One pointed to Tong, "That trouble-maker will have to be manacled to the floor. In fact, all of them for safety. You understand we can't have any incidents once we are in the air?"

The Policemen agreed, the Asians were herded into the chopper, perched in the dickey seats and their feet manacled to the floor. Tong was still in a rage, looking ready to kill someone, but there was nothing he could do, so he kept his mouth shut as the big trooper was standing beside the door, watching him. Charlie was ushered into a seat, his manacles attached to the ring in the floor. He sat passively, worn out by the whole day.

The chopper Pilot came out with a radio message making it clear what lay ahead for the Asians.

"The officers from the Federal Police will be flying in to Marree around 9 a.m. tomorrow. Looks like these two will be facing a barrage of charges, to which kidnapping will be added. They'll be spending a great deal of time at Her Majesty's Pleasure!"

Cosmo gave a shout from where he sat.

"Better add Tong's threats of murder to Chook and me while you're at it! I couldn't let anythin' happen to Chook, so I just went along with all the mess. Nuthin's Chook's fault."

Dave looked at the tired face of Chook, sitting quietly in the big truck.

He said, "If Charlie is to be believed and I don't see why not, looking at the lad, we can see he's not the full quid, so I'm prepared to drive with him in the Blitz to Marree, as long as he understands what Charlie wants him to do."

Poulsen went to speak with Cosmo and said, "We'll convey you and these perps to Marree in short order. The Army will have jurisdiction over you as they have been seconded by the SA Police. Sergeant Dawson will accompany Eddie in the Blitz to Marree, where you can phone your legal. But there will be a stay in the lockup for you and Eddie until we can get it all sorted. Can you tell Eddie what to do, so he fully understands?"

Cosmo nodded and shouted to Chook, "Listen mate, I need you to drive the truck into Maree. The Policeman wants to go with you and he will show you where to go. When we get there we'll get cousin Phil to come and help us. You're good to drive the truck. You can watch us flying off in the helicopter and we'll be waiting for you in Marree."

Chook looked miserable. He nodded his head, with his hair flopping over his eyes. He wailed, hugging the big dog, "But I gotta take Bitzer. Not goin' without me dorg!"

Dave Dawson made a grimace and Nick had a quick grin to himself, imagining what it would be like to have the big, smelly dog on the seat beside his boss all the way. But it seemed to be a moot point and Dave agreed the dog was able to come along as a witness.

Dave called to Nick, "OK, mate, you're in charge of our men. Put the radio back in usual signals and stay in touch. Don't think there'd be any trouble, but who knows! You drive south along the main road to Windani. When you get in, give Fardy some food stores and I'll check with him later. I'll have to stay overnight at Marree, but I'll ring my missus. We'll need to have Statements from Kate and Mungo Jack in the morning, so you'll be needed to drive them to Marree."

Nick grinned and couldn't resist a dig.

"Enjoy the dog's company, Sir!"

Dave was not amused and stalked off to Chook's truck. He got in the passenger side seat and said jovially to Chook, "Righto, mate, we'll go shortly. We can watch your brother get a ride in the Army chopper."

Chook pushed his door wide open and whistled and Bitzer galloped up and leaped in, nearly landing on Dave, but settling on the long bench seat where it was used to sitting. Dave waved ruefully from the passenger seat to Nick and his other men, who were chuckling to themselves. The dog was leaning cheerfully over Dave to dribble and grin.

Dave said to Chook, "We'll see how the Army chopper takes off. Lots of dust though!"

Sergeant Poulsen and the trooper clambered into the rear of the chopper, slamming the door, strapping in, while the pilot made his radio calls, began his rotation, building up engine speed slowly. The chopper lifted off the ground, raising a tornado of dust and debris, looking like a great grey insect heading in the direction of Marree.

Chook started the Blitz and as Dave Dawson showed him the way, followed the old road out to where it met with the road north. They could see the grey shape of the chopper away in the sky in front getting smaller and smaller. Chook was happier again, driving his beloved truck with the big dog beside him, with Dave suffering quietly but showing the way, so there were no troubles as they headed for Marree.

Chapter Fifty-Six

Nick went over to Ginger and Fardy who had got out of the Police vehicle to stretch their legs and watch the chopper take off. He clasped his hands over his head in a winning salute.

Ginger said with a wry smile, "Never though our trek would end like that! Great idea to get the Army involved. I wondered how it would work out for just you and Dave trying to grab the perps but, of course, no one knew the drivers from the Pedy had been doing the trip under duress and would be on your side."

Nick agreed. He said, "What a mess this has ended up, except for the quick intervention of the tribal men to help Kate Brenna get away safe. Goodness knows what would have happened to her if they had not been on hand. However, Poulsen will get things sorted out in Marree, so our help has finished for now. Let's have something to eat and a drink, before heading back to Windi. We'll be home by sunset."

They went to the back of their truck, pulling out some biscuits and rather stale cake, but which all went down with gusto and finished with some cans of soft drink.

Nick handed some food to Fardy and said to him, "You one good fella tracker, mate. You teach me? I'm a quick learner!"

Fardy grinned and shook his head.

"Nah, boss, white fella no see anyt'in'!"

They all laughed, suddenly relieved of the strain of their drama so they settled into the truck for the trip home, turning onto the better road that would take them south.

That evening as they arrived back in town many townspeople came out to give the Police truck a cheer and wave. As they turned into the Police yard, Nick suddenly had a thought about everyone wanting to know all the ins and outs of their trek.

He remarked to Ginger, "We'll have to take you, Mungo Jack and Kate to Marree in the morning to give your statements, so please don't say anything to any of the local mob till we get the legal stuff sorted."

Ginger nodded, "I'm so tired I could sleep on a rail, so I'll sneak into the men's quarters at the pub and sleep like the dead! Without Bones or Pup seeing me, I might add or I'll never be left alone!"

Nick looked at Fardy and said, "You did a very good job, Fardy. We'd never have got far without you. Reckon you know how to keep your mouth shut, eh? Dave said I was to give you some supplies, you OK with that?"

Fardy nodded and as they all wearily got out of the truck Ginger quickly disappeared down to the pub then Nick took Fardy to the back of the truck and dispensed supplies from the cache still there.

He clapped Fardy on the shoulder and said, "One day, I'll tell my kids that I knew the best tracker in the bush!"

Fardy giggled and sauntered off clutching his supplies, vanishing into the gloom like a shadow.

Chapter Fifty-Seven

The army chopper arrived at Marree and landed on the edge of the airstrip, ceasing its rotation so that the sudden quiet was almost deafening. The trooper opened the side door, followed by the pilot and they jumped to the ground, followed by Sergeant Poulsen.

He remarked to the men in a quiet voice, "I need you to back me up until Dave Dawson arrives with Chook in the Blitz. If they don't appear we may have to go back along the road for a recce. In the meantime, we need to get those Asians into the lockup, without further aggravation from them. I'll also take my weapon out in case of any funny business, so be alert. OK, let's undo the shackles first, leaving the handcuffs on till we get them put away."

The Army men nodded, the trooper took his big gun from over his shoulder and looked like business. They proceeded to undo the floor shackles and straps and Poulsen said in a stern voice, "Right, one at a time and no nonsense. The Army troopers are crack shots and I'm pretty good at shooting kneecaps out, so you'd never walk again!"

He beckoned to Tong.

"Out!"

Tong was livid with anger, but could hardly see any avenue of escape, clad only in his mucky shirt and under pants. He growled in his own lingo and dropped to the ground, where the trooper stood over him. Teo, looking very scared, followed meekly and also dropped to the ground.

Poulsen shouted to Cosmo, "I'll be back shortly, Charlie, so sit tight until we deal with these perps."

He and the troopers marched the bedraggled Asians across the main road into the Police station office and from there into the lockup at the back, where they were read their rights then placed in separate cells.

Cosmo was too worn out and fed up to care how long it took, sitting back in his seat resting. In the distance he heard a familiar sound and perked up. As the trooper and Poulsen came back, he shouted,

"By gum, that sounds like the Blitz! Good on Chookie! Can I get out now?"

Poulsen shaded his eyes from the late afternoon sun and sure enough, he could see dust coming on the road from the south. He and the trooper undid Cosmo's shackles and seatbelt, so, rubbing his ankles ruefully, he jumped down. They all went across to the Police station to wait.

Very soon, the old Blitz roared in from the main road, with the big dog stuck out of the driver's side window, barking its head off. Chook drew to a halt in front of the Police station and Dave Dawson clapped him on the shoulder, saying, "Great stuff, Chook, you're a good driver. Come and we'll find your brother."

The two army men came out, waving goodbye, went across the road to the airfield, clambered into their chopper, slammed the door shut and the chopper began its rotation. Everyone watched as it sped up in a great cloud of red dust and regally lifted off to head north.

Chook was pleased to see Cosmo and looking at him made whooshing noises, waving his hands over his head in imitation of the chopper. Chook, Dave and the big dog clambered down from the Blitz, Dave stretching his aching back.

Cosmo went to give Chook a hug and clamped his hand around the muzzle of Bitzer to stop him from barking joyfully.

"Boy, Chook, you nearly better than the big Army chopper, getting here so quick!"

Dave Dawson put his tuppence in as well, as they went into the Police Station office, "Chook is a very good driver and we had no trouble, other than the Blitz, being a Blitz, tends to want to throw everyone out going round corners. That right, Chook?"

Chook grinned, not sure what was wanted of him, but liked being called a 'good driver'.

Sergeant Poulsen said to Cosmo, "Charlie, you know I have to charge you as an accessory to kidnapping for now, but I understand you were under duress, so your legal should be able to sort that out for you."

Suddenly Chook, who was sitting on the floor with the big dog, came to life.

He said very emphatically, "Them bad men wanted to kill me! I done nuthin' to them! Then they wanted to kill Cosmo 'cause he couldn't find the ginger man. They took missie and I looked after her."

Poulsen and Dave looked at each other. They moved to the side of the room to have a conference. When they came back, Sergeant Poulsen said, "Charlie, what about I ring Bert Thompson, tell him in brief what had happened and also get your legal's number? You two stay here for a moment until we get that sorted out."

Cosmo went and sat on the floor with Chook while Poulsen went into the radio room, where he could be heard speaking to Bert Thompson. Dave came back with a phone number written on a bit of paper and handed it to Cosmo.

"That's all good, now your uncle knows the gist of things and here's the number for you to ring your legal. You should get onto that right away before it gets too late and he leaves for the night."

Cosmo got up and said to Chook, "I gotta ring cousin Phil, Chook, only be a minute or two, so you and the dorg sit here, OK?"

Chook looked worried, so Dave said to him, "You like a drink and some biscuits, Chook?"

Chook nodded and looked at his dog, "Bitzer needs a drink too."

Dave sighed, but produced a handful of biscuits and a can of soft drink and dutifully came back with a dish of water for the dog, who indeed needed a drink as well. Chook could hear his brother talking on the phone, so was happy for the time being.

When Cosmo came back he said, "Phil is talking to the Policeman, mate. We'll know what will go down soon. We'll be OK here now the nasty men have been shut up and Phil is going come and help."

Poulsen, was giving Phil Thompson the general story of the present fiasco and how he had already spoken to Bert Thompson regarding the welfare of Chook.

Phil spoke carefully, "Having heard from Charlie how he and Eddie were put under duress by the illegals, I will put off my work here so I can fly up in the morning. In the meantime, I can sort out some legal aspects pertaining to whatever charges will be laid for the Sims brothers. I will stand for both of them and the main thing is the care of Eddie for tonight. If he gets too stressed, he gets the shakes and sometimes falls into a fit, so you need to make sure he is OK, or a doctor may have to be called."

Poulsen said, "Well, he's sitting on the floor with Charlie, eating biscuits, with his arm around his dog, so seems quiet for the moment, but I'll have to put them both in a cell for the night. I have one they can share, so I'll get them fed and rested. We need to know the best way to handle Eddie, who I understand cannot read or write."

Phil considered for a moment, "That's correct, but he can also come up with good information when he is not hurried or frightened. I could bring a tape recorder with me and see if I can get his information down on tape. If he gets too stressed, he will forget things that may be cognizant to this case."

Poulsen said in agreement, "Surprisingly, when listening to what was being said in the office, Eddie suddenly blurted out about bad men wanting to kill him, then they wanted to kill Cosmo because he couldn't find the ginger man. It was the Asian men who took the girl and Eddie looked after her."

Phil said slowly, "That's all good and if we can get the full statement from Charlie, plus anything more from Eddie, that will change the whole aspect of their case. I understand you will take Statements from Kate Brenna and Ginger Martin and David Dawson and his driver will also give their depositions.

The Federal Police will add the harming threats to their charges as well. That's about all I can add for now. See you in the morning early and hopefully I can get Eddie placed in charge of his aunt and uncle for a custodial term."

Dave was listening to the outcome of the conversation with Phil Thompson, saying to Poulsen, "I can make my statement in the morning as Nick is bringing up Ginger and Kate, so he can drive me back. What do you reckon?"

Poulsen considered, "We'll get these two settled in a cell and get some food sent up from the hotel. Then you and I can go up to the house, where we can have a shower and my missus will see you get a bed for the night."

Dave yawned, "That'd be great if she won't mind, I'm bushed after such a big day. Just a thought, Chook won't be happy if the dog is not looked after."

The Sergeant pulled a wry face but submitted with good grace.

"Righto. I draw the line at the smelly beast being in the cell, but it can sleep under the cells and we'll give it some water and some of my dog's food. Hope it won't yowl in the night!"

They went to explain to Chook and Cosmo what would happen and showed Chook where the dog would sleep, so he was satisfied. The dog was chained up, the men were taken to the bathrooms and showered and then shown into a cell with two bunks.

Dave asked them, "That's all good, mates, now what would you like for tea? The chicken and chips from the pub is pretty good grub and I can make some cups of tea here for you."

They grinned and nodded. Poulsen went to both the smaller cells and asked the Asians what food and drinks they wanted but both refused to answer him, so he looked at Dave and shrugged.

He shouted into their cells, "OK. Bread and water for you two!"

He and Dave went away smiling for the first time that day.

Chapter Fifty-Eight

Early next morning, the phone rang in the pub office in Windani, where Ma Batley was looking at her never-ending paperwork, still in her dressing gown. She took up the receiver and was startled to hear Dave Dawson.

"Good morning Elsie, hope I'm not disturbing you so early?"

Ma laughed and remarked, "A woman's work is never done, Dave. What can I do for you?"

He snorted, "That's what my wife is always telling me! I'm still in Marree. Just need a message given to Nick, please. Tell him to get on the road pronto, as we got the Feds and a lawyer arriving early. Nick is bringing up Kate and Ginger to make their depositions, then bringing me back afterwards. Hope Kate is going OK?"

Ma nodded, "Jean has seen to her slashed foot and dressed it and other than being weary, Kate is fine. We breed our women tough out here! I'll get Bones and Pup to get the others up for breakfast and they should be able to get on the road in a half hour or so. See you."

She hung up and went to the kitchen where Bones and Pup were already making breakfast.

She asked Bones, "Could you go out and rouse young Nick and also get Ginger and Kate up, as they have to drive up to Marree early about making their statements. Something about the Feds arriving."

Bones went out into the pub yard and gave a huge, piercing whistle. Nick and Ginger's tousled heads poked out of the window in the men's quarters and Bones beckoned them in, pointing to his watch. They disappeared to get dressed so Bones went to Kate's room and knocked, to be greeted by a barrage of barking from Deefer, who was on guard.

Kate was already up and dressed, so she opened the door and Deefer flew out, gave Bones the greeting given to old friends, with plenty of licks and tail wagging.

Bones gave Kate the message, so she tied Deefer under her car, with water and food. She went with Bones to the kitchen, where Nick arrived looking as though he had shoved his head under the cold water tap. He looked tired after the efforts of the past two days but perked up at the smell of Pup's cooking and tucked into steak and eggs.

Ginger came in, so Ma relayed the message from Dave to them all. Kate looked a bit quizzical but got on with eating her breakfast with gusto, as she seemed to be hungry all the time, probably from missing so many meals lately.

Ginger sat down beside Kate with his meal and asked, "You feeling OK after your ordeal, Kate? How's the foot progressing?"

She smiled at him and said, "All good. Bit tired yet, but also interesting learning from the tribal men and another ride on a camel was a bonus! What do we have to do this morning in Marree?"

Ginger frowned for a moment, "Nothing really to be worried about. You'll have to write out your version of events and Nick and I have to do the same. Don't think they will need Jack, but we'll soon find out. Main thing for you is try not to leave anything out, however small it may seem."

Kate looked a bit perturbed, "I don't remember anything after I was jerked over the fence, as I was struggling and one of those Asian blokes hit me in the side of the neck and I went out like a light! Darn thing is still sore."

She showed Ginger the dark bruise on the right side of her neck.

He remarked, "That's used in unarmed combat training, so I'm not surprised you were knocked out! That's the sort of thing you need to write down for the Police. Also how you were treated after that."

Kate grinned through her teeth.

"I was as mad as a wet hen, I can tell you and gave that lot plenty of trouble, what with running away—didn't get far as that's when I cut my foot—plus I tried to strangle Cosmo, the driver of the rig I was in then generally gave plenty of sass. The tall bloke they called Cosmo, seemed to try and protect young Chook, the driver of the truck. The Asians were properly nasty and threatened to knife the young bloke if Cos didn't do as they wanted."

Ginger snorted into his cup of tea.

"Good on you, girl! Sounds as though you gave as good as you got! It was great that the tribal men were able to get you away in short order. You've got a good memory, so you'll have plenty to write down. It'll be quite a nice drive up to Marree this early in the morning so we can watch for all the birds—believe Jack gave you some bird lessons?"

Kate laughed, "I'm probably better at cattle and horse sounds, but still like my birds so I'll be watching more carefully in future. I'll go and get my bag out of my room—back in a second."

Just then, Nick drove into the pub yard in the Police truck, which had been refuelled, water and tyres checked and was ready to roll. Deefer gave him a proper dog's welcome, which made Nick laugh. He said to Kate as she came out of her room,

"Good to see young Deefer doesn't smell as bad as Chook's Bitzer! Dave had to ride in the front of the Blitz truck with Chook driving and the big dog beside him all the way to Maree!"

Kate pulled a face, "First thing I did when I got back was to have a shower and put Deef in it too! We both ponged, I can tell you! I smelt like camel and Deef smelled of whatever he'd been blissfully rolling in!"

Nick smirked and as Ginger joined them asked, "Who gets in the front seat with me—and *I* had a shower when I got here last evening!"

Ginger opened the front passenger door and beckoned Kate into it. He said mildly, "Best place to see all the birds, Kate."

The kitchen mob came out to wave them off, with Pup dipping and diving, shadow boxing and waving his fists over his head in a boxer's winning salute, which earned him a cuff around the ears from Ma, still in her dressing gown, her white hair standing up on end.

Chapter Fifty-Nine

As the Windani police truck motored into Marree, the occupants were amazed to see a very smart Cessna aircraft standing on the end of the airstrip, its white livery adorned with blue, red and silver flashes. The Pilot was busy pumping Avgas from drums under a tin shed, while the wind sock over his head hung as limp as a rag.

As Nick parked in front of the Police Station, he gazed admiringly at the sleek machine.

He said, with his eyes wide, "Wonder who owns that beauty! It's been my dream to get my Pilot's License and be able to own my own plane. Not often you see one as new as that out here."

Ginger laughed, "Right you are. Most aircraft out here are covered in dust and grime from their hard-working life. That looks like a city plane to me, but that's only a guess."

As they got out and stretched, Dave Dawson and Sergeant Poulsen came down the steps to meet them. They all went into the office where a second Policeman was busy with paperwork.

Poulsen shook hands with Kate, Ginger and Nick, saying, "Hello all. Nice to meet you in person, Kate. I'm Clive Poulsen. Over there is my 2-i-C, Josh Trembarth. Hope things have all settled down for you after your tribulations?"

Then he noticed Kate's bandaged foot an asked, "How'd that happened. Not from the knife wielding Tong?"

Kate smirked, "Nah, I got my bonds free while the blokes were otherwise occupied and tore off down the track, thinking I might be able to vanish into the bush, but ran over something that slashed my foot. That put paid to my escape for the moment!"

Josh was offering cups of tea all round, when Dave said to Kate, "If you want to use the amenities, go through to the back. The cleaner has already been in so things are reasonable."

She nodded and went out the back, where she was startled to see a tall, well-dressed man sitting on the steps of the cells, with his arm around Chook, who in turn had his arm around his dog.

After a moment, Chook recognised Kate and waved, calling, "Hello pretty missie."

She gave him a big smile and went about her ablutions. When she went back into the office, the tall man was there and came to shake her hand.

"Hello, Kate, I'm Charlie and Chook's cousin, Phillip Thompson an Attorney from Adelaide, who will be handling their case."

Kate smiled, a little over-awed, not sure what to say for the moment. Nick came over and said admiringly, "Guess who flew up this morning Kate, in the spiffing Cessna! Boy, would I love to own one like that!"

Phil smiled, a little ruefully, "Sadly, it doesn't belong to me, but to my law firm and is used for trips around the country areas that are difficult to access by road. In between work trips I get to do some piloting too, but end up having to read briefs half the time. I'm finished here for now and about to leave for Lyndhurst on business before heading back to Adelaide."

He turned to Poulsen, "I'll be in touch when I sort out what is needed for the Sims brothers. See you later."

He saluted everyone and went out to make his way across to the airfield. Nick looked longingly at the sleek aircraft and started to say, "I don't suppose I could—"

Dave laughed and said, "Go on, go and have a look, but don't be too long. We need to get these depositions under way."

Nick sprinted across the road with alacrity and caught up with Phil. They walked over to look at the Cessna, Phil climbing into the right front seat and strapping in.

In the office, Dave said to Poulsen, "Just a bit of light relief after all Nick's hard work with his driving and everything else he's done during out trek in the bush. Now, Kate, will you come over here and write out your statement. Josh will read it and then offer any help if needed."

He pointed to a small desk in a side room where Kate was given a pen and paper and left to gather her thoughts. It took her a while to get started but, once she got going, her pen seemed to flow across the paper very easily indeed.

After watching the Cessna take off, Nick came back with a big grin, so soon he and Ginger were recalling their own efforts in the kidnap case.

Finishing writing, they had their depositions counter-signed and officially stamped. Kate called Josh in to answer a couple of her questions, but after sorting that out she soon finished, signed her statement and had it counter-signed and officially stamped. She heaved a sigh of relief and went out to join the others.

The atmosphere in the Police station seemed to lighten and when a tray of hefty sandwiches arrived from the pub, everyone clapped. Josh came in with a big brew of tea and after serving everyone he went over to the cells to serve those in there. They could hear Chook yahooing, so he must have been hungry, but Josh came back shaking his head.

"Eddie is happy to eat whatever we bring him, but those Asians blokes still refuse to eat, so I gave their food to Charlie and Eddie."

Sergeant Poulsen smiled grimly, "We can't force those men to eat, but they've still got bread and water from last night. They'll eat when they get hungry enough."

Just then they were startled to hear a roar from the airfield, with a larger aircraft landing and traversing the concourse up to the end of the runway. The engine was cut, the steps let down and two uniformed men jumped out.

Nick went out to look, coming back with a grin all over his face.

"Like it here! Plenty of aircraft action! Looks like the Feds have arrived, judging by the insignia on this larger aircraft, plus some hefty-looking uniforms."

Poulsen looked relieved.

"About time, too! Josh, would you unlock the safe and bring out those packs we took from the Asians. Can't wait to get rid of that contraband. I gave them their clothes last night to change into as it got pretty chilly, but all I got for that service was a mouthful of curses from the Tong bloke."

He considered for a moment, "Dave, you and Nick stay here, but would you other folk mind going and sitting out the back to give us time to deal with the Federal Police. Josh, we need those documents we filled out last night, as well."

Kate and Ginger took their tea and food and sat out the back in the sunshine, looking around at the area in general. They felt so much more content after getting through all that was required of them.

Kate asked, "Now, all this hoo-har is over, what'll you be doing next?"

Ginger ran his hand over his shock of red hair and grinned.

"Back to exploration work with Jack, I guess. Our office is the bush and the ranges. Tough work, but someone has to do it! What about you?"

Kate gave the matter some thought.

"I'll be driving home in a day or so. Dad and the boys are having to shift cattle at present, to new feed and watering points. That's always a tough job and needs all hands on deck. Plus, my mother will be gagging to know all the ins and outs of the goings on here. Not looking forward to that, I can tell you! I'd rather forget it, except for the great tribal men and Mungo Jack—they were the real adventure."

Ginger agreed, "Don't know how the Fed Police will handling those illegals, plus theft, plus threats of violence, plus kidnapping, but my guess is that they will have to deal with whatever foreign embassy is belonging to those Asian men. It may take years to sort out, but you need to be aware, all of us may be called as witnesses when the whole caboodle gets into the courts."

Kate shrugged.

"Then I'll jump over that hurdle when it happens. Meantime, I would like to somehow get over the hurdle of dad refusing to let me own my own camel, so I can train it for the next races."

At that moment, the Federal Policemen, one putting away documentation in a satchel, the other man with a heavy kitbag of contraband thrown over his shoulder, came out to the cells with Sergeant Poulsen. The police were all armed and carefully unlocking the first door, took a subdued Teo from his cell, handcuffed him and went to the second cell to take out Tong, who was cursing and shouting imprecations in his native language. Poulsen shook his head at the other men and made a slash sign across his throat.

One of the Feds took a sidearm from its holster as a possible deterrent to bad behaviour. As they unlocked his door, Tong threw himself out, knocked the Policeman over, whose gun fell to the floor. Tong flew down the steps, heading for the old Blitz truck, which had been parked in the backyard alongside Cosmo's damaged vehicle.

As Tong forced the truck door open, the big dog charged out from under the cells, where it had been reclining without being chained. The dog, barking fiercely, grabbed Tong with a good bite to the behind, pulling him to the ground. Tong screamed as he fell and Cosmo, who had been watching from his cell, gave a great whistle and the dog, still growling, came back under the cells but with all his back hair standing up on end and his blazing eyes firmly fixed on the recumbent Tong.

There was dead silence for an instant. Ginger could feel Kate shaking with suppressed laughter, with Nick inside the office making curious coughing sounds.

The Federal Police, given time, recovered their sidearm and their cool, hoisted a howling Tong to his feet, handcuffed him and marched him and Teo at the point of the gun across to the aircraft. The Asians were bundled into the rear and manacled to the fittings. The door slammed shut and without due delay the pilot started his engines, taxiing to the runway and they were gone in a puff of dust.

The entire office staff, Josh, Dave and Nick and even Sergeant Poulsen couldn't keep a straight face. Ginger and Kate and even Cosmo hanging onto the bars of his cell, laughed till they were blue in the face. Chook, patting the dog through the cell bars, sang his own song to be part of the merriment.

The big dog grinned all over his face.

Chapter Sixty

After Kate and Deefer arrived back home, driving carefully with her still sore foot, there was a rapturous greeting from her mother, who grabbed Kate in a huge hug. Deefer ran around barking up a storm which set off all the working dogs.

Mrs Brenna wanted to hear all the general details of Kate's travail, but Kate, being fed up with the whole thing, told just a few main details, saying she would fill more in as she thought of things. She was feeling so relieved to be home and wanted to get back to the work of the station, plus needing to visit all her animals and birds.

Next morning, Kate put on thick woolly socks and her riding boots with her foot still bound up, felt quite comfortable. She went over to the horse paddock and was surprised to have the colt barge up to the fence in a flurry of dust to greet her.

She laughed at him, vaulted over the fence and hugged the colt round the neck. He shivered in delight and for once, stood passively, nuzzling her neck and then into a pocket to see if there were any handouts. Kate stroked him quietly and produced a couple of pieces of apple, which went down quickly. The colt then tore off round the yard, kicking and neighing, while the other two horses watched as though it was a mild amusement, coming over to greet Kate. She ruffled each horse and it made her heart sing to be home again doing her ordinary chores in peace and quiet.

Not all the quiet remained for long, as there was a warbling and chuckling from the tree above and her little magpie, Scruffy, came soaring down to land on her arm. Kate stroked the messy feathers and the bird lowered his head in pleasure, chuckling in his throat.

Just then Mrs Brenna came out onto the veranda with morning tea and rang the bell. Kevin came out of the shed and ambled over. He asked about Kate's trip back.

"You had no trouble driving with the bandaged foot? I could have sent the men over to bring you home."

Kate replied quite decidedly, "Everything was fine and I just puttered along at my own pace. Deefer was pleased to see our front gate and yodelled a lot with his head out the window after that! I'm still a bit limpy, so I don't know about getting on a horse for now."

Her father chuckled, "We don't need your help at present. We finished the transfer to the new paddock, Zack taking the bike and Fred deciding to ride Stalker, to give that one some hard lessons. Think it did that fussy animal a world of good. He came back in with a few more manners than when he went out, though we did have one good laugh out of him. Fred placed a long strap around the horse's neck and any time Stalker put his head down, feeling the desire to pigroot and chuck Fred, Fred pulled his head back with the strap."

Kate and her mother started to laugh.

Kevin smiled, "Stalker did have one last say. As the cattle were having a drink at the small dam, Fred took his eye off the main game and as Stalker went in for a drink, the horse put his head down and dumped Fred in the dam!"

Kate chortled and clapping her hands, she said, "Poor Fred, but it serves him right! He knows better than to take his eye off that horse, who likes his own way about everything. Stalker's tried to dump me a few times and I reckon he was grinning to himself, but as I always take goodies for handouts, he's been quite calm with me, in case I don't give him any! So far, so good!"

Later that evening as they finished dinner, Kate helped her mother clear up and they all sat about resting with cups of tea. Fred was interested to hear about Kate's winning streak on the camel belonging to Bones.

Kate was still very enthusiastic so she said, "I loved the whole experience. Once I learned the way the camel's stride affected my seat, really it was little trouble. Bones had been a cameleer for around forty years and so his experiences have been remarkable. He knows all the old Ghan watering holes and how those hardy men got the water out of deep wells. So, when I did so well around the yard and then across the back of town, we got on really quite quickly."

Zack was amazed. He said, "But weren't you frightened to get up on that tall thing? A horse seems high enough for me."

They all laughed and Kevin said, "Yes, but Kate has had a lifetime of experiences with her upbringing here and you've got a lot of stuff to catch up on."

May Brenna sighed into her cup of tea.

"No one could keep her off the darn horses all her life, so I guess the challenge of the camel was just another hurdle for her to overcome."

Fred asked, "How did you find that camel to work with, as compared to the horse, Kate?"

She thought for a while, then answered, "Bones showed me how not to walk behind them at any time as they can kick sideways and break your leg. I learned to take carrots for Bones' old Dandy, which she loves, walking beside her, talking to her all the time. She is older and quite a gentle creature and well-schooled by Bones—he was even taking kids for rides."

Zack looked perplexed, so Kate said, "Once I got the hang of the gait, Bones taught me to ride faster. Camels don't like to gallop as they run out of puff quickly. They prefer to canter for short runs but some of the older ones seem to like the competition, like Dandy. I was shown how to stick my heels in and flap the reins at the last moment and she just stretched out her neck and won by a nose!"

They all clapped, so Kate went and brought out her small trophy with great pride, giving it to them to look at the great crystal on the polished piece of timber.

Kevin said, "How did your young friends get on with their races?"

Kate chuckled.

"That was funny on both counts. Mark's young camel, Lucinda, was a bit upset with all the noise and lining up, but once he got her pointed in the right direction, she got the idea and came in second in her age race."

May asked, "How did he find time to school such a young camel, when his outfit are working full tilt all the time to take the big camels down to Adelaide?"

Kate considered for a moment.

"He told us she came into the yards and the older ones tried to bully her, so Mark put her in a separate paddock and gently got her tamed with good food and water. He got her used to being saddled, just like a horse really. Then he and Jason took turns in schooling Lucinda because she seemed so tractable and I guess it was a diversion from their hard and heavy work."

Zack was still thinking of how much he had heard about the bad odour of camels. He asked, "But everyone says they smell really bad. How'd you get over that hurdle?"

Kate laughed.

"You just don't notice it after a while, as the tame camels eat good fodder and they are groomed all the time, their shaggy coats being hosed down and brushed all the time, which they enjoy. I must say, Jason's older gelding was a great runner and he enjoyed his age race, a real pro, stuck his great legs out and at the end, won by a neck."

She said, looking sideways at her father, "I'd like to—"

Kevin threw up his hands!

"Don't start, young lady! We've enough trouble here with the camels, what with the fence breaking and trashing the waterholes. Last thing I would consider is a tame one joining in the melee!"

Kate shrugged, "Well, how about a compromise? Mark said next time he's got a weekend off, he could bring Lucinda over and I could practice down our roadway then he would take her away again?"

Everybody looked at her and then at Kevin.

He took time to consider.

"That's the sort of bargain I might be interested in, long as Mark doesn't leave the thing here!"

Kate grinned and saluted her father with a kiss on the cheek. She said, "Never know, I might be able to get Fred and Zack into the racing camel business as well."

There was a snort from the men and everyone laughed at the disgust on their faces.

Chapter Sixty-One

All systems were go at the camel catching pens, as all hands were working hard to get the next trucks loaded for the trip to Adelaide. The trucks were getting away as the dusk fell, as the night driving kept the camels as cool as possible.

Pete handed the lead driver his documents, banging the side of the cabin in farewell. The two trucks started of slowly, to concerted groans from the loaded camels and as the dust in the yards settled, all the men came into the sheds to wash and recover.

Pete threw himself into a rusty chair and shouted, "Hey Rangi, you got enough oomph to make us gallons to tea?"

There was a shout from inside and Rangi came out with a great grin across his brown face, followed by Jason, with all the billies of tea readymade which they dumped on the rickety table. Jason filled the pannikins and the men gratefully washed dust from patched throats. After a few minutes of relief, there was a small yapping coming from inside the shed and Jason looked guilty.

"Sorry Boss, I chained the little bloke to the leg of my bunk, so he wouldn't get run over."

The men laughed and Dan remarked, "Reckon, Lucky's being run over once in his little lifetime is enough for any good dog."

Pete simulated a big frown, "This ain't the place for dogs, you know that! Even rescued ones?"

Mark intervened, "Lucky's feet are almost healed, even though he might always have a limp in the hind leg—but Jase has some good news about the little dog."

Jason said, "It depends on what Pete thinks about the trip to Adelaide in the morning."

Pete groaned, while Jason went in to bring out Lucky, who was hardly recognisable as the decrepit and starving pup he and Mark had found at the Windani races. Lucky had turned into a fat, roly-poly little dog, who was people friendly and always wanted to be included in human activity, even when he was banned. The black hair around his eye and one floppy ear gave him a piratical aspect and his friendly nature had endeared him to all the men, in spite of Pete's threats.

Jason said to Pete, "I been speaking with my mum in Adelaide, told her all about this little bloke and how we can't keep him here. Mum lives on the Virginia side of Adelaide, near where we go in and she has offered to take Lucky. She's dog friendly and has an older dog that won't mind a bit of company. Mum has offered to meet us at Two Wells. Main thing is, Pete, do you reckon I can take him down tomorrow to give to my Ma?"

Pete looked at Lucky and sighed, "Yairs, but I tell you, Jason, if Lucky piddles inside my truck, you and he will be thrown out on the road! In the burrs!"

The whole camp roared and Lucky grinned as though he was in on the joke. Jason placed him on the ground and the little dog strolled around, giving a lick here and there and then he stood at Pete's feet, looking up at him with adoring eyes.

Pete picked him up, gave him a good pat, holding Lucky at eye level, said to him, "Don't you ever let this get out or I'll get a bad name as a softy!"

Pete placed the pup on the ground and then got back to work issues in his normal stern voice.

"Rangi, you need any stores this time around? Anyone needing anything personal, give a list to Jason and he can fill it out while he waits for me at his mother's place."

Jason made a mock face but was quite OK with everything now that Lucky's future was secure.

Chapter Sixty-Two

Towards the following weekend, the phone rang in Tindabulla office. Kate went to answer and was pleased to hear a night call from Mark on the satellite phone. She sat on the old chair and put her feet up on the desk, ready for a chat.

"Hello, good buddy, what's the go at your place?"

Mark replied, "My boss, Pete, has just gone down to Adelaide with the new transport of camels from our latest catch. I've got the weekend off and wondered if I can come over with Lucinda—we could have a bit of fun with her."

Kate grinned, "Sure. We've been busy here too, so I reckon I'm due a bit of time to myself. You want to camp over? If you bring a bedroll, there's the bunkhouse."

Mark said, "That'd be great. And I've got some good news for you. Remember the little dog we found in Windani in a terrible state? He's looking so much better with good food. The blokes here, even the boss, have really taken to him and fed him like a king! His front paws are not fully healed yet, but he can get around with care. I think he'll always have a limp from where he was nearly run over."

Kate growled in her throat, "Hate people who don't look after their animals! I could think of many nasty things I would like to do to them!"

Mark started laughing, "A nice girl like you! Anyway, there is good news as Jason's mum, Mrs Grandston, was told about the pup and decided she would like to keep him as a pal for her other dog. Jason's gone down with Pete to take the pup to his mum and we know the good lady will make a healthy dog out of the mite in no time."

Kate clapped and said, "Gina was smart when she called the pup Lucky. She must have seen into the future!"

Mark laughed and said, "We're not allowed to keep dogs at the camp, but Pete let Jason look after Lucky, on the premise that as soon as the pup recovered he had to go. Now there's a good home for him everyone is pleased."

Kate was also thankful and she remarked, "Nothing could be better for Lucky. So, what time do you think you'll be getting here Friday? Having been here before doing the camel catching, you'll know all the shortcuts across country. Come right up to the house and we can put Lucinda in the near paddock and get her settled down."

Mark agreed, "Probably be late afternoon by the time I get her loaded and trundle over in camel time."

Kate was pleased, "OK, Mark, that'll be fun. See you then."

They signed off and she went to bed feeling at last she knew someone that thought the way she did and was on the same wave length.

Mark arrived at Tindabulla on the Friday afternoon, just as the sun was fading in the west. Towing the trailer with Lucinda squatting on her stomach pad was always a slow business, but the camel looked not the least bit worried about her trip.

Kate took Deefer into the dog yard, much to his displeasure, in case the camel was frightened by his noise, then she went to meet Mark at the shed. She gave him a quick peck on the cheek and indicated the side gate to the horse paddock. Mark backed the trailer up and urging Lucinda to rise, escorted her into the paddock where Kate's two horses and the colt stood back eyeing the newcomer with surprise.

They led the camel to the trough, where she drank and then Kate pulled out some lucerne hay for her to browse. The colt was most fascinated, leaping and jigging round the camel, who chose to ignore him completely.

Kate and Mark laughed at the antics and she said, "He'll stop being a donkey shortly. Come and get settled in the bunkhouse then we'll have a cuppa."

They strolled over to the bunkhouse, where Mark met Fred, who showed him where the beds were and the shower in the outside amenities. They all went over to the house and as Kate made cups of tea and produced some scones, Zack appearing as though by magic from the shed and was all agog to hear about the camel.

He asked Mark, "I've never been close to such a large animal before. Does she bite?"

Mark laughed, "No, no often. Maybe a nip now and then but not meaning anything. I caught her when she was very young. She has a nice nature, like a good many camels so she tamed really quickly. I still treat her with respect, so become quite fond of her."

Fred looked at Zack, who was pulling faces.

"Ah, well, buddy, it's all a learning curve. Zack is more at home zooming up a windmill or fixing watering points and pumps. He's really good at mechanics, but the horses are still a bit strange to him and regarded with suspicion!"

Kevin pulled up in his work Ute, came up the steps, shook the dust out of his hat, throwing it onto a peg on the wall.

He came in to have some tea and greeted Mark, "Good to see you again, Mark. Many thanks for all the help you gave over at Windani, specially doing the chopper spotting."

Mark grinned, "I call *that* episode a learning curve! Flying in Pat's chopper for the first time, learning a lot of the technical stuff from him was a real eye-opener. He is very proficient and gave me the job of scouting the roadways— very different from looking at flat road maps. I had been thinking of getting a chopper License as it's a big help when rounding up the bigger herds of camels. Takes a lot longer on the bikes and trucks, which is expensive in time and cost and the chopper Pete hires now and then costs an arm and a leg."

Kevin agreed, "Maybe a good idea if your boss's outfit would pay for your lessons. I heard it is really expensive for lessons and then, of course, the outfit would need to buy the chopper, but it may be of benefit in the end."

After breakfast next morning, Kate and Mark went over to check Lucinda, to find the camel and the colt standing together near the fence. The colt looked just a wiry little fellow standing close beside the tall camel.

Kate laughed and said, "Looks like Bogey got over his fright and, perhaps, thinks Lucinda will look after him."

Mark shrugged, "Who knows what really goes on in their minds. We can only guess at what we know has been done by training."

He opened the gate, placing a halter on the camel, then leading her out into the front of the shed area. Kate shut the gate and followed.

Mark got his saddle and straps out of his truck and gave them to Kate. She held the halter, pulling it down and gave the order to sit.

"Hooshta, hooshta," pulling the reins down tight. The camel eyed her for a moment, gave a great groan and subsided onto the ground, folding her legs in neatly.

Kate blanched and looked at Mark, "Geese, Mark, does she really hate to sit? Does it hurt her?"

Mark chuckled, "Not at all. You don't take any notice of the groans. They do it all the time and it is only when there is trouble with the big males that it turns into threats and warnings and then you get right out of the road! We've seen some terrible fights and wonder if there will be anything left of them in the end, but after a lot of biting and kicking and thrashing their necks it all seems to get resolved somehow and they'll get onto the transport nice as pie. Now, hold the reins, walk alongside speaking quietly, so the camel knows where you are then slide into the saddle."

Kate had placed the saddle, cloth and straps on the camel the way Bones had showed her. Mark checked them with only minor adjustments to see that everything was tight and secure. Kate slid into the saddle, speaking softly all the while, she tightened up the reins.

She called, "Yalla, yalla," shaking the reins so Lucinda rose with the elegance of a queen, with Mark guiding her into the house yard.

He said, "Now, shake up the reins, boot her in the side and trot down the road a bit till you get the feel of how she goes."

Kate obeyed and was pleased at the instant response, so they rotted sedately down to the first gate, where Kate turned the camel and they trotted back. She waved in triumph to Mark, who stood laughing at the fence. Kate trotted back and forth several times, feeling quite firm in the seat with her responses to the camel's stride becoming easy for her.

She shouted, "This lady is so nice and quick, so easy—what a doll!"

Mark called, "Now give her a good flick with the reins and some hefty kicking and see if she will canter for you. This is what I have been teaching her for the races."

Kate turned Lucinda again and they flew back into the house yard at a good pace. May and Kevin were standing on the veranda, while Fred and Zack came out of the shed to cheer and whistle. Kate was delighted and slipped off her mount and bowed.

She shouted to Kevin, "See, dad, I would make a good racing rider—sure I can't have my own camel?"

Kevin shook his head and threw up his hands in despair and everyone laughed at him.

Kate turned to Mark with a grin.

"Guess that's big NO!"

Mark led the camel into the yards, taking the equipment off. Lucinda stood quietly looking over the fence and the colt came up to stand beside her, nudging her in the ribs. The camel didn't bat an eyelid, so the colt stood beside her like a little sentry.

Mark got out his curry comb and brush, showing Kate how to keep the camel coat in good order, brushing hard to get any detritus and rubbish out. Kate also had a go at the brushing and when the colt came over, she brushed him too, but he charged off around the yard, pigrooting and stamping.

Kate chuckled, "I guess that's too much attention for Bogey just yet."

Mark got out a firm brush, speaking quietly to the camel, walking with his hand along her side, he lifted each huge foot and brushed the sole clean. Then, with a hoof pick, ran it around the toenails to check for burrs or small stones that may have been lodged there.

He remarked to Kate, "Those great soft pads are really meant for sand and sometimes our harsh terrain can make injuries they can't recover from. Like your horses, good hoof treatment means a contented animal."

She replied, watching carefully, "Exactly the same with our horses, though they are good over rough ground, but the wretched galvanised burr can cause a heap of trouble. I do the same sort of checks after we've been out mustering— good maintenance really."

Mark looked at Kate, "Maybe we'll do this training for a while with Lucinda, as I don't see your dad changing his mind about your camel. That's if your folks are all OK with me coming over?"

Kate nodded.

"They'll be happy, I'll be happy and we can have a bit of fun away from work all the time."

Chapter Sixty-Three

Later that evening after all was settled down and still, Mark and Kate sat on the front steps looking out over the deep indigo sky full of icy stars.

Mark had been quiet for a moment, then asked, "Will you ever forgive those blokes who carted you off? I can't quite get my head around that happening in this quiet part of our world. It seemed like some sort of fantasy."

Kate considered for a while, then said, "Well, it was quite a farce. Seems Cosmo had been conned into being hired by those Asians, who had heard some myth about a skeleton made of opal hidden somewhere that only Ginger knew where. I was just the scapegoat as a bargaining power. Fat lot of good that did! But I tell you I learned a helluva lot from the Tribal men who rescued me. The stuff they know about their own country is amazing!"

Mark said thoughtfully, "We could learn a lot from their good knowledge if we weren't so full of our importance."

Kate sounded still amazed as she remembered Perce's help with her injured foot.

"Perce, the tribal man who helped spirit me away, just went and gathered—in the middle of the night, I might add—a heap of leaves he crushed, placed round my bleeding foot and then wove that bootee of reeds. I never saw anything like it!'

Mark added his thoughts, "Plus, to think that they had taught Mungo Jack to read the smoke signals and behold, next morning you are riding into town on a camel! Like something out of a movie!"

Kate reflected.

"It all seems like a mad dream by now. There is one thing that is bothering me, but I'm not sure how to find out about it."

Mark asked, "What's that?"

She said, "That young fellow, Chook, that got drunk and I pushed him in the trough, he was driving the big truck. Chook was quite kind to me, trying to be

267

helpful all the time, but he relied on Cosmo to tell him what to do. It was the Asians that were the horrors. I wonder all the time what has happened to Chook and if he is OK. I'd hate someone like that being stuck in jail when nothing was his fault. I sort of don't know where I could find out."

Mark thought for a moment, "Possibly Sergeant Dawson might fill you in, if you give him a call."

She looked at him with consideration.

"Do you think that would be allowed? We could have a go in the morning, while you're here—you were involved in the search. That would back me up that I'm not just sticky-beaking but quite concerned."

Mark patted her hand and nodded.

"Yeah, let's give it a go. All they can say is no."

Next morning they crammed into the office, while Kate looked up the phone book and patched a call through to Windani Police. She got Dave Dawson at first ring and introduced herself. Mark crowded into the phone to listen as well.

"Sergeant Dawson, this is Kate Brenna from Tindabulla."

Dave seemed pleased to her from her and asked, "How you doing, Kate? All going OK there? Hope you are fully recovered from your ordeal."

She replied, laughing, "Yes, all fine and dandy! Mark is here playing camels with me this weekend, so maybe I'll make Champion at next year's races. Just wanted to ask you a question, but I will understand if you can't tell me yet."

He said, "OK, fire away."

Kate explained, "I was wondering how that lad, Chook, got on with all the official hoohar? He would be missing his brother if he were stuck in jail by himself. He was quite kind to me, but intimidated by those Asians."

Dave answered promptly, "It seems his cousin, Phil Thompson, the lawyer from Adelaide, did a good job getting special dispensation for Chook, to be allowed into the custody of his aunt and uncle, the Thompsons, who have a small holding near Marree, called 'Yacca' it's easy to find off the main road, around ten miles out. Seems Chook lived with them after his mother died. They went in and took Chook home with them—and the big dog, I might add."

Kate asked tentatively, "Do you think I could ring them and just ask how the lad is going? I'd feel better if I knew he had settled down after all that happened to him."

Dave replied, "Can't see they would be put out by that. I can give you their number—hang on."

He ruffled some papers and came back online, "Here it is—copy this out," and read out a string of numbers.

Kate was really pleased, "Good on you, thanks very much. I'll follow this up and see what the Thompsons say."

She hung up the phone and she and Mark had a high five.

He said, "Good stuff! Ring now, while you're hot!"

Kate nodded, punching in the numbers and when a woman answered, she introduced herself.

"I'm Kate Brenna from Tindabulla. Sergeant Dawson has given me your number, as I just wanted to ask how Chook is getting on. Has he settled down after his troublesome time?"

Mrs Thompson chuckled. She sounded an easy-going lady with a warm voice.

"I'm Glad Thompson. Nice to hear you Kate and I hope you've settled down as well. Chook has his dog with him, though he misses Charlie for now, he is quite happy helping Bert with the animals and our market garden. He used to live with us so it's not any problem. I explained he just had to wait with us until Phil gets Charlie's business sorted out.

Kate was pleased, "That's really good to hear. How did Chook get to Coober Pedy in the first place?"

Glady said quite readily, "A couple of years ago, Charlie took Chook back there with him to teach him about driving and camping and all that they do there, but perhaps it wasn't the wisest thing for the lad after all. Would you like to come over one day and see Chook? He can't go out, but no one said anything about not having visitors. He talks about you as the pretty missie all the time!"

Kate laughed, looking at Mark with raised eyebrows. He nodded and wrote on a pad that he had the next Saturday off and could go over with her.

She asked, "Would it be OK if a friend and I came over next Saturday?"

Mrs Thompson was quite happy. She said, "That would be nice for Chook. Come for lunch and see what he's been learning to do here to help out."

Kate thought that would all be good, so she said, "Thanks, that'd be lovely. We'll see you then."

She shut down the phone and heaved a sigh of relief. Mark and she shook hands as a job well done. They went back out to the horse yard, where Kate showed Mark how she would start schooling the colt. Bogey was not happy to leave his new friend, Lucinda, but he had a halter and rope put on him and he was marched around the yard with a whip tickling his heels if he played up. He buckled and fiddled round but in the end trotted comfortably.

After schooling the colt Mark and Kate decided to harness up the stock horses, letting the working dogs out of their pen and whistling up Deefer. He came out from under his cool spot under the tank stand, carrying Kate's tatty old white jogger.

Mark and Kate laughed and she said, "For goodness sake, Deef, leave that rubbish behind—we're not taking your prize with us!"

Deefer was not deterred, so Kate grabbed the jogger and pitched it up on the tank. Deefer barked for a moment but she pointed her finger at him till he subsided. With all the dogs running amok around them, she and Mark trotted out of the house yards, riding down the roadway to check watering points and fences where there had been camel destruction.

Chapter Sixty-Four

Mark drove to Windani early on his Saturday off and met Kate at the pub. They went in to greet Ma and the girls and told them where they were going. Nick was in the kitchen having breakfast so he heard the news and promised to write their trip in the Police Station's log book.

They drove off in Mark's Ute and some ten miles or so south of Marree found the turn-off to the Yacca property easily. They were surprised to see the good growth of trees surrounding the property, which made it quite a spectacular spot in the more usual red desert.

As they drove into the house yard, Chook was jumping up and down clapping his hands. He flew to open Kate's door. She got out all smiles and was given a big hug.

Chook gasped out, "Been waiting and waiting for you, missie. Aunty Glad and I been cooking lots of good things for you."

Kate took his hand gently and showing him Mark, who was getting out of the other Ute door, she said, "This is another friend, Mark, come to visit you too. Mark is a camel catcher and a good camel racer."

Chook knew he had to have good manners or his aunt would frown, so he went shyly over to Mark and shook his hand.

There was a 'halloo' from the front of the house and Kate smiled to see Mrs Thompson, clad in a big apron over her dress, waving from the veranda. They ran up the steps, followed by Chook.

Kate said, "This is my friend, Mark, who had also met Chook at Windani, but don't think Chook would remember him."

Glady was pleased to see them arriving in good time, without any trouble on the road.

She asked, "Chook has been running round all morning making his favourite biscuits, so how about a cuppa to go with them?"

They agreed and Chook came proudly out of the kitchen with a tray of sweet-smelling biscuits, followed by Glady with the tea. They sat at a picnic table and chairs in the shade of some silky-oak trees, while Kate admired the big market gardens in the nearby fenced-in area.

She was fascinated, so she said, "I have never seen such a great garden, way out here. Even with good fences to keep out the roos. You must have remarkably good water here to keep it all in production."

Glady replied, "Our water comes from a side aquifer and is so filtered it is very pure and the soil around our area is good loam. We can sell as many vegetables as we can produce. Chook is getting to be a good market gardener, aren't you, Chook?"

Chook nodded happily with his mouth full of biscuits. The others smiled at him, pleased he seemed to have found such a quiet and peaceful family to help him.

They went walking round the gardens and Chook showed them where he had been helping with the gardening, then took them to see the horse paddock. The big dog followed them and seemed as happy as Chook. Kate felt quite relieved to see how the Thompson family was faring.

After they had viewed the garden, the duck pond and the fowl house, there was a call for lunch from the veranda. They were given a great spread of fresh produce from the gardens and met Bert Thompson, who had come in from the shed to join them.

He was a grey-haired long, lean stick of a man, who seemed quite an affable person, as he patted Chook on the back and told them how the lad was learning a lot of new things.

Chook nodded heartily, "I'm good at getting eggs and driving the tractor. Uncle Bert and me making good fences too. Lotsa roos round 'ere."

He looked crestfallen for a moment, adding, "Not allowed to shoot them but."

His aunt looked at him fondly, "Never mind, lad, good fences keep them off our vegetables."

After the meal, Kate helped Glady bring out cups of tea to the table with biscuits to follow. When they were relaxing, Bert started to sniff into the wind coming from the slope, somewhat ruefully he said to Chook, "Hey, young fella, I still get whiffs of that bad smell! Thought we had deodorised the shed enough. I'll have to apologise to our young friends here. Not good while they are eating!"

He shook his head and Glady started to laugh.

She said to Mark and Kate, "Don't start him, he'll worry though it all again!"

Mark was interested and said to Bert, "Go on, I love a good yarn with a cuppa."

Bert looked sideways at Chook, who was giggling.

He said, "Well, last week, Bitzer and our farm dog, Mulga, had been fossicking up the in the scrub. They came down running down the hill dragging something foul they had been rolling in. They wore ruffs of unspeakable filth around their necks with the pride of a teenager wearing her first Chanel No. 5. What a terrible sight!"

Kate was laughing and Glady frowned at her grinning husband.

She carried on with the story.

"It was very early in the morning when the stench hit us. The Boss here sat bolt upright in bed, his hair on end, his farmer's nose twitching at the miasma of pong the blew in through the bedroom window on the breeze. 'Glad,' he roared, 'what's that terrible smell!'"

Mark was looking mystified and Chook and Kate were both laughing outright.

Glady continued, "Both the dogs heard the roar from Bert and the possible threat in the voice of their lord. They bolted with their prize under the nearest shed. It fairly rocked with their fight to get under the most remote corner. The floorboards almost rose from the bearers with the intensity of the fetid stench!"

Bert was starting to cackle too and he went on, "Glad rushed outside retching over the veranda, while I made a beeline for the bathroom to swig water before I threw up. Chook was gargling in his room and ran out holding his nose."

Chook parodied himself holding his nose and making retching sounds.

He said, "I heard Aunty Glad swear! She said, bloody mongrels, I'll cut their throats when I get them!"

Everyone was laughing properly, while Bert tried to keep a straight face.

He said, "I told Glad our missing heifer musta died in the scrub, where we couldn't find her—except for the dogs! I'd have to go and burn the carcass or we'd be driven mad with the terrible pong when the wind is in the wrong direction. I went up to the shed and peered underneath, where two pair of eyes reflected guiltily in the dark and two tails thumped hopefully at me."

He grinned. "I yelled at them to get out here, stinking, mangey mongrels!" Bert shook his head.

"There was dead silence and only the rampant smell to mark the hideout of the dogs. I sighed and tramped off up the far paddock with a tin of fuel to arrange a funeral pyre."

Glady took up the tale, "Chookie and I could see under the shed the dogs had dragged in some lumps of festering skin from the unfortunate dead beast. I wondered what would bring them out of hiding once Bert had gone. I gave Chook some meat and bone scraps from the last night's meal and as he is good with animals, he coaxed and wheedled the dogs, who slunk out, thinking they would be forgiven. They were reeking—gawd, it was awful!"

Chook said, half holding his nose and mouth, "Bad smell nearly made Aunty Glad sick, but she tied dogs up and we hosed them down and I got soap and washed them good. Bad dogs!"

Bert nodded, "The rotting skin from the animal is still hidden in the depths of the doggy hidey-hole under the shed so Chook and I have wired around it, so the dogs can't get back in there. How long it'll take for the skin to rot away I can't imagine, so that's why I feel I need to apologise to visitors about the lingering smell. Bitzer and Mulga are tied up at night now, so they can't get into any more smelly mischief!"

As the tea and biscuits were finished, Chook seemed to be in a state of excitement and was whispering to his aunt. She patted his hands and remarked, "Chook has a surprise for you that we've been working on this morning. Hope you like ice-cream."

Chook flew into the kitchen and came out gingerly carrying a dish of multi-coloured ice-cream and some cones. He carefully measured out the ice-cream with a scoop and gave everybody a big dollop in the cones.

He settled down with a beatific look on his face, waving his multi-coloured ice cream and said to everyone.

"See, this is opal ice-cream—this the best opal ever!"

Epilogue

In his flat overlooking the river Torrens, Bon Campbell, now an elderly grey-haired man, sat at his desk, writing in his Journal and dreaming over the histories of his former extensive works in so many parts of inland Australia. They ranged from the Surat Basin in Queensland across to parts of the Northern Territory and most of the uplift area of South Australia. Bon's den had one wall of books, another of shelves of many mineral specimens that he took down now and then, using them to refer to the Journal, as to their origins.

On the back of his desk, balanced against a tray, sat a pave of immense amethyst crystals, glowing deep purple against the morning light. Bon sometimes wondered if it were some sort of magic that had overcome his common sense in the mountain cave of exquisite jewels, the setting like that only Aladdin could have dreamed up. When he ran his fingers over the great crystals in all their sparkling glory, he knew it was not just his imagination, but the event had also been shared by two other prospectors.

Bon knew full well that the opal dragon had never been found again or the whole world would have fought over it. He felt some sort of satisfaction to think the great beast still lay in state, like a shining, monstrous, almost alien being, safely away from the ravening lives of humans. Bon often thought, that along with the travel extracts from his lengthy Journal, the legend of the opal dragon would perhaps make a good story to write for posterity.

In the mountain retreat of the opal dragon the afternoon storm flashed and blew outside and the very rocks trembled in the onslaught. The crystals glittered in a speck of light from a fissure in the rocks, their myriad colours like cloaks of the Persian Kings.

The opal dragon lay in splendour on his rocky ledge, his siesta lasting millions of years. His iridescent bones contained all the colours of the known world and he rested in his eyrie, where perhaps the spirits of Arkaroo still lingered to keep him safe. The outside world of desert and mortal men fell into a line of his history that had no meaning in all eternity.

There was a rumble of seismic shift along the escarpment and the tiny light from the outside world closed when a rock fall filled it again. The glittering, coloured bones of the dragon seemed to make his great teeth form into a smile.

Only the rocks remained.